WITHDRAWN

Rise from the River

a novel by

Kathie Giorgio

MINT HILL BOOKS
MAIN STREET RAG PUBLISHING COMPANY
CHARLOTTE, NORTH CAROLINA

Library of Congress Control Number: 2014955695

ISBN: 978-1-59948-514-0

Produced in the United States of America

Mint Hill Books
Main Street Rag Publishing Company
PO Box 690100
Charlotte, NC 28227
www.MainStreetRag.com

It's been such a wild ride.
In continued gratitude for everyone
for your steadfast love and encouragement.
Thank you for hanging on tight.

No woman pops in for an abortion just because the clinic was handy. There is tremendous sadness, loneliness, in the cry, 'A woman's right to choose.' No woman wants an abortion as she wants an ice cream cone or a Porsche. She wants an abortion as an animal caught in a trap wants to gnaw off its own leg. —Frederica Mathewes-Green

...society as a whole must defend the conceived child's right to life and the true good of the woman who can never, in any circumstances, find fulfillment in the decision to abort. —Pope Benedict XVI

I was just guessing at numbers and figures,
pulling the puzzles apart.
Questions of science, science and progress
cannot speak as loud as my heart.
                                    —Coldplay
                                    "The Scientist"

The term "pro-life" should be a shorthand for respect for the sanctity of life. But I will not let that label apply to people for whom sanctity for life begins at conception and ends at birth. What about the rest of life? Respect for the sanctity of life, if you believe that it begins at conception, cannot end at birth. —Thomas L. Friedman

If a woman has [the right to an abortion], why shouldn't a man be free to use his superior strength to force himself on a woman? At least the rapist's pursuit of sexual freedom doesn't [in most cases] result in anyone's death. —Rep. Lawrence Lockman (Maine) in 1990.

CHAPTER ONE

Tuesday, September 26, 2006

Rainey

Conception: Formation of a viable zygote by the union of the male sperm and the female ovum, usually during intercourse; fertilization. Impregnation.

When Rainey Milbright slipped with her daughter into the dark park, she laughed, a quiet and deliciously evil laugh, and she felt like a child herself. "We're not supposed to be doing this," she whispered to Tish. "It's against the rules. The park is closed, but just this once, this one time only, I'm going to let you do something naughty. Only because we'll get home faster. We stayed too late at the custard stand. You've got school tomorrow."

Rainey tucked Tish's sweaty palm in hers and encouraged her to hurry. It was after dark and the park that ran along the Fox Riverwalk was supposed to be empty of visitors. Only the police, invisible in their black uniforms, skimmed through at measured intervals on their bicycles, scouting for intruders. Rainey hoped she would hear the smooth whine of their bike tires before they saw her. She would jump into the bushes, hide her daughter under the shelter of her shoulders, or stammer some lie about not knowing the rules, which were posted on large brown signs, lettered in gold, at each entrance to the park. Tish, she knew, would be delighted to be escorted home by the police. Rainey wondered if they would let the little girl balance on their handlebars, ride above their pumping legs. Tish's smile and excited scream of laughter would almost make it worth getting caught.

The dark settled around them and the steady scuff of Tish's sneakers against the pavement gave a rhythmic percussion to the soft drone of the Fox River. The quiet, the whisper of the river, and Rainey's own surreptitiousness reminded her of the times she went night-swimming in college. Sneaking out of the dorm into a warm and muggy Missouri night, gliding with friends across sidewalks and parking lots to the lake, discarding clothes in silver moonlight. Slippery-skinned bodies startled in the cold splash of evening-cooled water, and always the necessary silence. Just shared smiles and suppressed giggles.

Rainey glanced at her daughter, the result of one of those nights. An underwater soft-moon mating that left Rainey on her own. She was the one who instigated night-swimming during finals week in the particularly hot spring of her sophomore year. From that time on, she'd accepted her responsibility for first the conception, then the raising of her daughter.

"Look," she whispered now and Tish obediently looked where Rainey pointed. "Look how different everything is at night. See the swings? What do they look like to you?"

Tish shivered and Rainey felt the tremble of thoughts spreading from her daughter's eyes to her brain to her mouth. "Vines," Tish said finally. "They're like vines in the jungle."

"And the slide is an elephant!" Rainey said, happy to make the park a jungle in the middle of a Wisconsin fall, happy to make it green and humid and heavy with the sounds of birds and stampeding animals.

Tish smiled. "And the climbing structure...it's a...it's a...herd of camels."

With her words, the lush green jungle turned to the brown of a desert. Rainey squeezed Tish's hand and marveled at how a four-year old could use a sophisticated phrase like "climbing structure" alongside an impossible twist of imagination.

Earlier that night, they walked to the frozen custard stand, walked instead of drove because the air was cool and fresh and the leaves crackled much more sweetly under sneakers than tires. They slurped ice cream cones while sitting on a picnic bench. Tish's vanilla formed a drippy beard and mustache that oozed onto her shirt, and the taste of last summer mixed well with the brilliant fall sunset. Tish jabbered about each new color in the sky, comparing it to pumpkins and tomatoes and cotton candy, and Rainey just couldn't interrupt the steady stream of words and exploding sky to tell her daughter they needed to go home, to return to the routine of bath time and bed. When they finally threw away their cone wrappers and left, it was past dark. Rainey considered taking the bus home, circling around instead of cutting through the park the way they came, on the path that was the easiest, fastest way back. But it was late and there was still Tish's bath and the every-night struggle into pajamas and through tooth-brushing. There was also the quickly decreasing time for Rainey's own sleep before she left Tish next door with Doris, her landlady and babysitter, and rushed off to work in the morning. So Rainey chose the Riverwalk; she chose to break the rules.

They continued on, changing bushes to sand dunes, trees to pyramids, and it seemed to Rainey that the night went from cool to overwhelmingly hot. She panted and Tish panted with her, and they looked ahead for an oasis where there would be water and the sweetness of shade, even though all around them, it was already dark and a river flowed beside them, flecked with moonshine.

Rainey was certain she saw him first, before Tish did; the shadow that Rainey thought was a policeman stepping out of the bushes, a brave sheik after desert smugglers. But there was something about his posture, his body looming large, as he stood spread-eagled over the path, and there was nothing in his face that shone out of the blackness. Before he even took a step toward her, Rainey knew, and she grabbed her daughter's shoulder.

"Tish," she whispered. "Tish, run back to the climbing structure. Climb to the highest part where the little house is and sit there and don't move until I come get you."

"Mama?" Tish's head swiveled between Rainey and the man that was moving closer.

"Tish, run!"

And she did. She was a good girl, she almost always did what Rainey told her to do. Her footsteps rattled back up the path, but then Rainey thought she heard Tish stop. She tried to look over her shoulder, to see if Tish was still moving, still running, but the man was on Rainey then, shoving her off the path through the bushes to a little clearing right next to the river. The soft rush of the water grew suddenly louder as he pushed her to her knees.

"No!" she cried once. She had to say it, even though she was no match, even though she already knew she had no choice.

He grabbed her ponytail with one hand, and with the other, he undid his pants. "Suck," he said, the word flying out loud and ugly. He pulled her head forward and she felt his penis, hard, full, against her lips and she pulled away, looked down and noted the charcoal of the skin, mottled with gray and brown. "Suck!" he said again and brought both of his fists against her temples so that her ears rang and she shut her eyes. Opening her mouth, she took him in.

He held her head as she gagged, but tried to swallow him whole. She thought about clamping her teeth down, biting with all her might, then running, but she was afraid for Tish, afraid she wouldn't find her in the dark, afraid the girl's little legs wouldn't be able to move fast enough and then he would catch them both. He moaned, a guttural sound that encouraged Rainey; maybe he would finish fast and it would be all over. But when she tasted him, tasted just the beginning of salt, he pulled away and knocked her backwards. She fell hard, arched over a large rock, and for a moment, she couldn't breathe and there were stars and she was only dimly aware of her skirt being sliced away.

Sliced. She felt the final tug as the blade of what must surely be a knife ripped through the waistband. And then he cut away her panties at the crotch and she felt the smooth coldness, the slimness, and then he held the edge against her naked thigh.

"Feel this?" he said. "This what'll fuck you if you make a sound. Any sound. Got it?"

She opened her mouth, tried to find air.

As if he was testing her, he ran the knife across the inside of her thigh and the pain seared through her, white hot and flashing like the sun rolling out of an eclipse. She cried out, just a small yelp, and he backhanded her across the jaw.

"You don't get it? You don't understand? Make a sound and this what'll fuck you, bitch."

And he slid the knife into her.

She stopped breathing, stopped moving, her entire body coalescing around the blade, so cold and thin, so small.

"Better," he said, pulling the blade out and rolling her over, stomach-down, on the rock. She tried to go limp, but he kneed her against her ribs and so she cooperated when he lifted her on all fours. She gasped when he pushed his way inside her, all in one move, and she fell forward on her face, scraping her cheek, her nose, against the rock and into the grass. Then she braced herself on her forearms and held steady against him. Her palms and knees embedded themselves into the ridges of the rock. He gripped her by her breasts and he bit into her neck, hard enough that she knew he must taste blood, and she wondered for a moment if he was a vampire. A vampire in the desert. Her body felt as if it would break. As if it was already broken. Held together only by the envelope of her skin, her bones rattling loose inside.

Not a vampire. She remembered the game she played with Tish an insane few minutes before, and she opened her eyes and tilted her head, trying to see back over his shoulder, trying to see through the bushes. But there was only his body, heavy, his eyes wide open and huge, and then his face dropped again. She felt his teeth once more at the back of her neck. She remembered not to cry out as he tore into her skin.

An animal. He had to be an animal. She tried to think of a creature of the desert who would bite and chew, a violent and large beast, but she couldn't come up with a one. She could only think of camels, Tish's herd that was the climbing structure, and camels, though suffused with heat, would never do more than spit. She wasn't being attacked by a camel.

A wolf then. Were there wolves in the desert? She closed her eyes and he became a wolf, gray and thick with fur, teeth sparkling with saliva, and Rainey became a piece of meat. You're a steak, she said, you're a steak, a T-bone, a porterhouse. She fell into that, became red and raw and flaccid. She held her eyes closed and her edges began to soften, to blur, transforming into the mottled red and white marble of raw steak. Her knees and elbows seemed to unlock, to crack open like an eggshell, and slowly and easily, she crawled away from her body, leaving the meat behind.

Reaching the bank, Rainey looked back and saw herself, arched over the rock, caught under the wolf. Her blouse and cami were crammed like a noose into her armpits and her panties hung in shreds around her waist. Her teeth and gums were bared in a grimace so harsh, and her eyes clamped so tight, Rainey thought of a skeleton and recognized what she would look like in death. Quickly, she turned away and glanced down.

She was dressed. Her skirt, still whole, fell neatly to mid-thigh and her blouse and cami were tucked in. Rainey stretched her limbs, still strangely unhinged, and looked toward the river.

The moon stippled down in a million flecks and created a steady path on the current. Rainey leaned over, wanting to dip her hand in, to touch the water and the shine and the movement, to grab it like the tail of a kite that would pull her to safety. But as she leaned, the moon didn't wait, and instead shifted and cast its glow onto her. Warmed in the light, in a shower of glisten, Rainey raised her face and basked. For that moment, all was soft.

But then a grunt interrupted the light. Blinking, Rainey remembered Tish and she turned toward the bushes, thinking she could find her daughter and run home, leaving her body behind to deal with the wolf and the rock and the strange silent struggle. She would bathe Tish and put her to bed, as she planned all along, and then head straight into a steaming shower. Drown herself in heat and sibilance and the rainbeat of water.

But an odd tingling sensation rolled over her torso and Rainey glanced back at her trapped body. The wolf's hand tremored over her breasts, her ribcage, and down. "C'mon, baby," he whispered into her body's ear and she heard it from a few feet away. "Sweet Jesus, girl, you know you want it."

What was he doing? His hand disappeared between her legs and Rainey crept over to look. Ducking down, she saw his fingers working her folds apart and there was the glitter of pink. "No!" she said, she had to say it again, and she tried to crawl back to the river, to the shower of moonglow, but his thumb found its way and focused itself directly on her clitoris. The wolf's humping rode Rainey's body forward against his thumb, creating a constant and dominant friction.

Like a shot, Rainey was soaked through with an awful pleasure and sucked back into her body like dirt in a vacuum. Digging into the rock, she fought the sensation, but his grip caught her up in a cage. The heat of his breath and his relentless thumb forced her body to respond outside of her will. She strained toward the river, toward the moon and its shine, the warmth and the shield it gave her, but he zeroed his thumb in further and he laughed.

"See, baby, you want it! All you bitches want it!"

He increased his rhythm and held his hand steady, never allowing her to escape from the climb she didn't want to feel. As she found herself taken and taken and taken, her body rose higher and the pain fractured mute and blunted. She went blind into white and fell into the throb, the heat and the static, finally releasing and crossing the pinnacle of orgasm. He said, "Oh, yeah, baby, that's a good girl," and he pushed hard, his semen flowing from him, filling her, then down her legs to the grass.

He dropped her, shuddering, back onto the rock. She felt its edges against her breasts and stomach. And she wanted to die. Right there. She wanted his knife to find her and take her and slice her and kill her. She never wanted to face anyone else ever again. No one.

But Tish. Her eyes flew open and she grabbed onto the grass.

She heard the rush of his zipper, the jingle of his belt. Then he delivered a kick to her ribs and her breath was gone again.

"Don't you forget, woman, you liked it," he said. "Don't you go crying to anyone because they'll see it on your face. If I'da let you talk, you'da begged for it. You come find me another night and I'll take care of you again."

The bushes rustled and she heard his step on the path. There was a pause and she stiffened, waiting for him to come back, but then she heard him say something, too low for her to make out. A soft sound answered, a kitten's mew, and he was off down the path, his feet moving swiftly back the way Rainey came. The way she walked with her daughter after eating ice cream cones and admiring the sunset.

Rainey tried to sit up. She was on fire and her ribs felt like they were going to split through her skin. Holding onto a branch of the bush, she tried to stand, but her hand slid down, stripping leaves, and she sat hard upon the ground again. She fought against the pain, against the blackness that beckoned at the corners of her eyes, a dark and silent lake, promising peace, promising escape.

But she had to get to Tish.

Bracing herself first on her knees, she forced herself upwards until she could stand and look over the bush. Rainey was naked from the waist down, her panties sliced, her skirt gone, her shirt and cami straggling damp from her armpits. She began to shake as she covered herself the best she could.

That sound again, like the cry of a kitten. Rainey looked over the bush, and saw the form that she suddenly knew would be there. "Tish," she said and her little girl looked up, her face as white as the moonlight. Rainey stumbled through the bushes and fell beside her. Rolling Tish into her arms, they lay on the grass together, and Rainey tried to stop her own trembling even as she tried to stop Tish's. She kept repeating Tish's name, a whisper, a soft comforting sound, and she tried to cover them both, to warm them in a blanket of "Tish, it's okay, it's okay."

Time seemed to slow down and, as they rocked, Rainey felt the grass grow flat and cold. Tish didn't make another sound. Finally, there was the soft whine of a bicycle tire, the gentle jingle of its chain. Rainey sat up, pulling Tish with her onto her lap, using her child to cover her nakedness as much as she could. "Help," she said then, at first softly, like her mantra of comfort, but then louder, more strident. "Help!" she howled, throwing her head back, looking up at the moon, forcing the word toward the stars to shine on them both and bring them rescue. Only when the brakes squealed, only when the bike dropped and the policeman ran toward them did Rainey begin to cry. To cry and rock and hold her child, who curled warm in her lap and pressed silently against her.

Wrapped in a warm blanket, Rainey lay on a stretcher in the ambulance, not listening to the paramedics as they said soft things to her, touched her arm, attempted to take her blood pressure. Once she assured them several times that she had no neck pain, the paramedics were willing to pass on the backboard, but they insisted on the stretcher. Rainey gave in to this, as long as Tish was able to be on the stretcher with her, not on a different stretcher, not seated on the other side of the ambulance, not in the front seat with the driver. Rainey only wanted to look at her daughter, to watch Tish, who sat at her waist, holding her hand, but looking down at her lap and not saying a word. Rainey remembered her thought from earlier, that Tish would be so excited to be escorted home by a policeman on a bicycle; yet now, with the siren shrieking and squawking radio calls all around them, Tish didn't look up once. Rainey squeezed her hand and was reassured when the little girl's fingers replied.

When they got to the hospital, Rainey and Tish were rolled inside. The ER was in its usual state of chaos and Rainey was grateful when they were brought to a room away from the rest, a room not with curtains, but walls and a door. A nurse lifted Tish off the stretcher and then gently pulled their hands apart. She led Tish to a soft chair, a chair that reclined, a nurse explained, and then she pulled on the handle and tilted Tish back. But Tish tucked her legs beneath her and curled her arms around her own waist. Rainey submitted to the gentle hands of another nurse who removed the blanket from her shoulders and helped her from the stretcher to stand on a paper mat. Carefully, this nurse removed Rainey's shirt and cami, and the remains of her underpants, dropping them to the mat, the sound a sigh like snowfall. When Rainey was naked, the nurse had her step aside and she folded the mat up entirely around the clothes and then she quickly left the room without a word. Rainey wondered what she would wear home. The nurse who helped Tish covered Rainey with a hospital gown, faded, but soft, and settled her on the examining table. "You're a little bit shocky," she said, her voice barely above a whisper. "Let me get you a heated blanket. One for your little girl too." And she left as well.

Rainey rubbed her arms, took as deep a breath as her aching ribs would allow. "Tish," she said. "Tish, are you all right? Did he touch you? Did he hurt you?"

Tish glanced at her, shook her head, then closed her eyes. Rainey wished for sleep for her, a sleep that would take over and wipe out the memory of everything she'd seen. How much did Tish observe from the other side of the bushes? How much did she hear? The bushes were taller than Tish, maybe she hadn't seen anything. Maybe she only sat on the path and waited for her mother to come out. Maybe she only heard the sounds, felt the reverberations shaking the ground. For one quick moment, Rainey was grateful that the rapist convinced her to stay silent; the image of Tish sitting there, listening to her mother's screams, was too much to bear. Maybe there was some good in the forced silence. "Try to sleep," Rainey said. "We'll go home soon."

The nurse came back in and wrapped them both in heated blankets, Rainey first. Rainey sighed as the heat slid through her skin. Tish burrowed into hers, pulling it over her nose, and seemed to drop off.

"Is there someone we can call?" the nurse asked. "A family member who can come to take you home?"

There wasn't family close by. Rainey chose to move to Wisconsin when she became pregnant with Tish. She needed distance from her mother's sad and betrayed face, from her father's scowl and constant complaining that she'd gotten herself knocked up and now she couldn't finish college and she'd better not expect him to support her and her baby. She left their house in St. Louis in the middle of the night, sneaking out just as she snuck out of the dorm for night-swimming, for a night of love and conception, and then she drove north to birth her child. She chose Wisconsin before she left, opening her atlas to a map of the midwest, closing her eyes, turning a magical three times, then dropping her finger down. She discovered a town west of Milwaukee, with the native-sounding name of Waukesha. Rainey felt an earthy rush of excitement as she drove off into the darkness, her disapproving and disappointed parents asleep behind her, and her own hand tucked over the life inside she swore she would protect.

She was all of nineteen years old and she still believed in the magic of spinning three times.

There were no brothers or sisters to call; Rainey was an only child. Tish's father, a young man Rainey had been dating for about six months by that night-swimming night, provided a steady check each month and was otherwise absent. He'd never seen Tish, but he went on to graduate from that Missouri college and he lived now somewhere in Tennessee. He was a name on a check that Tish didn't know about, and Rainey could only hazily remember his face. She remembered nineteen-year old love, though, and her memory of that night was always warm. Even now, she told herself she wouldn't change it, wouldn't alter it, and each time she looked at her daughter, she couldn't imagine a life without her. While Tish was an accident, she felt like a plan. A firm surprise step in Rainey's life that she never would have missed.

But for family, there was Doris, Rainey's landlord and the woman who cared for Tish during the day, before and after school. She lived on the other side of the two-story duplex Rainey rented from her.

"Rainey?" the nurse said and shook her gently. "Someone to take you home?"

Rainey blinked and looked at the clock hung solidly between two prints of flowers on the exam room wall. It was just before ten. Doris would be in her nightclothes by now, wrapped warmly in what she called her duster, but she would be awake. And she'd be well aware of the quiet next door and she'd be wondering why there was no sound of splashing bath water, or of a young girl singing an off-key lullaby. "Please call Doris Granger, my next door neighbor," Rainey said and gave the nurse the number. "Tell her to use her key to go inside and bring me some clothes."

The nurse nodded. "Is she someone you would be comfortable with knowing what happened?"

Rainey thought of Doris being told only to come to the hospital, to bring clothing. In the half-hour it would take for Doris to dress, then go to Rainey's to pick out pants and a shirt and decent underwear, and drive through every stoplight to get there, she would pass all possibilities through her mind. She would consider that Tish was murdered, Rainey attacked, the blood of Tish's killer sprayed on her clothes. Rainey shook her head, clearing her thoughts. "Please tell her immediately what happened. Then she can be prepared."

The nurse took Doris' number and left. Rainey sat and watched Tish. And she waited for Doris.

Rainey and Tish loved Doris. With her own mother's abdication to a relationship of infrequent phone calls and random practical packages in the mail, Rainey felt that Doris stepped in, became a mother and grandmother both. She was at times a bit too religious for Rainey's taste, wearing a variety of crosses, in silver, in gold, some plain, some with Christ stretched across, his head tilted toward a concave chest. Doris read to Tish from a book of Bible stories sometimes, and offered frequent promises to pray for Rainey's health, her job, her life, but Rainey found all that easy to overlook. That was just the indoor Doris and Rainey loved her, but she loved the outdoor Doris even more.

Every day, Doris decorated her front yard with a variety of stuffed animals. A large English sheepdog always sat on the front porch, sometimes joined by another and a litter of puppies. Multi-colored sheep grazed on the grass, alternating with cows and a horse. A bald eagle sat on a fencepost on one day, a chicken the next, a garish plaid vulture on the third. Rainey loved best the large six-foot neon green ape that sat on a wooden glider under the maple tree. Doris even provided fluorescent yellow fake bananas by its side. On rainy days, there was only the sheepdog on the porch, protected by the overhang. In the winter, the stuffed animals cavorted in the snow, standing firmly on brightly colored plastic sleds Doris bought for them at the Wal-Mart. She scoured Goodwill weekly for these orphaned stuffed animals. Tish played in the back yard, where Doris provided a swingset and a sandbox, but she loved to run among the animals in the front yard. Rainey knew that passersby sometimes startled at the sight of her lean and quick daughter moving like a dark sprite among all that stuffing.

A doctor hurried in, brandishing a clipboard. A policeman stepped in behind him, and a policewoman followed last. They nodded at her, then stood off to the side, both folding their hands in front of their belts, each of which held a gun. "Ms. Milbright?" the doctor said.

She nodded. "Rainey."

He blinked at her. "I'm sorry?"

"My name is Rainey." She looked toward the blanketed lump in the recliner. "That's my daughter, Tish."

He stood next to the table, gently shook her hand. "I'm Dr. Bradford," he said. "And this is Officer Robert Stanton, and his partner, Officer Sarah Freeman. They'll be working with you on this case."

The officers stepped forward, each offering a hand, and Rainey greeted them politely. Sarah held her hand for just a second longer, patted her gently on the shoulder. Then they stepped back and resumed their posture. Rainey wondered about being a "case."

"Is Rainey short for Lorraine?" the doctor asked.

Rainey winced. Everyone asked that. "No, it's just Rainey. My father named me, it was raining the day I was born, big storms. Knocked out the power, though the hospital had a generator. My mother spelled my name though. Wrong. She gave me an E-Y instead of just a Y."

The doctor smiled. "Well, all right then, Rainey. Are you comfortable with your daughter here? Would it be better if we talked alone? One of the nurses would be happy to—"

"No," Rainey said. She looked at Tish, who hadn't moved. "Please. I need her close." Rainey felt the tears surge up again and she wiped them impatiently away. "I think she fell asleep."

"It's okay." Dr. Bradford put a finger to his mouth, then made a show of tip-toeing over to the recliner. Rainey caught Officer Sarah rolling her eyes and Rainey almost barked a laugh. The doctor carefully removed the top of the blanket and peeked in. He nodded, then returned to Rainey. "She's got her eyes closed," he said. "And she's breathing deeply, so it looks like she's out. She didn't suffer any injury?"

Rainey remembered hugging Tish on the ground while they waited for rescue. Tish felt cold, but all together, all of a piece. She remembered Tish shaking her head when Rainey asked if she was hurt. "I didn't notice anything," she said. "But I don't know what she saw. She hasn't said anything since I found her."

"Could be shock." Dr. Bradford sat down next to Rainey and continued talking in a soft voice that Rainey had to lean to hear. "My understanding is that you were attacked on the Riverwalk tonight while you were walking through with your daughter."

Rainey wished they would go back to just talking about names. She wished she was in a room that didn't have police officers in it. She wished that this was just another middle of the night ER visit when her daughter woke up with croup and a fever. Rainey's voice suddenly left and she nodded.

"You were raped?"

She nodded again.

"And you're not sure how much your daughter witnessed."

Rainey looked over his shoulder at the recliner. There was no movement. She struggled, cleared her throat, forced her voice out, though it was clogged and weak. "I told her to run, but when I came out of the bushes, she was sitting on the path."

Dr. Bradford touched her arm, so lightly, she could only just barely feel it through the blanket. "There are some things we have to do that will probably seem cold and awful to you after what you've already been through. But we have to collect specimens which will help to identify your rapist, if the police find him. I also want to do an examination to make sure you're all right, that you didn't suffer any internal or external injuries, beyond what I can already see."

Rainey thought it was odd that he referred to the man as "her rapist." Like she owned the man who attacked her. Like she knew who he was or that he was a part of her life. Her mother, her father. Her friend, her daughter. Her rapist.

The doctor set aside his clipboard and glanced at the nurse as she came in. "Do you know if your rapist used a condom?"

A condom? "No, he didn't."

"All right. We'll talk about options as we go along."

Rainey shuddered. She remembered reading a newspaper article about a woman who asked her attacker to use one of the condoms she had in her purse and he was actually willing to do so. Rainey was amazed by the article, and thought about putting condoms in her own purse, but she never got that far. She certainly never thought to ask her rapist about protection. He wouldn't let her speak.

The nurse pulled up a chair and held Rainey's hand as Dr. Bradford asked for details on the rape. The officers each pulled out small notebooks and seemed to be jotting down everything that Rainey said. She tried to recall it all and she stumbled over her word choice, trying to pick the clean words, no slang. Every time she mentioned a body part, she looked over at Tish. The doctor and nurse looked too, and so did the officers, but Tish remained buried and silent, apparently asleep.

"Okay," the doctor said finally. The nurse captured Rainey's other hand and held it tightly between her own. "We're going to give you an internal exam. It will be a little different than what you're used to…we'll be doing a pubic hair combing, trying to collect anything that belongs to your rapist. And we'll have to collect specimens from your mouth and your vagina. It will be uncomfortable, I know, but it really will help in the long run. We want to make sure this guy never hurts anyone else again."

Rainey tried to think of that, of his being out there, waiting to attack someone else. But it was hard to fathom. It felt like her rapist was waiting that night for her alone. Her rapist. All hers. "My mouth?" she said. "But…he didn't come when he was there." She blushed and suddenly her blanket was too hot. She wished she could throw it off and wrap it more tightly around herself at the same time.

"We'll scrape some of the cells from the inside of your cheeks. There might be evidence there. We'll also be taking blood to establish a baseline and begin checking for STD's. If your rapist has an STD, it won't show up tonight, but you can start treatment just in case, if you wish. You'll be retested periodically over the next several months to make sure nothing develops. But if anything new develops in further testing, we'll know it came from him."

Rainey hadn't even thought of that possibility. Suddenly, a man skulking in the bushes, waiting to jump out and attack her, attack a woman, seemed very likely to be covered with disease. "AIDS?" Rainey said softly.

"You'll be tested for that too, but your chances of contracting AIDS through rape are statistically very small." He turned to the officers. "Robert and Sarah, I'd like to start examining Rainey now. Can you wait outside please?"

They both nodded and Sarah said quickly, "We'll be just outside the door, Rainey, okay?"

Rainey nodded and wondered what they were waiting for. She didn't think her rapist was likely to show up at the ER, ready to attack her again. Still, she felt a sense of safety, knowing that there were officers at her door, and a doctor and nurse here in the room with her and her daughter.

Dr. Bradford turned back to her after the door closed. "Now are you in good health?"

Rainey relaxed as the doctor ran through the usual litany of pre-exam questions. She was familiar with this, knew the answers, and she could pretend that she was just there for her annual physical. He asked her for the date of her last period and she gave it, but then she flinched and sat straight up. The blanket fell off her shoulders. "Oh, God," she said, her voice suddenly back and strong. "Could I get pregnant from this?"

The nurse jumped up and covered Rainey again. "I'm going to get another heated blanket," she said.

Dr. Bradford looked at his calendar. "It's not likely, given today's date and the date of your last period."

"But my cycle is always irregular. I can go for the usual twenty-eight days one month, and then go for forty the next."

Dr. Bradford frowned. "Well, we can think about that. If you're worried about pregnancy, there is something you can take. The morning after pill. It's like taking a handful of birth control pills at once. Are you on any contraception?"

"No," Rainey whispered. "I'm not involved with anyone."

The doctor nodded, then stood to place both his hands on Rainey's shoulders. She recoiled, his touch feeling like an invasion. He stepped quickly back. "I'm sorry," he said. "It's going to be okay. Really. We'll just take this step by step."

A week ago, a few hours ago, Rainey would have welcomed a touch from a man. A good man. Now, she couldn't stop herself from trembling.

The nurse returned and supported Rainey's back as she was eased into a lying position on the table. Rainey forced herself not to jerk. "We'll start with the pelvic exam," Dr. Bradford said.

Rainey heard the clang as the metal stirrups were pulled out and snapped into place. The nurse settled another warm blanket around her and Rainey longed to tuck her head under, like Tish, and just go to sleep while the doctor did his work.

"You might want to look into counseling for your daughter," Dr. Bradford said from somewhere between her knees. "Here's the speculum. It'll be cold."

Rainey stared at the ceiling and tried not to think of the knife.

"And for yourself too," the nurse murmured.

Rainey frowned. "What?"

"Counseling."

There was a sudden slice of pain and Rainey yelped and snapped her knees together.

"Easy," the doctor said. He touched her knees, carefully opened them, and Rainey began to cry. "It's okay. Just take deep breaths. You have an injury here…a cut?"

"It's from the knife," Rainey whispered. The nurse's grip on her hand tightened. "He told me to be quiet and I made a noise and he…used the knife."

The room spun away and Rainey fell deep into the shock of her experience. Sounds rose out of her as harsh and unstoppable as a convulsion. She felt an increase in heat and then she heard the soft sound of rain and felt it drizzling her kneecaps. Soaking in the warmth, she tried to steady her breathing, to soften her cries, and she realized the nurse was draped across her, hugging her, rocking and shushing her just as Rainey rocked Tish on the Riverwalk. The raindrops were Dr. Bradford's palms, patting her knees in a smooth and calming rhythm. "Easy, easy," he kept saying. "Just breathe."

"I'm okay," she said finally. "Let's just get this over with."

Rainey breathed through all the collections and blood-lettings. Dr. Bradford sutured the cut inside her and Rainey gripped the nurse's hand until they both heard knuckles popping. Rainey laughed then, just a little, and the nurse smiled back. Rainey left the room for x-rays, but only after the nurse promised to not leave Tish alone, not even for a second, and Officer Sarah reassured her she would stay outside the door, while Officer Robert accompanied Rainey to the x-ray room. Eventually, they all gathered in the exam room again, and Dr. Bradford presented a brown paper bag.

"Here are the clothes your neighbor brought in." He set it on her lap. "You've got the cut that extends to deep inside of your vagina and several tears. I'm giving you antibiotics for those to prevent infection, and that will cover the bite marks on your neck too. As you heal, the sutures will dissolve. You have cracks on several of your ribs, and these are bound to be very painful over the next several weeks. You have extensive deep bruising, particularly on your face, but also on your ribcage and back, and gouges on your knees and elbows and palms. I'm prescribing a painkiller, which you can take as necessary. When the pain eases, you can just use ibuprofen or acetaminophen, which will help with the swelling too." He handed her a baggie filled with packets of pills and two slips of paper. "We'll send the test results to your doctor, so you should make an appointment with," he looked at his notes, "Dr. Johansen in a couple days so she can go over them with you. In the meantime, like we said, you might want to think about checking into counseling for both you and your daughter." He gave her a brochure. "Here's a list of providers specializing in rape recovery. Don't be afraid to come back here or call if you need help." He stepped back.

It struck Rainey how organized her situation was, how easily her injuries were categorized. One after another, ticked off, and the treatment presented. All black and white. Just step forward. But it felt like she was stepping into a quagmire. Into a sea of purple and green. "So can we go home now?"

Dr. Bradford shook his head. "Not quite yet, I'm afraid. From here, your neighbor will take you to the police station. Officer Robert and Officer Sarah will want you to describe your rapist again, to try and get a composite of him. And they'll want to take pictures of you, the extent of your injuries."

Rainey slumped. All she wanted to do was go home. Go home, shower, and then sleep for as long as she could stay under.

From his post near the door, Officer Robert said softly, "We know you're tired, Rainey. But this has to be done, especially while your memory is still fresh. We want to get started trying to find him."

Dr. Bradford tentatively touched her shoulder. "I wish I could do more, Rainey. I'm sorry this happened to you. It should never happen at all. Not to anyone." He quickly squeezed her hand, then left before she could say goodbye or thank him. The officers followed him out.

The nurse opened the bag. "Do you need help getting dressed?"

"No, I don't think so. I'll be fine." Rainey looked inside and smiled when she saw her favorite battered gray sweatshirt and a soft pair of yoga pants. "So Doris is still here?"

"Yes, she's in the waiting room. Just come out when you're done."

When Rainey stripped off the hospital gown, she startled at the dark patchwork on her own skin. Purple and red bruises fanned over her ribcage and spotted her breasts. The pain rushed up again, as if the physical sight of her attack brought it right there with her, in that room, not out in an abandoned park next to a whispering river.

Where she wasn't supposed to be in the first place. Where she chose to break the rules. With her daughter in tow.

"*It's against the rules,*" she'd said to Tish. "*Just this once, this one time only, I'm going to let you do something naughty.*"

Rainey wanted to relegate the whole damned thing to the back of her mind, the back of her life. But it was right there with her, not only in the room, but in her own body, on her skin, branded onto her bones.

She dressed quickly, hiding the evidence. Being covered in familiar clothes helped, but she really wanted to get home to her own shower. Carefully, she unwrapped Tish. The little girl slept with her arms around her legs, her cheek resting on her kneecaps. Fighting her own pain, Rainey scooped her up and instantly, Tish molded tightly to her body. Rainey felt the warm hug of Tish's arms around her neck, and the answering squeeze of Tish's legs around her waist. "Tish?" Rainey whispered. "Are you okay? Are you awake?"

There was only warm breath against her neck.

"We're going home now, baby. Just one more stop first." Rainey carried her from the room. Immediately, the officers flanked her and supported her arms as they moved down to the waiting area. Rainey's ribs and shoulders screamed and she felt like her legs weren't working quite right. She looked up in time to see Doris barreling down the hall. Rainey wanted so much to open her arms to her, to fall into the older woman's embrace. But she couldn't let go of her daughter.

"It's okay, it's okay," Doris said and wrapped herself around Rainey and Tish both. "Don't drop her. Do you want me to carry her? I can carry her. Let me help."

"Oh, Doris," Rainey said. Her teeth began to chatter. But as Doris' hands tucked into Tish's armpits, Rainey felt her daughter's body tighten its hold. "She doesn't want to go."

"It's okay, it's okay," Doris repeated. She walked backwards in front of them, and she rubbed Tish's back.

Rainey felt close to tears again. "I just want a shower."

"Then that's what you'll have. And I'll sit there with you the whole time. I'll make you hot chocolate and tuck you into bed."

Rainey shook her head. "We have to go to the police station first."

Doris looked at the officers. "Really? This child needs some sleep. Can't this wait until tomorrow? I can bring her to you in the morning."

Rainey wondered who the child was. Tish? Herself?

Officer Robert shook his head. "I'm sorry, we have to do this now, but it won't take long."

They moved down the hall, Doris leading the way, but looking over her shoulder, Rainey holding Tish, and the two officers on either side of them. Rainey could see Doris' old Toyota Camry parked illegally right outside the entrance. "When I go under that shower, I don't think I'm ever going to want to get out."

"You will, honey, you will." Doris opened the passenger side door. "And I promise there will be more warmth waiting for you. I'll get every blanket in the house. Your side and mine."

Rainey slid into the front seat. There was no discussion about putting Tish in the back or wrapping a seatbelt around her. Even the officers didn't say anything. Rainey became Tish's seatbelt and the more she hugged, the more she felt Tish hug back. Rainey no longer thought that Tish was asleep and she wondered if she ever was, but the girl kept her eyes tightly closed.

Rainey closed her eyes too and rocked as Doris started the Camry and followed the squad car. Rainey rocked all through the dark streets. She tried to push every thought out of her mind, every flash of the attack, every worry about Tish, every throb of her ribs. She tried to just sink into the rhythm.

But the pain wouldn't let her forget.

At the police station, Doris stayed in the waiting room, Tish curled and still pseudo-sleeping on her lap, while Rainey sat in a back office with Robert and Sarah, who showed her sketch after sketch of eyebrows, eyes, noses, hair. They seemed to grow more and more frustrated as Rainey pushed each sketch aside.

"I'm sorry," she said. "It was dark. So was he. I didn't see much. He was big, probably about six-three, and he felt heavy to me. Two-fifty, maybe three hundred pounds?"

Officer Sarah wrote everything down, even though it seemed she'd written it all in the examination room too. "What about his face?"

Rainey closed her eyes, tried to remember, but all she saw was shadow. "I just know he was dark. Black." An image of swirls against the sky came to her. "His hair was really curly. He had white teeth. And brown eyes."

Sarah wrote all this down, then looked at her expectantly.

Rainey felt like she failed a test. "I'm sorry," she said again. "That's all I know. It was just too dark."

Officer Robert sighed and pushed his chair back. "It's okay. If you remember anything else, let us know. Sarah has to take some photos of you now. These will be used against him if we ever catch him."

Rainey thought she heard a note of hopelessness in his voice and she wondered why they were even bothering with the photographs. Her rapist would never be caught. She knew that. She just observed too little…her body and her mind recorded every blow, every word, every place he molested, inside and out. But she didn't know what he looked like.

"His voice was husky," she offered. "He used a lot of curse words. He didn't speak proper English."

"Any accent?" Robert asked.

"No." Rainey looked at the floor, trying to avoid the officers' crestfallen expressions. It was hopeless. She was hopeless.

Officer Sarah took Rainey into another room, where she carefully photographed every inch of Rainey's face and body. She had Rainey take off one article of clothing at a time so that Rainey was never fully naked, and she appreciated that. By the end, Rainey had to hold onto the wall for support. Exhaustion coated her skin and weighed down her eyelids like silver dollars. She leaned on Sarah on the way back out to Doris and Tish. While Sarah and Robert both helped Rainey into the car, Doris buckled Tish in the booster seat in the back.

"Take care, Rainey," Robert said. "Let yourself heal. We're going to do everything we can. We'll be in touch."

Sarah, gently stroking Rainey's hair back behind her ear, whispered, "I'm so sorry, Rainey. I'm so sorry."

Rainey knew she would never see or hear from either of them again.

As Doris pulled away, Rainey turned sideways in her seat, so she could watch Tish. Rainey's vigilance grounded her, preventing her from drifting off into a twilight sleep. She focused on the warmth of the shower that would envelope her soon. Drown her. She would raise her face to the full moon of the showerhead, and in that steam and heat, she would let herself howl. If only she had the energy.

CHAPTER TWO

Doris

At a few minutes before seven, Doris realized that Rainey's alarm clock was probably preset and she reached out to smack it off before it rang. She often heard the siren sound of Rainey's alarm through the wall, on her own side of the duplex. The alarm was harsh and shrill, but Rainey said it was the only thing that would knock her out of a dead sleep. But she needed that dead sleep now. She hadn't been under that long, no longer tossing in the bed like a storm, no longer moaning like her skin was being peeled away. The painkillers must have finally kicked in. Doris stood at the foot of the bed and watched Rainey breathe.

There were just so many bruises. So many bruises on this child's face. The swelling forced Rainey's mouth to stay open and she snored, a delicate sound in the chaos of color, and then on the exhale, the smallest of sighs, a note so thin, it reminded Doris of a rubber band, pulled taut. Doris smoothed the sheet and blanket and tucked them softly around Rainey's shoulders. She'd gotten a glimpse of the bruises on Rainey's stomach and back as she helped Rainey into her nightgown the night before. Doris wanted to keep those wounds warmly hidden away. She laid a hand against Rainey's cheek—it was cool—and then she moved down the hallway.

Doris found Tish lying in her bed, staring at the ceiling. Doris sat next to her and stroked her arm. "How are you, hon?" Doris asked. Tish just shrugged. "Are you ready to get up?"

Tish sat up quickly, then glanced toward the door. When she looked back at Doris, her eyebrows were raised.

"Your mama is sleeping. I think we'd better let her stay that way. She needs rest. How about some breakfast?"

Tish threw back the covers and reached for her robe.

"Okay, good, you must be hungry. We're going to stay over here, all right? Maybe we'll go over to my side after school. But I want to stay here close to your mama, just in case she needs anything."

Tish led the way downstairs, then sat at her place at the table. Doris began raiding the refrigerator, pulling out eggs and bacon and cheese and milk. She wanted to feed Tish, to fill her up with good food and good health, just the way she wanted to cover Rainey in warm blankets. Enough food, enough heat, then everything would be all right. She knew her three-egg omelet was Tish's favorite meal. How such a little girl could pack so much away! Doris found sandwich bologna, another Tish favorite, and decided to throw that in too. Mushrooms, black olives, maybe even pickles. All Tish delicacies, all foods that made Tish lick her lips and crow with hunger. "You want to try pickles in your omelet, honey?"

Tish swung her legs and stared at her placemat.

Doris noted the silence, waited for it to break. She gave Tish a cup of apple juice, then began cooking the omelet. She wondered if the aroma would float up the stairs and wake Rainey, if Rainey would feel hungry, if she would even be able to eat with that swollen mouth. Doris considered getting out the blender and making a shake. There was coffee ice cream in the freezer, Rainey's favorite. She could add milk and chocolate syrup and maybe Rainey could put her lips over the straw and gently sip with the least amount of pain. Or she could use a spoon. Doris glanced over at Tish. Tish never sat so still. There was always something to play with, a salt shaker, a spoon, a napkin. Even her own fingers would do. But now, she sat still and quiet. Doris thought she seemed like a mirage.

"Honey," Doris said, checking the bubbling eggs. "Can you tell me what happened last night? What did you see?" She waited, holding her breath, but Tish didn't answer, another Tish abnormality. Tish typically talked with an unstoppable enthusiasm and Doris punctuated their conversations with "Uh-huh." Doris threw in the rest of the ingredients and began to fold the omelet. Then she tried again. "Did you hear anything? Your mama says you haven't said a word since you were in the park. What happened, hon?" Doris flipped the omelet onto Tish's special Winnie-the-Pooh plate and decided on another tactic. "Your mama said you called the climbing structure a herd of camels! Was that fun?" But when she turned, Tish was no longer in the room. "Tish?"

After setting the plate on the table, Doris looked into the living room. Tish knelt backwards on the couch. She held the curtain away from the window and looked outside. Doris could hear her sucking on her arm. "Tish?" She sat down next to her.

When Tish looked at Doris, her eyes were wide and glassy. Then they seemed to sweep over, tears covering her cheeks in a sheet. Her lips tugged down and then her mouth opened and while her tongue curled and she took wracking breaths, no sound came out.

"Oh, sweetheart!" Doris grabbed her and held her in a hug so fierce, Tish began to gasp. "It's okay. You don't have to talk about it, you don't have to remember it, just forget it all, okay? Forget everything you saw, everything you heard. Your mama is all right, everything is going to be just fine. You wait and see. Your job is just to forget." Doris sat back. She took her shirt sleeve and dried Tish's face. "Come on, your omelet is ready. I even added bologna and pickles, just for you."

Tish took Doris' hand as they returned to the kitchen. As she watched Tish eat, Doris grabbed a fork and swiped small bites of the omelet. It was amazingly good with bologna and pickles and everything else. Doris thought that she'd have to make one like this just for herself, and maybe for Rainey too. "But if you do want to talk, you know you can talk to me, okay?"

Tish nodded and smiled, showing eggy teeth.

"Do you want to talk? About anything? You usually sing to me at breakfast."

Tish looked down, then picked at another forkful.

So Doris gave up. There would be no words out of this child this morning. "It's okay, Tish." As Tish resumed eating, Doris started cleaning up the kitchen. It was always odd being in here, in this side of the duplex where everything was the opposite of hers. Mirror images. She automatically turned to the right to get to the fridge, but it was on the left. Rainey put things in her cabinets differently too, and Doris had to keep reminding herself that it was all right for Rainey to have her own system. Doris would do things differently, of course, and she owned the entire place. But Rainey paid the rent faithfully, after all, and she filled this space with warmth and Doris' life with companionship, and so she should be allowed to make things her own. It was her own, Rainey's own. Doris couldn't imagine anyone else living here.

Doris heard the chair scrape back and she turned to collect Tish's things. There never was a bath the night before and Doris wondered if she should draw one before Tish got dressed, teeth brushed, backpack on, in time to take her off to 4-K. Rainey normally got Tish dressed and fed, and then Doris took over from there, and so the feeling of being out of order kept nagging at her. She touched Tish's Winnie The Pooh backpack, and for the first time, she noticed how gloomy Eeyore looked.

"Tish," she said slowly. "How do you feel about going to school today?"

Tish, standing next to the table, looked away.

"Do you want to go? Or do you think it would be better to stay home, just for today? Take a little break?" Doris herself always believed in staying busy, that work kept your mind off your problems. But this was a pretty big problem, and the school likely needed time to adjust to Tish's not speaking. But then, maybe Tish would speak in school, when the teacher called on her. "School might be a good idea."

Tish shook her head, tightened the tie on her robe, then moved into the living room. Doris heard the television turn on and then the tinkly music of children's programming drifted into the kitchen. Doris thought about insisting that Tish go to school, but when she glanced in and saw Tish lying there on the couch, slippered feet drawn up, thumb in her mouth, that thumb that hadn't been in Tish's mouth for a good six months, she relented. She looked for the school's magnet stuck among others on the refrigerator and then she retrieved her cell phone. But punching in the school's number made her hesitate.

This wouldn't be the first time she called Tish in sick. Doris was listed on the school's records as Tish's daytime caregiver, someone who could be trusted to make decisions and take her to and from school on a regular basis and in emergencies.

But this was different. When the school secretary asked the reason for Tish's staying home, what should Doris say? Tish was sick? She wasn't. She was in shock? Doris wasn't sure. But Tish was silent and that silence showed just how wrong the world was on its axis this morning. How much did the school need to know?

They'd need to know that Tish wasn't talking, certainly. Would they need to know why? How much did they need to know about Rainey? How much would Rainey want them to know?

Doris tucked her phone back into her pocket and walked slowly up the stairs. On the way, she pulled the afghan from a close-by rocker and tucked it snugly around Tish. Tish's lips, pouted around her thumb, tugged upwards in almost a smile. Doris sighed and smiled back. She could at least supply a meal and warmth. She wished she could supply more.

Leaning over Rainey, Doris felt the same need. She smoothed the covers, tucked in the blankets again, stroked Rainey's hair back from her forehead and cheek. Rainey's eyelids fluttered. "Rainey," Doris said. "Rainey, hon, can you wake up for just a second?"

Rainey's eyelids stopped fluttering, then stuttered up like old windowshades. Doris was stunned to see only white and she stepped backwards. Then Rainey's dark brown irises tumbled down, returned Rainey's soul to her body, and she looked directly, if sleepily, at Doris. She blinked.

"Rainey, I think Tish should stay home today. Do you want me to call the school?"

Rainey nodded and her eyelids began to droop.

"No, wait, hon. They'll ask me why she's staying home. What should I tell them?"

Rainey's eyes shot back open. "Oh, god," she moaned. "What should we tell them?" Her voice came out low and moist.

"I think…" Doris touched Rainey's hair, stroked a blanketed shoulder. Tucked it tighter…warmth. "I think we should just tell them the truth. They're going to have to know anyway, especially if Tish takes a while to start talking again. I couldn't get her to say a word at breakfast. She didn't even sing."

Rainey held Doris' gaze. The pain there was almost more than Doris could take. She thought about Tish downstairs, thumb in her mouth, and for just a moment, Doris thought about suggesting the same thing to Rainey. Maybe a retreat, a regression through time, would help.

Then Rainey nodded. "You're right. They should know."

Doris walked to the foot of the bed, tucked in the blankets there. She added another, a throw, to cover Rainey's feet. Feet were always the coldest. "Do you want me to bring you your phone?"

"You tell them." Rainey's eyes closed. "Please, Doris." Her head slunk down until the blanket pooched around her cheeks, leaving only her pale forehead and a few strands of hair visible.

After giving Rainey a final pat and waiting until her breaths went from jagged to even, Doris straightened herself. Returning downstairs, she patted Tish too, on her way to the kitchen. There, she brought cell phone out again and stood next to the fridge, dialing the number that appeared on the school magnet.

"Blair Elementary Attendance!" the secretary cheered into the phone.

"Good morning." Doris worked at keeping her voice strong and steady. Maybe they wouldn't ask anyway. And then she could tell them later, once she figured out exactly what to say, how to say it. "I need to report that Tish Milbright won't be in 4-K today."

"Is this her mother?"

"No, I'm her caretaker. I've called in before."

"Oh, yes, Mrs. Granger, we have you on file. Reason for the absence?"

And there it was. Doris hesitated. "Well…it's kind of a complex situation. Would it be possible for me to speak with Tish's teacher?"

The secretary paused, then said, "Let's see if she's in her room. I'll transfer you."

During the minute that the recorded music played into her ear, Doris tried to prepare her speech. Words flew in and out of her mind…attack, rape, Rainey, silence, Tish, rape, silence. Rape. Rape! Right in front of a four-year old.

"Mrs. Whitstone here, can I help you?"

Doris startled. "Oh, hello, Mrs. Whitstone. It's Doris Granger, Tish's caretaker."

"Good morning, Mrs. Granger! I hear Tish won't be in school today?"

"Well, no, and there's a special circumstance I need to tell you about. Tish's mother asked me to call you and explain." Doris closed her eyes, then carefully selected from the pile of words, tasting each for delicacy and truth. "Last night, Rainey was attacked and raped." She heard the teacher's gasp. "And apparently, Tish witnessed it. They were walking home on the Riverwalk."

"Oh my god."

Doris nodded. Three simple words, but the horror was clear. "Rainey got pretty banged up. And Tish, well, Tish seems to have stopped talking. She hasn't said a word since the attack. She wasn't hurt, she's not bruised, I don't even think she was touched. But she's just…mute."

The teacher stumbled a bit over her own words, then gained purchase and momentum. She talked about supporting Tish, having her see the school counselor, maybe see a therapist outside of the school as well. Doris said that Rainey was already considering this. And then they agreed to give Tish that day and the next off, and then she should be back at school. That would be Friday, so Tish would go for one day, then have two days off, then be back to a normal routine. "If her mother agrees, of course."

After thanking Mrs. Whitstone and promising to share the plan with Rainey, Doris checked on Tish, then sat down at the kitchen table. She decided to give herself a break, a second cup of coffee, a doughnut from Rainey's secret stash above the refrigerator. As she raised the mug to her lips, though, she noticed how her hand shook. And then, as she sipped, the teacher's words rang through her ears again.

Oh my god.

The horror, the shock. Each word saturated with an emotion that couldn't be fully expressed by the words, but by the sounds of them. And yet the words the teacher chose were the ones that Doris used daily, in reverence and awe. *Oh, my God.*

Setting the coffee down, Doris folded her hands, then rested her forehead on her fingers. She tried to pray, but after the "Oh, my God," she was surprised at the words that blazoned across the insides of her eyelids, a hidden marquee in bright and angry red:

"Where were You? God, where were You last night?"

Doris' fingers unfolded and covered her face as she began to cry. More words came to her, as they always did, words memorized in love and in faith, words learned and tucked away for later comfort. These came from Proverbs 14:26.

In the fear of the Lord is strong confidence: and his children shall have a place of refuge.

Where was Tish's refuge? Where was Rainey's? Where was God?

And where was Doris' comfort? The words she knew so well, kept prepared for such a situation, weren't bringing her the comfort she thought they would. The way they always did. But then again, such a situation didn't really work here. It didn't fit. This was a situation never ever imagined.

There was a soft touch on her arm and Doris immediately pulled Tish onto her lap. The child didn't cry, but began to rock, and Doris rocked with her, trying to find a rhythm that would bring them comfort. Comfort for Tish, and comfort for herself as well. And somehow, comfort for the battered body that lay hidden in blankets upstairs.

His children shall have a place of refuge. That's what they all needed right now. Doris rested her chin on Tish's head and looked around at Rainey's kitchen. Which Doris owned and provided. For now, Doris would provide the refuge. She would offer comfort as best she could.

But God was Doris' comfort.

Where was He?

Foreign words, foreign thoughts. A foreign, unthinkable, alien situation. Doris closed her eyes and rocked, breathing in the scent of Tish's shampoo and little girl sweat. And something else too.

Fear. Fear emanated from Tish like a sheen. Doris could feel its spark.

She held on tight.

CHAPTER THREE

Tish

I saw them. I saw him. He did stuff to Mama.

He made Mama hurt.

Mama put his boy-thing in her mouth. And he said suck. I suck on suckers. I suck on popsicles. Grape and root beer are my favorites.

I used to suck on my thumb. I am sucking on it again.

I cried. I didn't know what to do. Then the man left and Mama cried and then I was scared. She said help.

Doris says, "Say something, Tish." Mama says it too.

I can't.

I am sucking on my thumb. It tastes like eggs and pickles. It is my boy thing. He said suck. And then he will go away.

CHAPTER FOUR

Rainey

Week 1: During the first thirty hours after conception, the zygote remains a single cell, but then it divides into two. Fifteen hours after that, it divides into four. And at the end of three days, it looks like a berry, made up of sixteen cells. It's now called a morula, which is Latin for mulberry.

At the end of its first week, the mulberry becomes a blastocyst. It is the size of a pinhead, but composed of hundreds of cells. Cilia, tiny hair-like projections in the fallopian tube, gently hold the blastocyst and push it on its journey to the uterus.

When Rainey woke, she held still for a moment and wondered why she was in bed. It felt late to her, and she could hear the sounds of the television downstairs in the living room. Tish was up. Tish was never up before Rainey.

But when Rainey tried to move, she remembered.

Everything hurt. The only way to keep pangs of pain from cascading over her entire body was to hold absolutely still and take the shallowest of breaths. She ran her tongue over her lips and the motion made her face sting. If Tish was downstairs, Rainey had no doubt that Doris was here, taking care of her. It sounded like the playtime music from Nick Jr., so it had to be Tish. If it was Doris watching television, the house would be flooded with the dramatic swells of the daytime soap operas. Stories, Doris called them. Rainey wondered for a moment why Tish wasn't in school.

Then she felt again the weight of Tish against her, folded against her body, not saying a sound, not even opening her eyes. Tish was home from school. Was she hurt?

Rainey remembered asking, and Tish shaking her head. But she never said the word. Never "No."

Rainey tried to sit up and a sound escaped from her before she could stop it. She sounded like a cow in heat. Despite the pain, Rainey smiled. If Tish was there, she'd be giggling.

Before Rainey could get to her feet, Doris appeared in the doorway. "Tish is fine," she said. "Stay in bed, Rainey."

Grateful, Rainey sank into the mattress, maneuvering onto her back as Doris tucked the comforter around her shoulders. "I remember now…you woke me up earlier. You called the school?"

Doris nodded and sat on the edge of the bed. "She's still not talking. I called Mrs. Whitstone and explained what happened and she felt that Tish should stay home for a couple days. Just to get herself together."

Rainey waited for her body to settle and all the shouts of pain to quiet into whispers. She wondered what she looked like. She remembered the spatterings of bruises over her body the night before; her skin looked like a piece of desperate modern art. For a second, a second only before her mind shadowed her memory, Rainey remembered feeling like a marbled porterhouse steak and it seemed she looked like one too. By now, the bruises would have deepened and sprouted more color. Black. Purple. Deep, deep red. Had Tish seen her that morning? "I guess that makes sense. It's really hard to imagine her in school today, as if nothing happened. I'm glad she's home. Thanks, Doris."

They sat like that for a second. Rainey felt like she should be doing something, but she didn't know what. This whole day just felt odd, out of routine, no schedule at all. Tish not at school, Doris here instead of in her own side of the duplex. And where was Rainey supposed to be?

Work.

Rainey nearly sat bolt upright; in her mind, she did, but her body shrieked and clung to the mattress. "Doris, my job! They're probably wondering where I am!"

Doris shook her head. "No, hon. I thought of that. I called them early this morning. I only said you were sick, though…I didn't know what you'd want me to tell them."

Rainey sighed and settled back. Doris' lack of words caused a momentary relief that calmed her heart rate. Though she thought it odd that Tish's teacher would know what happened before Rainey's own boss. It seemed out of place. Perfect, really, just so with the jumbled-up nothing's-where-it-should-be feel of this day.

Doris patted her hand. "Is there anything you need? Are you hungry?"

Hunger. Rainey focused on that, fighting her way down to her basic bodily functions which must be under her bruises somewhere. She felt a twinge. "I think so." She shook her head. "I think these pain meds are leaving me sort of goofy."

Doris smiled. "Why don't I get you a nice bowl of soup? I made a huge crock pot of chunky tomato and vegetable yesterday. Had to do something with all the tomatoes and zucchini from the garden. Let me heat some up. That'll feel good down to your bones."

Rainey nodded. She recognized the ting of a headache. "Maybe some coffee too? And some water?"

"You bet. Just rest. I'll tell Tish you're awake." Doris pushed herself off the bed.

"Has she seen me today?"

"I don't think so. I stayed over last night and sat with you until seven. She was in bed until I got her up." Doris hesitated by the doorway. "I'll try to prepare her a bit. Your face…well, your face takes a little getting used to, I think."

She didn't leave and Rainey waited, wondering if Doris needed instructions on how to prepare Tish. And what could be said, really? Your mother looks like she's had the crap beaten out of her, so be ready. But Tish already knew that, didn't she. Rainey started to scrunch down, thinking to pull the blanket up to her cheekbones, but then Doris brought in a new thought.

"Rainey…should I call your parents?"

The zing that went through Rainey took her breath away and snapped her arms down straight to her sides. Her entire body felt like it suddenly went on full alert. "No," she gasped. "No, Doris, I don't think that's necessary."

"But, well, they should know, shouldn't they? Maybe they could help?"

Rainey forced herself to take a deep breath against the ache in her ribs, forced herself to slope her body against the sheets, her head against the pillow. Maybe she would need to find someone to help, but who, if not her parents? Doris was, after all, an old woman. Maybe this whole thing would be too much for her. She worked hard, taking care of Tish during the day, and she was always there for Rainey too. But now, caring for a child who suddenly wouldn't talk and a woman who…well, it would be difficult, wouldn't it. Rainey cleared her throat. "Do you want me to ask around? See if I can get some help here, so it's not so much on you?"

"Oh, no!" Doris immediately came back over to the bed and fussed over the covers. "I just thought…well, I thought you might want your mom, Rainey. With all this."

Rainey thought of her mother, the way she turned her face away while her father ranted about Rainey's becoming pregnant with Tish. Slut, he'd called her, and her mother hadn't said a word. She hadn't raised a hand or her voice. And in the four years since Tish was born, Rainey hadn't seen either of her parents. Her mother was only a voice on the phone, a name on the cards and packages she sent. Her father…her father was lost in the background. "No, Doris, I really don't. I don't want them to be bothered."

"All right then." Doris stroked Rainey's hair, then left the room.

Rainey sank down further, feeling the comforter slide against her face. Odd how something that felt so cool could also feel so warm underneath. She closed her eyes and folded her arms across her chest. She could feel herself breathing. With the warmth around her like water and the cool of the material against her face like a breeze, Rainey thought of night-swimming again, so long ago. She remembered thinking of it last night, before the attack. Before the rape. Those awful sounds of a few hours ago rose up for a moment, and Rainey shook them out of her head and instead focused on the memory of her college friends' soft laughter, the water undulating with under-the-surface secret movement. The water buoyed her and she felt sinewy and sleek, her skin glistening with the moon. Dwayne, her young lover, swam around her like a snake, an eel, and the press of his body against hers was delicious. She remembered mating in the still spring-chilly lake, her legs wrapped around his waist as he used the wake from others' play and the flutter-kick of his own feet to enter her, only their heads above water, everyone around them slow-motion cavorting, maybe mating themselves, no one paid attention. Tish's moist and shimmering conception. Rainey remembered the intensity of the underwater orgasm, her struggle to remain silent and not roar with glee and the swell of life at the moon, and she wondered now if she would ever want a man to touch her that way again. She remembered last night's orgasm, so animal, so out of her control, so not a part of her own desire, and she shuddered.

Not like that. Not like that. It wasn't supposed to be that way.

Slut, her father called her.

On that night in the moon water, that night with her friends and the song of waves and soft voices, she wasn't a slut. She was alive. But last night. Last night under a different moon and with the river running by her, not supporting her, not holding her up, but running away…

Last night, Rainey was her father's daughter. Last night, she felt, she was everything he thought she was.

Rainey felt a touch and opened her eyes to Tish. Tish's small hand splayed against Rainey's cheek, her thumb touching what must be bruise or a cut, from the spark that went through Rainey's awareness. Her hand shot up from the comforter and slapped Tish away, then immediately, as Tish jumped and pulled back, she clasped Tish's fingers and squeezed them tightly.

"Honey," Rainey said, "I'm sorry, you startled me, and you touched an owie place." Tish's eyes filled. "It's okay, it's okay, I know you didn't mean it." Tish pulled back, trying to escape, and Rainey held on, despite the shriek of pain that went up her arm, down her shoulder, to her ribcage. "Tish, stop it, don't go. Stay here with me."

Tish's fingers and arm went limp. Tish was never limp. Even in sleep, the child was like electricity, a volt of energy.

Rainey patted the empty pillow next to her. "Doris is making me soup. Maybe even crackers." She tried to smile. "Oyster crackers, honey, and maybe I'll share some with you. Wanna come in next to me? You can turn on the television, if you want."

Tish climbed in, but while she reached for the remote and turned on the TV, her eyes never left Rainey's face. When the jazzy soundtrack from Blues' Clues filled the room, Tish set the remote down, hesitated, then lifted the blanket and looked under at Rainey's body.

Rainey was never so grateful for her old and ratty nightgown. Tish wouldn't see anything other than worn and familiar flannel. With a sigh, Tish replaced the comforter and nestled into the pillow. Rainey let her watch the TV show for a while, then she touched her hand. "Tish, are you all right?"

Tish nodded.

"Did that man…" Just mentioning him made him rise up again, a shadow against a black night sky. Rainey closed her eyes, swallowed, then tried again. She felt Tish's fingers squeezing hers. "Did he hit you? Step on you? When he left?"

Tish shook her head, that same motion from the night before, but she didn't release Rainey's fingers. She didn't go limp. Rainey relished her grip.

"So you didn't get hurt?"

Tish turned to her then, going up on her knees, her face as white and full as the moon the night before, and the tears that rushed forth were not individual drops, but a wave that covered Tish's face and flowed off her chin. She shook her head again, then pointed at Rainey.

Rainey fought her aching ribs, sat up, and hugged Tish. "Yes, Tish," she said. "Yes, he hurt me. But I'm okay, all right? I'm fine. I'm right here and I'm okay. Honey, what did you hear? Did you see what he did to me?"

Tish sobbed and Rainey felt the nod against her chest. "Oh, baby," she said, and she remembered the man again, her rapist, the brutality, the wolf that he was, sinking his teeth into her neck. What would that look like to a four-year old? Like grizzly bears? What do lust and violence look like? Lions tearing at a kill? A felled and bloody wildebeest? And what does it do to a four-year old when that bloody wildebeest is your mother?

She let Tish cry until her breaths caught, and then deepened. Rainey used the sheet to wipe Tish's face and nose. Rainey tried to say that it would be all right, that things were fine, but her own throat constricted, as if her rapist's hand was there again, his teeth against her neck. So instead, Rainey sat back with her daughter snuggled in her armpit and they both watched the television.

Doris showed up with a tray and two steaming bowls of soup. "This'll warm you," she said. "This'll do you both good." There was a mug of coffee and a glass of clinking ice water and a Winnie-the-Pooh cup filled with chocolate milk. And one large bag of oyster crackers.

"Look," Rainey said. "We don't even have to share, Tish. Doris thought of everything." She struggled to sit back up and Doris caught her under the arms. Scooting her up like a baby propped on a pillow, Doris set Rainey into a sitting position and she placed a bolster behind her. Tish scooted up on her own. The tray went between them.

As she ate, Rainey savored the feeling of tomato warmth sinking down her throat and puddling into steaming comfort at her core. Tish slurped noisily beside her and Rainey swallowed a plea to be careful around the comforter. She watched Doris help Tish sprinkle oyster crackers over the soup surface until it looked like a pond covered with cream-colored lilypads. Oyster crackers were the first finger-food Tish went for as a baby, spurning the usual empty-circle Cheerios for the solidity of a hexagon. Rainey remembered that baby toothless mouth gumming the salty snack and grinning, Tish's drool turning into a paste. Ever since then, the house was never without oyster crackers in the cupboard.

Rainey thought, for a moment, of conception, the possibility of pregnancy, of a new baby, a child emerging from the heartlessness of rape, and she wondered if the soup was nourishing more than herself. If there was already a hungry little mouth sucking the soup from her own stomach, taking what it needed to grow. The child of an animal. A brute. A wolf, or maybe, from Tish's perception, a grizzly bear.

What would such a child be like?

Rainey shuddered and dropped her spoon. Doris glanced over. "You okay?"

Rainey nodded. "Just still a little shaky. When am I due for more pain meds?"

Doris checked her watch. "In about ten minutes. Guess it won't hurt you to have them a little early."

As Doris disappeared into the bathroom, Rainey looked at Tish. As a baby, she was seven pounds five ounces of pure screaming sweetness. Even through all of the colic and temper tantrums, Rainey detected a purity in Tish, a depth in those eyes that revealed the caring and compassion that would steer the child to bring home dead birds and animals. Doris graciously allowed these animals to be buried in her back yard, complete with glued popsicle sticks for headstones, and made-up names so the creatures wouldn't be buried like strangers. There was that soft smile and graceful movement that exposed Tish to the future, as a woman who would love well and who would never want to hurt anybody.

A child who named a dead squirrel Nutty Frank and buried him with tears and a prayer learned from Doris would never be a monster. Never an animal herself.

What would this new child, if there was a child, be like?

And Rainey wondered, as she slid her hands under the comforter and cupped her belly, if there was a child, would she even give it the chance to show what it was like? Or would it follow the path of the earlier brother or sister, the earlier mistake, a high school mistake, the one before Tish? The one Rainey's boyfriend convinced her not to have.

Rainey swallowed the pills Doris brought her, then closed her eyes. When Tish kissed her, when she and Doris tiptoed out of the room, bringing the tray with them, Rainey pretended not to hear.

At fifteen, Rainey fell in love for the first time, in that wonderful blinding way that adolescents have, before they are afraid of rejection and abandonment and isolation. Of course he would fall in love with her, this seventeen-year old junior in high school where Rainey was a freshman, this boy who dressed cool and played on the basketball team and had dimples so deep, they creviced the corners of his mouth even when he was deadpan. Her love for him was so powerful, so all-encompassing, taking over in squiggles on her notebooks, hot entries into her journal, daydreams that kept her from answering teachers' questions, that she knew he would fall for her too. He had to. At fifteen, Rainey felt that love was a magnet, that if she loved someone, her love would draw him in. And it did. That, and a deep V-necked white sweater that exposed the smooth curves of her new and profound breasts if she bent just the right way, and she did, scooping things out of her backpack when he happened to be passing by. There was also a short black skirt that swirled and pressed against her thighs as she made extra trips to the salad bar, which was happily next to the table where he ate lunch.

They dated for six months, moving swiftly from held hands at the movies to dancing pasted together at school events to the reclined seats of his father's car. She loved him, she did, and his touch felt so good and she kept letting him go just a little further. Over the sweater, then under, and she swore she felt the skin on her breasts stretch taut with need under his fingertips. Her nipples became impossibly erect and his tongue against them was the only antidote. Over the skirt, then under, over the panties and then under, and when his fingers entered her, when he clumsily and then not so clumsily massaged her clitoris, she felt the world fall away and open up for her, only for her. She stroked his sex as well, learning the different shades of rigid and smooth, curling a finger around a head that seemed artfully, amazingly swirled, and she even, at his fifth request, took him into her mouth and tasted a boy for the first time. He tasted like salt. Like potato chips. Like pretzels. Like the way she imagined the ocean would taste.

So when, one night in his bedroom, when her parents thought his parents were home and they weren't, Jeff asked to go all the way, when he said in a soft and so strained voice, "Please, Rainey, let's make love, I want you so badly," it seemed only natural to give in. To cave to this love and need and desire that overwhelmed her, that made her entire body flush, that made her dream of marrying him, turning twenty years old with him, thirty, forty, bearing his children, making love to him night after night after night in a fantasy world where love and passion never died.

The first time hurt and she cried, but then they did it again and again and again and soon it didn't hurt anymore, but seemed to become an expression. The rhythm, the spasms, his gasps against her neck and erupting from her own throat, all spelled love. Rainey and Jeff 4-ever.

Rainey never thought about birth control. Neither did he. Who thinks of such things when you are fifteen and in love so deep, there isn't room for practicality, for sensibility?

So her period went missing. A whispered consultation with her girlfriends led Rainey to slip out of school at lunchtime for a trip to the drugstore where she bought a pregnancy test. She blushed and told the check-out girl it was for a friend, but the check-out girl just shrugged. Rainey figured there were many pregnancy tests bought for friends, and she burned with embarrassment all the way back to the school. The next morning, Rainey and her friends congregated again in the girls' restroom behind the added-on gymnasium, a restroom where nobody ever went except for occasions such as these, occasions where privacy was an absolute necessity for the tears or cheers that would follow. One of her friends read the directions aloud and Rainey, behind the closed door of a stall, carefully peed in a cup, not trusting herself to aim just right onto the stick, and then she dipped the stick into it. The stick looked a bit like a thermometer and she thought about how it was about to predict the temperature of her future. Hot if it was negative, and the fever of her life could continue uninterrupted. Cold as death if it wasn't. She took the stick and set it on the counter by the sinks, so she and her friends could watch the little oval window where she hoped her fever would appear, but worried about the lack of heat. It was supposed to take three minutes.

It only took one for the test to turn out positive, but they waited the three anyway, in case it changed its mind. In case there was a mistake. Rainey cried, leaning against one friend, then the other, and a third threw the result into the garbage.

"Maybe you guys can get married," one said, and Rainey thought of that, thought of her dreams where she made love to Jeff every night and filled their house with beautiful babies. But she was always older in those dreams, and the babies came after years in college where she and Jeff made love in dorm rooms and classrooms and football fields under the stars.

"I don't know," Rainey said.

"Rainey, you have to tell your parents," another friend said.

And Rainey went colder. Tell her parents who went to church every Sunday? Her mother told Rainey about the facts of life by giving her a pamphlet and blushing, and her father never did anything but sit behind his newspaper and smoke. Rainey didn't talk to either one of them much, but she knew they had expectations. A pregnant daughter, still in high school, wasn't one of them.

"I can't," Rainey said.

"Then you have to talk to Jeff."

That seemed like the right thing to do. So Rainey pulled herself together and got through the school day. She threw up at lunch and felt faint in fifth hour, but then she and Jeff went to his house where his parents wouldn't be home until six, and Rainey's mother thought her daughter was at the library, studying. Rainey waited until after they'd made love, of course. She waited until they were lying together, and she was full of his semen, she felt it as it trickled out from between her legs and coated her thighs, and she thought about how she never considered his semen dangerous before. She waited until he held her tucked against his chest and his hand was lazily stroking her bottom. She felt him sigh and she was happy and she knew he was too. So she held onto that, breathed it deep into herself, and she told him.

"Jeff. I took a test today. I'm pregnant."

His body stiffened. Everything went rigid and the force of it tossed her to the other side of the twin bed. She stared at him and his eyes were wide.

"You're what?"

She swallowed. "Pregnant. I guess we should have been using birth control."

He blinked. She touched him, tried to stroke his chest, take his hand, but his skin was cold as metal. He was as cold as the test predicted.

"Jeff, we need to do something. What do you want to do?"

She felt his shift away from her. The mattress dipped and then he rolled over, sat on the edge of the bed. She looked at his back as he said, "Abortion, I guess."

She shuddered as the vision she'd been working on all afternoon, of the two of them in a simple one-bedroom apartment, loving each other and caring for their baby, beating the odds by working and parenting and staying in school, dissipated. She didn't know how abortions were performed, but suddenly, she saw herself on a table with a vacuum between her legs and a tray full of sharp instruments at her side. "Oh, God," she said.

He turned then. "You have to, Rainey. We can't have a kid now. Christ, you're only fifteen."

She was, but she felt older as she looked down at her naked body, still full and flushed from lovemaking. She always felt older with him.

He nodded. "We don't have to tell anyone. I'll pay for it. We'll go to the clinic downtown, the westside. I can drive."

Rainey placed a hand over her tummy. She felt her own softness. Then she said, "Okay."

He took her there on a Saturday, when their parents thought they were going to the mall. Jeff sat in the waiting room and Rainey lay on her back on the paper-covered steel surgical table and, in a twilight sleep, she opened her legs and heard the doctor talk to her in a soothing voice as he probed and scraped and removed her body of what she thought she did not want. She didn't know what the doctor said, but his voice was nice.

Afterward, she leaned against the car as Jeff told her he thought they needed to date other people. That they were too serious about each other and that's what landed them in this trouble.

Rainey knew the truth though. She knew he hated her body now, hated the way it sucked in his seed and created a life he didn't want or care for. Her fifteen-year old body was no longer for making love, but for making trouble. Making babies. Unwanted babies that had to be scooped out and flushed away.

She cried all the way home.

Then she locked herself in her room, told her mother she was experiencing a painful and heavy period, and she lay alone in her bed and waited for the bleeding to stop. She didn't talk to her friends, who called and called and called. She certainly didn't talk to her parents. And Jeff never called again. In the hallway at school, he looked away. He began dating a sophomore.

Rainey learned about rejection and abandonment and isolation. At fifteen.

Over the years, Rainey thought every April, on that particular date, about that little flushed-away baby. She'd realized it was the right thing to do, that at fifteen, she wasn't ready for motherhood, and at seventeen, Jeff certainly wasn't ready to be a father.

But then Tish happened. Rainey was nineteen when she became pregnant, twenty when she became Tish's mother, much older, she felt, and more responsible, and while there were times when single motherhood was hard, she never regretted keeping this wild dark-haired girl.

Now, drifting in her bed between drug-induced sleep and a foggy wakefulness, Rainey placed a hand on her bruised stomach. Older skin now than the fifteen-year old's that momentarily protected and cuddled an unwanted fetus. Older than the twenty-year old who produced a glorious cracker-eating child. But Rainey's skin was still soft. She was only twenty-four.

Rainey wondered if there was a baby there. If her genes and her rapist's were colliding together as she and he did the night before, in violence and power and fear, and if that blend would create a child. And if it did, what would she do?

Rainey let her hand fall away. When she cried, it hurt in so many ways, her bruised and cracked ribs aching with the pressure of sobs, the skin on her face burning from the salt of her tears. And inside, so far inside, it hurt the most of all.

When Rainey woke again, it was in the midst of a dream. She relived the rape, on the rock, by the river, under the man, but in the fullness of daylight. She saw it all. Spotlit by the sun. She saw it happen again. And when she pulled herself away, when she yanked herself from drug-induced sleep into the quiet of her bedroom, she was saying that word she so wanted to say the night before, but was threatened into silence. No. She just wanted to say no. She wanted to scream it.

And that's how she woke herself. With a scream.

Frozen, her mouth still in an O, she looked toward the open door. Did anyone hear her? Was Tish in the hallway?

There was no one. The room and the hallway were silent, and Rainey could still just hear the sound from the television below, and a low drone that must be Doris' voice. Relief flooded Rainey even as pain rose again in her consciousness.

She didn't want anyone to know. She didn't want anyone to ever know everything that happened last night. How she reacted. How her stupid body reacted. For the second time in only a few hours, Rainey wanted to die.

How could she? How could she come during a rape?

Slut.

Rainey felt sick and she struggled to get out of bed, to get to the bathroom, her little and private bath that was just to her left, just beyond the dresser. But she was stiff and in pain and her body again wouldn't do what she wanted it to do. She made it halfway to the bathroom, gagged, then vomited on the floor.

She was holding onto the wall when Doris came flying in. "Oh, honey," she said. Tish was right behind her, her eyes wide, her hand held tightly to her mouth. Rainey realized Tish was sucking her thumb.

"I'm sorry, Doris, I just couldn't make it." Rainey wiped her mouth with the back of her hand. "I just got so sick all of a sudden." She felt what remained of the dream, what hadn't flown out of her and landed in a puddle on the floor, settle itself like a yoke on her shoulders. She slouched. Her stomach burned.

"It's probably the pain pills." Doris wrapped an arm around Rainey's waist, helped her back to the bed. "Here, let's change your gown." She turned to Tish. "Sweetie, go downstairs and get me some paper towels please." She waited until the little girl walked away, and then she said to Rainey, "Let's get you changed before she comes back. She doesn't need to see this."

Rainey flinched. "Neither do you," she said. "I can do this myself."

But Doris whisked Rainey out of her gown before Rainey had a chance to say more. Doris blocked the door while rummaging through the dresser for another gown and Rainey looked down on herself, thinking she was prepared for what she'd see, she'd already seen her aftermath body yesterday. But she wasn't ready at all. Bruises scattered over her body like the rapist's road map, a crazy path of stops and starts, bridges and tunnels and dead ends. Doris pulled a soft yellow nightshirt over Rainey's head and Rainey settled it over her hips. Then she lay back down in the bed. "I want to take another shower," she said. And another and another and another, she thought. I don't think it will ever be enough. I don't think there's enough hot water in the world.

"Okay. Just let me know when you're ready. I want to be close by." Doris arranged the blankets, then took the paper towels from Tish who silently appeared in the doorway.

"Hi, sweetie," Rainey said. "What have you been doing today?"

Tish shrugged.

"Watching television?"

She nodded.

"What did you watch?"

Tish's mouth opened, but then she glanced quickly at the window. Moving to the foot of the bed, she held onto Rainey's toes.

Rainey sighed and found herself wanting to somehow kick-start Tish, ignite her voice. Tish said she saw, but what exactly had she seen, in the night and through the bushes? What was going on in that dark cork-screwed head? Asking direct questions didn't work, and Rainey was too tired right now to think of any other battle plan. So she twiddled her toes under Tish's fingers and Tish smiled. Rainey tried to smile back. "I'll just rest for a little bit. Make sure the nausea is gone. Then I'll take a shower. Maybe get dressed."

"You're not getting dressed. Not today. Too much bending and twisting." Doris swept up the last of the paper towels and then stood there, looking at them, as if unsure what to do next. "If you want, you can put on your robe and come downstairs and sit on the couch. Or the recliner, the recliner would be better. But that's about it today. You don't want to push yourself."

Rainey frowned. That's exactly what she did want to do. Move, work. Brush Tish's hair, make dinner, get a load of laundry going. Anything, just to keep moving forward. Moving away, leaving last night far behind. Bring back the normal. "Doris, I'm okay."

"I know you are. But let's just take it easy for now."

Rainey closed her eyes. She felt Tish squeeze her toes. "Love you, baby."

There was no answering "Love you." There was always an answering "love you," an offer and gift routine conversation that Rainey adored and counted on. The air felt hollow without Tish's voice. She heard Doris and Tish leave the room, Tish's footsteps light, Doris' heavier and slower. They didn't close the door.

Tish's silence felt, for a moment, judgmental, and then Rainey stepped in to find reason. Tish was four years old. Rainey argued with herself, tried to tell herself that Tish's lack of response was because of the trauma of the night before. That it wasn't because she knew Rainey's secret. How would she know? She was a baby, she didn't know anything about anything.

Except for what she witnessed.

Behind her eyes, Rainey went over the night again, picking apart every step, every decision, trying to find where she went wrong.

Choosing the Riverwalk was definitely a mistake. There'd been other rapes there, Rainey read about them, felt sad and amazed and angry that such a thing could happen in her own town at such a beautiful spot. The Riverwalk was originally left open twenty-four hours a day, but the night seemed to draw an element that made the safety of the daytime disappear with the river current. And so the curfew was established, as well as the night-time flights of the police on bicycles. But it wasn't all that late last night, late for getting a little girl into a warm bath and then off to bed, yes, but surely early for rapists. Didn't they come out, arm in arm with robbers and murderers, after everyone else, everyone kind and good, was safely behind closed doors? Didn't they go after stupid women who stole into dark parks after midnight when the good and kind people were fast asleep? Not after mothers. Not after a mother with a four-year old little girl, still sticky from frozen custard and immersed in an imaginary desert.

Rainey squeezed her eyes tighter. What had she been wearing? What about her gave the clue that she would be an easy target? Her skirt…she'd worn it to work. It was short, yes, but professional. Black. Snug-fitting at the waist and over the tummy, and a little bit of flirty frill at the bottom. No slit though. She'd worn black opaque nylons and before they went to the custard stand, she kicked off her low heels and slid the nylons off her legs. She tugged on white ankle socks and sneakers. It was after work and they were walking, and Rainey wanted to be comfortable. So she wasn't wearing stiletto heels or thigh-high lace-up leather boots, the type of thing that Rainey and her friends back in college pointed out to each other and giggled and called fuck-me shoes. Hooker boots. Whore heels.

But she was bare-legged. Bare-legged under a flirty short skirt. Maybe similar to the one she wore in high school, the one that beckoned to Jeff during her trips to the salad bar.

Her blouse. What blouse was she wearing? It was a simple white oxford, rolled up at the sleeves after work. A lace cami underneath. How far did she have the blouse unbuttoned? Rainey swallowed. She did unbutton it at dinner. Down three or four buttons, letting the cami fully peek out. Tish liked to see the lace. She said it looked like swirly ocean waves against her mother's skin. Rainey loved that description; Tish had never seen the ocean, but the lacy curves and curlicues were a lovely image. For now, the lacy camisole was the only way Rainey could give her daughter the ocean, and so she was more than happy to unbutton a few buttons to let her daughter see and imagine.

Did Rainey button it back up before going to the park? No. She didn't. Was that it then? A red flag? A white flag of surrender?

Rainey clutched the collar of her nightshirt. Did that white oxford and white lace beneath glow in the moonlight? Did it show her to be a woman who wanted it? Who wanted a man to take her?

But she had a little girl.

Rainey's body reacted though. What did that mean about her? *Slut.*

"Oh, God," she said, and this time, she made it to the bathroom in time. She forced herself. She didn't want an audience as she threw up her shame and her fear and her pain. She threw up silently, making sure that she would remain alone. She didn't want any help.

Then she took off the nightshirt and stepped into the shower. Hot tap on full force, cold just the smallest of turns. A tiny concession of comfort for a woman Rainey knew now to be despicable.

Two days later, Rainey's alarm went off and she got up at the routine hour and slowly dressed herself. The pain was still there, but lessened, an undercurrent instead of a roar, although the bruises had taken on a deeper, more violent purple. She tucked the Tramodol in the back of her medicine cabinet the night before and switched to ibuprofen. And now, while she didn't dress for work, deciding to take the rest of the week off, she chose the softest of jeans, a long-sleeved t-shirt and sneakers, and prepared to go downstairs, make breakfast for her daughter, and get back to it. A normal life. As normal as it could possibly be now. Even though the clock pointed to the same time it did every morning, nothing felt the same. Even as she placed her feet on the same path, left turn out of her bedroom door, five steps down, turn right into Tish's room. The same as always. But inside, drop dead different.

Tish was still sleeping when Rainey went into her room. Quietly opening the closet door, she picked out Tish's clothes: her favorite pink denim overall jumper, a white blouse with pink piping, and white sneakers with pink hearts on the toes. Rainey set these on the end of the bed, then went into the dresser and added little undies with pink dancing teddy bears and a pair of white tights, which she knew Tish would protest. Tish preferred bare legs ending in bobby socks, or better yet, sandals, but it was fall and getting chillier and Rainey was determined to win this battle. She stared for a moment into the disheveled drawer at the sea of pink and white and sometimes a bit of purple, and she wondered if she would ever convince Tish that there were other colors besides pink in the world. From the second drawer, she took a brush and a pink and white scrunchy. She put the brush in her back pocket and the scrunchy around her wrist, and then she turned to find Tish staring at her from her pillow.

Already the unusual, on this attempted path of normal. Tish always slept until Rainey kissed her awake on her cheek. But this morning, wide brown eyes. Unblinking.

"Hey, sweetie," Rainey said softly, then bent down and, through the sudden painful squeeze of her ribs, kissed Tish. "Time to get up and get ready for school, okay? I'll meet you downstairs."

Tish sat up and frowned.

Rainey nodded. "It's time to get back, baby," she said. "Think of all the get-smart stuff you've missed!" She left the room quickly to avoid any silent arguments, and to set out apple juice and oatmeal with just a touch of brown sugar and maple syrup stirred in. From the kitchen, she could hear a few thumps and bumps upstairs, so Rainey knew that Tish obeyed and was up, getting dressed and making her bed. A softer sound from the shared wall in her kitchen let her know that Doris was awake as well, and that she was more than likely aware that Rainey was up and back in the game. Rainey hoped Doris would stay over there as she asked the night before, in a quickly whispered conversation just after tucking Tish into bed. Rainey asked for Doris' help in seeking out normal, a return to an everyday life. Even though there were going to be so many things to trip over. If all was normal,

Rainey would wait for Tish to finish her breakfast and at the door, she would slip Tish's backpack over her skinny shoulders and then hustle her over to Doris. Doris would be waiting at her own front door. Rainey would kiss Tish on the top of the head, wish her a good day, and then drive off for work, waving out her car window at the little girl who always waved back. So did Doris.

But this, the blue jeans, the t-shirt, Tish making her bed, but not saying a word, the aroma of oatmeal, the soft sounds of Doris making her own coffee and likely heating up a homemade muffin on the other side of the wall, this wasn't normal. It was a mix of normal—the bed-making, the oatmeal, the sounds from the other side of the wall—and the abnormal—the blue jeans and t-shirt, the silence, the undertone of pain, the realization that she wouldn't be bringing Tish to Doris, but to school. To talk to her teacher. About her daughter and rape.

But it was close to normal, and it would have to do. Rainey settled herself to focus on the automatic, on what she'd be doing on any morning, the actions that were still here, even though the world was so different.

Tish appeared a few minutes later, her shirt neatly buttoned, her overall dress buckled, and her bare legs sliding beautifully into her socks and neatly Velcroed shoes. She attempted to move quickly into her chair, but Rainey stopped her.

"Tish, where are the tights I put out for you?"

Tish shrugged.

"It's too chilly for just socks. Go back upstairs and get the tights." Rainey was stunned when Tish's eyes brimmed over. Tish was always exuberant, rarely given to tears. "Sweetie, it's not that big a deal. Go get the tights. I'll help you put them on."

There was a hesitation, and in that hesitation, Rainey wondered if Tish was really ready to go back, when tights instead of socks could make her cry. But then she was gone. Rainey listened to the footfalls up the steps, down the hall, then the double-clunk of dropped shoes. The slam of a dresser drawer, the top one, Rainey knew, then softer footsteps back down. In the kitchen, Tish stuck out her feet as Rainey slid the tights over her toes and heels, up the calves and thighs, and settled the elastic band around the tiny waist. Then she put Tish's shoes back on, patting the heels, and swinging Tish's legs neatly under the table.

"I'm going to drive you to school today, okay? I want to talk to Mrs. Whitstone." Rainey settled down opposite Tish with a cup of coffee and her own bowl of oatmeal. Tish, she noticed, kept stirring, but nothing made its way up to her mouth. "Tish, you have to eat. You won't learn if your stomach is empty. Empty stomachs lead to empty heads," Rainey said, quoting Doris.

Tish nodded, then took the tiniest of bites. Her appetite must have kicked in against her will, because she sighed and began to scoop up great mouthfuls.

Rainey ate with her, and she measured her words carefully, turning them and rearranging them, before she spoke out loud. She decided it was best to offer up a question, rather than a command. "Tish, do you think you'll be able to talk at school?"

Tish dropped her spoon. She clapped both hands over her mouth.

"Tish, honey, I know it's hard. But it's been a couple days. You need to talk. How can you ever learn if you don't talk? You have to ask questions to learn. You have to talk to ask questions."

Tish's eyes remained round over her fingers.

"You can't even write yet, Tish. How are you ever going to tell me things that you want?" Rainey leaned forward, a sudden idea making her eager. "Tish, it's September. In three months, it will be Christmas. How are you going to tell Santa your list? What will you do when we go to see him and you sit on his lap and he says, 'Ho, ho, ho, little girl, and what do you want for Christmas?'" Rainey deepened her voice for Santa and she hoped for a smile, and maybe a blurt of desired treasures.

Tish breathed in quickly and Rainey leaned back, triumphant, thinking the inhale was in preparation for speech. But then Tish pointed at her.

"Me? But, Tish, how can I tell Santa what you want, if you won't tell me?"

Tears appeared for the second time that morning and then she let her head fall forward on the table with a clunk that made Rainey wince.

"Tishy," Rainey whispered. "I miss your voice." She waited, but Tish made no move. "Okay, then," she said and sighed. "We'll just have to see how it goes." This wasn't going to be an easy battle, like the tights. She couldn't reach in and pull Tish's voice out. No matter how much she wanted to.

Rainey got up to clear the table, but stopped for a moment to stroke and brush Tish's hair, pulling the corkscrews into the constraints of the scrunchy. Tish sat up, drained her apple juice, then went into the living room to watch television until it was time to go.

When they left for school, Rainey knew that Doris was standing at her front window. She turned to wave. "Tish," she said, "wave to Doris. She's watching you."

Tish lit up and waved vigorously. Behind the window, Doris laughed.

More than likely, a second cup of coffee would be poured and ready for Rainey in Doris' kitchen when she got back. The door to the right, identical to Rainey's and nestled next to it, would be open, and through the screen door, there'd be the smell of blueberry muffins and butter, fresh and strong coffee, and Doris' voice would call out, inviting her in. Knowing this made it easier for Rainey to get herself and Tish into the car, to drive toward an impossible discussion about an impossible situation.

At the school, Tish accepted another kiss before running off to the playground. Rainey wondered if she would talk secretly to her friends, but Tish immediately climbed onto an empty swing. Up in the air, she wouldn't have to talk to anyone. Rainey couldn't help but marvel at Tish's ingenuity and she watched as Tish's friends circled in front of her daughter's flying sneakers. They smiled and waved and Tish smiled back. Silently. Rainey went into the school in search of Tish's teacher.

Mrs. Whitstone was at the board, writing capital and lower case letters, when Rainey walked in. "Hello, Mrs. Whitstone," Rainey said.

The teacher whirled around. "Rainey! Oh my god, how are you? Are you all right?" She immediately pulled a chair and Rainey sank gratefully onto it. She noticed how Mrs. Whitstone's eyes flickered over her body, then rose slowly to her face.

"I'm doing okay. Listen, Tish is coming back to school today. And she's still not talking."

Mrs. Whitstone sat behind her desk. "It must be some sort of defensive reaction that she's having. Not talking must make her feel safe somehow."

Rainey nodded. "That could be. I haven't had any success at all getting words out of her. I've asked direct questions, everything. I even told her if she didn't talk, Santa wouldn't know what to bring her." The teacher's jaw slackened and Rainey suddenly felt like the cruelest mother ever. Her daughter witnesses a rape and Rainey threatens her with no Christmas?

"Well, Rainey, when Mrs. Granger called, I did go ahead and contact our guidance counselor. She's at another school today, but she said that as soon as Tish returned, she would make a special trip in to see her. Maybe she can help."

Rainey remembered the emergency room doctor and the nurse, urging her to get counseling for Tish. And maybe for herself too. "Okay. I think…I think we're going to need a lot of help. Please, would you call me after school today and let me know how things went?" Rainey braced her arms on the desk, then pulled herself carefully to a stand.

"Certainly. If you'd like, I'll call you at lunch, so you know that everything is okay. I know you're going to be worried." Mrs. Whitstone stood and held out both hands to Rainey. "It will be okay, you know. I'll do everything I can to make it so. Tish is a strong little girl."

Rainey smiled and released her hands into Mrs. Whitstone's grasp, relishing the warmth of the gesture. "Oh, thank you, Mrs. Whitstone. That would really help." Rainey's eyes involuntarily filled, just the way Tish's did at the breakfast table. "This is just so difficult. I never thought…"

Nobody would, Rainey thought. Nobody would ever think of such a thing. Who would ever think, while watching your daughter be born, watching her grow and sing and play, that one day, she'd witness a rape? That she'd see her mother attacked. Nobody would.

Did the rapist? Did he picture such things?

Did he choose her specifically because she had a little girl?

Mrs. Whitstone squeezed her fingers. Rainey shuddered, quickly swiped the tears from her cheeks, and left the room.

Going down the hall, Rainey noticed that the other teachers turned quickly away when they saw her. Rainey felt branded somehow, as if her bruises and cuts put her into a new herd. The Herd of Stupid Women Who Get Raped In Front of Their Daughters. She pictured the imaginary herd of camels from that night, lumbering through the playground, and she saw herself, lurching with them, blindly, into the dark. Rainey wondered how many were in her herd, if she would ever get to see someone else, talk with someone else, who really knew what this was like.

To be held down like that.

To be so afraid to move or to scream, not just because you might die, though that fear was there, it certainly was there, blown up bigger and bigger with every pump of your heart, but also because you might just cause your little girl's death as well.

She staggered for a moment, grabbed onto the wall to steady herself. Then, carefully, she made her way to the parking lot.

Rainey decided there would be no herd. How could there be? Who else in this world was as stupid as Rainey was that night? And who else would react the way she did, the way her body did, the way she so tried to stop, but in the end, caved in to?

There was nobody else. She wished the ground would just open up and swallow her, not take her from this life, from Tish, but provide her with a special underground tunnel, where no one would ever see her again.

Rainey sank into her car. She shut the door and locked it. She never drove with her door locked. She never thought of it before.

Tish might find her safety in silence. Rainey would look for it in Doris. In blueberry muffins and fresh coffee. And in a kitchen that wasn't her own, but a mirror image, not touched by any of what happened in the park.

Who would have thought. About any of this, that any of this would be possible, could happen, could affect a life, multiple lives, in this way. Rainey didn't want to think of it anymore. She wanted normal. She needed it.

CHAPTER FIVE

Doris

Doris was just hanging up the phone when she heard the car pull into the driveway. She glanced over at her table, where her Bible sat closed next to her coffee mug. The slim satin ribbon bookmark split like a snake tongue out of the Bible, marking the place that Doris read after her first cup of coffee. Usually, after breakfast in the morning and right before going to sleep at night, she opened her Bible randomly and read whatever presented itself. It amazed her how often she would feel comforted or soothed or suddenly uplifted in a flood of joy by these out-of-nowhere words. But these last few days, she felt like she was seeking something specific, instead of waiting for a surprise. She told herself she was looking for healing for Rainey and for Tish, and she wasn't sure how to provide it. What words, what phrases, what memorized verses wasn't she remembering? She told herself that this was what she was looking for.

But she knew better. And Doris relied on the truth. To her, the word held a capital first letter, just like the B in Bible, the He when referring to God. While she searched for the right words, the right phrases, she was really looking for herself. Doris wanted an explanation. She needed it.

Doris heard Rainey's first careful steps on the porch and thought how only a few days ago, Rainey's footsteps almost always rang out in a run. Doris waved and called toward the open screen door. "Come on in, Rainey. How are you feeling? Did you talk to Tish's teacher?" Rainey's face was check-marked by the screen, turning her a silvery gray, and she nodded. Doris noticed how even that small movement seemed cautious, watchful of sudden pain. "Come have a cup of coffee. I have some fresh-baked coffee cake. The kind you like, with all the cinnamon crumble on top."

"Oh, Doris, you are a godsend." Rainey opened the door and her face fell clear. She patted Doris' arm, then continued past her to the table. "I was all prepared for blueberry muffins, but this is even better. Thank you for baking it."

Doris liked to think of herself as a Godsend from time to time. She liked reading Bible stories to Tish and answering the little girl's questions. She knew that Rainey and Tish didn't go to church, and so she busied herself as a Godsend in Tish's life. If Rainey preferred to sleep in on Sunday mornings, if she and Tish liked to stay tucked up in Rainey's bed until noon, and then come downstairs and surround themselves with the Sunday comics and sales ads and fresh-made pancakes that Doris served up every week, as soon as she came home from attending 10:30 mass, then Doris would be Tish's church. Doris knew better than to judge.

Do not judge by appearances, but judge with right judgment, it said in the Book of John, Chapter 27, Verse 4.

And Doris knew too, that once the pancakes were eaten, she and Rainey would return the dishes to Doris' side of the duplex, and then they would sit on the porch all Sunday afternoon. Doris would have another cup of coffee and Rainey would drink iced tea and Tish would dance with Doris' stuffed animals. Those two next door might not go to church, but those Sunday afternoons were holy in Doris' book.

Doris loved Tish and she loved Rainey. They could enjoy their Sundays together and Doris would see to it that Tish would grow up knowing God.

Knowing God. Doris knew that if Tish would talk, her voice would be suddenly adult and it would be tinged with the poison of accusation. She would ask, "Okay, Doris, why did this God of yours do this? Why did this happen to my mom?" And Doris, who had an answer for everything, didn't know what she would say. She hadn't found an answer yet. Already, she'd spent hours paging through the Bible, trying to find the right words. But she kept hearing her own words, sharply close to what she imagined Tish's would be:

"Where were You? God, where were You that night?"

Now, Rainey started to sit down, but, seeing Doris' Bible, she quickly corrected herself and moved to a different chair. She didn't push the book away, Doris noticed, just removed herself from it. "Tish didn't seem too happy about going back to school," Rainey said. "She was in tears twice before we even left."

"Tears?" Doris busied herself getting out a second mug, putting the coffee on the table, setting the platter of coffee cake just so. "That's not like her, though she has teared up a lot the last few days. What was it about?"

Rainey wouldn't look up. "First, it was because I wanted her to wear tights instead of socks."

Doris thought quickly. The little girl's legs were encased in white as she went out to the car. Good for Rainey! She stuck to her guns on that one. Doris knew how convincing Tish could be. A tilt of her head and suddenly, she was too adorable to say no to. Or she pitched a temper tantrum. She wasn't so adorable then.

"And then…I asked her if she would talk at school, but she wouldn't answer me."

Doris shook her head. "It is odd, this not talking. I can't count the number of times I wished that little girl would hush, just for a minute, to let me hear myself think. And now I don't know what to do with all this silence."

Rainey nodded. "That's not what made her cry though. I told her—" Her voice broke. Doris patted her shoulder and then Rainey tried again. "I told her I missed her voice. She sounds like a chipmunk. A chirpy little chipmunk. I always thought it would be so hard when her voice started to change, to get deeper. I never thought about it disappearing. I never thought —" Suddenly collapsing into tears, Rainey leaned into Doris' side. "Oh, God, Doris, I know it's only been a few days. But it feels like years. I just wish I knew exactly what she saw, so I could try to explain it to her. Though I don't know what I'd say. He was…so brutal."

Doris thought about her own struggle to find the right words, the right answers, the right way to explain God's presence in this situation, or His lack of presence, which she wondered about, but couldn't accept. She hadn't even thought about a more concrete explanation that Tish would be looking for, a physical explanation. She'd need to know what she saw, what she heard. Tish didn't even know where babies came from yet. She didn't know about intimacy between a man and a woman. And what she saw was nowhere close to intimacy. Doris wrapped her arms around Rainey's shoulders, lowered her face against Rainey's skull, smelled her shampoo.

She wanted to feed Rainey. To make her warm. She turned to fill a mug of coffee, set a warm piece of coffee cake on a pretty blue dish.

Rainey sat up, wiped her eyes, then circled her hands around the mug. "I just don't know what to tell her, Doris."

Doris sat down with her own mug and plate. She thought of her capital T. "You have to tell her the truth, honey. You were attacked. By a very, very bad man. Plain and simple."

"Plain and simple." Rainey took a sip of coffee, a bite of the cake, but she seemed to have difficulty swallowing. "The things he had me do…I keep going over it all in my head. Watching myself step by step. Wondering what I did wrong."

"Wrong?" Doris leaned over her Bible and grabbed Rainey's hands. "You did nothing wrong! All you did was try to come home."

"Yes, but through a park after it closed. In the dark. And Doris… well…should I have dressed different? Should I have had on sweats or something?" Rainey's words came out in a rush and Doris heard the tremble. "Do you think maybe he liked my legs or my chest? I had on a short skirt, that new black one with the flounce I bought for the office, and I took my nylons off before we left home, so my legs were bare. I had my blouse unbuttoned a bit so Tish could see my lace, maybe he saw that as a sign that I, well…" Rainey bit her lip, looked at the table. "Wanted to be with someone like him?"

Doris shuddered. Who would want that? Who would ask for such a thing, go out looking for such a man? "Rainey, you're a beautiful woman. You're beautiful even in sweats. I think…I think he would have attacked anyone that came along. It didn't matter who she was or what she looked like, as long as she was female." Doris thought again of the way Rainey looked at the hospital, staggering down the hall with Tish in her arms and a police officer on either side. Just beaten. Beaten and used. Doris remembered thinking she looked like a dog's old raggedy toy, chewed and shaken and ripped to shreds.

Rainey nodded, sat back, then continued eating. "At least I'm feeling a little bit better. I'm still sore, but not as bad." She glanced at the clock. "I should probably call my doctor's office. The hospital was supposed to send all the results of my tests over there."

"Tests?"

"Yeah, you know. Like for STDs."

Doris ran her mind over the letters, trying to come up with something, and she couldn't. She looked at Rainey.

"Sexually transmitted diseases. Like VD. Or AIDS."

Doris' mouth dropped. She hadn't thought about that, about the possibility of the rapist having a disease, of his passing it on to Rainey. The attack seemed like enough, the violence of it, the forced sex, the taking without asking. The taking away of all that was private. Doris hadn't even been able to get up the courage to ask Rainey about the details of the attack. The possibility of disease seemed like a sinking to an even lower level, a new wound. Something that maybe wouldn't heal with time. Something that would allow the rape to last a lifetime.

"The doctor said it wasn't likely, but I have to be tested. Even if these tests come out negative, I have to keep getting retested, for quite a while, I guess." Rainey looked down into her mug. "For pregnancy too." She said the word quickly.

A baby. Another consideration that Doris hadn't thought of. "They won't be able to tell that right away, will they?" She knew that tests were faster these days; she saw the advertisements on television.

There was no more waiting for the rabbit to die. Doris remembered the guilt she felt over that rabbit, her rabbit, when she found out she was pregnant, so many years ago, and one after one, everyone crowed, "The rabbit died! The rabbit died!" That was how her doctor told her, over the phone. It was what her husband said, when she called him at work, whispering her news. And it was even what her friends at church said. But Doris thought it was sad, that in order to be declared with child, a rabbit had to lose its life. A female rabbit, that Doris always pictured as pure white, with pink inside its ears and a pink triangle nose. It was in memory and secretive honor of that white rabbit that she chose a soft blue bedding set for her son's nursery, soft blue with clouds of white bunnies crouched on it, holding orange carrots in their prayered front paws.

Rainey shrugged. "I don't know. They seem to be able to know a lot." Suddenly, she froze, then looked at the clock again like it had a secret answer. "Oh, shit!"

"What?" Doris pulled her sweater together, folded it over her breasts, crossed her arms to keep the sweater closed. She didn't like it when Rainey swore, and she always encouraged her to leave such language at the office.

"Sorry, Doris, I didn't mean to say that." Rainey looked back at her. "The doctor said something in the hospital…something about taking the morning after pill. It was a way of making sure I didn't get pregnant. But I didn't take it…At least, I don't think I did. I think I said I would think about it, and then I forgot." She glanced at the clock again. "I wonder if it's still possible or if it's too late."

Doris remembered a sermon from church last spring, or maybe it was summer. The priest, Father Markham, talked about evils like abortion and infidelity. He spoke of legalized ways of getting around sin, such as the morning after pill, which he said was a way to swallow abortion, to take it inside and let it do its dirty work. "A morning after pill…isn't that the abortion pill? Isn't that like having an abortion?"

Rainey blinked. "The doctor said it was like swallowing a week's worth of birth control pills, all at once. I guess…I guess that means if a pregnancy was starting, it would wipe it out. I hadn't really thought about it."

They sat quietly. Normally, Doris would have cleared all remnants of breakfast off the table by now, had her stories on the television, and been well into her daily chores. Today was Friday, which was normally the day Doris reserved for errands or pleasantries, like shopping at the Goodwill. But the last couple days, taking extra care of Rainey and Tish, set her schedule on its ear. She was working on bathrooms today, which was a Thursday chore. By now, she should have the televisions going on both the first and second floors, playing them at full volume, so she could hear the dialogue as she scrubbed and flushed in the powder room down the hall, the full bathroom upstairs. Rainey would be at work, Tish at school. Tish at school was the only normal thing about this day so far. Yet that wasn't really normal either…Doris already knew Tish wouldn't start talking at school. That would be too easy.

Even the day wasn't normal. It was Friday, but she was doing Thursday things.

She glanced at the phone, then over at Rainey. She felt a wash of guilt, but she shrugged it away. "Rainey, I need to tell you something."

Rainey pushed away her plate and mug. The plate bumped gently against the Bible. "What is it?"

Doris tried to smile. "Well, you know how the other day, I asked you if you wanted me to call your parents?"

The guarded look that came over Rainey whenever they talked about her parents or her home shifted over Rainey's face, lowering her eyebrows, turning down the corners of her mouth. "Yes, I remember. I told you I didn't want you to call them."

"Well…" Doris played with the satin bookmark. "Right when you pulled into the driveway, I just got off the phone with your mother."

"What?" Rainey stood up in a movement that was probably meant to be abrupt and angry, but was instead painfully slow. "I asked you not to do that! I said I didn't want them!"

"I know, I know, but…" Doris stood up too. She was so sure when she made the phone call before, but now, looking at Rainey's bent body, suddenly bent a little more, she began to wonder if she was wrong. "I just felt that they needed to know. You're their daughter, they'd want to know if you were hurt. And you are hurt, Rainey."

Rainey began to shuffle toward the door. "I don't want them, Doris. They won't help."

"They might. I would, if you were mine." Doris followed, wanting to grab Rainey's elbow, to lower her back into her chair at the kitchen table. That urge to feed her came again and Doris wanted to put the entire pan of coffee cake in between them both, the pot of coffee too, and give them each a fork and just dig in. "Rainey, hon, I just thought you might need your mother. I prayed on it, and it seemed like the right thing to do. They're…well, your mother said they would be on the road within an hour. They'll be here by tonight. I said they could stay here, on my sleeper sofa." Doris looked at Rainey's back. She'd stopped moving and stood in the middle of the entryway. "I'm sorry. Do you want me to try and reach them again? Tell them not to come?"

Rainey jolted forward again, making it to the door. She braced herself against the jamb. Doris noticed that Rainey held her breath until she was fully upright. Then she ran her hands carefully over her ribcage and down, breathing out in a soft sigh. "You prayed on it," she said, her voice quiet and chill.

"Yes. You know I do. I do for everything."

Rainey turned slowly, supporting herself on the door jamb, switching hands as her body swung fully around. She pointed back down the hallway, to the Bible on the table. "Do you really think there's anything in there," she said, "for me? For me and Tish? Is there anything in there for us now, after this? How can there be anything to pray about?"

The answer to that was just what Doris had been looking for. Seeking. Doris tried to hide the frantic panic that poured over her. "Of course there is," she said and she searched and searched her memory banks for something, anything, that would help. She wanted to help, she always wanted to help, especially Rainey and Tish. They'd been her family now for four years and suddenly, she needed to find just the right words. She wanted to find a key, a potion, a magic bean that would set everything to rights.

The Truth.

But as the verses flipped through her mind like index cards, nothing lingered. Nothing resonated.

Only her own questions. *Where were You? God, where were You that night?*

Doris didn't even have an answer for herself. She looked at Rainey, still by the door, her face open, her eyes wide. She'd lowered her hand; she was no longer pointing at the Bible. But she was looking at Doris straight on. She was waiting for an answer.

Doris remembered the words she looked at this morning, words she looked up specifically, not at random, and thought would help. *"O Lord my God, I cried unto thee, and thou hast healed me,"* she remembered reading. But they didn't bring peace, not this time. Instead, she found herself asking, "Didn't they call for help, God? Didn't Rainey call? Why didn't You help them?"

Where were You? God, where were You that night?

So now, with Rainey standing there, holding on to the door, holding herself upright under this new pain, Doris searched some more. She bought herself some time by returning to the kitchen, then bringing back her Bible. She stood in front of Rainey and made a show of flipping through the pages, as if she was looking for just the right passage, which she was, of course, at the same time that she was looking through her memory. Trying to find an answer. Trying to find the Truth. Finally, she cradled the open Bible in both hands, closed her eyes and quietly recited, *"Come, and let us return unto the Lord; for he hath torn, and he will heal us; he hath smitten, and he will bind us up."*

Hosea 6:1. The Old Testament. It was all she could come up with. And it felt so inadequate. Doris was stunned with the Truth of that. The Bible's words weren't supposed to be inadequate. God wasn't supposed to be inadequate.

When Doris opened her eyes, Rainey was staring at her. Rainey's breath became heavier, her chest rising and falling rapidly under her t-shirt, her cheeks flushed. Doris wanted to put out a hand to her, to tell her it was okay, it was all right, there would be no more pain. But Doris couldn't…she knew now she didn't know all that for sure. She didn't seem to know anything.

"What does that even mean, Doris?" Rainey said, her voice low and hoarse. "He has smitten? Torn? Does that mean God did this to me?"

"Oh, no, honey! God wouldn't—" But Doris stopped. God didn't do the rape, no. But He didn't stop it either.

Where was He?

Rainey lurched away. Doris could see the ache that pushed its way through Rainey's joints and muscles. Doris wanted to tell her to stop, to stay and watch television with her while she cleaned the bathrooms, to lay on the couch and Doris would cover her with an afghan she knit herself. She would keep her filled with coffee and warm cake. But Doris stayed silent. The screen door opened and closed, the shriek of old hinges echoing the sound Doris felt trapped in her throat. In a few seconds, there was an answering shriek from Rainey's door and then more noises on the other side of their shared wall. It sounded like Rainey went upstairs. And then there was the soft distant rainfall of the shower. Another shower. Rainey took one last night. She took one this morning, before bringing Tish to school. Doris heard every single one.

She told herself to get moving, the bathrooms needed cleaning, she'd already missed the first half of her story. But she stared at the Bible and she couldn't move. She wanted to turn more pages and find the comfort that she'd always found there. But now, with the unfamiliar mid-morning sound of Rainey in shower after shower after shower, Doris just didn't know where to turn.

There was no comfort in coffee and fresh-baked coffee cake. Not even in Rainey's favorite, not in sugar and crumbled cinnamon, baked to a crunchy crust. And there was no comfort in the Bible. In Truth.

Doris just didn't know where to look next. She wasn't used to being a seeker.

After clearing the breakfast dishes, Doris made all the usual moves to clean her bathrooms. She emptied the little garbage cans. She tossed the bath rugs out into the hallways. Her bucket of cleansers and rags and sponges waited by the toilet on the first floor.

But then she followed her thoughts outside. Moving around her yard, she rearranged that day's episode of stuffed animals. She added the rooster, Tish's favorite, to the fencepost and replaced the green gorilla's stuffed bananas with a bowl of birdseed. Doris loved the way the birds settled next to the neon green fur, even sometimes perching on the ape's head, as if stuffed green gorillas were as natural in the wild as cardinals and blue jays and robins. She thought her sheepdog patriarch looked harried today, so she put the mother dog and puppies back inside. Then she added something new, something she'd been waiting to surprise Tish with. The majority of the animals came from the bin in Goodwill, but this one, she found at the church rummage sale the weekend before. New animals debuted on Friday afternoons in her yard and each one celebrated its new homecoming with a sleepover that first night in Tish's bed. Removing the glorious purple cow from its hiding place in her coat closet, Doris settled it next to the sheep so they could graze together. She thought of the little rhyme she planned to teach Tish on the day the cow appeared:

> *I never saw a purple cow*
> *I never hope to see one,*
> *But I can tell you anyhow,*
> *I'd rather see than be one.*

She wondered if Tish's sudden bark of laughter would bring her voice back. If she could trick Tish with joy and surprise back into normal.

Then Doris got in her car and drove off toward downtown, just a mile or so away. Maybe a stop at the library, she thought, or a trip to the Tres Chic Used Boutique. Doris bought quite a few of her clothes from there, and it was where she found the terrific hot pink overall dress that Tish was wearing to school that day.

All the way into town, at every stop sign and stoplight, Doris could see her church's steeple. It towered over the town and Doris looked for it wherever she went. It was like a beacon, showing her the way home. She always liked to think of it as a big pointed finger, made out of Milwaukee's historic cream city brick, directing the way to God. She kept the finger in sight, as if it was beckoning her, as she drove past the library and then Tres Chic without a glance, even though she'd taken herself away from her chores with the thought that she'd shop there. It just didn't seem right, cleaning bathrooms on this day. Not when Rainey was back in the shower again. Not when Doris couldn't provide her with any answers, and not when Doris couldn't find any answers for herself. She parked in front of the long row of steps leading upward to the church's entry. The doors were thrown open, the way churches always used to be, welcoming, all day and all night, and Doris took this as a sign that the church was where she was supposed to be.

Each week, it seemed to take her a little longer to get up the stairs to the church, but so far, Doris refused to give in to age and go in the handicapped entry around back, where there was a parking lot and a door that led to an elevator which would raise her up to the church proper. That time would come soon enough, she figured. For now, she put her knees and hips to work, her arms swinging encouragement. But in the middle of a weekday morning, with no other church-goers there to chat her up, to take her mind off the step followed by step followed by step, the journey seemed to take forever. On this day, for the first time, she counted the steps and discovered, after attending this same church for her entire life, that there were thirty-three. She wondered about the significance of that as she stood puffing at the top. Thirty-three. Christ was supposed to be thirty-three years old when He was crucified.

And the "supposed to" in that thought robbed Doris of the breath she was trying to catch. It was another first. A few days ago, the sentence would have been, "Christ was thirty-three years old when He was crucified." There was no *supposed to* about it. Or there didn't used to be. That thought, the simple addition of two words, rattled her.

Everything was changed. In just a few days, from a Tuesday to a Friday, everything was changed. Even things that were supposed to be unshakable. Like faith. Faith, by definition, was supposed to be unshakable. At least, by Doris' definition. A rock. Faith was supposed to be a rock.

"So we fix our eyes not on what is seen, but on what is unseen, since what is seen is temporary, but what is unseen is eternal." Second Corinthians. Chapter 4, Verse 18.

But Doris was shaken.

Making her way into the church, she blinked as the muted stained glass lit the air with dust-mote smears of red and green and yellow. Everything always looked holier in a church, she thought, whether it was full of people for the celebration of a mass or a wedding or the somber slow quiet of a funeral. Or if it was empty, like on this day. There was something about the orderliness of the pews, the hymnals standing at attention in their holders, the stained glass, the statues, and of course, the gigantic crucifix that overlooked everything from above the altar. Doris always felt humble when she was here, humble and quiet and meditative. But now, as she looked up into the face of the twenty-four foot tall Christ, looked into His closed eyes, she didn't feel holy at all.

"Where were You?" she whispered. "Weren't You there? You know what a beating feels like. Why didn't You stop it? There was Tish! There was a little girl!" Doris felt dizzy from looking up and she stepped backwards, grabbing onto a pew. "She's only four," she said. "How can you be four years old and witness something like that?" She moved into the pew and sat. "How is that even possible?"

"Doris?" The familiar shape of Father Markham moved out from the little dressing room to the side of the altar. He was folding something. "Is that you?"

Doris wondered if she didn't say anything, would the priest just go away? But she was raised to answer to priests, and to answer immediately and politely. "Yes, Father."

Father Markham had been Doris' priest for the last eight years. He'd grown familiar to her now and, like all the priests before, seemed to embody the church, give it a life of its own. It took Doris a while to get used to his looseness, his easiness. But now, when she came in to volunteer for a bake sale or a rummage sale or to weed the beds of the Garden of Prayer, she often found herself answering his smile with one of her own, even slapping him lightly on the arm when he made a bad joke. Now, he walked across the altar, genuflected (that answered a question Doris always had, if the priests genuflected on the altar when they were not performing a mass), and then stood in front of her. He was folding a chasuble, she saw now, a beautiful shimmery green one. "I was going through all the cupboards," he said. "So many people have donated beautiful chasubles to the church for our priests to wear. With only me left, it just seems like so many. I hate to see them go wasted, but how do you give such gifts away?" He formed the Eucharistic robe into a neat square. "I thought if I just straightened them up, made them orderly, then… well, then they wouldn't take up as much space and it wouldn't seem as excessive and then it would be okay." He laughed softly, his voice a hushed echo in the body of the church.

She smiled back and touched the light-shot material. It felt soft and airy, almost like water running between her fingertips.

"Is there something I can help you with?" He moved to the far end of the pew, went inside, then sat next to her, giving her the center aisle. To escape in, she presumed, if she didn't want to talk. Or if she'd been interrupted in the middle of a sacred conversation.

"I don't know," she answered honestly. "It's just…well, a friend of mine has been hurt. Really hurt. And I can't seem to find any answers. I always know just what to say to people, what verse to offer. But there doesn't seem to be anything for this. And that just amazes me." She took a hymnal from its holder, flipped through it. "It scares me, actually. I've always had answers. God has always given me answers. But not this time."

"How was she hurt?" The priest settled back, lowered the kneeler, propped his feet on it. He seemed so relaxed, like he was in his own living room. He also seemed smaller than when he was on the altar, preaching.

Doris wondered about discussing such things with a priest. Rape. An awful act. But to bring it up to a priest, a priest who was celibate…what would he know? Doris settled her shoulders, stared straight ahead. Father Markham was a man of God. And God wasn't giving her any answers right now. Maybe the priest, even though he knew nothing about even proper intimacy, of what happens between a man and his wife, could come up with something. Doris knew her Bible. But the priest should know it better. He should know the ways of God. So she said it straight out. "She was raped on the Fox Riverwalk a few nights ago. Father Markham, it's my neighbor. My tenant. Rainey."

The priest drew his head back, then tented his fingers into prayer formation. "Oh, gosh, how awful. I read about that in the paper. She's your neighbor?"

Doris nodded. "And I babysit her little daughter. Tish. And Tish saw the whole thing. Rainey…well, she hasn't told me all the details, but she was brutalized. Her face is bruised, her ribs are cracked. There's more bruise than normal skin right now on that girl. It's just painful to look at her."

"Awful," Father Markham said again. He flexed his fingers, curling them into his palms and then flinging them into a tent again. Doris was reminded of the little game she played with Tish, flapping her fingers into a church crowded with wriggling people. *Here's the church, and here's the steeple, open the door and see all the people!* Tish always crowed in delight at all the finger-people waving in a row. "Wasn't she in the park after it closed? What was she doing there with her little girl?"

"Trying to come home." Doris swallowed. "She wanted to get Tish home for her bath and it was late, so she took a shortcut through the park."

Curl, tent, curl, tent.

Doris closed her eyes and dove in, into what she was sure was a murky puddle of blasphemy. "I just want to know where God was." She wanted to close her hands over his and squeeze, draining some of his strength, his faith, into her own fingers. "How could God let that happen? To Rainey? And to a little girl?"

And how many times had Doris been asked that by grieving or angry church members over the years? How could this happen? How could that happen? And every time, Doris answered. She put her arms around those people and she spoke in a low voice and she answered. But not now. Not for herself. Now, the words she murmured into their ears, God's ways are His own, and we just have to accept His actions on good faith, seemed empty, mocking, almost insulting. Good faith. Fixing your eyes on the unseen. The eternal.

Faith was supposed to be a rock. But even rocks could split. They could shatter.

Father Markham crossed his legs. "We both know His ways are hard to figure sometimes. Rainey might not know His purpose for a long while. It will take a lot of prayer to bring healing."

The same thing that Doris whispered to others. All those times she whispered, it made sense. To her. Had it made sense to them? Or did they feel just the way she did right now? Lost. Angry. "Father Markham." Doris stood up. Her hip brushed the folded chasuble and sent it slithering to the floor. "This is a four-year old little girl. A baby. Maybe there was a reason God wanted this to happen to Rainey, though I can't imagine what that would be. Why would any woman need such a horrible thing to happen to her? But to a four-year old…to have her see something that she shouldn't even know about yet…and to see it happen to her mother…Oh, God, it just makes no sense." Doris sidestepped out of the pew and walked down the aisle. She usually wanted to linger in church, to soak it in, but not today. Not now. It was a mistake to come here.

Church had never been a mistake before.

"Doris, stop a minute." Father Markham followed her. Doris didn't stop, but moved more slowly, her head turned to show she was listening. "You know I could throw all the old platitudes at you. God works in mysterious ways. Everything happens for a reason. God never gives you more than you can handle. I know they don't seem to work right now, they don't make sense, they don't fit. But that's sort of the point, isn't it?"

Doris stopped. "What point?"

"That faith isn't supposed to just work when it's easy. It's not supposed to be applied only to things that can be explained. There's a reason it's called blind faith…sometimes we just have to feel it, even if we can't see it or explain it. God was there, Doris."

To see what isn't seen. Doris' definition of faith. So we fix our eyes not on what is seen, but on what is unseen, since what is seen is temporary, but what is unseen is eternal.

Doris swung around and looked right at Father Markham. She stared into his eyes and saw what was there, kindness, faith, a desire to help. But she said, "And He didn't save a four-year old little girl?"

Father Markham blinked, then bowed his head.

"'Let the little children come unto me, and do not hinder them, for the kingdom of Heaven belongs to such as these,'" Doris said. She looked over the priest's shoulder at the tall figure of Christ, arms outstretched, nails pounded into palms dotted with red. She found herself wondering if Christ's imprisoned hands kept Him from beckoning to Tish and Rainey, from lowering His arms around a little girl and her mother.

But how foolish. Christ came down from the cross centuries ago. His arms were free while Tish's tongue was now in prison. And Rainey…Doris thought of the way Rainey moved across her porch this morning, of the sound her throat made when she cried. Doris thought of STDs and the possibility of an unwanted, violently bred baby. Rainey was in Hell. There was no kingdom of Heaven on the Fox Riverwalk. No Heaven in Rainey's interminable showers either.

Then Father Markham looked up. "Doris?" he said softly. "They're alive, aren't they? Rainey wasn't murdered? And the little girl…the rapist didn't touch her?"

It was Doris' turn to blink.

"God was there, Doris. What happened is just unthinkable. But maybe what didn't happen is even more unthinkable. Beyond it. Abominable." He held his hands out to her, palms out, then turned and walked back up the aisle.

Doris waited until Father Markham scooped up the chasuble and disappeared into the side room. He remembered to genuflect. Then

Doris left the church, counting the thirty-three steps backwards as she returned to her car. As she counted, she tried to find comfort. In the priest's words, just as she tried to find comfort in the Bible. In hot coffee and cinnamon coffee cake. And in the fact that Rainey and Tish were still alive and breathing.

Even if they were battered. Even if Tish wasn't talking, and even if Rainey could be diseased or pregnant.

Doris tried to find comfort. She looked in the Bible. She talked to a priest. She raised her face to a crucifix and she attempted to soak in the words of advice and care and compassion offered in God's house. But there just didn't seem to be any comfort anywhere today. Not even in the warmth of two sustained lives. Lives that she was grateful to have right next door. Two lives that she loved very much.

For the first time ever, Doris Granger couldn't deny being angry at God. She couldn't deny the Truth.

CHAPTER SIX

Tish

Mrs. Whitstone at school says, "Talk, Tish." The helper lady says, "Talk, Tish. Ah, ah, ah. Oh, oh, oh. La, la, la. Can you say something? Can you say Mama?" Doris says, "Talk to Mama, Tish." I need to talk to Mama.

Mama says Please and it makes me sad.

Mama says he is a bad man. He is a mean man. He's not in jail yet. And he said to Mama, "Make a sound and this is what will stuck you." And I tried not to make a sound. But then I looked and the leaves crunched and then he stuck Mama. He stuck her lots and she bleeded and she broke and she cried.

He's not in jail yet. He said, "Make a sound and this is what will stuck you."

My mama is sad too. She got stuck. I looked and the leaves crunched.

So now I'm quiet.

CHAPTER SEVEN

Rainey

*Weeks 2—3: By the time it reaches the uterus, the rapidly
dividing ball of cells has separated into two sections.
The blastocyst hatches, tumbling out of its surrounding
membrane. Using little pin-like projections called
chorionic villi, the blastocyst digs into the rich uterine
lining, connecting as much of itself as possible with the
woman. At this point, the blastocyst changes its name
again and becomes an embryo. The embryo and the
woman share hormones and other essential fluids. This
process is called implantation and it marks the real start
of growth. Of pregnancy.*

Tish was in bed by the time Rainey's parents showed up. It
was dark outside and Rainey curled up on her couch, an
afghan wrapped around her waist, and she listened to Doris
in her kitchen, back again on this side of the duplex, stacking the
dishwasher. Rainey wanted to do it, but Doris told her she didn't
want her bending. And, Rainey knew, Doris wanted to be close by
when Rainey's parents walked in the door.

Rainey understood that Doris meant well, but the idea of even
seeing her parents in her own home on a normal day was unthinkable.
She walked out of their door, her childhood door, so many years ago,
and her parents never told her to come back. Never asked to see their
own grandchild, who was the proof, Rainey knew, of her father's
charge of slut. Unthinkable. So much was unthinkable. And now, to

have them coming here for this, supposedly to come to her rescue after she'd been raped, after she'd been walking where she shouldn't, with a child who shouldn't have been out that late at night, a school night, Rainey couldn't believe that either. To Rainey's father, Tish should never have been conceived at all. Rescue? She doubted he was coming for that. And her mother was never much for rescue either. She only went along for the ride, her husband at the wheel in all aspects of their life. And she was good at looking away.

At the sound of a car, Rainey stared out the window. The headlights veered in and the glow tucked itself against her garage, then went dark. Doris leaned in from the kitchen, drying her hands on a towel. "Is that them?"

Rainey nodded. She had no idea what she was going to say. But her parents, especially her father, would be sure to demand some kind of explanation.

Doris tossed the towel back into the kitchen, then went and held the front door open. Rainey supposed she should be the one doing that. But the afghan, which warmed her a moment ago, now held her firmly on the couch. Her limbs wouldn't move. "Hello!" Doris said and Rainey heard her parents call back and she wondered at the lightness of their voices. As if they were any parents just coming to visit their daughter, doting grandparents to visit their granddaughter. Not coming to see if Rainey was still alive, if she was still whole, to see how she could have been so stupid as to get raped.

Doris stepped back and Rainey's parents walked into the room. Seeing her, her mother drew in a breath so sharp, it shattered the chill autumn air. She dropped her suitcase right there and moved swiftly to the couch.

"Rainey," she said. "Oh my god, Rainey." She reached out and touched Rainey's face, cupping her cheek. The bruises were still there. While they were healing, they seemed to look a little worse each day. Rainey was waiting for the soft yellow that would mean they would soon disappear, so she wouldn't see a reminder every time she looked in a mirror to wash her face or brush her teeth.

For a moment, Rainey leaned into the softness of her mother's palm, but then she pulled back. "I'm okay, Mom," she said.

"You certainly aren't." Her father came and sat down too, on the coffee table. He didn't touch, but Rainey saw his fingers twitching. "My god, Rainey," he echoed. "What the hell happened?"

Doris quietly disappeared into the kitchen and Rainey listened to the sounds of coffee being prepared as she considered how to tell her parents about the attack. She'd been struggling over this all day, ever since Doris confessed to the phone call this morning. She didn't know exactly what Doris told her parents, but Doris didn't know the details of that night, and so her parents wouldn't know either. There would only be that one word. Rape. And that Tish was there. All day, Rainey talked it out in her mind, working a variety of sentences, mixing phrases and words, and nothing seemed right. Everything was just so blunt, so harsh.

"He raped me," she said now, rolling all of it, the twists and the turns of it, into one simple sentence, one that she could say fast and then clamp her lips together over the unspoken details. She just couldn't bear the details.

Her mother cried. There wasn't a sound from her, just tears scribbling down her cheeks. Rainey waited for, and received, questions. They all came from her father. Where was she that night, what was she doing? Where was Tish? What did the man do to her? To them? Rainey supplied one-word answers. Fast, fast. The final question, *what did the man do to you?*, she ignored, turning her face away and looking back out of the window.

Doris came in with steaming mugs and slices of the coffee cake from that morning. "I thought you could use this," she said. "When you're ready, I'll get you settled on my side of the duplex. I have a very comfortable sleeper sofa in the living room. There's a powder room downstairs too, though when you shower, you'll have to go upstairs." She smiled. "It's just like Rainey's, only in the reverse."

Her parents didn't glance up, Rainey noticed, though her mother did reach for a cup of coffee. Her hands shook and she quickly nestled the mug in her lap to steady it. Rainey took one too, for the warmth.

"So how bad are you hurt?" her father asked. "And Tish…is she hurt at all?"

At the mention of Tish's name, Rainey tilted her head. Normally, there weren't voices in the duplex at this time of night. It was another glitch, another unfamiliarity, and Rainey wondered if her daughter would wake at the sound. Tish wouldn't recognize the voices; she'd never met her grandparents. She'd spoken to her grandmother on the phone, but that voice, distorted by the miles and tinniness of a phone headset, of cell phone towers, wasn't anything like the one in the living room now. Though Rainey's mother hadn't said much. It was a man's voice that would wake Tish, and for a moment, Rainey panicked, wondering what Tish would think if she woke and heard.

"Sh," Rainey said, and pushed her hand down over her lap, trying to lower a volume she couldn't touch. "Tish is asleep, I don't want to wake her." Everyone glanced toward the stairs. "She wasn't hurt," Rainey said. "She's fine. She went back to school today. But she's not talking, and we don't know why." And then she listed her own injuries, the ones they could see, some of what they couldn't. She left out the what-ifs, the possible pregnancy, the maybe disease.

Her father shifted on the coffee table, setting some newspapers rustling. Doris quickly gathered them and took them into the kitchen, to the recycling bin under the sink. "What time of night was this?" he asked.

Rainey shrugged. "About eight, I think. It was dark. We went out to get some frozen custard as a treat after supper —"

"So why did you go through the park then? After dark? What were you thinking?"

As if Rainey hadn't already asked herself that. As if she hadn't asked it a million times, and the count was still going up. "I just wanted to get home. It was late and I had to get Tish to bed. It was a school night."

Her father got up and began to pace. "But for god's sake, Rainey, it was after dark." His voice rose again. "You don't ever go to places like that after dark. You know better."

"Please," her mother said. Even on her lap, the mug began to tremble. The coffee threatened to slosh over.

Rainey noticed Doris go up the stairs. There was a click, and Rainey knew the door to her daughter's bedroom was closed. Doris came back down, but stopped halfway, sitting on the steps, ready to run up or down, wherever she was needed. While she smiled at Rainey, Rainey couldn't help but glare back. See? she wanted to say. This is why I didn't want them here.

Her father stopped pacing. He started to shake his finger in the air, but then he rammed both hands into his pockets. "This should never have happened. It wouldn't have happened, if you were older and smarter and used some common sense. You're just so damn irresponsible."

Rainey allowed her head to drop against the back of the couch.

"Rainey is a great mother," Doris said, speaking through the rails of the banister. "She's wonderful with Tish. And Tish is just glorious. What a bright little girl. Why, just the other day—"

"A bright little girl who isn't talking. Because her fool mother kept her out too late on a school night. For ice cream!"

Rainey felt her mother grab her hand and squeeze. She didn't squeeze back. She shut her eyes and her father's voice filled the blackness.

"And what kind of a girl goes walking through a park late at night, Rainey, huh? What kind of girl? Maybe the same kind of girl who gets herself knocked up swimming naked with a bunch of boys at college?"

Rainey heard her mother's cry, Doris' exclamation, but Rainey couldn't make sense of their words. And it didn't matter. Slipping her fingers free of her mother's, Rainey stood up and headed toward the staircase. As she walked up, steadily, slowly, a hand on the banister grounding her, she said over her shoulder, "I didn't ask you to come here. You need to go." If there was a reaction, she didn't wait to hear it. She stepped carefully around Doris, and she heard Doris rise to her feet after she went by.

Upstairs, she looked in on Tish. She slept, undisturbed by the voices below. She looked just like herself…there was no difference from just a few days ago. Asleep, she was just Tish. Not a little girl who'd witnessed a rape. Not a little girl who'd fallen so completely silent.

Carefully, making sure the latch slid slowly into place, dulling the click, Rainey shut the door behind her, then slid down with her back to it. She and Tish would stay here, in this little room glowing with the blue from a nightlight, until her parents went away. Until they were gone and all was quiet again. Rainey knew her father's words would echo for her over and over again. But Tish didn't need to hear. She'd already heard more than any four-year old should.

Rainey wasn't sure how long she waited as she heard people moving around downstairs, the clicks of lights being turned off, her front door closing, the resounding thump of the deadlock as Doris locked it for the night. Rainey was momentarily grateful for Doris, grateful that she had a key to Rainey's side of the duplex, grateful that she was taking her parents away, if only to the other side of their shared walls. But then Rainey remembered that her parents wouldn't even be there if it wasn't for Doris. Anger warmed her cramped body, but then eased away. It was impossible to stay mad at Doris. She did too many other good things, and even this, this bad thing, was done out of love. And out of ignorance. Rainey didn't like to talk about her parents. She was sure her parents didn't like to talk about her. She wondered if the 5x7 photos she sent of Tish were framed and displayed anywhere in their house.

But no harm done. Rainey wasn't so sure she believed this, but she repeated it to herself anyway.

As she waited, making sure that no one was coming back, Rainey dropped off to sleep for a bit, her head resting on her bent knees. But her cracked ribs couldn't tolerate that for long and she woke abruptly, gasping for breath. Tish shifted. Rainey slowly flattened her legs to the floor, watching the little girl while she rolled over and threw her blankets off, then was still again. Getting painfully to her feet, first one knee, then the other, then a foot planted, then the other, holding on to the door for support, and then letting go, Rainey tucked Tish back in, then went to her own room and prepared for bed.

Rainey closed her eyes and was willing herself to sleep when she heard the click. The tumbler of the deadlock turned and slid back. Carefully, Rainey rose to a sit. Was it Doris? Coming back to check on her?

But there were bumps and thuds downstairs. Doris could move through Rainey's place in the dark, she knew it so well. And the footsteps on the stairs…they were too light, even if Doris was trying not to wake Tish.

In a moment, as quick and sudden as a gasp, the sounds and the dark and her fear and that night brought her rapist back to Rainey. He was here, he'd found her somehow, and he was coming back to take care of her again, just like he said he would. Rainey's skin felt like it was tightening, sucking in on itself over her bones and tissues, and she could hardly breathe. Getting out of bed, she crept to the door, willing herself to look into the hallway, to see him, to make sure he wasn't going into Tish's room, to wave him in to her room if she had to. If she had to, to keep him away from Tish. Holding herself up against the door jamb, Rainey leaned, then leaned some more, until she could peek around the corner.

And there was her mother, moving slowly down the hallway, one hand on the wall.

Rainey's breath flew out of her like a flame and her muscles let go and she slid to the floor.

"Rainey!" Her mother was there, pulling at her, lifting her up. "Rainey! What are you doing! What's wrong?"

Rainey tried to find her feet, her legs, tried to find any bone that wasn't turned to water, that would help her to stand up. Would help her to step away from the tremendous fear that left her sprawled and without form on the floor, half in and half out of her bedroom. "I thought…" she said. "Mom, I heard you, and I thought…"

"Oh, baby." She helped Rainey to the bed. "I'm so sorry. So sorry. I didn't know how to tell you I was coming, I thought you were sleeping, I had to wait until your father was sleeping too, you know…to come see you. I got the key from Doris."

Rainey fell against the mattress, let her head sink into the pillow. Her mother pulled up the covers, tucked her in, just as Rainey tucked in Tish a little while ago. Then her mother sat down next to her, wrapping her arm around Rainey's shoulders. Rainey felt the weight, so foreign to her now, and she stiffened. "Why are you here, Mom? I told you both to leave."

Her mother sighed. "I just wanted to talk to you. I just wanted to make sure you're okay. You know, those things your father said... Well, you know your father—"

"He was right though, wasn't he, Mom." Rainey thought about how Tish would curl into Rainey's side when they sat like this, how she would become an extension of Rainey's ribs and breasts and hips. She felt how contracted she herself was, now in the daughter role, that even with her mother's arm snugged around her, there was a stripe of sheet showing between them. "I was stupid. I know it."

"Oh, baby. Oh, God, Rainey, oh, sweetie." She hugged Rainey closer and Rainey felt the stripe begin to close, despite her own resistance. "You're not stupid. You're not. Honey, well..." She rocked Rainey, the way Rainey remembered from when she was small, the rock she used with Tish, the one Doris held her in the other night at the hospital. That easy sway, left to right, left to right, skin to skin, head tucked under chin, and the rhythm as steady as breath. "Honey, all mothers make mistakes. All mothers, you know."

Rainey looked at her mother then, at the tears that caught and pooled on her lower eyelashes before sliding down her cheeks. Her mother's arms tightened and she continued the sway. Rainey leaned into her, curved herself into her mother's ribs and breasts and hips, and began to cry. She wept the gray and red-flecked smoke of grief and fear and pain that seemed to dissipate into a fog as she was encompassed by the warmth of the embrace. The warmth of her mother.

Eventually, Rainey was aware of being placed back against the pillow, of the sheets and blankets pulled up over her shoulders, tucked under her chin. She turned onto her right side and curled into a C, just as she did as a child, her face toward the door, and she sensed her mother leaving the room. Behind Rainey's closed eyelids, in a mind just moments from sleep, she pictured her mother drifting down the hall, looking in on her granddaughter, a granddaughter she'd only seen in photographs which might or might not be on display in her own house, whose silenced voice she'd only heard on the telephone. Then she went down the stairs and through the front door. Rainey heard the door lock, pictured her mother turning the key, testing the knob, making sure all was safe, her daughter was safe, her granddaughter too, and in her bed, Rainey felt warm and powerfully sleepy and surrounded with sanctuary. With shelter. A shelter she knew would be gone as soon as she opened her eyes in the morning to the purple-pink bruises on her body and the silence of her little girl. But for now, she fell into sleep the way Tish did, and like Tish, in sleep, she was the same as she was before.

The first thing Rainey did the next morning was look out the window. Her parents' car was gone. After breakfast, she and Tish went over to Doris' side, and after Tish was settled in front of the television and Saturday morning cartoons, Rainey sat down in the kitchen and accepted a cup of coffee. Doris' living room was as usual, perfectly put together, and the sofa bed only seemed a comfortable couch against a powder blue wall. There was no evidence that Rainey's parents were ever there. As if to make that so, neither Rainey nor Doris talked about it.

As Rainey sipped her coffee though, and ate the fresh blueberry muffin Doris pulled out of her oven, she glanced often through the doorway at the couch. Silently and secretly, she wished for her mother. And she wished her mother saw Tish, sitting there now, awake and brimming with dark curls and her sweet smile. Maybe, once clasped in the surprise of her grandmother's embrace, Tish would find her voice again. And maybe, if Rainey was rocked often enough herself, rocked and held by her own mother, she would begin to feel better too.

But her mother was gone, sitting beside her father in the passenger seat, her father as always behind the wheel. Her mother would be looking out her window, seeing all the passing trees and meadows and factories and homes that lined the highways between Wisconsin and Missouri. Rainey thought she could see a flash of something in that face that stared blankly out. Pain? Regret? Or just the settle into the same pattern. A seat by her husband, Rainey's father, who always held the wheel. And an empty back seat.

Three weeks after the rape, Rainey sat on the edge of an examining table. She glanced at the door, and then parted the edges of the paper gown draped over her, opened to the front. Her skin was a soft pink, just tainted here and there with the briefest of yellows, flowing smooth and round over her breasts, then down to her stomach, her puckered belly button, then V-ing out to the curve of hips and the fullness of thighs, and finally dropping over the edge of the table to her calves and ankles and her feet. Her feet were hidden, tucked into a white pair of socks which Rainey carefully selected that day to make sure there were no holes in the toes.

Rainey marveled that the bruises were almost gone. Three weeks after the attack, and outwardly, she was close to looking like herself again. Rainey squinted until the random yellow and pale, pale green disappeared and she tried to tell herself that everything was back to normal. She was back to normal. And while Tish still wasn't talking, she would soon be back to normal as well. A week or two, and it would be like nothing ever happened.

That's what she tried to tell herself. Every day. And every night, as she tried to sleep.

Her rapist was still at large, as the police officers liked to say. Rainey shoved away the shadow that loomed suddenly at the corners of her eyes. Yes, he was at large, and yes, he was large. In her memory, he was larger than could ever be possible. He blocked out the black sky, pierced here and there with stars that sparkled. But she preferred to think that he'd disappeared. Slid into the mirage of that desert night by the river and wouldn't be back unless sand and heat and the rolling hills of camels were conjured up again. Rainey wouldn't allow that. She would only dream of oceans from now on. And jungles. And fields as green as the crayon in Tish's schoolbox.

He disappeared and all was returning to normal. Or would be soon.

She told herself.

Well, maybe. Rainey snapped her gown shut. The pressure of the paper over her breasts made them ache against the restraint. An ache and sensitivity Rainey remembered well. And there was the in-home pregnancy test she took yesterday morning. But even those were faulty. Stress screwed up a woman's cycle. There'd never been such stress as now. And Rainey's cycle was never regular to begin with.

She took that test alone this time, not in the company of suddenly serious friends from high school. There was no collective gasp. There was just Rainey and the result, the fast-appearing positive, just as fast as the one in the school restroom, and was now shoved to the bottom of her garbage can. The same place that first pregnancy test, taken so long ago, ended up. Later on this day, Rainey would go home, bag up that garbage, take it to the big bin in the garage, and tomorrow, garbage day, she would haul it out to the curb. To be taken away. Out of her existence.

But the result wasn't going anywhere.

Her hand started to float toward her stomach, and Rainey pulled it back, set it deliberately next to her hip, flattening her fingers over the coldness of the examination table. She would not let herself touch her stomach. Not in that way. Not with that special curve in her palm. There was no one in there. There couldn't be, no matter what the stick at home, in the bottom of her garbage can, said. Peeing in the cup here, undergoing a professional and medical test, would prove just that.

That's what she told herself.

She startled when her doctor opened the door. "Hi, Rainey," Dr. Johansen said and she came to stand by Rainey's side. The doctor took her hand.

And with that, Rainey knew. Dr. Johansen, while a warm and demonstrative woman, never held Rainey's hand before an examination before. Rainey closed her eyes.

Dr. Johansen squeezed. "Rainey, hon, the test came out positive. You are pregnant."

Rainey couldn't open her eyes. She couldn't nod, couldn't talk. Any movement, any breath she would take, would make it all real. Would make it normal, a new normal, when this couldn't possibly be normal. She felt her arm stretched, heard wheels, and knew from the downward tug that Dr. Johansen settled herself on the stool by the side of the table. All without letting Rainey go.

"The test was a weak positive, indicating you're still early on. Which would coincide with the date of the rape." A pause, a squeeze. "Rainey, has there been anyone else? Any chance that this isn't his?"

His. Her rapist. And now, a bizarre member of her family. Both he and his child going into places she didn't want them to be. Taking a deep breath, she opened her eyes and looked at the doctor. "No. There's been no one else. Not for a long time."

Dr. Johansen nodded. "Okay. Oh, hon, I'm so sorry."

The sincerity in her doctor's voice allowed Rainey to cry. Her arms started to go around herself, but she slapped her hands back on the table. She wouldn't embrace it. She wouldn't. Dr. Johansen stood up, wrapped her arms around Rainey's shoulders, and swayed.

When the sobs slowed, Dr. Johansen gently lowered Rainey to her back. "I'm going to examine you, okay? See how things look. Make sure that healing has taken place."

Rainey allowed the doctor to raise her feet into the stirrups. She was glad she'd kept her socks on. The stirrups would have added even more cold. Rainey didn't need more cold. She was, she felt, an iceberg. Her teeth chattered.

The examination was quick and Rainey was soon upright again. Her gown crinkled open, but Rainey didn't care. Let her body be exposed. Look what it had done. It sucked in her rapist's semen, sucked it in like sustenance, and made a baby. A fetus. Rainey jolted as she remembered her orgasm, the spasms, and she wondered if that's what drew the sperm in. If her body hadn't reacted, if she'd stayed still and impassive and just let herself be used, would the sperm have gone so deep? Deep enough to make a baby? She remembered telling herself that night that she was a piece of meat, a T-bone. But a piece of meat doesn't get pregnant.

And what kind of a girl goes walking through a park late at night, Rainey, huh? What kind of girl? Maybe the same kind of girl who gets herself knocked up swimming naked with a bunch of boys at college?

Baby number three. All of them unplanned. Two conceived during times of joy. One conceived in darkness.

Slut, Rainey thought. Sluts get pregnant.

Baby one, gone. Baby two, speechless. Baby three… forcefully implanted.

Dr. Johansen pulled Rainey's gown shut, tying it with the little paper streamers. "Everything looks fine. Typical for this stage of pregnancy. Your cervix is closed. The cut you had in your vagina is healed over, and there's no sign of infection." She took Rainey's face in her hands, looked directly into her eyes. "Hon, there's time. Okay? It's early. You're only three weeks into this. You have until twelve weeks to decide what to do."

Rainey looked down at herself, now hidden in grainy green paper. Green like the bruises once were. "Do?"

"Rainey, you know the options. They're all there for you, whatever you feel is right. You could choose to abort."

Abort. Baby number one. Abortion, Jeff said, and now, Rainey heard again the scrapes and the suction, felt the probing and then the bleeding that lasted for weeks and led to an emptiness she never understood. Was the void from the loss of the baby? Or the loss of Jeff, that first love that was supposed to evolve her somehow into a Woman, a woman with a capital W, a Wife, a Mother. Instead, for the longest time, she was nothing. Hollow.

Dr. Johansen continued. "You could choose to have this baby."

Like she had Tish. Baby number two. The loneliness of that pregnancy, the laboring for eighteen hours in a room full of strangers who became for that time her best friends, then disappeared on the day she was wheeled to the door of the hospital with the baby tucked into her car seat and cradled in Rainey's arms. When the sliding doors opened, Rainey stood and she walked to her car in the parking garage, left there the night she drove herself in, pulling to the side of the road during contractions, flattening the gas pedal between. She carried her newborn, clamped the carseat into its base, and then she drove herself and Tish back to their apartment. For the first three weeks, it was only Rainey and her healing body and her crying baby, and she thought she would go insane. She only took three weeks maternity leave, it was all she could afford, and the unsuccessful scramble to find affordable childcare took every bit of energy out of her. She met Doris in a grocery store, where Rainey was draped over the constantly crying Tish, cradled in blankets in the metal seat of the cart. Doris descended on them both, rocked Tish into silence in one arm, rocked Rainey in the circle of the other arm, and by the end of that afternoon, Rainey moved out of her apartment and into the duplex, with Doris right next door. Rainey was lucky, she knew she was lucky, and Doris was here with her still. But this new pregnancy…this pregnancy was different. Unwanted, unplanned, as Tish was, as that first baby was, but darker in so many ways.

"Or you could have the baby and adopt it out," Dr. Johansen said.

Adoption. Going through the pregnancy with an alien in her belly, nine months of being a vessel for possible evil, explaining in some way to Tish why her mama looked different, and then, after, answering the impossible question of where her fat belly suddenly went. Disappeared, like her rapist, into the desert.

Three choices, all of which seemed like no choice at all.

"Rainey, you've got time. You don't have to decide right now. Okay? And I'm here, any time you want to talk about it. I'm here, no matter what you decide. No matter what you decide, it's all right, hon. If you decide to abort, I can do it, you won't have to go anywhere else. This clinic does abortions…I do abortions, you won't have to go to a stranger. If you have it, I'll be with you the whole time. All the way through. It'll all be okay."

Rainey shuddered. If only it was that easy. All right, okay, going back to normal…these were no longer concepts she could expect. On a black night, next to a river, she was seeded. Planted. And now the world was inside out.

At work, everyone knew that Rainey was The One Who Was Attacked That Night. On her second day home, two days after the rape, Rainey had Doris call her in sick again, and ask specifically to talk to Rainey's boss. Just like she carried the news to Mrs. Whitstone, Doris also explained it all to Michelle, the office manager. On her first day back at work, Rainey found Thinking Of

You cards heaped on her desk, baskets of fruit, some bouquets. None had been sent to her at her house.

"We weren't sure what to do," said a co-worker, trying to explain. "It wasn't like you had the flu or a heart attack or your mother died. Somehow, it seemed…too personal to send these to your house. Too intrusive. We wanted you to know we were thinking of you, but we also knew that you needed time."

Rainey wondered if their hesitation wasn't about intrusiveness at all, but about keeping her the way they knew her. If they wanted to keep her in their state of normal. If it was easier to keep her as Rainey the Receptionist instead of Rainey the Raped. She'd scooped the cards into a grocery bag, the flowers and fruit into a garbage bag and pitched it all into a dumpster behind the grocery store on her way home. She hoped no one saw; she didn't want to hurt their feelings, just as they didn't want to hurt hers. But she didn't want these reminders anywhere close, not at work, not at home.

Now, coming back to her desk after her doctor's appointment, Rainey wondered how long it would be before everyone knew the new secret. She probably wouldn't be showing by the end of twelve weeks, she remembered that, but there was so much more that gave it away. Would she have to run down the hall to the restroom to throw up? Would an afternoon exhaustion hit her like an undertow, pulling her toward sleep as her body struggled to come up with the energy to keep two alive, not just one? How long would it be before everyone realized that her rapist left something behind that night, that might not fade away like her bruises?

Sitting at her desk, waking her computer, Rainey glanced at the time in the lower right hand corner of the monitor. Four o'clock. Doris would have Tish at home by now. Tish would have her favorite afternoon snack, chocolate milk in her Eeyore cup and a brown sugar cinnamon poptart. Always a brown sugar cinnamon poptart, no matter how Doris plied her with fresh-baked treats. The snack had to be in front of the television set, playing the DVD of her choice. Tish always needed some down time right after school, as if the strain of 4-K, of learning the alphabet, the numbers, learning to play with other children, suddenly drained her and she needed to regress a bit before she could pop back up. And pop back up she would, hitting the ground running, as Doris liked to say, like a jack in the box that suddenly had its spring fixed. Like the brown sugar cinnamon poptart in the toaster. When Rainey got home, Tish would be out with the stuffed animals, dancing around them, and probably jumping over and over again the purple cow that had become her new favorite.

Not singing though. Tish's constant movement was back, but her voice remained still. At times, Rainey saw her lips moving, her mouth open and close, as if she was speaking in her mind. But nothing came from her throat. At times, Tish would come to rest beside the purple cow, lean in and poke her nose inside the soft flap of its ear. Rainey wondered if Tish whispered to the cow, if the cow held Tish's voice secret. If the cow held all Tish's secrets from that black night by the river.

Opening a file, Rainey prepared to finish the afternoon correspondence. Everyone had their letters and robot emails to her by one and she spent the afternoon writing new ones when necessary, and filling in online and hard copy forms with the appropriate names and addresses and dates. It was mindless work, but she loved it. In her own way, she knew that the tasks she did kept the office moving. Take a basic bolt out of a huge machine and it grinds to a halt. Rainey didn't mind being that bolt.

To her computer screen's left were a series of photographs of Tish. Her newborn in-the-hospital picture that showed a grimaced bright red face and squeezed-shut eyes. Professional portraits from every birthday, showing the growth of hair from shiny brown ringlets to corkscrews, smiles from gummy to gap-toothed to brilliant, cheeks from baby-pudgy to slim. There were a few candid shots too, of Tish learning to walk, to run, to dance with the stuffed animals. One of Rainey's favorites was of Tish with the green ape, each of them with a banana in hand.

Once Doris entered their lives, things smoothed out for Rainey. While Tish could be a handful, Rainey no longer felt completely the isolation of the single mother. She still made all the decisions herself, of course, but she had someone to bounce those decisions off of. With the advent of Doris, Tish went from being a crying, demanding blob of skin and leaky orifices to a pink and shiny baby. With some of the pressure lifted, Rainey was able to see the joy that was her daughter.

Now, simply, as if by accident, Rainey's hand dropped from the keyboard and rested on her lap. She allowed her thumb to stroke where her tummy curved out. Just a few times, quick taps to a secret spot. To a secret interloper.

Motherhood certainly hadn't been all bad.

But.

While Tish's father was not a presence in their lives, he was responsible. The checks arrived every month without fail. And whenever Rainey thought of him, she remembered soft water, stroking waves, the clasp of wet and strong arms around her, smooth and slippery skin a pleasure against hers. What would she remember of this baby's father? What would she think of if she looked upon this child's face?

Tish looked like her father. Would this one? Would it be dark?

For a moment, Rainey froze and examined her thoughts. Was she racist, wondering if this child would be dark-skinned like its father?

But the father was dark-skinned. And Rainey and Tish weren't. Would this child be different? Was Rainey a bad person, a judgmental person, to even think of this?

As if that was all she had to think about. This child, this situation, was dark in so many ways that didn't even figure in the color of the child's, or the rapist's skin. Would the darkness be more than skin deep, would it permeate, sink in, to the child's core? Would whatever sent that man on that path, walking by the Fox River to rape a woman, to beat her, not even caring that she had a little girl with her, would that same thing be in this child too? What would it inherit from its father? Would violence be in its blood?

Rainey pulled her thumb away. It wasn't a child. Not yet. It was a floating mass of cells that she could get rid of, if she chose to. Even if it grew, even if arms and legs sprouted and it stretched firm against her, it didn't have to become a child. She could heft it around like a sack of groceries for nine months, drop it, and hand it off to a woman who wouldn't think of dark nights every time she looked at its face. Who wouldn't look at the hands and notice the resemblance to fists. Brutal fists. What would happen when the child's voice deepened?

Rainey slammed her own fists on her keyboard. Grabbing the picture of Tish with the ape, she hugged it to her chest, hugged it hard, even after she heard the glass in the frame snap. She had a child. She had a child.

Baby number two.

"Rainey…are you okay?"

Rainey looked up. Her office manager, Michelle, leaned over the high ledge of Rainey's desk, her barricade, Rainey liked to call it. It was the closest to an office as she would ever have. Carefully, Rainey set the photo down. A crack ran down the center of the picture, and as Rainey leaned back in her chair, half of the glass tilted and fell onto her desk. It didn't seem like there was enough force, but it shattered. Rainey and Michelle both looked at it.

"I'm okay," Rainey said. "Guess I'd better clean that up. And maybe it's time for some coffee."

Michelle smiled and agreed. "I think that's a good idea. I heard someone brought in doughnuts too."

After Rainey offered to bring Michelle a cup of black coffee and a powdered doughnut, she ducked down the hall to retrieve the dustpan and brush broom. She again relented and let her hand stroke once, twice, over her tummy. She just couldn't seem to stop herself. But after two times, she did. And then she kept herself busy.

Rainey hesitated before pulling into the driveway. She loved this moment, when she saw Tish before Tish saw her. There were Tish's crazy curls, popping in and out and behind the stuffed animals in Doris' front lawn. From across the street, it was a slatted view through picket fence and Rainey always thought of an old-time film, flickering on the screen. Tish, absorbed in the animal world, rarely looked up to discover her mother, and Rainey sat, engine idling, watching the jack-in-the-box action. There was a wild assortment in the yard that day and Rainey knew that Tish was behind it. Doris always had a bit of a plot to her daily choices. She might go with a farm theme, or a bird theme, or a zoo. The sheepdog was always on the front porch, and the green ape was pretty much a fixture too, except for when it was raining, and lately, so was the purple cow, but today, the rest of the lawn sprawled with animals of all genres. Snakes coiled around the feet of sheep and the rooster sat on the back of a gray hippo, a newcomer that Doris bought the week before. And through it all, the sprite, the brown curls, the slim and tender body, dressed as usual in pink, pink jeans and a pink and white striped shirt, ducked and dodged and Rainey saw the brightness of Tish's smile. Quickly, Rainey opened her window and listened.

All that activity, which should have been punctuated by shrieks and laughs and high-pitched nonsense words, was instead accomplished with silence. At times, Rainey thought she heard the swish of Tish's pink sneakers against the grass or the brush of her jeans against processed fur, but that was it. Then suddenly, Tish dropped out of view.

Rainey closed her window and pulled into the garage on her side of the duplex. She went in through the back door, automatically preheated the oven for whatever she was cooking that night; she couldn't remember what it was, but it was likely that it needed 350 degrees. Then she walked through the living room, out the front door, across the porch and down the steps to the front lawn.

Tish knelt next to the purple cow. Her arm was slung over the beast's shoulders and her head tilted against it. Two best friends taking a break.

"Hi, baby," Rainey called.

Tish swooped up and turned in a movement so quick, she became a blur. But then she was solid in Rainey's arms. Rainey remembered that just a few weeks ago, this was always accompanied with cries of, "Mama! Mama!" Now, there was just the beat of Tish's heart against Rainey's stomach.

Her stomach. Rainey turned quickly sideways and Tish looked up, her eyebrows raised. The question was there, even though Tish never made a sound. You okay? You hurt, Mama?

It was a question Rainey didn't know how to answer. No, she wasn't hurt. Well, yes, she was. The knowledge of the pregnancy was a new and fresh wound from the rape, three weeks after the fact. A bruise so deep, it didn't show yet on her skin.

But it would. It wouldn't stay hidden forever.

"How was school?" Rainey asked. Tish shrugged, took her mother's hand and pulled her toward Doris' door, where Doris waited with Tish's backpack.

"She seemed to have a good day," Doris said. "The teacher said she was fine."

Tish's day had to be interpreted now by the teacher and by Doris, and then by Rainey herself. Rainey wondered if Tish would let her know if someone got it wrong, if someone saw a good day when it was bad. She wondered how she was ever going to know anything for sure again, when it came to this silent daughter.

"And how about you?" Doris handed over the backpack and then glanced down, as if she could divine an answer with x-ray vision. While she didn't know about the at-home pregnancy test, she did know about the doctor's appointment. "Everything go…okay?"

Rainey nodded. "I'm fine. We'll talk about it later, okay? Why don't you come over around nine or so, after this one is tucked away in bed?" She caught Tish's ringlets in her fingers, let the brown laced with gold trickle through and around her knuckles like the rich discovery of jewels.

"Sure. Tish and I baked brownies this afternoon. Mint ones, your favorite. I'll bring them over with a fresh pot of coffee. And in the meantime…" She leaned down to Tish, whose lips had taken a sudden downturn. "Here's a couple brownies for the princess. Just for her." Doris presented a paper plate covered with bright red plastic wrap. Two Tish-sized brownies were inside. Tish lit up, took the plate, and carefully balanced it to her own door.

"Thanks, Doris." Once inside, Rainey automatically flicked on the television and knew that Tish plunked herself down on the sofa. Her thumb would be in her mouth again, and Rainey pondered bringing it to Tish's attention. The thumb, like the silence, was no longer jarring, but an everyday thing again. Rainey took the brownie plate away just as Tish peeled back the wrap. "You can have one for dessert if you eat your supper and one before bed. Not now."

Tish sighed, but didn't argue. It was hard to argue when you wouldn't talk.

In the kitchen, Rainey looked in the fridge and found the two chicken breasts she remembered to pull out of the freezer this morning. Dusting them with seasoning salt, she placed them in the oven, and then searched through her cupboards for a rice mix that Tish would eat. Supper started, she opened the backpack to see what Tish's day brought.

The backpack wasn't quite closed. A roll of heavy paper, thick, stuck out of the top. Rainey figured it was from Tish's art class and she set it on the counter to look at last. Then she tossed aside a notice of a PTO meeting and the hot lunch menu for the next week. There was a note from the guidance counselor, saying Tish cried during their session that day, but didn't speak. The counselor felt it was positive that Tish was at least able to cry. There was a note from Mrs. Whitstone too, saying that she heard Tish hum during reading circle. But as soon as she commented on it, Tish stopped. Rainey cursed the teacher for commenting. Let it build, she thought. Let the hum build. Maybe, if no one noticed, if no one said anything, that voice would surge back. Settle on Tish as easily as the thumb returned to her mouth. After zipping up the backpack, Rainey picked up Tish's artwork.

As Rainey unrolled it, she saw only black. Black swirls, made with thick paint, coiled from one end of the paper to the other. There wasn't any white left anywhere. Rainey wondered if Mrs. Whitstone saw it. Or the guidance counselor. She wondered if this was what made Tish cry.

She brought the painting out to Tish and sat by her on the couch. Tish's eyes were glazed, her mouth pouted and pulsing around her thumb. "Tish, honey, this is…really pretty," Rainey lied. "But I'm not sure what it is. Is it night time?"

Tish blinked a few times, then popped her thumb out like a cork. She smiled for a moment at the sound. Then she nodded. She ran her fingers over the painting, nodding the whole time. Near the bottom, the swirls changed, became broader, and at first, Tish trickled her fingers over it. Then she looked at her mother and made swooping motions with her hands.

"Waves?" Rainey guessed.

Tish nodded again.

"Is it the river? At night?"

Tish turned back to the television and brought her thumb to her mouth. The moist sounds reminded Rainey, in a way, of the river. The rhythmic sucking against the bank that night.

Rainey rolled the paper back up and brought it to the kitchen. Standing by the fridge, she tried to decide what to do. Every child knows that a spot on the refrigerator is a source of pride, and it was no different for Tish. But to bring the darkness of that night into the house…yet it was Tish's artwork. What would it mean to her if her mother didn't display it?

The chicken sent an enticing aroma into the air and Rainey heard the soft bubble of the rice on the stovetop. Holding the rolled-up picture with one hand, Rainey stirred the rice with the other. The motion brought the boil under control and the violent hot water soothed and fell into tiny bubbles through which Rainey could see the rolling grains of brown rice. Nutrition for her daughter. Nutrition too for Rainey. She glanced down. Nutrition for what was inside too. A nutrition Rainey wasn't sure she wanted to share. It was supposed to be all for Rainey and for Tish.

Rainey clanged a lid over the pot and then turned back to the refrigerator. After mothering for four years, Rainey knew that there was more than one way to bring nutrition to a child. To nurture her. There was artwork on the fridge.

As she unscrolled the painting and captured it with clamped magnets, Rainey saw a flash of pink. It was on the back of the painting, the lower right hand corner, and so she hadn't noticed it before. Rainey curled the corner toward her, bending down and turning her head to see it past its upside-down perspective. A pink stick figure. Tucked behind the river, away from all the swirls.

Or beneath it so deep that no one would ever see.

Rainey grabbed a scissors and carefully sliced that corner away, freeing the pink stick figure. She clamped the bottom of the painting firmly to the fridge, then lifted the pink girl to the corner of the freezer, as far away from the painting as she could get. The pink girl got her own magnet and was surrounded by the white clean surface, far away and above the swirling black river and night time below. Rainey wondered for a moment if it looked like the girl was going to Heaven.

But then she decided it just looked like the little girl was safe. Rescued. Pulled away.

When Tish came in for dinner, answering immediately and obediently her mother's call, she glanced at the fridge. Her eyes widened when she saw the cut-away corner. Rainey pointed to the pink girl above. "She's here, Tish," Rainey said. "See? I saved her. Look how far away from the river she is. She's safe, way up here, and there's no one there to hurt her."

Tish sat at her place, the chicken steaming, the rice too, creating a sheen of moist sparkle on her face. She looked at Rainey.

Rainey patted the pink girl. "She's safe," she repeated. "You're safe, Tish."

Tish picked up her fork and began to eat.

Rainey was just putting Tish's snack time dishes into the dishwasher when she heard her front door open. Even though she knew it was Doris, as promised, coming over with a plate full of mint brownies and a pot of fresh coffee, Rainey's heart still did a dive and then a jump. Sounds did that to her now, as did cars driving by late at night, throwing light into her bedroom. She tried closing the blinds, but found she couldn't. If the blinds weren't open, how would she ever spot her rapist if he came back? Even though he caught her at the river, even though he didn't know her name or her address or even what she looked like in broad daylight, Rainey was scared that her rapist would find her. And Tish. He'd find them both. He found them that night, he could find them again. Safety wasn't always as easy as she promised Tish, it wasn't as simple as putting a pink stick figure on the upper corner of a refrigerator. Rainey felt hunted, and she felt she must have been hunted as soon as she started down the Riverwalk. When she thought back to that night, it seemed she knew he was stepping out of the bushes before he even did. Doesn't prey have a sort of second sense, doesn't the skin tingle right before the hunter appears?

He found her that night. And he was still at large, after all. She didn't talk about the terror, and mostly, she kept it shoved deep down. But a simple sound of a door latch could send fear flying out of her skin like sweat.

And now, he could come after a piece of himself too. Something he left behind. Something he planted into her body, making her even more his own. Without even knowing her name.

Simply, Rainey placed her hand flat on her belly. A movement of protection. But then she pulled her hand back.

Taking a deep breath, she turned as Doris walked into the kitchen. Sure enough, the plate was there, heaped with far too many brownies for the two of them, and steam rose steadily from the glass decanter in Doris' hand. "Is she asleep?" Doris asked.

"I think so. She's in bed, anyway." Rainey took down two mugs. First, Doris' favorite, one made at the local Walgreens with a smiling photograph of Tish splashed across the front. Then Rainey's favorite, a deep blue and clear bell-shaped mug. As she set the mugs down on the table, Rainey wondered for a moment why the Tish photo mug wasn't her favorite, but Doris'. Instead, Rainey loved the deep crystal blue of the other. It was a peaceful color, the blue of the ocean or the night sky right before it went to black. In the morning and last thing at night, Rainey always needed some peace. Life as a young single mother wasn't easy. There were bills to pay, to worry over, there was a little girl to raise and raise right, there was always the next step on a never-ending list of things to do.

And now, she really needed the peace brought by the blue mug. Right now, and every second forward, she really needed the night sky to stay that deep blue, spurning the black, but of course, it never would. But Rainey held the sky blue constant, wrapping both of her hands firmly around it. Cobalt, she thought. Was cobalt blue? Did loving this mug over all others mean she was a bad mother? Was she a bad mother for letting Doris use the Tish mug? Was she a bad mother because Tish was no longer talking? Because she briefly considered not putting Tish's artwork on the refrigerator? Was she a bad mother for taking Tish into the park that night?

And what kind of a girl goes walking through a park late at night, Rainey, huh? What kind of girl?

Rainey sat down suddenly, her legs gone.

"Rainey?" Doris asked. "You okay?" She reached over, grabbed Rainey's shaking hands, stilled them. "You're so cold." She squeezed Rainey's fingers, then rewrapped her hands around the mug. Filling the mug with coffee made it even bluer. Then Doris pressed her own hands over Rainey's, smoothing her fingers around the glass, pressing like she was making a sculpture.

Rainey caught her breath. Breathed in, breathed out. "Doris, would you have done what I did?"

"What? When?"

"That night. It was so late and I still had to get Tish in the bath and then to bed. I still had to load the dishwasher, put the laundry away. You know all the stuff. And the bus wasn't due for another fifteen minutes, and in that time, I could get us across the park and home." The warmth from the cup seeped through her fingers and ran up her hands. Rainey pressed harder, urging the heat to flow throughout her body.

"Well." Doris set two brownies in front of Rainey on a paper plate. Doris always brought over paper plates because she didn't want Rainey to use her own dishes and add to her chore list. "I'm an old lady…I wouldn't have been able to get across the park in fifteen minutes. I guess I would have waited for the bus. You move faster than me."

Rainey looked at the brownies. Doris always made them so pretty. The dark brown ran rich as mud. Near the top, the brightest of green shot through, reminding Rainey of leprechauns and summertime lime slurpies bought at the PDQ. "It was so dark, Doris. I just…I just didn't think. It was only the park, you know? We walk through it all the time. I know every inch of the Riverwalk."

"Sweetheart." Doris poured her own coffee. "You're only twenty-four. You're young. It was just a park, to you."

"Is that it then?" Rainey tore her hands away from her mug. "I'm young? Am I stupid? Not even thinking that a dark park could be dangerous? It was dark! It was night!" She echoed her father's words. "For god's sake, what was I thinking?"

"Rainey." Doris nudged the plate forward. "Rainey, that part is over now. Eat your brownies. If you keep looking back, you'll never move forward."

Rainey felt herself puncture. It was those kinds of sayings that always deflated her. They were supposed to sound wise, but they probably came from a bumper sticker. Or the Bible. Doris was full of the Bible, full of saints and apostles and disciples and shoulds and should nots. "Is that from the Bible, Doris?"

"No. I saw it on a bumper sticker today. Guess it just fell out of my mouth."

This made Rainey laugh and suddenly, she was safely in her kitchen again. Her daughter was sleeping upstairs and her neighbor was here, with a pot of strong coffee and Rainey was about to sink her teeth into dark chocolate, shot through with summertime. Rainey picked up a brownie, and felt the chocolate begin to melt from the heat infused in her fingers. She bit. The house hummed its silence around them.

Doris ate her own brownie, then leaned forward. "So. Tell me what the doctor said."

Rainey clenched her fingers, then stopped, worried that her mug would shatter, like the glass in Tish's photograph that afternoon. "I'm pregnant." It was just like when she told her parents, flat out, that she was raped. No introduction, no prelude. The words just so blunt, so outright. *He raped me. I'm pregnant.* Again, she rolled all of it, the twists and turns of it, into one simple sentence, one that she could say fast and then clamp her lips together over the details. The details, then. The decisions, now. She just couldn't bear the decisions.

The words hung between them. Rainey pictured them first in baby blue, the result on the home pregnancy test, crammed now in her garbage can in the garage, and then pink, like the stick figure, but they quickly ran to black. Like the river. She sipped her coffee.

"His?"

Rainey glanced up. "Doris, whose else would it be?" Honestly. Doris knew her every move. Did she think Rainey was having sex with co-workers in closets during the day? "The doctor said I'm only three weeks along. I have until twelve weeks to decide what to do."

And Rainey waited. This was where the wise and helpful quote should turn from bumper sticker to Bible. The good Christian in Doris would have her toss the immediate response onto the table. Abortion is evil. Abortion is wrong. To have an abortion is to kill a baby. What did that pro-life bumper sticker say, the one Rainey saw on so many cars around town? *Abortion stills a beating heart.* Even a beating heart caused by rape.

But Doris said nothing.

Rainey looked up, surprised. Doris had her hands around the Tish mug now, and she held it the way Rainey did hers. "The doctor said I have three choices. Have the baby and keep it. Have the baby and adopt it out." She took a deep breath before she said the word that she knew Doris was waiting for. Armed with a Bible. "Abortion." So blunt. So outright. *He raped me. I'm pregnant. Abortion.*

But Doris just nodded.

"Doris," Rainey said. "I know what you're thinking. Go ahead. Tell me."

Doris cleared her throat. "You know…" she said. There was a hesitation, and then she spoke slowly, pulling each word out as if it was hung somewhere in her throat, needed to be tugged loose, rolled out onto the table. "You know that abortion is an abomination in the eyes of God."

Rainey closed her eyes. She hadn't expected anything else. But still, it cut. An abomination. What happened was an abomination. The rape. And she, Rainey, was an abomination. She nodded.

"But…I don't know, Rainey. I don't know. I wish I did."

The break in Doris' voice caused Rainey to fly her eyes open. Doris had tears streaming down her cheeks. She'd never seen Doris cry. Not even the night of the rape. Nor the days after. Rainey grabbed for Doris' hands, and they held onto each other, with their mugs, the blue night sky, Tish's smiling face, between their circled arms.

"I've always thought of abortion as something promiscuous women did when they, you know, slept around and got pregnant. I never thought about it like this. You aren't promiscuous. You don't sleep around. This isn't your mistake, Rainey. This was done to you."

Rainey kept her fingers entwined with Doris'. "I keep thinking about him. You know. Him. And what if…what if this baby is like him?" Rainey thought again of the darkness of the rapist's skin. But she knew she was talking about so much more than that. The darkness this child could be infected with went much further than skin deep.

Doris sat back suddenly and Rainey found her hands flat on the table. "A good man," Doris said, then stopped. She cleared her throat, closed her eyes, then tried again. *"A good man out of the good treasure of his heart bringeth forth that which is good; and an evil man out of the evil treasure of his heart bringeth forth that which is evil.'"*

Rainey shuddered. An abomination. Her rapist loomed larger than life between her and the river. He blocked the moon. There was no shine of goodness on him anywhere. Even the moon didn't cast its reflection on him.

"But Rainey." Doris wiped at her eyes, then sat briskly forward. "Rainey, the child is part you too, right?"

Part Rainey. A part she didn't want to remember. A part Doris didn't know about, a part nobody knew about except for her rapist. Her body in spasm that night. A dark part of her she didn't recognize, she didn't even know was there before the rape. If her rapist was evil, and if an evil part of her came out that night, what if those forces blended together?

An abomination.

"I don't...I can't think of it as anyone right now, Doris. Not part of me at all. I can only think of him." That was all Rainey could say. No more details. No more decisions. She sat back and shared the silence with Doris, while Tish, she knew, slept above them. Up high, like the pink stick girl, held safely with a magnet on her freezer. Rainey wanted to think that Tish slept peacefully. And inside Rainey, she knew the cells were doubling, tripling, quadrupling themselves. At some point, in a split second, a blink of an eye, the intake of a breath, a new heart would leap out of nothingness and begin to beat. In the dark. In the darkness of Rainey's own body.

"Say something," Rainey said. "Say something, Doris, say something strong. Comforting. Please." Not from the bible, she wanted to say. From a bumper sticker. From a book, any other book. But Rainey fell silent.

Doris closed her eyes again. Rainey felt compelled to do so too. She didn't know if Doris was praying or thinking, or a little of both, but Rainey tried to join her in it. She heard when Doris inhaled, then spoke softly.

"Wait on the Lord; be of good courage, and he shall strengthen thine heart; wait, I say, on the Lord."

Rainey opened her eyes and looked at Doris. For a moment, her neighbor's face was upraised and it was like peace itself rose over her body and up to her chin, and then over it, blanketing her skin. But then Doris opened her eyes too and looked back. And her gaze dropped to the tabletop and below, where the unknown lay hidden in Rainey. Doris frowned, the skin puckering that looked so peaceful just a second ago. So certain.

"Okay," Rainey said. "I'll wait. I have nine more weeks." She folded her hands over her abdomen and slouched in her chair. It was, she felt, not an embrace or a movement of protection. It was simply an acknowledgement of what was there. What had to be dealt with.

Details. Decisions.

She waited as the coffee cooled and the rest of the brownies remained uneaten. When Doris left, after going upstairs and glancing in at Tish, then kissing the top of Rainey's head, Rainey put their mugs in the dishwasher, then turned it on. She checked the doors and the windows, a new nightly routine, and shut the lights off, one by one. She used to leave the stairway light on, but no longer. She didn't want to make it any easier for her rapist to find the path to her bedroom door. She checked on Tish, smoothed her hair as much as the corkscrews would allow, pulled the pink blanket to her chin. In sleep, Tish's thumb had fallen out of her mouth, but her lips remained in a circle, and so Rainey kissed them. Tish kissed back, then sighed, emitting a sound so soft, Rainey nearly missed it. But she captured it and held it, long after it was gone.

Before climbing into her own bed, Rainey looked out the window. Everything was dark and quiet. The favored blue of the night sky was gone, leaving behind that classic black, littered with stars that didn't brighten the ground. Only the occasional car drove by. It was silent next door too, and Rainey knew that Doris was in her own room, on the other side of Rainey's own wall, probably already asleep.

Rainey thought about closing the blinds. But then she left them open, just in case.

Huddled in her bed, Rainey listened to the sound of nothing, all the snaps and cracks of a silent house that was never truly silent. She thought of her mother, here on a visit that was so short, sneaking in, creeping up the steps, and finally sitting next to her daughter on this bed, holding her, rocking her. Rainey felt again her head tucked under her mother's chin, and she felt the warmth of those arms around her. She thought of Doris that night, kissing the top of her head, just the way a mother would, before going out the door to her own home.

Rainey's mother never knew about that first child, the one aborted when Rainey was only fifteen. She knew about the second child, of course, and turned her face away, said nothing, when Rainey's father berated her, slapped her down, refused to offer any help or support for a child that would be his tousle-haired granddaughter.

But the night they were here, Rainey's mother crept away from her father. She slipped here, next door, and stumbled up the steps to sit beside Rainey, to hold her. And she peeked in on the granddaughter she never saw before.

Pulling the covers up to her own chin, as she'd done to Tish in Tish's pink room, Rainey stared at the black sky through her window. Her locked window. In the morning, she decided, she would call her mother. She would call after her father, now retired, settled in their den with a second cup of coffee and the morning game shows on the television. Her mother could answer the phone and carry it to the back patio, sit in the sun, and listen.

Rainey would tell her mother about this third child. Maybe she wouldn't look away. Maybe she could help her daughter decide what to do.

Maybe.

Rainey closed her eyes, bringing the black of the night sky under her lids and into her sleep.

CHAPTER EIGHT

Doris

D oris set aside her Bible, carefully stroking the soft satin ribbon in place, folding the ancient cover to a close. She'd had this Bible for almost as long as she could remember. It was inscribed to her on her First Communion, from her mother. "To my baby," the inscription said. "Daddy and I are so proud of you. You are a little bride of God today. Keep the faith always." Doris did feel like a little bride that day, dressed in her flowing white gown that reached just past her knees, her feet tenderly tucked into brand new lacy socks and white shiny mary-janes. The veil placed on her smooth brown hair was double-tiered and she wore one layer over her face, just like a real bride at a real wedding. When she went up to receive communion, it was the priest that lifted the veil away so she could poke her tongue out at him and receive the host. Receive the body of Christ and take Him into her bloodstream. The priest married Doris to God that day, and Doris felt strongly that she was looking through the priest to the face of God, as He took her as His little bride. God smiled at her as she held the wafer carefully balanced on her tongue, keeping her teeth far away, as she'd been instructed in catechism. Of course, God smiled at all of them that day. There were twenty little brides at First Communion. And twenty-three little boys too. Doris wasn't sure what to call them; she never was. If the girls were the brides of God, and God was the groom, what would the boys be? Grooms didn't marry grooms, at least, not back then. But all of the first communicants that day balanced wafers, all tried valiantly not to chew.

Behind Doris, in the first pew not reserved for the little brides and boys, another boy, older and not wearing a suit, but a pair of jeans and a neat button-down shirt, chewed so loudly, she heard his lips smack. She turned to look at him, and he grinned and said loudly, "It tastes like dog food, doesn't it?" His father whacked his shoulder and while Doris was scandalized, she had to push down a giggle as she faced forward again. The wafer, she thought, tasted more like notebook paper than dog food. The boy, four years older than Doris, grew up to skip school and wear leather and ride motorcycles. For a while. Then he married Doris.

Doris remembered wondering once, when she sat in her high school confirmation class, if God was a bigamist, with all these little brides. And the boys too, however one wanted to interpret that. The unbidden thought that He was marrying children, that God could be a pedophile, flitted across her mind that day too, and like now, she shook her head to rid herself of that curious blasphemy.

God would never do such a thing.

So she shook her head and kept the faith, just as her mother told her to, and she was reminded of this every time she opened her Bible. Through it all, she'd kept the faith. Church every Sunday and holy day. Reading the Bible first thing in the morning and last thing at night. Volunteering at the church.

"So we fix our eyes not on what is seen, but on what is unseen, since what is seen is temporary, but what is unseen is eternal."

Doris kept the faith.

And the whole time she did, through all the years, Doris also had plenty of opportunities to be angry at God.

But she pushed them all aside. Until now. Now there was a bruised Rainey and a silent Tish. And a little nameless third.

Doris' Bible sat between her cooled coffee and nibbled-on breakfast bran muffin. Like always, she'd opened the book at random.

She found herself in Job 34: 23 - 28, but what she'd read just hadn't helped much.

For he will not lay upon man more than right; that he should enter into judgment with God. He shall break into pieces mighty men without number, and set others in their stead. Therefore he knoweth their works, and he overturneth them in the night, so that they are destroyed. He striketh them as wicked men in the open sight of others; Because they turned back from him and would not consider any of his ways: So that they cause the cry of the poor to come unto him, and he heareth the cry of the afflicted.

Usually, when Doris read, she found answers, sometimes answers she didn't even know she was searching for, and she was able to enter her day humming and prepared. But today, she was zig-zagged. One line led her to feel she found an answer, and then with the next, she found questions. If God did strike wicked men, if He overturned them and destroyed them, then surely the rapist would be found and brought to justice. But if God heard the cry of the afflicted, why didn't He hear Rainey that night? Why didn't He hear her now? Was He listening to Tish's silence at all?

And the opening line of the verse haunted Doris the most of all. *For he will not lay upon man more than right.* To Doris, that sounded like one of the platitudes Father Markham mentioned, the one she herself often used with grieving or stunned members of her church…God never gives us more than we can handle. If this rape was something that God laid upon Rainey, and He never laid upon man more than right, did that mean that Rainey somehow deserved it? That it was right for this to happen to her? And that she was somehow supposed to be strong enough to handle it?

Why would God think any woman could handle the brutality of rape? Of being held down against her will, of her body being used for a purpose it was never intended for?

And it wasn't like the rape just happened to Rainey on that one night. For that bit of time. It didn't stop, it kept on happening. Every day, there was more to consider. More to go through. It might be over for him, as he went out looking for other women, but for Rainey, the violation kept growing, sticking its legs like spiders into every part of the web of her life. Every part. Her daughter, her friend. And its effect on her body was still ongoing too. And would be for the next nine months.

If that's what Rainey decided to do.

But despite this, Doris was supposed to keep the faith. And Rainey wasn't supposed to receive more than she could handle. And then Tish. Wasn't this more than any four-year old should handle?

Doris stood up, shaking these thoughts out of her head as violently as her teenaged consideration of God as a bigamist and pedophile. Today was Friday, and she was back on her normal schedule, which meant her house was clean and she was free to do as she pleased. Go to town on errands. Visit friends. Sit and read the newspaper on her front porch, while nursing a second and longer cup of coffee. She liked, on Fridays, to make a tour of the Goodwill, to see if anything popped up during the week. Friday was the best day, before the weekend scavengers descended. Doris pressed her lips together as she cleaned up her breakfast, trying to decide what she wanted to do, if she wanted to do anything at all. Even with Friday being Friday again, she wondered if her life would ever feel returned to normal.

She brought her Bible up the stairs and to her bedside, where it would wait for her and her final night time read and prayer. She wondered what she would read at random that night.

And then she wondered if she would open the book at all.

Doris had plenty of opportunities to be angry with God. On this morning, she felt every one of them descend on her, like the weight of fallen angels.

Shaking her head, she retrieved her purse and headed out into the day.

The Goodwill offered up a stuffed and striped rhinoceros, which would look just wonderful next to the gray hippo. Doris paged through the children's clothes, hung in a splash of color on the back wall, scattered in sizes and colors, and found a great pair of pink overalls for Tish, shot through with a stripe of purple. Knowing what she was after now, Doris quickly located a lavender long-sleeved t-shirt to wear with the overalls, and in the shoe section, there was a pair of pink and purple striped sneakers, with a bright white rubber toe and hot pink shoelaces. They didn't even look worn and Doris knew without looking they were in Tish's size. Doris loved it when things fell together like this. It was like it was all laid out for her, just waiting for her discovery. Tish would be delighted and Doris knew that as soon as Saturday arrived, there would be a flash of pink and purple and Tish would leap in front of her, arms and legs akimbo in the biggest Look-at-me posture, complete in her new ensemble. It would have to be washed and dried by Monday, so she could wear it again to school. With Tish's bounce and skip, her wide smile flashing as she twirled, the clothes wouldn't just be worn. They would be debuted.

Doris always presented all new stuffed animals to Tish with a poem or a little story, like the purple cow rhyme. The gray hippo last week was easy; Shel Silverstein's "Recipe for a Hippopotamus Sandwich" earned Doris a huge and happy Tish smile. As Doris stood in line to check out, she wracked her brain for a rhino poem, but she came up empty. She shrugged. It would come. She had faith it would come.

As always, Doris kept the faith.

She had faith in so many things. Entire outfits falling together at Goodwill. Bins tossing up stuffed animals that would fill in her yard like missing puzzle pieces. And poems to give as gifts. Her mantra, repeated often throughout every day, was "God will take care of it," or "God will make do." God will provide, as she was taught in catechism.

But imagine. Imagine a God who popped silly rhymes for stuffed animals into Doris' head not taking care of a woman being raped. Not lifting away her four-year old, or helping that four-year old to shut her eyes, block her ears. Imagine having faith in such a God.

Doris shook her head. Hard.

In the car, she thought she was turning toward the coffee shop, but when she reached a certain intersection, she turned right. Then she stopped at a florist's. She knew where she was going now, the path she was on, as certain as the path to a new outfit in Goodwill. Where she was going, she never arrived empty-handed.

Doris had many opportunities to be angry with God.

Kneeling in front of her husband's grave, Doris plucked the dead flowers out of the plastic holder and tucked in the fresh. "Hi, hon," she said. It was getting harder to sit on the ground at her age, but carefully, she slid her hips sideways over her folded calves and came to what she thought of as a ladylike pose. One arm propped her up, her legs curved gently to her side and she sat upon her husband and considered him. She looked at the final date on the stone, stronger and more resonant than the period at the end of a sentence. June 27, 1998. "Gone eight years already, hon," she said. "Hard to believe."

And it was. Eight years ago, when she was sixty-eight and Harvey was seventy-two, she had some aches and pains in the morning, but just moving down the hall to the bathroom and then down the stairs to the kitchen loosened her up and by the time she sipped her first jolt of coffee, she was pain-free and young again. Half an hour later, she'd already read her Bible verse and was humming to the song on the morning radio show. When the stairs creaked and then were echoed by Harvey's chair, announcing his arrival, she slid a plate full of yellow scrambled eggs, three slices of bacon, and a perfectly toasted English muffin in front of him. She always set out the full array of jams and jellies; orange marmalade, apple butter, raspberry, boysenberry, and the old stand-by, grape, because even after almost forty-seven years of marriage then, fifty-five now, if Harvey was still alive, she could never predict which mood went with which flavor. As Harvey dug into his breakfast, she always wrapped her arms around his shoulders and kissed his neck, receiving a warm "Mmmmm" in return. No matter what. No matter if they'd fought the night before. No matter if the bills were overdue. No matter if it was the days following the diagnosis of congestive heart failure. Always a kiss, and always warm appreciation.

Even on the day after she found their five-week old son dead in his crib first thing in the morning. That morning, the morning after the worst day of their lives, she wrapped her arms around her husband's shoulders and kissed his neck, just like always, even as tears rolled down her cheeks and into the open collar of his shirt. She knew she soaked his chest. His tears soaked her hair. Yet still, no matter what, she hugged and he said, "Mmmmm."

It was like faith. Like reading the Bible every morning, and reading it every night.

Doris turned now to the little headstone by her husband's. Forrest James Granger, it read, and in italics underneath, "Our little man."

For five weeks and two days, Doris rocked him, nursed him, saying softly, "What's the matter, little man?" when he cried, whispering, "Good morning, little man!" when his eyes first opened at daybreak. For five weeks and two days, she relished going into the nursery at first light, raising the blinds just the tiniest bit so she could see the curve of his cheek and the flare of his eyelashes, just so she could watch the exact moment when those eyelashes flickered and then Forrest opened his eyes onto the world. By the time Harvey came down to the kitchen, not only would breakfast be waiting for him, but so would his son, sucking on one fist while waving the other, fresh in a clean diaper and sleeper, tucked in the bassinet under the kitchen window. But that morning, the day Forrest should have turned five weeks and three days old, Doris waited longer than usual for his eyes to open. And then she looked closer.

Doris had plenty of opportunities to be angry with God.

Replacing Forrest's flowers now, she glanced at the little angel she insisted be carved in the lower right of the headstone, and then at the little angel she insisted be carved in the upper left. The angel on the left looked down on where Forrest rested, and the angel on the right looked toward Heaven.

The priest who then reigned at Sacred Heart, not Father Markham who came five priests later, told Doris and Harvey that there weren't any angels for their little boy. Babies who died before baptism, this priest insisted, went to a place called Limbo. Without baptism, the baby wasn't cleansed of sin and wouldn't be allowed into Heaven.

Forrest was to be baptized the following week, when he was six weeks old. Doris already had his christening gown bought, a beautiful thing, even though Harvey insisted that boys didn't wear gowns. To appease him, she'd also bought a pure white sleeper which Forrest would wear under the gown.

She still remembered Harvey surging to his feet, knocking his chair over, that day in the priest's small office. "What sin?" His hands grasped the priest's desk for support. "He was five weeks old! All he could do was poop and pee and eat! Babies can't sin."

Even deep in grief, Doris shuddered at the words poop and pee being uttered in the presence of a priest.

The priest folded his hands and Doris wondered if the man's every thought was a prayer, a conversation with God. "All children are born with the stain of original sin, Harvey. Baptism purifies. Your son left us before baptism. I'm sorry."

But still, Doris insisted on the angels in the headstone. At the funeral, when she and Harvey were allowed a last glimpse of their son before the tiniest of caskets was closed, Doris slid a small bottle of holy water from her purse. Her hands shaking, she soaked her fingers with it, then touched Forrest's forehead, his chest, his left shoulder, his right. His forehead glistened. Then she pulled the little white blanket up to the baby's chin, tucking him in for the final time, sending him off on an unexpected and terrible journey, and she collapsed, spilling the rest of the holy water on the floor.

It was Harvey who helped her up. Harvey who gently closed the lid and then leaned heavily against her, crying with sobs that she knew she couldn't appease with a "God never gives us more than we can handle." And it was Harvey who, after wiping his eyes and nose, picked up the empty holy water bottle and pitched it hard into the garbage can just before they walked into the body of the church for the funeral. Doris could still hear the solid thunk of that plastic bottle hitting the bottom of the can. A harsh metal sound, unfitting, foreign, in a church filled with hymns and her own quiet cries. It was Harvey's last time in a church, until his own funeral. Doris continued on alone.

Every Sunday morning after their son's death, she lost her husband. Week after week, year after year. She felt the absence of her son in her arms and the vacancy at her side in the pew. The possibility of losing one more thing, her rituals, her church, her faith, seemed like the edge of insanity. And so she stayed, murmuring the same words each week, listening to sermons that sounded alike after so many years, and offering up prayers.

Platitudes? Maybe so.

Now, Doris pictured her little man in his casket, just as he was fifty-three years ago. Fifty-three years of floating in Limbo. The casket was white and lined with white satin. He wore his white sleeper, and over it, the stunning white christening gown, beaded with seed pearls in the shape of a cross from his chest to his tummy and over his arms. She hoped the white blanket was still pulled up to his chin. So much white for this little baby. White for innocence, for purity.

In a baby stained with original sin. A baby floating forever in Limbo.

When Doris pictured Limbo, she pictured millions of little babies, little souls, floating like the mobiles above their empty cribs. They couldn't walk yet, they couldn't crawl, what else was there for them to do but float, suspended from some unseen ceiling beneath the floor of Heaven? Babies lost in miscarriage, babies born with their umbilical cords around their necks, babies born too sick to breathe more than a few seconds. And babies like her own, who in the middle of their sixth week of life, just stop breathing somewhere in the night. No cry, no whimper, no thrashing in their blankets. Just stop.

Doris kept the faith, even then. She had her moment with the holy water, she had her angels. And then she stuffed her anger deep down her throat and offered up prayers and Bible verses instead. She went to mass every week and joined her voice to the congregation's, over and over and over again, hugging the familiarity to herself, hugged the consistency, the longevity, and so she repeated her faith too. Over and over, she said the words. And over and over, she kept the faith, despite the questions burning her throat. Questions that she swallowed.

Five days after they buried Forrest, Doris opened her Bible in the morning and read from Matthew 18:11—14:

For the Son of man is come to save which was lost. How think ye? if a man have an hundred sheep, and one of them be gone astray, doth he not leave the ninety and nine, and goeth into the mountains, and seeketh that which is gone astray? And if so be that he find it, verily I say unto you, he rejoiceth more of that sheep, than of the ninety and nine which went not astray. Even so it is not the will of your Father which is in Heaven, that one of these little ones should perish.

That was where Doris placed her hope that day, even as her faith kept her reciting in mass. She placed her hope in a God that would find this little flock of sheep in Limbo, all those little sheep away from the millions of souls that must roam Heaven, even as Doris shook away the question about God creating Limbo in the first place. Sometimes it was easier to find comfort in hope than in anger. Sometimes certain questions just hurt too much, piled pain upon a pain that was already unbearable.

"I love you, little man," she said now. Reaching out for Harvey's gravestone, she raised herself up on its shoulders, as she often leaned on him in life. Brushing off her pants, she stood quietly until the chiming of the town's church bells, signaling noon and lunch, quieted. "Rest easy," she said. "Both of you."

She turned to go, but then looked a little longer at Forrest's grave. He was a baby that was so wanted, so hoped for and loved and delighted in. Yet God took him away and chose not to provide any others. And now there was this new baby, tucked deep inside Rainey. A baby much more purely stained with sin than Forrest ever was. Would God take this child away too?

Doris patted the small stone. If God was a loving and caring and sensitive god, surely He would.

Yet right here, in the green well-trimmed grass, here was proof...

Doris shook her head quickly, violently. So many times shaking her head that day. She turned toward her car and decided she would treat herself to a lunch at the little deli in town. She would see friends there, and their chatter would clear her mind. And that afternoon, after school, she would present Tish with her new outfit and show her the stripey rhino which would take its place in Doris' yard.

And God help her, she would come up with a rhyme for a rhino.

After school, after Tish's snack and down time in front of the television, Doris stood on her porch and watched the little girl walk through the stuffed animals. Tish wasn't running today; her stride was slow and thoughtful, and while she wasn't sucking her thumb, she was running her index finger over and over her lips. Doris saw this gait before and she remembered when it used to be accompanied by a whisper as Tish talked out her problem, thought out her answer. Sometimes she would turn to Doris for answers, but mostly, she did it on her own, and by the time she turned to Doris, it was with a clear face and a bright smile. Doris would ask her what she was thinking about, and Tish would tell her, supplying Doris with the whole question and then the answer, and then Doris would hug her and say, "You are such a smart girl, Tish." And she was.

Doris also used to think it was amazing how Tish could talk so constantly. Before Tish, Doris had always attributed a steady stream of chatter to a steady stream of nothing much going on in the brain. It was amazing how noisy an intelligent, introspective child could be. And now, Tish's silence was even noisier.

Doris waited for the answer to come to the little girl, but it stayed away. The wrinkle of thought remained firmly between Tish's eyebrows. Finally, Doris moved down the steps, carrying the rhino and the bag from Goodwill. "Hey, Tish," she said, taking a seat. "Come see what I've got for you."

Tish looked up, her gaze unfocused as her thoughts were interrupted. Then she locked onto the bag in Doris' hands and she moved quickly to the steps, sitting down next to her, her little hip sinking into Doris' full one.

"You okay?" Doris asked.

Tish nodded.

"Is something wrong?" Doris draped her arm around Tish, gave her a shake. "You don't usually walk like that unless you're working something out."

Tish shrugged. At another small shake from Doris, Tish stuck out her tongue and touched it. The look she gave Doris then was one of pure pain. Her face drew long and her eyes rounded like spotlights and her mouth gapped and sagged.

"Sweetheart!" Doris dropped the rhino and the bag and swept Tish into her lap, rocking her. Doris never forgot how to rock a child, any child, even though she only rocked Forrest for five weeks and two days. Doris rocked until she felt the stiffness melt from Tish's spine, until Tish's arms came up and circled around Doris' neck. Then, carefully, Doris sat Tish up, spun her so she straddled Doris' lap and faced her, and she pressed her forehead to Tish's. "Tish, does it hurt when you try to talk?"

Tish's skin rubbed against Doris' as she shook her head. No. Then she turned and pointed at the street.

"It hurts…the road? The car? The world?" Doris guessed.

Tish pointed at the driveway. Then the garage. The door to her side of the duplex.

"It hurts your mother?"

Tish nodded vigorously.

Doris' mind cranked, trying to follow Tish's silent train of thought, trying to match her mind to a four-year old's. "Honey, how does it hurt your mom?"

Tish's face transformed to an expression so bewildered that Doris felt the ground open beneath her and she and Tish sat at the edge of a dark canyon, too dark to know what was inside, but dark enough to know it was deep. Tish didn't know the answer, she couldn't explain. And neither could Doris. How could Doris fix it if neither of them understood the problem?

"Honey, it won't hurt your mom if you talk. It will help her. It hurts her that you won't talk. We both miss your voice."

A face ripped in two. That was the only way Doris could think of to describe Tish's next expression. Like she was just being torn in half. Quickly, Doris fell into that steady rock again, trying to mend the girl back together, trying to close the canyon. Then Doris reached for the rhino, tumbled to the bottom of the steps. "Look what I got today. He's going to be the hippo's friend."

And Tish lit up. She beamed the way a four-year old should, when presented with the improbability of a rainbow-striped rhino. The afternoon lightened, the canyon seamed together and disappeared under the blanket of Doris' grass, and whatever the problem was smoothed away from Tish's face. For now. Doris laughed out loud.

Tish sat the rhino on her lap, hugged his neck, and looked at Doris expectantly. Doris leaned back and, squeezing her eyes shut, prepared to recite the poem she found in one of the many children's books of poetry she kept around for the stuffed animals, and for Tish. Especially for Tish. There were two shelves in Doris' living room especially for children's books that were for Tish and Tish alone.

Her girl.

Well, Rainey's girl. But hers as well.

Doris recited.

I left our rhino in the rain;
all night he's been outside.
The rain has soaked him to the bone,
right through his rhino hide.

He's my responsibility.
My folks said, "Don't forget…"
But somehow I neglected him,
and now he's soaking wet.

And both my folks are all upset
and feel I can't be trusted.
I left our rhino in the rain,
and he rhinocerusted.

Tish's mouth opened and her tongue wagged and her shoulders shook, in her new and silent version of laughter. Doris watched her and in her own silence, she prayed and prayed and prayed that God would set this one thing to rights. Please, God, she thought. Give the child her voice back. And give her back to us.

Doris kept the faith.

Tish sat and patted the rainbow rhinoceros and Doris knew there was no danger of this one being left out in the rain. She started putting the stuffed animals in her yard when Tish was six months old. She and Rainey were well-established as neighbors by then. Even before Tish and Rainey, Doris put the stuffed English sheepdog out on her porch during the day. Doris was allergic to dogs, she could never have one of her own, and to her, the porch was lonely without a dog sitting upon it. So a stuffed dog had to do. Harvey brought it home to her one spring, a spring before Doris' one pregnancy and birth. Before Forrest. Harvey told her he saw it in the window of a gift shop and something about it seemed perfect for their porch.

So it was Harvey that started it all, really, by placing that dog on the porch. And once he started, and once Forrest was lost to them, Doris found she just couldn't stop. The dog went outside every day. And every night, he sat sentinel by the door. A guard dog.

Now, like the books, they were all for Tish.

"Look what else I have." Doris presented Tish with the bag.

Tish pulled out the overalls and shirt and held them in front of herself. She placed the sneakers next to her own feet and then struck a pose like a supermodel. Doris clapped. "You'll look beautiful."

They both turned at the familiar sound of Rainey's car. Doris listened to the cut of the engine, the garage door closing, then the back door of the duplex, Rainey's footsteps, and out she came to sit next to them. Rainey admired the rhino and the outfit, she laughed at the second recitation of the poem, and then Tish took off at a run through the animals. She attempted a cartwheel, but her legs stayed bent, and it looked more like an odd sideways somersault.

"Has she been okay?" Rainey asked.

Doris noticed how tired Rainey looked. She made a note to bring over some hot lemon tea that night. It would help Rainey to sleep, and also help with any queasiness, should that be starting to develop. "She's been fine. She said something odd though."

Rainey startled. "She said?"

Doris cursed herself for her own choice of words. "Well, no, she didn't talk. It was…well, she answered, you know." Doris told Rainey of her conversation with Tish.

Rainey frowned. "So she thinks she'll hurt me if she talks. I wonder what that means, where she got that from."

"I don't know." Doris folded the new outfit, placed it on Rainey's lap. "Rainey…maybe it's time Tish saw someone else besides the counselor at school. Maybe someone from that list the hospital gave you."

Rainey played with the sneakers, tying and untying one shoe. "I suppose. I was hoping that she'd just sort of handle it, you know? Everyone always talks about the resiliency of children." She slumped. "I'm not feeling so resilient myself. Mothers are supposed to be resilient too, aren't they?"

Doris put an arm around her and rocked her just a bit. Rainey joined in and they swayed together.

"I keep wondering how a therapist can help Tish. I mean, she's not talking. What can a therapist learn from a silent child that we can't?"

"I don't know. Maybe he'll be able to tell something just from what her body says."

Tish went running by and Doris watched the skip in her step, so different from the slow walk of before. Tish did a twirl, her arms spinning, and her face split open with a grin as she shook her hair at the sky. To Doris, Tish looked for all the world like a happy and healthy four-year old, a child who was well-loved, a child who could be expected to be afraid of thunderstorms, to wish on white dandelions and pennies in wells, and who would sing off-key in the bathtub while draping her pink body in a magic cape of iridescent bubbles.

Yet Doris knew better. There was that silent tongue. There was whatever it was that Tish saw that night, that Tish heard, and that she kept locked away in her memory like poison. Like a secret weapon. One that could kill the world. Or just hurt her mother.

Just. As if Rainey wasn't already more hurt than could be imagined.

Hauling herself up, Doris caught Tish and gave her a kiss and a squeeze. She also offered her usual promise to set out the animals first thing in the morning, so Tish could wake up, slip out of her warm bed with the rhino tucked under her arm, and place him in his new home. Then Doris went inside to cook her supper as Rainey went in to cook theirs.

Doris hesitated at the bottom of her stairs and looked up. She knew where everything was up there, she knew where everything was in her whole house. Her Bible waited for her on her bedside table, and if she kept the routine, if she followed the usual path of her evening, she would watch television, bring a snack of tea and cookies for Rainey, take a bath (she showered and washed her hair on Tuesday, Thursday and Saturday, and took a bath on Monday, Wednesday and Friday), brush her teeth, then settle into bed and reach for a Bible verse. What would she read in her Bible that night? Did God know she was having doubts? Would she open the book, the Good Book as they always called it in church, and would she see an answer? Did God know she was angry? Did He even care?

Or would she see what she really wanted?

An apology.

An apology for everything.

Doris had many opportunities to be angry with God. Her throat burned with them all.

She shook her head. Quickly. Violently. Then she continued on to her kitchen.

CHAPTER NINE

Tish

I didn't do what Mama said. I always do what Mama says, but I didn't. She told me to run to the climbing structure. She told me to stay there. I didn't.

I sat down.

Mama got hurt.

He said make a sound and this is what will stuck you. I made a sound. The leaves crunched. It was teeny tiny, but I made it, and he hurt her.

I made a sound. I didn't do what Mama said.

He said suck and he will go away.

I suck. My thumb is always wrinkly now. It's gross. The kids laugh at me. They call me baby. They sing, "Tish can't talk, Tish can't talk!"

I can talk.

But I can't.

Mama got hurt. I didn't do what Mama said.

CHAPTER TEN

Rainey

Weeks 4 & 5: Inside the amniotic sack, the embryo is surrounded by fluid. The nervous system is developing, and the foundations for major organs are in place. The embryo is now around 2 millimeters long.

A groove forms on the outer layer of cells and then folds to form a hollow tube called the neural tube. This will become the brain and the spinal cord. At the same time, another tube-like structure forms, and it will eventually be the heart. The embryo already has some of its own blood vessels and so blood begins to circulate. A string of these blood vessels becomes the umbilical cord.

Rainey stood in the doorway and watched her daughter sleep. One thin arm was slung over the rainbow-striped rhino. Rainey smiled. She never knew what would show up in Tish's bed next. It was always a surprise. What wasn't a surprise was the teddy bear clutched in Tish's other hand, crushed to her cheek. Teddy, the unimaginative name Rainey gave to the bear when she was oh so tired and had just moved in to the duplex four years ago, was always there. Doris gave Tish the bear on that move-in day. She'd gone out that afternoon and bought it, so that Tish would have something soft to sleep with that night, and every night from that point forward.

In the moon-washed darkness, Rainey cupped both her hands under her abdomen. She'd been sick at work that day. Mid-morning. She had a bagel for breakfast and coffee and it was still an hour and a half until lunch and first her stomach growled, and then it heaved.

She barely made it to the bathroom in time. Luckily, no one else was in there. Rainey reminded herself of the constant light graze she had to follow while pregnant with Tish. If she kept her stomach almost completely full at all times, she might be able to keep the nausea under control. The tea Doris brought that night helped, and Rainey added teabags to her mental checklist of things to grab before work in the morning.

Sitting out on the porch with Doris earlier, watching Tish play, and then sitting with her in the living room, sipping tea, Rainey hadn't been able to bring herself to tell Doris of the nausea. Feeling it was one thing. Saying it out loud made it all even more real. She told Doris she was pregnant; that made it real. The vomiting made it real. But saying to someone, saying to Doris, "I had morning sickness today," calling it that, not saying an upset stomach, or the flu, or food poisoning, that made it somehow more real yet. It acknowledged that a pregnancy, a baby, was underway and already changing who Rainey was. Already affecting her. A baby, if she let it go that far. Physically, and in her own mind.

Rainey wasn't able to tell her mother that morning either. After she threw up, Rainey took her cell phone and stepped out to the parking lot. Leaning on her car, she called her mother. When her mother answered, when Rainey heard the cautious voice over the phone, "Hello?", a question, cautious because her parents didn't have caller ID yet, and who would be calling at that time in the morning, on a weekday morning, when her mother should be rinsing the breakfast dishes, her father reading the paper and watching game shows, no one ever called then, Rainey hung up without saying a word.

She just couldn't. Who could ever say those words? "Mom, I'm pregnant. And my rapist is the father."

Now, Rainey leaned against Tish's door jamb. In her sleep, Tish's mouth grew slack, and her thumb slid wet and shiny onto the pillow.

If Rainey ended the pregnancy now, right now, she wouldn't have to go through all of this. She would bleed, yes, but her hormone levels would drop and she'd be herself. Her body would be all her own again, in a way it hadn't been since the night before the rape.

But Rainey stood and looked at Tish, sleeping. The blanket barely moved, so gentle were her breaths. And Rainey's hands cupped her abdomen.

Turning quickly, Rainey headed down the stairs. She kept the lights off, moving through the dark, not wanting to draw any attention to her house. But then she turned down the basement steps, and there, she turned on a lone lightbulb. No one would see her down here, no one would be alerted to her presence.

Searching the shelves, she pulled down one box, put it back, then pulled down another. She set it on the washing machine and opened the flaps. There were the soft scents of baby powder and Dreft laundry detergent and a faint sour smell of spit-up, something that Doris assured her could never be completely washed away.

One by one, Rainey lifted out the impossibly small clothes. Tish's wardrobe grew monumentally after they moved in next to Doris. Until then, Rainey made do with the three sleepers that she'd purchased on clearance at a discount store. She held them up now, one pink, one lavender, one yellow. Silver snaps and booted feet, and special little cuffs that folded over baby fingers to keep the child from scratching herself. Tish came home in the pink. It had been too big and Rainey felt so unprepared. She never expected the smallness of that baby. The fragility. And how every single need had to be filled by Rainey and Rainey alone. Until Doris, there was no one else. Rainey wasn't prepared for how exhausting that would be.

Then she pulled out all the Doris clothes, rainbows of sleepers and overalls and teeny tiny dresses that surrounded Tish's baby body like the petals of a sunflower. Each week, Doris hit the Goodwill, and each week, she came home with a fistful of treasures. And Tish, dressed in the found treasures, became a treasure herself that Rainey loved beyond reason, loved with the fullness of a mother for her child. Her beautiful little girl.

With Doris there, with all the relief and support and strength Doris brought, Rainey was able to see her way past the exhaustion and the overwhelm and instead, glory in her daughter. The first smile, the first laugh, the first tooth, rolling quickly to the first crawl, the first step, the first flat-out run and then the first day of preschool. There were other days too, so many days that Rainey wondered if she'd done the right thing by keeping Tish, too many days that she cursed a late night spent in the water of a still spring-cold lake. The first virus, the first stomach flu, impossible amounts disgorged from a child who couldn't yet toddle to the bathroom. The first tumble down the stairs. The first shouted "No!", the first full-blown temper tantrum in the middle of a grocery store, complete with the first, "I hate you!" Rainey remembered stamping her own foot, shouting, "I hate you too!", then running out of the store with her daughter under her arm, her groceries abandoned, sure that Child Protective Services would be at her door within hours. What kind of mother yelled "I hate you!" at her daughter in a grocery store, even if that daughter was being particularly hateful at the time? Even if that daughter was the first to yell those words, "I hate you!", and she seemed to deeply mean each of the three syllables?

What kind of mother does that? Maybe the same kind of mother who brings her daughter through a dark park after curfew, even if that daughter needs to be bathed and tucked in for sleep and the park is the quickest way to get her there.

And what kind of a girl goes walking through a park late at night, Rainey, huh? What kind of girl?

There were also the glorious moments not talked about in any baby book. The first time Tish shouted, "Oh, shit!" in front of Doris in a perfect imitation of Rainey, and the look on Doris' face! Rainey tried to reprimand Tish, but instead laughed so hard, Tish joined in until she wet herself. Oh, the mess.

The evening romp of a little girl through impossible stuffed animals. Corkscrews spinning. Arms wide like a windmill.

And the sweetness of that chirpy little girl voice. Right now, Rainey would even be happy to hear, "I hate you!"

Rainey carefully folded the clothes and returned them to the box. She thought about keeping the box down, maybe taking it up to her room, looking at the little clothes from time to time. When the nausea hit. The fatigue. And with this pregnancy, if she kept this pregnancy, when the fear hit.

Could she do this all over again? A second child, all by herself. The child of a dark man who, instead of holding her close and making love to her in the waves of midnight lake water, snarled and bit her neck like an animal. As she lay next to a river that she couldn't quite reach. Sprawled. Thrown there.

Rainey tried to move on. She tried to push it away, to move up the stairs and prepare for bed, which was just what she was supposed to be doing. She wasn't supposed to be down this basement. She wasn't supposed to be looking at baby clothes. But what loomed was that face over her shoulder. That dark face whose ears stuck out of either side of his head like alien cauliflower.

His ears.

Rainey blinked. Her rapist had large ears. Did she tell the police that, when she described him? Would that help? She made a mental note to call Officer Stanton or Officer Freeman in the morning, and she felt an odd sense of pride wash over her. She remembered something, maybe something that would help them find her rapist and then she wouldn't have to be scared anymore.

She thought of Tish upstairs, of herself standing in the doorway and watching her little girl sleep. She wondered if she could stand in this new child's doorway, see his profile in the darkened room, and not be reminded of the night of his conception. She often thought of Tish's conception, especially whenever she saw Tish around water. In the tub at night. At swimming lessons. On those too-rare days when Rainey brought them for picnics on the beaches by Lake Michigan. Or by the river, the Fox River, that flowed through her town just a few blocks away.

By that river. She'd even thought of Tish's conception on that night. Would she ever be able to look at this unborn child sleeping and not see what she couldn't see then? Her own daughter, on the other side of a bush, watching as Rainey was brutalized. Watching her brother's conception? Her sister's?

Rainey felt a wave of nausea, followed by a slap of fatigue. Quickly, she shoved the box back up on the shelf, so hard, it thudded against the wall. Rainey shuddered at the sound. She could end this all tomorrow, if she decided to. It could all be over.

Though she knew it wouldn't be over, even then, even if that was what she decided. There was that other baby too, the one she aborted in high school. She thought of that first baby, not when reminded of its conception, but on the day of that pregnancy's termination. April 14. She wondered if that day would ever mean anything else to her. This many years later, it was still a day circled in red in her mind. Is that how she would remember this child too? Would she have two death days to remember? And Tish's birthday? The day she let one live? One out of three. More dead than alive.

Heavily, she walked up the stairs. She stopped again at Tish's room. Tish hadn't moved, but the moon had. It lit now the foot of Tish's bed and Tish was in darkness. Rainey knew she was there, though. She didn't know how she knew; she just did. Even though she couldn't hear it, couldn't see it, she felt Tish's breath stroke evenly against her arm.

At the foot of the bed, laid out for the next day, was Tish's new outfit. More pink, though at least this had some purple in it. And even that, overalls, shirt, shoes…well, even that had to be taken under consideration, didn't it. A new baby would need new things. If it was a boy, it could never wear Tish's pink-obsessed clothes. And this time, there wouldn't be a child support check. Even if her rapist was found, how could he support a child from jail?

Until he got out.

Rainey took a step backwards. This pregnancy, this baby, was his too. Would it bring him to her after he got out? If her rapist was ever found and put away? Would this child be like a treasure map, marking her with an X, when her rapist was released?

Would it help him find her now?

Rainey held in her shriek, then ran silently throughout the dark house, her path memorized and sure, checking the locks again on the doors and the windows. They were all locked, she checked them twice already. Then she climbed into her own bed, after taking one fast peek outside, the moon and streetlight frosting the yard and sidewalk in silver. There was no one out there.

For now.

But there was someone inside. Rainey touched her abdomen one more time. She could end it all tomorrow. Sever any connection her rapist could have with her. Rip that treasure map right in half. Keep the treasure in the other room an only child.

Sever it all. More dead than alive.

But she didn't. Rainey let another week go by without a decision. Hopelessness stopped her, prevented her from moving ahead, after she spoke with Officer Stanton and reported the rapist's cauliflower ears. Officer Stanton was polite, and he asked that she call him Robert, and she thought she heard the sound of a pen on paper, but really, the ears didn't seem to make any difference in finding the rapist.

They would never find the rapist.

The nausea continued and built in intensity. She drank hot lemon tea in the morning, once she got to work, and she drank it again before going to bed at night. She tried eating smaller meals, she tried sucking on peppermints and eating saltines while drinking white soda. But nothing seemed to work. She was sick and she was hopeless and she was stupid. Pregnant. Just pregnant.

And babies suddenly populated her entire world. Wherever Rainey went, to the grocery store, on a walk at lunch, to the library for Children's Story Hour with Tish, mothers with young babies stepped in front of her. She turned and they were behind her. If she looked over at the car next to her at a stoplight, she would see a mother speaking into the rearview mirror, and in the back seat, there were waving hands and wails. Babies cried in strollers, in pouches, slept in the arms of their mothers. And the mothers looked happy and harried and exhausted. They were everywhere, it seemed. No place was free from babies.

Just as no place was free from shadows that appeared from the edges of her eyes. From around corners or from the inside of alleys. As soon as it began to grow dark, Rainey went inside with Tish and locked and closed the windows and doors.

Rainey listened too. Not just for the turn of the doorknob, or the unexpected creak on the stairs, but for Tish's voice. She listened for a subconscious hum as Tish hovered over a coloring book. A throaty bark when she sneezed. A sudden laugh at the surprise of cartoon explosions. Rainey waited for a sound, but heard nothing. The silence, instead of becoming the norm, seemed to deepen every day. There were just no sounds at all.

But Rainey did hear the sound of her mother's voice. Finally, in the middle of the week, after another run to the bathroom and a case of the dry heaves, Rainey returned to the parking lot and called her mother. "Hello?" her mother said, her voice even more cautious than before. A second strange call in the middle of a weekday morning.

But this time, Rainey answered. "Mom."

"Rainey!" Just as she predicted, Rainey heard the scuff of her mother's shoes as she quickly retreated. The sound of birds confirmed her mother was on the porch. "How are you? Are you all right? I've been wanting to call —"

"Mom," Rainey said. And then she sobbed.

Her mother at first cried out, but then, she began to hum. And Rainey recognized the tune. A lullaby sung in her ear when she was little, and even when she was older, if she was home sick with a fever. Her mother hummed into the phone and Rainey wrapped her free hand around her middle and she swayed.

"Mom," she said finally. "Mom, there's something awful."

"What? Is Tish okay?"

"Tish is the same. Not talking. But Mom…" Rainey knew she had to say the words. What was happening was already real anyway. But it felt like there were so many levels of real, so many to work through before this became clear and the truth, and not something she imagined or dreamed. Nightmared. "Mom, I'm pregnant. The rapist left me pregnant."

The gasp was so loud, Rainey nearly fell off her feet. She leaned against her car.

"Oh my god, Rainey." The gasp left her mother breathless. "Oh my god."

Rainey listened as her mother's breath mixed with the birdsong in her parents' back yard in Missouri. "Mom, I don't know what to do."

"It's not…you're not very far along, right? A few weeks?"

"Five. I have to make up my mind by twelve weeks. After twelve weeks…well, after that, I won't have any choice but to have it."

"But you could still give it up. I mean, if you have it."

Rainey closed her eyes. "Yes. I suppose that choice would still be mine."

She waited for her mother to tell her what to do. Her mother always told her what to do. Get her homework done. Brush her teeth. Don't wear so much make-up.

Though her mother didn't tell her what to do with baby number two. She just turned her face away and let Rainey's father do the talking. The yelling.

As if on cue, Rainey heard her father's voice, calling from inside the house.

"Rainey, I have to go. Your dad wants to do the grocery shopping today, and he wants to find a new snowblower, before the snow starts. We don't need a new snowblower, but you know your father. He says there's these lightweight ones now, that even I could push."

Not that her father would ever let her mother push the snowblower. Her job was to sweep the steps, Rainey's to shovel the sidewalk while her dad blew out the driveway. The heavy job, fit only for a man. Rainey wondered who did the sidewalks now.

"Okay, Mom. I just…I just wanted you to know."

"Call me. Every week, call me. Or I'll call you. Please, honey."

Rainey blinked. Her palms sweat with the surprise of it. "I will." She suddenly felt herself smiling and she couldn't have said why. "I will, Mom. I promise. Every week."

"No matter what. Okay? No matter what."

"No matter what."

And then her mother was gone. But Rainey heard her voice for the rest of that day. And that night too, when she went to bed. She heard her mother's hum. Into her pillow, Rainey hummed too.

One night, after Tish went to sleep and Doris said goodnight, Rainey went through the list provided by the hospital and selected a therapist for Tish. She chose a woman. Everyone around Tish was female. Doris, Mrs. Whitstone, her best friends, her own mother. There were boys in her class, but Tish was still at an age where she ignored them. Tish only rarely heard adult male voices, and then usually in passing. Her grandfather never came to the phone. Rainey just couldn't imagine that Tish would talk to a man, especially after the night that brought all of this onto their shoulders. That made it necessary for a four-year old girl to see a therapist. A little girl who, until that night, spent most of her time talking and talking and talking.

The first appointment with Tish's therapist was just with Rainey. With a voice that still shook after five weeks, Rainey told the therapist about the attack and what she thought Tish saw.

"And Tish hasn't spoken since that night?" Nanci asked.

Rainey shook her head. "Not a word. She, well, she kinda talks with gestures and with pointing and with her face. She's working with a guidance counselor at school and with a speech therapist. But it hasn't helped."

Nanci nodded. "Muteness isn't a completely unusual reaction to a trauma like this," she said. "It could just be that Tish saw something that night that she doesn't have the words for."

Rainey stared. Of course Tish wouldn't. Why would a four-year old, any four-year old, have words for something like that? A four-year old shouldn't have words for sex, let alone rape, attack, blow-job, doggie-style. Rainey tried to fight her tears, but knew after five weeks that it was a losing battle. She dissolved.

Nanci came around her desk and kneeled in front of Rainey. She offered tissues. "Rainey, I know you're concerned about Tish. But are you taking care of yourself too? This happened to you, you know. Tish saw it…but it happened to you. Tish wasn't the only one who was traumatized."

"I'm trying," Rainey stammered. She didn't know how to finish that sentence. "I'm trying," she said again. She just didn't know what it was she was trying to do.

"Are you seeing anyone? I can give you some names."

Rainey had that list from the hospital that brought her here, for Tish, but she nodded anyway. If some of the names were doubles, then maybe that meant they were especially good people.

But then she found herself unable to lift her eyes to Nanci. Even if they were good people, why would they want to talk to a mother like Rainey? Why would someone like that want to talk to Rainey at all?

And what kind of a girl goes walking through a park late at night, Rainey, huh? What kind of girl?

The kind of girl who gets herself knocked up three times. And yet only has one child.

Rainey wasn't so sure she could face good people.

While Nanci wrote, Rainey blew her nose and dried her eyes. "My caretaker, Doris, was talking to Tish the other day, asking her questions. Tish will nod yes or shake her head no. And she said that Tish thinks that talking will hurt me."

Nanci looked up. "Hurt you."

"Doris tried to tell her that it's her silence that's hurting me, that it would make me feel better if she talked. But Tish just wouldn't have any of it." Rainey tried to smile. "She's stubborn."

Nanci handed her the list. "Stubbornness will work in her favor, I think, with her recovery. Why don't you bring her in after school tomorrow? We'll start with twice a week and see how it goes."

Rainey stood up. "Okay. But…how will you know?" She realized how rude, almost accusatory, that sounded. "I mean, how can you talk to her if she won't talk to you?"

Nanci smiled. "We'll play." She motioned around the room and Rainey took in dolls and dollhouses, a child-sized kitchen set, some balls and blocks. "Kids say a lot by how they play."

Rainey thought about Tish's drawing that was no longer stuck to her fridge, but thumbtacked to the wall heading down the basement stairs, with all the other pictures Tish made. The black of the swirls, the pink of a little girl all the way on the other side of the paper. The pink girl remained on the freezer. Rainey moved around Nanci's room, touching the things that she knew her daughter would touch as well. She picked up a baby doll, smoothed its hair, tugged down the little dress. Everything in this room was so warm, and she hoped that warmth would melt right into Tish, make her feel safe again. Make her talk again. Make her feel like the little pink stick girl way up high at the corner of the refrigerator. Rainey glanced at Nanci. She only told the therapist about the rape, about what happened. She hadn't mentioned the pregnancy. She wondered if she should. Tish didn't know about it, so did her therapist have to know? She noticed that Nanci was watching her closely and she quickly put the doll back down. "I think Tish will like it here. You have wonderful toys." She returned to her chair and picked up her purse.

"Rainey." Nanci crossed the room, put her hand on Rainey's shoulder. "Is there something else? Is there something you need?"

Rainey shook her head, turned away, but then stopped and sighed. "I don't know if this is important. It's something that Tish doesn't know, but there is something else that could affect her. Maybe. I don't know if Tish will ever know this. Because…I don't know what's going to come of it. Maybe nothing. I don't know."

Nanci led her back to the chair. "What's that?"

"The rapist left me…" There it was again. The chance to say it out loud. To bring it into the room with someone else, to have someone acknowledge what was going on inside. But Rainey couldn't. Not with a stranger. Not with someone who was going to be helping her silent daughter, silent because of what Rainey did. So she talked around it. "At the hospital that night, the doctor offered me the morning after pill. But in all the chaos, I forgot all about it. I've had a pregnancy test. It came out positive. My doctor confirmed it." It was easier to say, 'The test came out positive,' than 'the rapist left me pregnant.'

Nanci took in a quick breath. Rainey heard it.

"It's been five weeks since the rape. I haven't…I haven't made any decisions yet. I just don't know what to do." The tears again. Rainey quickly grabbed for more tissues.

"Oh, Rainey." Nanci took Rainey's hand and squeezed it. "My god, you have a lot to deal with. Honestly, I don't know how you're still standing." Quickly, impulsively, she grabbed Rainey in a hug. "Let me help. Please. Don't worry, Rainey. I'll help Tish. We'll find her voice again. And you start getting through this too. In a way, you have to find your voice again as well."

Rainey wanted to ask her just how to do that. Where to start. But she wasn't even sure who she was anymore, or if she even deserved help. Especially from good people. She thanked Nanci, promised to keep her informed about what was going on, and returned quickly to work.

For the third day in a row, despite the lemon tea, Rainey had to run to the restroom to throw up. As she straightened from the toilet, tears of strain running down her cheeks, she heard the restroom door close. Someone had come in while she was there. Someone must have heard.

And Rainey knew then she had to get out. Before anyone knew for sure. The people at work just couldn't know until Rainey knew what she was going to do. When she made a decision. For now, she had to get out.

After rinsing her mouth and washing her hands, Rainey went straight into her manager's office. "Michelle," she said, "can I talk to you for just a moment?"

"Sure, Rainey." Michelle stretched, then sat back. "How are you? I mean…is everything going okay?"

Even after five weeks, no one knew what to say.

"Michelle, do I have any vacation time coming?" Rainey sank in the chair in front of the desk.

"Vacation? Well, sure. You haven't taken any yet this year, have you?"

Rainey shook her head. "Not really, just two days." Even working full time, taking vacations just wasn't in the budget. In preschool last spring, Tish bubbled over with her friends' summer plans. Disneyworld. The Grand Canyon. Washington DC. One child even went to Paris. Rainey took two days off, framed them around a weekend, and took Tish to an amusement park just over the Wisconsin/Illinois border. They stayed in a budget hotel that at least had a swimming pool for Tish and a hot tub for Rainey. And they walked on the shore of Lake Michigan, collecting water-smoothed stones and sea glass and shed seagull feathers. Tish had a glass bowl in her room filled with what they found. Rainey tried to tell herself the lake was different and foreign, a new experience for Tish, because this was Illinois's portion of Lake Michigan, not Wisconsin's. Tish loved every minute of it. But Rainey still felt like she'd let her daughter down.

"Then you have three weeks minus two days."

"Okay. Can I take them? Starting today?" Rainey leaned forward. She willed herself not to cry. "Michelle, I really need the time off. I really need to…well, you know. Just try to deal with all this." Without thinking, she gestured toward her stomach.

Michelle looked, then looked lower, and Rainey was able to see the shiver that ran through her. "I understand, Rainey," she said. "You also have ten personal days, you know. You could take up to five weeks, and still get paid, and not put your job in jeopardy."

Five weeks. That would take her to ten weeks into the pregnancy, with two left over to make her decision at twelve weeks. Or, if she went ahead and made it, no weeks at all left. "Thanks, Michelle. I don't know if I'll need all that time, but I'll keep you posted. I hate to leave you guys like this, but…" Rainey held out her hands, palms up. She tried to find the gesture for "I need help," tried to say the words, but couldn't. She remembered Nanci, just an hour before, saying that Rainey needed to find her own voice again too. Until right then, Rainey wasn't aware of just how much she'd lost it. Tish didn't have the words for what she needed to say. Neither did Rainey.

Michelle nodded. She came around her desk and hugged Rainey. "It's okay. Really. Take the time you need. This…this just can't be easy. I can't even begin to imagine, Rainey."

Neither could Nanci. *Honestly, I don't know how you're still standing, Rainey.*

"If you need more time," Michelle said, "well, remember, you have sick days too."

Rainey wondered for a moment if Michelle wanted her to leave. If she wanted her to take day after day after day off so that her job would be in jeopardy, so that she could be fired, so that the company could learn to get along without her. Could replace her with someone else. Someone normal. It couldn't be easy for Michelle either, having to walk by a raped woman every day. A woman who had been in the news. Having to talk to her, having her type your letters, field phone calls. Michelle said it couldn't be easy for Rainey, but Rainey knew she wasn't the only one having a hard time. This wasn't easy for anyone. Not anyone who had any kind of connection with Rainey.

So if this was difficult, how would they deal with a raped co-worker who was pregnant as a result? Would there be an office baby shower with multi-colored balloons and a big cake and punch with ice cream floating in it for a receptionist heavy with a child conceived next to the river in the middle of a dark park? A park where she should never have been in the first place?

Rainey glanced at Michelle's face, saw the concern, and she shoved the thoughts away. Maybe it would be easier for the company if she just disappeared. Maybe it would be easier for her if she started all over again, at a different job, with people who didn't know about the rape, about who she was. But she wasn't going to worry about that right now.

Rainey thanked Michelle again, then returned to her desk. She stayed only long enough to grab her purse. She thought about taking some of her things home, particularly the photographs of Tish, but then she decided to leave them behind. This wasn't the time. Right now, she planned on coming back. Then she walked out the door to her car. She didn't want to go home right away though. Doris would be there, wondering why she was home early, and right now, Rainey just didn't want to explain anything. So she pulled her car out of the parking lot, idled for a moment at the next intersection, and then she decided where she was going to go.

The park. She hadn't been there since the night of the rape and she wasn't sure what drew her there now. She just wanted to see it.

In the middle of a weekday afternoon, the park was filled with a quiet kind of life. There were children, but they were young, not yet school age, and mothers sat on benches and talked and chided their children when they shrieked too loudly. Rainey sat in her car and watched for a bit, wondering if the mothers would still bring their children there if they knew what happened in that park five weeks ago. To a mom and a little girl. Would they feel safe? In the bright sunlight, danger seemed very far away.

Rainey got out of her car and began to walk along the Riverwalk. The grass was green and gold, the river a root beer brown flecked with blue from the sky, and the little children whooped and screamed from the climbing structure and swings.

The river burbled a cheery accompaniment alongside her, just as it had that night. People smiled at her as they passed, some raising a hand in greeting. Rainey found herself wanting to demand their location that night. Where were you? Why didn't you raise a hand then? Even though she knew they were nowhere around. They were all at home, where they were supposed to be. Where she was supposed to be.

Because the park was closed. Because only Rainey was stupid enough to walk through it at night, and drag her child with her. At night, this safe park went through an awful transformation.

And what kind of a girl goes walking through a park late at night, Rainey, huh? What kind of girl?

Slut.

Rainey stopped by the spot where she knew it happened. She turned toward the river, as if she wanted to admire it, watch its soft flow with the light of day bouncing from it. She knew if she looked over the bushes, she'd see the rock that bent her back, that bruised her skin. She knew the soft patch of grass, just to the right of the bushes here, was where Tish sat. She wanted to sit there herself, to try to make herself the size of a four-year old, to see what Tish might have seen, but Rainey's entire body went into a shudder so hard, she bent double. Quickly, she ran down the walk, away from that spot and the pain and the shadow that ran after her. Finding a bench, she sat down and tried to control her breathing.

Digging through her purse, she found the list that Tish's therapist gave her. Running her finger down the names, she saw Rape Crisis Center. That's what this was, wasn't it? A crisis? Even if it did happen five weeks ago, and it was dark at the time, instead of a sunny Tuesday afternoon?

Flipping open her cell, Rainey dialed the number. But when a woman answered, the only thing Rainey could do was cry. Just like when she called her mother. Just like when she talked to Nanci. Rainey damned the tears. They were there, they were always there, it was no wonder her voice was drowned.

"Are you okay?" the woman called into Rainey's ear. "Please… tell me where you are. Tell me what's happening. Where are you? Are you being hurt?"

"No," Rainey finally sobbed out. "It was five weeks ago. I was raped five weeks ago."

"Okay," the woman said. "Okay. Take a deep breath, all right? Deep breath. Breathe in, breathe out. You're fine, just talk to me. And breathe."

Rainey closed her eyes and listened and breathed. Her chest hurt, as though she'd been running a marathon. But the tears thankfully slowed.

"The rape was five weeks ago?" the woman asked.

"Yes. And I just found out…well, I found out two weeks ago, that I'm…" Rainey was outside. She was near where it happened. A few steps ago, on that night, she was still Rainey. Still alone, just one woman in her body. Then a few steps later, she wasn't. And here she was again. On the phone with a Rape Crisis Center, with a woman who encouraged her to breathe. With a woman who would have talked to other women, many women, maybe, who were about to say what Rainey was about to say. "I'm pregnant." The word sounded overloaded in her ears. But she said it. She didn't say the test was positive. She didn't say her doctor confirmed it. She just said it flat out, and she said it again, straight into the Rape Crisis Center ready ear. "I'm pregnant."

The woman let her own breath sharply fill the phone. "And it's his?"

"Yes."

"Oh, honey."

Rainey cried again, but softly now. "And I have to know…I have to ask someone…"

"Go ahead. I'm here. Go ahead."

Rainey felt stupid. She thought how stupid she would sound, asking this. Pregnant three times, and she didn't know this answer. But she needed to. "Can…does a woman's orgasm make it easier to get pregnant?"

"What?"

Rainey's head spun and she tried again. "During the rape… well…I came. Is that why it happened? The pregnancy? Did I make it easier for the sperm to…to…"

The woman on the phone exploded. "Okay, what is this? Some kind of a joke?"

A joke.

"Who do you think you are? Listen, there are women out there who—"

Stunned, Rainey snapped her phone shut. Her tears stopped as if slammed against a wall, and against that wall, Rainey deflated. Her body slumped forward and she held her head in her hands, convinced that if she didn't, she would have kept rolling to the ground, where she would have curled into a ball and begged to disappear.

She was a slut. She was a slut, wasn't she? Coming during a rape. She must have wanted it. That's why she went into the park that night, she knew there was danger, it was a dark park, it was at night, other rapes happened there. But she went anyway, she just had to, even with her child. Her baby.

And what kind of a girl goes walking through a park late at night, Rainey, huh? What kind of girl? Maybe the same kind of girl who gets herself knocked up swimming naked with a bunch of boys at college?

Pregnant three times and only twenty-four years old. Pregnant from a high school boy, a college boy, and now a rapist. A rapist that made her come. Even in the middle of impossible pain and humiliation and fear.

Because she must have liked it.

A joke.

She was a joke. Who did she think she was? Calling for help.

She wore a short skirt, didn't she? With a little flounce, what did they call it in the magazines, a flirty little flounce. And her blouse was unbuttoned. And at home, late at night, after Tish went to sleep, late at night when it was dark and the moon shone in and covered Rainey's bed, back when the open curtains were for the moon's company, not protection, didn't she like to throw back the covers and masturbate? Touch herself in the light of the moon and imagine a man there, a man who would touch her where the moon touched and come inside her and make her cry out? Didn't she do that, almost every night, it seemed, before the rape? Make herself cry out, and then smack a hand over her mouth to keep from waking Tish? A hand with slick fingers, that smelled of herself, smelled of Rainey, smelled of slut?

Women who get raped don't come. They cry. They cry and they scream and they die. But Rainey didn't do any of those things, did she? She stayed quiet when he asked her to, took him in her mouth when he insisted, opened her legs when he ordered her to. She didn't fight. She came.

There was no help for her. There was no help anywhere. Not from good people. No one would help her. She was a joke, the woman on the phone said. She was a slut, her father said. And her own voice said it too. Who did she think she was?

Her abdomen pressed against her legs and Rainey felt uncomfortably full. Slowly, she straightened up, neatened her hair, pulled down her jacket. This was her punishment, she supposed. This fetus. This baby. This reminder of what she did, what she didn't do. If she got rid of it, would that make it even worse? If she kept it, would it help her to become a better person? A better woman, a better mother?

She thought of Nanci telling her that she needed to take care of herself. Would taking care of this baby, wrapping her body around it, growing it full, be taking care of herself? Would it make her who and what she was supposed to be? Could she raise her head then? Would she make the right decisions? For everyone?

Rainey remembered again the soft voice of the woman on the phone, before it grew hard with hatred. *Breathe in, breathe out.* And that's what Rainey did. That was all she knew how to do. She sat on the bench and closed her eyes and breathed. She listened to the river as it chanted alongside her. Its voice sweet and melodic.

But not forgiving. Never forgiving.

It was 12:30 in the morning when Rainey's cell phone rang. She kept it on her bedside table every night now, instead of down in the kitchen, on the counter next to her purse. She kept it turned on too while it recharged, ready in case of a stray noise that had no obvious origin. Like the locked windows, it was just a new part of normal. Rainey startled, didn't recognize the number, but saw that the area code was Missouri.

"Hello?" she whispered.

"Rainey, it's me."

"Mom? What number is this? Why are you calling now?"

The sound that emerged from her mother was like a sly chuckle. "I got myself a cell phone. So I can call you whenever I want, without your father knowing. I'm going to keep it in my pocket all the time, on silent, but if you call, it will vibrate and I'll know it's you. It's just for us."

Just for us. A secret. How long since Rainey and her mother had secrets? Rainey remembered long afternoons, two kitchen chairs draped with blankets, she and her mother underneath in the blue-tinted makeshift tent, sharing diet soda in plastic teacups, saltine crackers with cheese. It always had to be cleaned up by the time her father came home. The chairs back under the table, the blanket returned to the closet upstairs. "Wow, Mom."

Her mother laughed again, lighter. "How are you, honey?"

"I decided to take some time off of work. I'll still get paid, but I'm using my vacation and personal days. I just need to figure this all out."

"That's good. I think that's good. And you're still…"

Her mother couldn't say the word either. "Yes, Mom. I haven't made any decisions yet."

"Okay. I just wanted you to know that whatever you decide, whatever, hon, I'm with you. Okay? I'm with you."

"I just don't know what to do."

"I know."

Her phone to her ear, Rainey closed her eyes and listened to her mother breathe. Breathe in, breathe out. And her mother hummed. Rainey must have fallen asleep like that, because in the morning, she woke up, her alarm going off, the sun on her pillow, and her phone propped under her ear. Your call has ended, the screen said.

Rainey clicked "okay."

Rainey was at home two days later when her phone rang again, this time in the middle of the afternoon. Tish was at school, brought in for the second day by Rainey rather than by Doris, a fact she seemed to accept with just a small lift of her eyebrows. "Mama's just taking a little break from work," Rainey said and Tish nodded. Doris was probably off to the grocery store. That's what she usually did on Thursdays, Rainey knew, and Doris drove off sometime after lunch.

The cell phone screen said the number was unknown. It kept ringing. For that moment, for three foreign rings, the phone became another shadow that Rainey had to watch out for. Did her rapist find her? Had he found her number and when she answered, she was going to hear that voice again?

Rainey never wanted to hear that voice again.

She answered and held her breath. She hoped for the voice of a telemarketer who had the awful job of tracking people down in the middle of the day. But instead, Officer Stanton identified himself.

"Ms. Milbright," he said. "Rainey...we've made an arrest."

Rainey sat down. She was standing by her kitchen counter, there was no chair, so she sank to the floor. "What?" She could have, she thought, walked to the table, sat there, or moved into the living room and sat on the couch. But there was just suddenly no energy to move her legs. She braced her back against the cabinet.

"We think he's the guy who's been doing all the rapes along the Riverwalk. There've been two more since you. And then this one, we caught this one in the act. Last night."

Two more. Rainey didn't know. She hadn't been watching the news or reading the paper. Even the comics seemed too difficult to comprehend right now. "Two more?" she said.

"Well, three, if you count the one where we caught him, last night."

Rainey thought of that woman, saved in the middle. Maybe saved before he invaded her mouth. Before he bent her backwards. Before he cut. Rainey wasn't sure if she counted that woman or not. What was she wearing? Did she have her daughter with her?

"We'd like you to come down here, for a lineup."

Rainey immediately went cold. "I can't…" she said. "I can't see him right now." Like she could see him later. Like she was in the middle of an important meeting, but would make an appointment for the next day.

"It's okay, Rainey," Officer Stanton said. "It's not a lineup like what you've probably seen on television. We show you photographs. You won't actually have to be near him."

Photographs. Just pictures. Pictures didn't breathe, didn't stare at you, didn't hold out knives. Didn't look you straight in the face with the truth.

Sweet Jesus, girl, you know you want it.

Rainey violently shook her head, nearly dropping the phone.

"Rainey," Officer Stanton said when she didn't say a word, "it's really important. It would help us to get him behind bars."

Which was where she wanted him. In a cage with no door, no keyhole, no way out at all. Photographs could put him there. It would only be photographs. "Okay," she said. "I think I can do that. When would you like me to come?"

"About an hour?"

Rainey agreed. Glancing at the clock after she hung up, she realized that an hour would run right into the time she was supposed to pick up Tish and take her to her therapy appointment. Rainey had actually grown to like waiting for Tish in Nanci's small, but comfortable waiting room. She felt like some of the help being offered to Tish could leak out under the door, soak its way through the carpet, and up to Rainey. She always felt better when she left with Tish, as they both waved goodbye to a smiling Nanci. Therapy by association. Now, she picked up the phone again and called Doris. She explained the situation in a voice she hoped was steady and asked if Doris could deal with Tish.

"Sure, hon, that's not a problem," Doris said. Rainey could hear the sound of Muzak in the background and knew she was right in her guess about the grocery store. "Are you sure you can do this by yourself?"

No, Rainey thought. "I think so," she said. What other choice did she have, really? Someone had to pick up Tish, and there was no one else but Doris. Rainey adopted Officer Stanton's voice. "It's not like I have to be in the same room with him. It'll just be pictures."

"All right, then." Rainey could hear Doris' doubt, but she knew the same options were running through her neighbor's mind as well. There was no one else to get Tish. "We'll be waiting for you when you get home. Oh, Rainey. I hope it's him. I hope they got him."

"Me too," Rainey said. And she did. She wanted him caught, put away where she didn't have to worry about him anymore, didn't have to worry about corners and shadows and phone calls in the middle of the afternoon.

She would take her phone with her. Her mother was just a speed dial away. On her secret cell phone. Their secret. Rainey pictured a blue blanket tent and immediately felt warmer.

Even though that tent would have to be quickly whisked away, hidden in the upstairs closet, before her father came home. Would her mother answer, no matter what? Even if her father was right there?

Her father was always right there. And Rainey was her mother's secret.

But still. She'd fallen asleep the night before with her mother's breath in her ear. Her hum, held as familiar and dear as a blue blanket made into a tent.

Rainey went upstairs to change. She got as far as stripping down to her bra and panties when she froze. What do you wear to a lineup?

Her rapist wasn't going to see her, but what should she wear to stand in front of a group of photographs, a group of strange men's faces, and point the right man out? If she could point him out…it was so dark that night.

But there were those cauliflower ears. Rainey would look for those ears on this day.

She stood at her closet. What would the police officers think if she wore what she wore on that night? A short skirt. A white blouse, unbuttoned to expose the lace of her cami. Would they skim her with their eyes? Would they know?

Slut.

Would they let her rapist go?

Rainey pulled on jeans and a long-sleeved plain red t-shirt. Then she pulled off the red and put on a blue instead. From blue, she went to black. Instead of letting her hair flow freely over her shoulders, she tugged it back, fastened it in a low ponytail that hung against her neck. Neat white socks, white sneakers. No jewelry except for the four tiny silver studs in her ears. Then she went off to meet her rapist.

Not to meet him. Identify him. Point him out. See if he pointed back at her.

Oh, yeah, baby, that's a good girl.

To see his photograph. Just to see his photograph. It might not even be there. It might not even be him.

Rainey hoped it was. She hoped he was behind bars. In a cage where beasts belonged.

But where did she belong?

Rainey shook her head and focused on her driving. She needed to arrive safely.

At the police station, Rainey was led into a small room with no windows. There was a table and three chairs. Officer Stanton greeted her and urged her again to call him Robert, and then Officer Freeman stepped forward, smiled, and said to call her Sarah. Rainey found herself smiling too. It was a warm greeting and the room felt almost festive. The officers were excited, hopeful, and Rainey caught it from them. They sat on one side of the table and Rainey settled across from them. There was a wide mirror across one wall and Rainey figured that there were people on the other side of it who could see her, who could watch her reactions, but she didn't ask if this was the case. She didn't really want to know. She didn't want to feel spied upon; she wanted this to be a happy, not a suspicious, occasion.

"Okay, Rainey," Robert said. "I'm going to leave you with ten photographs. Sarah, here, will stay in the room with you while you examine them, but she'll move over to the door, so she's out of your way and you can concentrate. She's here if you need her, for anything, a drink of water, a cup of coffee, if you have a question, anything like that. You can study the photographs for as long as you need to. If no one looks familiar, that's okay, just tell us. When you're ready, Sarah will let me back in."

Rainey nodded. The party atmosphere shifted and she suddenly felt like she was on some sort of bizarre reality television show. A twisted Candid Camera. She folded her hands tighter than a prayer. Robert picked up a stack of 8 x 10 photographs, tamped them together like an ungainly deck of cards, and then placed them in front of her. Rainey had to fight down the urge to cut the deck. After briefly touching her shoulder, Robert quietly left the room. Sarah moved to stand by the doorway, one hand on the knob. "Go ahead," she said. Her tone was so friendly.

The first man in the pile of photographs stared up at Rainey.

Carefully, with just the tips of her fingers, Rainey picked up the pictures, then dealt them out in a strange game of solitaire. Rapist Roulette. Two rows of four. One row of two. Ten men looked up at her from the flat of the table. Some had mustaches or beards or both and some were clean-shaven. Rainey couldn't remember the rasp of stubble against her skin that night. She noticed that none of the men were bald, they all had curly hair, though some wore it longer than others. And all of their faces were blank. No one stared at her with the hunger of an animal in his eyes. No one bared his teeth, ready to sink them into her neck.

Rainey sat with the ten men, her hands folded. She looked at their eyes. She tried to find hate there. But she hadn't seen his eyes, had she? It was dark. He was just a shape.

His eyes were dark. She remembered. Brown. Intense. Crazed.

Rainey pushed back her chair and stood, staring down at the photographs. Then, one by one, she picked them up and held them over her head at arm's length so that they looked down on her. As her rapist had that night. She turned away from the fluorescent lights so that each picture went into a blur, a shadow. And Rainey looked at the outline of each held-up face, tracing the lines from neck to ear to hairline to ear to neck, five times over.

On the sixth, there were cauliflower ears. When Rainey saw the shadow, saw the ears, she began to shake and she dropped the photograph. Turning away from it, she sat down in her chair and held herself, rocking, first forward and back, then the side to side sway. Rainey rocked herself. She immersed herself in the motion. She felt for her cell phone in her pocket.

"Are you okay?" Sarah appeared by Rainey's side. Without thinking, Rainey leaned into her, and she was amazed when Sarah's arms wrapped around her shoulders, hugged tightly. Rainey stopped rocking, breathed deeply, then nodded. Sarah waited a moment, rubbing Rainey's back, then returned to the door.

Leaving her chair, Rainey examined the final four photographs, ignoring number six on the floor. Then, she picked him up and tried again.

And dropped him.

Those ears. And the intensity of his eyes. The hair in relief, coils against the moonshine.

Carefully, she stacked the nine innocent men to the left hand upper corner of the table. Then she picked up number six and centered him. Nodding at Sarah, Rainey sat back down and waited for Robert's return.

She was tempted to reach out and turn the photograph face down. Smack it against the table so that the only thing she could see was the white backing. She was tempted to pick up the photo and rip it in half. And in half again. And again and again and again until there was nothing left but the confetti of memory, gray and white and black and brown, so light and small, it could blow away in a breeze and never be thought of again. She could blow it away, sending her own breath across the table. Her own breath to chase him away forever. Him and his cauliflower ears.

Instead, Rainey folded her hands and looked at her rapist's face. He had a flat nose, a smooth complexion. His eyes seemed blank, but if Rainey looked hard enough, she could see the wolf. If he smiled, Rainey knew she would see the flash of white, white ridges which sunk into her neck that night. Which left a mark still. Rainey saw it every morning when she dressed, every night when she undressed before crawling into bed. She knew exactly where the scar was and her fingers could find it without searching. The mark would always be there, and Rainey felt marked like a vampire's victim, though she didn't believe in such horror. She knew real horror, horror that couldn't be tucked away with the end of a movie, the close of a book. Rainey wondered if the flesh of last night's woman still remained in the crevices between her rapist's front teeth, in the grooves of his molars. The tearing teeth. The chewing.

Rainey heard the door open and in a moment, Robert slid into his seat, Sarah beside him. "You found him?" His voice remained calm and quiet; he didn't show a bit of surprise or excitement. He was tucked in, and Rainey appreciated that. The party atmosphere no longer felt right. If Robert raised his voice, Rainey knew she would fall apart, her entire body breaking into the confetti she wished the photograph to be. Her rapist to be.

Rainey's own voice was gone. Lost in the teeth of this photograph, this rapist, lost in his memory. She nodded. She wanted to ask about the other women. Were they okay? Were they bruised? Were they cut? Did they also carry this man's child in their bellies? Were they all going to give birth to a pack of pups that could someday hunt as a group, could bring down women, could kill?

Were the women here? Were they in other rooms, with ten photographs in front of them too? Could Rainey sit with them, get together with them, form a bizarre club, a club of women who knew? Who understood?

Could they hold each other?

"Are you all right, Rainey?" Sarah leaned forward, touched Rainey's hand.

Rainey nodded again, then cleared her throat. She forced her voice to return. "Yes," she said. "I am. I was just...well, I was wondering."

"Go ahead," Robert said. "It's all right. You have the right to ask all the questions you want, Rainey. You're the one who knows. You're the one who can give us the answers and help us to put this guy where he belongs."

Rainey looked again at the picture, the cauliflower ears, the flat affect. She hadn't thought of it that way, that it was her word that would take care of this, would lock the man away in prison. In a cage. Which was where he belonged, she told herself. "The other women...Did the other women say..." Is this him? she wanted to ask. Did they say so too?

Robert sighed and sat back. "They haven't seen the photos yet, you're the first one here. But Rainey, I wouldn't tell you if they did. I want this to be your answer, your realization. You were there. I don't want anyone else putting doubts in your mind."

Or removing them, she thought. Suddenly, she just wasn't sure.

For a moment, she closed her eyes. She saw the shape, the shadow, saw the ears outlined by the moon, heard again the soft whisper of the river. What could have been Tish's whisper too. Then she opened her eyes and looked at the photograph and saw the ears again. The cauliflower. There was more too. She could hear him.

She could hear him.

She thought of her hesitation by the phone, when she nearly didn't answer it that afternoon because she was afraid she would hear his voice. And she never wanted to hear his voice again. But she knew exactly what it sounded like. She knew it was exactly him.

She looked at the picture again. "I'm sure this is him," she whispered. "But you know...it was dark that night. He talked to me. Is there a way...is there a way I can hear him speak? His voice?" She couldn't believe she just asked to hear what she never wanted to hear again.

Robert sat back. "A voice lineup? Sure, we can do that. You'd have to be in the same room with him though. Do you think you can handle that?"

Rainey suddenly saw him there, her rapist, in front of her. Saying those words again. She shoved her chair back, stood up, ready to run.

Robert grabbed her hands. "No, it's not like that. I'm sorry, I didn't mean to say it that way. I would be here with you, and so would Sarah, and we would set up a screen, from the doorway to here, so you couldn't see any of the men. Another officer would bring them in, one by one. They would each say something, but Rainey, it would have to be something that the rapist actually said to you, okay? It would have to be his words. That would guarantee that you're hearing what you heard that night."

"Oh, god." Rainey pulled her hands away, then folded them again, this time to keep them from trembling.

"Can you do it?" He leaned forward. "I mean, you don't have to, you seem pretty positive that this is this guy. Your reaction was very strong. But there's no doubt that a double-recognition, that picking him out from his picture and his voice, would help in court."

So it was a two-way mirror. Robert had been on the other side of the glass the whole time. There were probably others too. And while it felt intrusive before, like Rainey was on the slide of a microscope, now it made her feel better. Safer. It wouldn't be just her and Robert and Sarah, here in the room with the ten men. With her rapist. There was a whole roomful of people just on the other side of that mirror. A roomful of people who could save her, if they had to. Just as that last woman was saved, just the night before.

And then Rainey could go home. Tish and Doris were waiting. And when the phone would ring, or the doorbell, or when Rainey was out walking or driving, when she was just sitting on the porch, she wouldn't have to jump and startle at every small sound, every change in the light or motion out of the corner of her eye. She wouldn't have to watch and be afraid to blink. She could go to bed at night without triple-checking all of the locks.

And maybe, if he was locked up, if she could tell Tish that, Tish would speak again.

"I can do it," she said. "It's okay, I can do it. I just want to make sure."

"All right. I'll look in your folder, at the report, at everything you told us he said. But is there anything in particular, anything that stands out in your memory? That you can still hear him saying? Maybe something that he said in a special way?"

Rainey swallowed. There was so much.

Suck.

Sweet Jesus, girl, you know you want it.

Oh, yeah, baby, that's a good girl.

But she didn't want to say those. Not in her own voice, not out loud, not to anyone. Just like she didn't want to let her pregnancy out into the air of reality, she didn't want those words there either. Not the ones that marked her, like his teeth. That branded her. That let Robert know, Sarah know, the whole world know, what her rapist already knew.

Slut.

When Rainey said that she was pregnant, when she admitted it to Doris, to her mother, to Tish's counselor, and to the lady at the Rape Crisis Center, when she finally connected herself and the developing cells inside her to her voice and to sound and words that someone else could hear, a friend, a relative, a stranger could hear, she wished she hadn't. Almost as soon as she said them, Rainey wished she could take them back into herself, tuck them back as far inside as the fetus itself. But there was no going back then.

And there was no saying these words now. This truth. Rainey couldn't say the words that went round and round her head so many times a day, even more times at night. She couldn't say them and risk Robert and Sarah staring at her, pushing back their chairs, and walking away, leaving her there all by herself. They would ask her the same question that the lady from the Rape Crisis Center did.

Okay, what is this? Some kind of a joke?

Just who do you think you are?

But there were other words. He said other words. She closed her eyes and remembered.

"This what'll…" she said and stopped.

Robert squeezed her hands and Sarah was suddenly there again, an arm around her shoulders.

"This what'll fuck you…" Rainey said, "…if you make a sound. If you make a sound, this what'll fuck you, bitch." The words were heavy in her mouth, hard against the sides of her throat, cutting off her breath. "He had a knife."

"Okay," Sarah said and squeezed. "Okay, Rainey, it's all right. You sure you want to do this?"

This what'll fuck you. He had a knife. But not this time. This time, there would be police here. Nothing could happen if there were police here. Robert was here and Sarah had her arm around Rainey's shoulders. There was a team behind the mirror. "Yes," she said. "I can do this."

Robert and Sarah left for a while, then came back with a wide wooden screen carried between them. The door was propped open and they set the screen up, creating a hidden passageway. Rainey couldn't see anything, just the very top of the doorway. When everything was ready, Robert had Rainey sit back in her chair and make herself as comfortable as possible. Robert and Sarah each stood behind Rainey, and they both put a hand on one of her shoulders. Rainey liked the weight of their hands, the grip of their fingers. She felt protected.

Robert leaned down close to her ear and said, "They're going to be brought in one by one now, Rainey. They are not in the same order as they were in the photographs, okay? It's all different."

She nodded. And then she reached up and clasped the officers' hands. Rainey's hands were shaking and she could feel that Sarah's were too. Neither officer let go.

There were shuffled footsteps. Then voices. One right after the other. Low voices. High. Slurred and sharp and soft and mean and flat. Some accents, some not. And over and over, the same words, again and again, nine times repeated.

This what'll fuck you if you make a sound.
If you make a sound, this what'll fuck you, bitch.

And then her rapist was there, all around her. He was there and she saw the cauliflower ears, the hair ringleted against the moon, felt the rock against her back. Felt the knife as it slid inside her. Rainey's feet hit flat on the floor and she shoved back, colliding into Robert who scrambled to stay standing and yet he never let go of her hand. There was more shuffling as the man was led away.

But not fast enough. He began to shout, and Rainey heard every word, felt every letter as it smacked against her. "You bitch!" he shouted. "You bitch! If I ever get my hands on you —"

Rainey threw herself out of her chair. She rolled under the table and curled herself into as tight of a ball as she could. He was there. She had to protect herself.

His voice, in mid-shout, broke into a gurgle. There was a grunted order from a police officer and then the slam of the door. Robert knelt on the floor beside her and clutched her fingers. Rainey felt her breath rattling from her chest, impossible to grab back, and she choked. Sarah ran from the room and Rainey felt suddenly bereft. She wanted to call for Sarah, ask her to come back, but Rainey's voice was gone again. Disappeared. Shattered.

Then Sarah came back in with a cup of water held in front of her like a healing potion. Robert helped Rainey to her feet and back into the chair, and Sarah handed the cup to Rainey. When the water spilled, shook free from the cup by Rainey's trembling fingers, Robert held it for her and she sipped. She sipped some more and the water slid cool and smooth down her throat, opening the passageway, bringing moisture to everything that suddenly went dry with fear. A fear so intense, it robbed her of her breath. She sipped again and soon, she was able to hold the cup herself. Breathe in, breathe out, she thought, and she heard it in Nanci's voice, a part of her therapy by association. Her shoulders slumped and both Robert and Sarah relaxed next to her.

"Guess we know which one it was, huh?" Robert asked and smiled.

Rainey tried to smile back. "Was it…was it the same as the photo I picked out?"

He hesitated, then nodded.

"So…so what happens next?"

"He'll be held. There'll be an arraignment, and then we go from there. With this many rapes, it will likely go to trial."

This many rapes. Not just her. He wasn't only her rapist anymore. He was theirs. Three other women. One who was saved. Four altogether. "But he's…he's not loose anymore?"

"No." Robert stood up. "No, Rainey. Not loose anymore." Sarah gave her a quick hug and a smile, and then she was gone.

Rainey pictured her rapist. Behind bars, in a cage. Where he belonged. Pacing. Shouting. Abruptly, she wondered what the other women wore for their rapes. Why they went into the park after dark, when there were so many signs posted, saying, no, don't go here, don't be stupid. Were they all stupid? Did they form a little stupid slut society?

But Rainey didn't go to the park alone. She went there with her little girl. She was the most stupid of them all. The Slut Queen.

Suddenly, she was exhausted. "Is it okay if I go now?"

"Sure. I wanted to ask you though, before you leave…" Robert paused and Rainey felt herself automatically bracing herself. What else could they want her to do? "I just wanted to know how you are. How you're healing. You look good. Is everything okay?"

For a moment, Rainey was pleased that someone who knew what she went through said she looked good. Robert saw her on that night, right afterwards. He saw the blood and the bruises. But now, maybe she looked like nothing ever happened. And maybe it could go back to being that way too.

Except Rainey knew better. She knew something was fundamentally changed.

"I'm okay," she said. "Well, as okay as I can be. I still hurt, sometimes, in my ribs and my back. But I guess that's not the worst of it."

Robert, who'd started to smile, stopped. He leaned forward. "The worst? What else, Rainey? What's wrong?" He frowned, shook his head. "God, that's a stupid question. There's so much that could go wrong, I know that. Have you tested positive for something? What did he have?"

Rainey suddenly felt sick with disease. She wasn't, at least not yet. There was so much testing still left in front of her. She didn't even know for how long. "No," she said. "No, it's not that. It's just…"

And there she was again. Not with a stranger this time, but not with a friend or family member either. Rainey knew by now it was best to just say it fast and flat out. She'd suffer the consequences later.

"I'm pregnant," she said.

Robert sat back down. "Oh, no," he said. "Oh, man, Rainey, I'm so sorry." He rubbed a hand across his face. Rainey noticed it looked like he hadn't shaved that day. "I'm going to put that in your record," he said. "Maybe that will help…it'll show even more damage than what the photos saw. That will make the case against him even stronger."

Rainey grabbed the edge of the table. She thought of her rapist yelling, of his saying, *If I ever get my hands on you…* "I thought you said he was locked up!" she said. "I thought you said he wasn't loose anymore!"

Robert quickly took her hands. "He's not," he said. "He is in a cell. But this might just make sure he stays there. For as long as possible."

Rainey pulled away. She didn't want to think about her rapist's release. Not when she just started thinking of him as locked up. "Please," she said. "I just want to go home now."

"Do you think you're okay to drive? You can stay here for a while, have a cup of coffee, get settled back down. You can even go into a little lounge we have, if you want. We have doughnuts." He smiled. "Or I can have Sarah give you a ride." Robert leaned over the table, looked directly into her eyes. "It's okay. Whatever you need, Rainey, just let me know."

She shook her head. She stood and was relieved when her knees didn't wobble.

Robert took her elbow and walked her to the door. "Thanks, Rainey. We'll let you know as things happen. You were a big help. The best."

Rainey couldn't believe he just said that. As if being raped was heroic. As if she was a superhero. Wonder Woman. Wonder Slut, who gets herself raped and puts her daughter in danger, all in a single bound.

Wonder Slut. Rape her and watch her come. Watch her reach orgasm even as she's hurt. Watch her become pregnant.

Rainey felt soaked through with shame, with guilt. She couldn't look at Robert anymore. She ducked her head, rounded her shoulders, and quickly left the station.

All she wanted now was to go home and see Tish. She would feed her, bathe her, tuck her in bed at eight o'clock. She would lock all the doors and windows. Three times. For tonight, she would. Then maybe, she could stop. Because her rapist was in a cage now.

Where he belonged. Where she knew he belonged, even if she wasn't sure for herself, where she fit in all of this.

How long would he be there?

But even with the locking, three times over, there would be a difference, she hoped, starting that night. When she left the blinds open in her room, it would be to let the moon back in, as a friend, not as a beacon that could point out danger. Even so, she would keep the covers firmly pulled up to her chin, not bathe and stretch her body in secret passion in the silver light. She would keep her own fingers on the outside of the blankets. Rainey didn't think she would ever make herself cry out in the light of the moon again. She didn't deserve to. Not with herself. Not with anyone else.

Even with her rapist behind bars, it couldn't all go back to normal. As she got in the car, she put on her seatbelt, hesitated, then made sure the lap belt was securely below her abdomen.

At home, Rainey and Tish ate supper at Doris', because Rainey just didn't have the energy to cook. Besides, Doris said she had hot dogs and macaroni and cheese, and they all knew whose favorite meal that was. Tish jumped up and down, clapping her hands, and then she made little happy squeaking noises. Abruptly, she slapped her hand over her mouth and dashed from the kitchen.

Rainey looked at Doris, who shrugged. Remembering the teacher who pointed out Tish's humming and then Tish stopped, Rainey wondered if she should just let those joyful squeaks go, not mention them, when what she wanted to do was grab Tish, shake her, make the squeaks come back, form into words, into sentences, into whole conversations. Rainey glanced toward the living room, then slumped against the counter.

Doris slipped an arm around her. "So," she said quietly. "Was it him?"

Rainey nodded. "I picked him out twice. In his photograph and with his voice. It was him."

"Oh, thank God," Doris said. "Thank God." She squeezed Rainey, then turned toward the bubbling macaroni on her stove.

"He knew it, too," Rainey said. "He began to yell at me. He said if he ever gets his hands on me…" Rainey didn't know how to finish the sentence. Her rapist wasn't given the chance. But she knew. She knew he'd kill her, if he ever found a way to get his hands on her again.

Doris deserted the macaroni and swept Rainey up in a hug. "Oh my God," she said. "Oh, how awful. Rainey…did you see him?"

Rainey shook her head. "No, he was behind a screen. I just heard him. The police never left him alone with me." She thought of her hurtle beneath the table. "I wasn't ever in danger. Not really."

"But it must have felt like you were."

Rainey shuddered. But then she stepped back. "It's okay. He's behind bars. Officer Stanton said he wouldn't be out anytime soon."

Leaving Doris to her cooking, Rainey went out to the living room. Tish was kneeling on the couch, looking outside, sucking her thumb with such vigor that the room was filled with the rhythm and slurp of it. Rainey sat beside her, ran her fingers through her daughter's hair. "Tish, honey," she said. "The police called me today. That's why I didn't pick you up from school. I was down at the police station."

Tish spun around, caught her mother up in a wide-eyed stare, sucked her thumb in so hard that Rainey thought her entire fist would disappear.

"They got him, honey. They got the bad man. He's in jail now. He's all locked up."

Tish stopped in mid-suck, her cheeks pulled in, her lips puckered. Then her jaw relaxed and her thumb slid out, wrinkly and red, and she rested her hand in her lap.

"So you see?" Rainey scrambled for something to say, to say it in the way a four-year old would understand. And in a way that would unlock Tish's voice. "The good guys got the bad guy. He's in jail, in a cage. With lots and lots of locks. Forever. He can't hurt me ever again." Rainey took her daughter's hand, dried her thumb on her pants. "He can't hurt us ever again. Okay?"

Tish smiled. But she glanced outside.

"It's true, honey. So…" Rainey hesitated, unsure if she should ask, but then she decided to. Tish was a direct thinker. If it was black, it was black. If it was white, it was white. Rainey thought again of the black river that Tish drew. The river was black. That night was black. It was darker than anyone could ever imagine it, and Tish and Rainey experienced it, went beyond dipping their feet into that dark; they immersed their whole bodies. Tish was right and she'd said it in a way that couldn't be clearer, even without her voice. But the little stick girl, hanging above on the freezer, was pink. And safe. Tish was safe. And Rainey so wanted her voice. She cupped Tish's face in her hands. "So can you talk now?"

Tish pulled away. She shrugged, then lowered herself into the couch, slouching down so that her back curved like a U into hips that went up into the pointiest of knees. The television was on, but soft, and Tish looked toward it. Her hand floated up, her thumb propped and ready, but then Tish sighed and brought her hand to rest on her stomach.

Rainey looked at it there, cupped on the little pouch of girl-tummy, and then down at herself. At the way her hand automatically now rested on her own stomach. Even though she didn't know yet who she was protecting. The fetus or herself? Or was she even protecting at all; maybe she was hiding. Squashing. Did Tish know? She'd already seen what no four-year old should see; did she somehow know something she couldn't possibly?

Tish did not know where babies came from.

Tish's shirt rode up with her slouch, and the pink skin of her stomach crinkled. Rainey remembered blowing kisses there, when Tish was a baby, and then a toddler, and how Tish would vibrate with laughter, bumping her tummy against her mother's face. Rainey still blew kisses there, especially after bathtime, when her little girl wriggled naked and delicious before her, popping out of the fluffy towel like a jack-in-the-box nymph. Rainey loved that little tummy.

The new tummy, if there was one, wouldn't be pink. Well, it could be, but there was a chance it wouldn't be. It could be dark. Like that night. Would Rainey ever be able to blow kisses on that night?

Tish, the direct thinker, knew how black that night was. She'd said so without ever saying a word.

Rainey touched Tish's hand, stroked the thumb whose skin was beginning to smooth out. At least Tish's thumb was out of her mouth. It was small, but it was a step. With her mouth uncorked, maybe sounds would come soon after.

Rainey went into the kitchen to help Doris with dinner.

Doris came with Rainey and Tish back to their side of the duplex because the therapist, Doris said, wanted to call and talk to Rainey about the session that day. Doris whispered this while they were cleaning up, and she told Rainey that Nanci would call while Tish was in the tub, so she'd be out of earshot, and that Doris would keep an eye on the soapy little girl until Rainey was done.

Rainey was already exhausted. She wondered what it was the therapist had to talk to her about, why it couldn't wait until the next session. When Doris chased the silently laughing Tish up the steps, Rainey brought her phone to the living room and waited. Almost as if Nanci heard her settle on the couch, the phone rang.

"Hi, Rainey!" the therapist said. "I was sorry to miss you today, but I heard it was possibly for a good reason. What happened at the line-up?"

Quickly, Rainey filled her in.

"That's wonderful! Did you tell Tish?"

"I did. She hasn't said anything, though. But she did pull her thumb out of her mouth. I'm hoping that's a good sign." From upstairs, Rainey heard the water filling the tub and Doris sang a song about a rubber ducky. Normally, Tish would be singing right along, and Rainey waited, hoping the high shrill voice was about to break through the soap bubbles, but Doris was the only one she heard.

"It is a good sign, Rainey. And I hope it does make Tish feel safer. I wanted to talk to you about our session today…it was a really good one, and I didn't want to wait to tell you."

Rainey leaned forward.

"Tish gravitated toward the dolls today," Nanci continued. "She's been playing with the Legos mostly, but today, she settled down by the dollhouse. She focused in particular on the mother and father dolls. Or the man and woman dolls, I suppose."

Rainey nodded. She wondered if most of the children in Nanci's practice would think of the dolls as Mom and Dad. But not her daughter. How did her daughter think? Mama and Bad Guy?

"I know this isn't going to sound particularly positive, but it really is, Rainey. Tish displayed a little bit of violence today, when she was playing. She laid the woman doll down flat on the floor, right on her face, and then she hit the woman doll over and over with the man doll."

Rainey grabbed for the afghan. This was good news? Her daughter was recreating the scene and it was a good thing? "Oh my god," she whispered.

"I know. I know, Rainey, how that must sound, but see, she's showing me what she saw. She's showing me how she saw it, how she's remembering it, and that will help me to talk to her, to help her. See? She is communicating, Rainey. I remembered how you asked me how I could help if Tish wasn't talking, but she is. In this new and silent way, but Rainey, today, she shouted!"

A sound came out of Rainey then, but she couldn't have said what it was. It was all of it, just all of it, and it undid Rainey just then. It unstrung her like a bale of hay with its wires sliced. She went in all directions. There'd been the line-up and the voice and the photo, there'd been the decision of what to wear, what do you wear to a line-up, and there was the idea of three other women, one caught in the middle of the act, and there was the pregnancy, and now there was this. This. Her daughter using a male doll to beat up a woman. Instead of putting them in a pink convertible together. Instead of sitting them at a kitchen table together, or even laying them in a bed together. She had the man beating the woman.

Rainey made that sound, that unidentifiable sound, and then she made it again and she sobbed.

"Rainey!" Nanci's voice came quickly over the phone. "Really, honey, really, it's a good thing. I mean, nothing about this situation is good, you know that. But what's important is recovery, it's helping Tish understand what happened, and understand what is going to happen now and making her feel safe again. She has to feel safe, Rainey. Right now, she doesn't feel like she can talk, but she's finding a way to talk to me anyway. And with the man being captured… Rainey, really. It's a good thing."

Nanci was beginning to sound ragged and breathless by her last word, and Rainey tried desperately to get herself back under control. "I'm sorry," she gasped. "I'm sorry. It's just so much…"

"I understand." Nanci seemed to wait while Rainey gathered herself, began to breathe more deeply. "I think it's a step forward, Rainey. A positive thing. But I also know, really, I do, how hard this is. That something like this can be seen as a positive step, when it's coming after something that never should have happened at all."

Just like that, Rainey's voice was gone again. Was Nanci placing blame? Was she saying what Rainey herself thought, what her father said out loud, that Rainey never ever should have done what she did that night? That all of this was her fault?

"It shouldn't have happened to Tish," Nanci said softly. "And it shouldn't have happened to you, Rainey. It shouldn't ever happen to anybody."

She wasn't. She wasn't placing blame. "Thank you," Rainey whispered.

They finished the call. When Doris came down a few minutes later, leading a clean and prancing Tish, she took one look at Rainey and offered to get Tish her snack, make sure she brushed her teeth. Rainey agreed and found herself only able to sit and stare straight ahead until it was time to go upstairs, tuck her daughter in, kiss her forehead. With the warmth of her daughter's skin pressed to her lips, Rainey shook herself and pulled herself to her feet once again. She tugged the blanket up to Tish's chin, made sure Teddy was tucked in too, promised Tish she'd see her in the morning, and then she returned downstairs, where she knew Doris was waiting.

Rainey filled Doris in on the therapist's phone call, and then she reassured Doris that she was fine, she was just going to sit and watch television for a little bit, and then go to bed herself. Just as Rainey kissed Tish, Doris kissed Rainey on the forehead before leaving for her side of the duplex.

But Rainey never turned the television on. She sat on the couch and stared at the blank screen, and she thought about calling her parents. Letting them know that her rapist was caught.

She wondered about who to call, which parent, which phone. For the longest time, after dinner, before the phone call from Nanci, she sat and watched Tish playing with some pink and white Legos and she wondered if both her parents would want to know about the line-up. Her mother would, she was sure of that, but her father? Would he want to hear this too?

Somehow, having the rapist behind bars, felt like maybe her father might lift some of the blame from Rainey. The police hadn't, after all, put Rainey behind bars. And Nanci, right there on the phone, didn't seem to blame Rainey either.

Though, she supposed, they didn't know the whole story. They didn't know what she did, what her body did, during the rape.

Slut.

What is this, some kind of joke? Just who do you think you are?

Since she hadn't heard from her father at all since her parents' visit a few days after the rape, she wondered if she'd been disowned. If that was the final straw, if her father was a camel, like the camels of the desert night by the river, but with his back broken. If her stupidity was just too much for him to handle now. Rainey's daughter stopped talking, her father stopped caring. Because Rainey was just that kind of girl.

Though there was her mother. The surprise of her mother. Rainey still held the feel of her mother that night, sneaking in after her father went to sleep, climbing up the stairs to Rainey's room, rocking her. Rocking her deep. And she had her mother's whispered voice on the phone, humming her to sleep.

Her mother would definitely want to know.

But after Doris left and Rainey sat in her living room, picked up now, neat, television off, lights dimmed, she realized she wanted both her parents to know. She wanted them to know that her rapist was in a cage and that she was the one who put him there. So she picked up the phone and called her parents' landline. It was her mother that answered.

"Rainey!" she said and Rainey smiled. It was almost automatic, but a good kind of automatic. Her smile reached toward her mother and Rainey was suddenly delighted to hear her mother's voice. "How are you?" And then in a whisper, "Why are you calling this phone?"

"I wanted to talk to you both," Rainey whispered back. And then, aloud, she said, "I'm fine, Mom. It's been…well, I guess it's been a good day. I wanted to let you know that the guy who raped me got caught. He's in jail."

Rainey heard her mother gasp and then the scrape of a kitchen chair across the floor. "Oh…oh, that's wonderful. I'm so glad. He's… it was really him?"

Rainey sank into the couch. "Mom, put Dad on the extension. I want him to know too." She waited while her mother called and then there was a click and the sound of the television floated over the wires.

"I'm here," her father said. "Hello, Rainey."

So Rainey told her parents about it. The phone call, the hesitation, the trip to the police station, the photos, the voices. "It was him. I know it." She decided to leave out her rapist's shouted threat. She wanted her parents to think, like Tish, that the rapist was forever gone. "And well, I guess I took care of it. I took care of it, didn't I?"

"Yes." Her mother's voice was warm. "You did. I'm so proud of you."

Rainey held that pride to herself, as she waited to hear what her father had to say.

And then she thought how quickly that pride would go away if she told her mother her deepest secret, her body's deepest betrayal. And she wondered if her mother told her father about this new pregnancy. Another pregnancy. The third.

So quickly, Rainey was cold.

Her father said nothing, but she could still hear the television.

Her mother jumped in. "And Tish? How is she?"

So maybe Rainey hadn't completely taken care of it. "She's still mute. But I have her with a therapist. I'm hoping, now that the guy is in prison, maybe she'll start talking again. She knows there's nothing to be afraid of anymore."

They talked a bit longer, Rainey's mother filling her in on the weather, the neighbors, a light discussion filled with the gap that was Rainey's father. At one point, Rainey heard the softest of clicks. The sound of the television disappeared.

"Dad?" she said.

"He hung up, honey." There was a hesitation and Rainey knew that her mother was hovering, caught in the need to do what her husband wanted her to do, which was hang up, just as he'd done. It was expected. "Oh, Rainey," she said finally. "This is so good. I'm so glad. Maybe now things can get back to normal."

Rainey so wanted to think that too. But it wasn't back to normal yet. Nothing was back to normal yet. The only difference between this night and the last was that there was a man behind bars and Rainey didn't have to worry about him finding her anymore. At least for now.

But she still had to worry about what he left behind.

"Mom?" Rainey said. "Can you tell Dad something for me?"

Her mother paused, but then said, "Of course, hon."

"Can you tell him, please, that there were three other women? Besides me, I mean. That man…he got three other women after me."

There was silence. And then her mother's voice fell back to a whisper. "Oh, how awful. Yes, I'll tell him."

"Okay." Rainey swayed in her seat.

"Honey," her mother said. "Give our love to Tish. And I love you too." Then she dropped to a whisper again. "And call me whenever you need to. Okay? Whenever you need to."

"No matter what," Rainey said, just as her mother said it too. Rainey felt her smile come back, though she knew it wouldn't stay. "Love you, Mom. Bye now."

The phone in her lap, Rainey sat in the dim living room. She thought about those three other women, the last, caught in the act. Their rapist's act. She wondered if they were sitting alone in their living rooms too. Or if they had family around them, or a daughter upstairs, or if they held phones still warm from conversation.

She wondered if he did the same thing to them. If their bodies responded. If he called them good girls, if he brought their bodies to an awful release. One that they hated, as much as she did. She wondered if they were that kind of girl too. Like she was.

Slut.

So stupid. Rainey sank sideways and curled up on the couch, drawing her knees up. She lay there and hated her own stupid self. She hated everything that got her there, to that moment. First boyfriend gone, a child dead. Second boyfriend gone, a child upstairs, silent, witness to something that no child should ever see. Voice robbed. And now, a rapist locked away, and another child whose life hung in the balance. In Rainey's balance. The child, the fetus, whatever it was, was locked away inside of her. Its father was in prison. So was the fetus.

And so was Rainey.

In the heat of hatred, Rainey still felt cold. She pulled the afghan over herself again. In the silence of that living room, in the silence that poured from her daughter's bedroom upstairs, Rainey burned with ice-cold as she clutched Doris' blanket to her chin.

CHAPTER ELEVEN

Doris

After putting Tish to bed and kissing Rainey goodnight, Doris cleaned up her own kitchen, washing the dishes, the pots and the pans. She had a dishwasher, but tonight wasn't a night for a dishwasher. Doris had to do something with her hands, something more than rinse and stack. So she attacked the stuck-on pieces of macaroni at the bottom of the pot. She scraped at the cheese, hardened and crisp, on the edges of her dishes.

And she thought of her response when she heard that Rainey identified the rapist. When Doris realized that he was locked away, behind bars like the animal he was. *Thank God. Oh, thank God.* It was an automatic response, an utterance she used millions of times when things went well. Thank God the storm didn't blow her roof off. Thank God the car started on a freezing cold morning when even her exhale seemed laced with ice. Thank God when Tish, as a baby, finally stopped squalling with colic and began to sleep through the night for Rainey, and sleep through the afternoon in a luxurious nap that allowed Doris a cup of coffee and sometimes a few winks herself.

And now, thank God that this monster was behind bars.

But why were there four women out there who had to go through this violation first? This horrible intrusion in their lives, in their bodies, that left them bruised and battered and soaked through with humiliation? Doris saw humiliation on Rainey's face, in Rainey's posture, whenever she talked, however briefly, about the attack. Doris didn't understand it, didn't know why the humiliation was there, but she saw it and knew that it saturated Rainey with a terrible poison. And why was there now a tiny baby floating inside of Rainey, a baby born of this humiliation? There was evil in the world, there was no doubt of that, but why would evil be allowed to beget evil?

Where was God?

Doris hated that question. She always tried to block it, whenever it threatened to rise up into her mind, into her voice. She tried to keep it out of her prayers. But it seemed to be steadily rising in her now, like a shout, and she wanted to shout it for Rainey, for Tish, for all three of the other women. She wanted to shout it for this baby. And the worst part of wanting to shout was knowing that, no matter how loud her words were, she likely wouldn't get an answer.

Doris sighed, putting away the final pot. Then, getting out a chopping board, she began to stack raw carrots, celery, potatoes and zucchini. She would fill a crockpot with vegetable soup, let it cook overnight, filling her house with the aroma of good nutrition and health, and offer it to Rainey for lunch tomorrow. Doris tried to think of that, of warmth and vitamins and nourishment, but when she placed the vegetables on the cutting board, she chopped them with a large knife, bigger than necessary, and her gusto, she knew, was bigger than necessary too.

Doris felt like an angsty teenager, or a toddler, with all questions and demands. Why? Why? Why? And where was God?

A whole life of faith. A whole life of believing and gratitude and acceptance.

Well. Maybe not a whole life. Some things, she knew, were hidden. Pushed down. Buried and denied.

Doris thought of her own baby, of Forrest, gone to Limbo at five weeks and two days old, and she sliced through acceptance, changed it to tolerance. To putting up with.

To just not thinking about what she couldn't even begin to understand. Because sometimes, there was nothing else to do but stop thinking, when there was never a chance of an answer.

When Doris was Tish's age, four years old, she was already going to church every Sunday. She wore dresses over lacy anklets in the spring and summer, thick and itchy tights in the fall and winter. White mary-janes evolved to black mary-janes, and then white mary-janes in a larger size as the seasons passed. Doris whispered her sins through a screen to a priest, to God's ear, when she was seven; she wore her veil and married God when she was eight; she confirmed her belief and undying faith when she was twelve. She professed her love for Harvey in front of God on her wedding day; she prayed for Forrest's health every day of her pregnancy and she called to God for help during the pain of labor. And every day and every night, for years and years and years, she opened the Bible her mother gave her for her First Communion, she opened it at random and read the words that she honestly believed God hand-picked for her.

But when Forrest died…well, when Forrest died.

Doris slammed the knife onto the counter, scooped up the massacred vegetables and threw them in the crockpot.

When Forrest died, she asked the priest why. She asked God why.

Doris added several cans of beef broth, stewed tomatoes, poured in tomato juice.

When Forrest died, she asked herself why she couldn't have gone into the nursery a little earlier, roused the baby, reminded him to breathe and to live. She wondered what kind of mother wouldn't know when her child passed away in the middle of the night. What kind of mother wouldn't notice the absence of her baby's breath in the house.

Doris scattered in a few spices. Garlic, onion flakes, a touch of chili powder. Italian seasonings. She dropped on the glass lid, flinching at the fragile sound of glass against ceramic, then turned the switch to low. Going out to the living room, she settled in her recliner as she did every night, and she held the remote in her hand. But she didn't turn the television on. Instead, she listened for the sounds from next door. If this was a normal night, if the world was suddenly returned to normal, Doris' house would be filled with the sounds of next door all night long. The sound of Rainey bathing Tish, tucking her into warm and fresh pajamas, pulling back the covers on the bed, kissing her goodnight. Making sure that she had Teddy. Making sure that Tish was safe. Every mother makes sure that her child is safe. What kind of mother wouldn't?

What kind of mother was Doris anyway?

For the last five weeks, there were no normal sounds. On this night, it was Doris who bathed Tish, and Tish who pantomimed the sounds she would typically make. She pantomimed normal. But nothing was normal.

Nothing was normal for the longest time after Forrest's passing too. Doris remembered.

One night, about two weeks after Forrest's funeral, Harvey rolled toward Doris in bed. She held her Bible in her lap. She hadn't opened it yet. Harvey touched her, stroking the side of her cheek, then her shoulder, running his hand down her arm and then he held his fingers pressed against hers, where hers pressed against the Bible. "What kind of God," Harvey asked in the softest of voices, the most hurt of voices, "lets a perfectly healthy baby boy die?"

And what kind of mother? Doris wondered that night. What kind of mother?

They hadn't really touched each other in bed much since Forrest's passing. She kissed Harvey's neck every morning, she cried on his shoulder, he cried on hers. But no real husband-and-wife touching. Doris felt his fingers on hers and knew that if he reached for her now, if he tried to find comfort in her body, she would break into pieces. There was no comfort there. Not in her. She no longer knew what was inside her body anymore. Who was there in bed with her husband? Who didn't walk into that nursery until it was too late?

She wanted to give Harvey an answer, to say something that would make sense, that would redeem God. And she wanted to tell Harvey that she wondered the same thing. That her body and mind were wretched with questions.

But she said nothing. His pain was too great, and so was hers. If the hurt was put together, blended, it would drown them both.

Doris was sure of that. They would stop breathing, just the way their baby did.

Eventually, Harvey fell asleep and his hand fell from hers. Doris opened the Bible. Her eye was drawn to the middle of the page, to Psalm 10, line 16.

The Lord is King for ever and ever: the heathen are perished out of his land.

The heathen are perished out of his land.

Was Forrest a heathen? Because he wasn't baptized? Was Doris, because she didn't have the sense to check on her son in his time of need?

Why did she fail?

Doris wanted to throw the book across the room. She wanted to see it smack against the wall and fall to the floor, its pages bent and ripped. She wanted to slam it shut, then open and slam it shut again. And again. She wanted to tear the pages into shreds, cram them in her mouth, chew them, spit them on the floor.

But she didn't. She stroked the satin ribbon into place and closed the Bible, setting it without a sound on her bedside table. Then she turned out the light and settled down to sleep by her husband.

The words burned in the darkness behind her eyes. Heathen. Limbo. For a small baby boy, five weeks and two days old. Stained with original sin, the priest said. A baby boy. Born out of the love she shared with Harvey. A love that was kept private from the rest of the world. But a love she relished.

Heathen. Original sin. Five weeks and two days old.

Doris and her husband were drowning.

Doris thought of the angels she insisted grace her child's headstone. She wondered if they did any good at all, if they brought real angels to her little man's side, if they kept him company while God looked away. While God turned His back.

Doris fought the tears that night with Harvey, and she fought them for months until they finally dried, she thought forever. She slipped back into a life of routine, of regularity, of normal, church like clockwork every Sunday, reading the Bible morning and night, "Oh, thank God!" popping out of her mouth at every appropriate time. And silence at others, silence at times when the questions and accusations and demands threatened to come up from the dark, from the past she tried to bury. From the grave where her baby was buried.

And now here it was again. Doris flipped the remote over and over in her hand. She thanked God when Rainey and Tish appeared in her life. Forrest was gone for so many years by then, forty-seven years, and Harvey for three when she saw Rainey in the grocery store that day, crying over the tiny baby in her cart, crying as if she just didn't know what to do or where to turn anymore. With Rainey and Tish next door, with them in her life every single day, Doris found new things to thank God for. For the pleasure of a little girl's smile first thing every morning. For the softness of voices over shared cups of tea or coffee in the early evening. For the surprise and startle of burnished spring curls and the sing-song of a nonsense rhyme sung out of tune in the middle of a jungle of stuffed animals. For another woman, just as sodden with the love for a child, sitting next to Doris on her front step, offering company. Company in a day that would otherwise be empty of family.

Now that elfin voice was silent, wasn't it. And the dark circles under Rainey's eyes didn't seem to ever be going away. Deep inside Rainey, there was another who was silent for now, and might be silent forever. And somewhere in town, hidden away in their own homes, were three more women. Dark circles under their eyes too, maybe. Bruises. And in the prison, there was a man who left his mark on them all.

Thank God for that. Thank God for the man being behind bars.

And Rainey and Tish were still here. Tish danced in silence among the stuffed animals, a rainbow-striped rhino under her arm, and Rainey still sat beside Doris, even if her leaning asked more for comfort than offered company. But they were still here.

Oh, thank God.

Setting aside the remote, Doris let the darkness descend on her. Overtake her, though its weight was thinned with the growing aroma of fresh vegetable soup, bubbling away in the crockpot. There would be nourishment tomorrow. She would feed Rainey. Rainey was still here.

Oh, thank God.

But where was He?

The next day, Doris found Father Markham behind the church, in the Garden of Prayer. It was used for prayer, of course, but mostly, it was used for photographs at weddings and confirmations and on First Communion day. All the little girls and boys would line up with their parents, waiting to stand under the vine-covered arched trellis, to have their pictures taken in their white dresses, in their black suits, surrounded by the bright reds and purples and yellows of God's spring flowers. On this day, Doris found Father Markham on his knees, weeding, when she came around the corner. He was wearing jeans and a t-shirt. When he realized Doris was there, he stood and wiped his hands on his back pockets, and Doris read on his shirt, "PTL anyway!"

"PTL anyway?" she asked.

Father Markham looked down. "Praise The Lord anyway," he said. "Last year's confirmation class had this made for me. I used to say it to them all the time. I say it to all the confirmation classes. You know. No matter what happens, praise the Lord anyway." He sat down on a white scrolled bench, placed before a pond replenished by a constantly flowing fountain.

When Father Markham took over the church eight years before, he purchased a special heater for the pond and the fountain so that people requiring prayer would be able to find the purity, the clarity, of bubbling water, even in the dead of winter, even in Wisconsin. Doris thought it was foolish at the time, but since then, she found herself out there in February and March, standing in front of the fountain. Not usually praying, but hoping for spring. Hoping and praying, she thought, really weren't all that much different.

"You haven't been coming to mass," Father Markham said.

"No." The decision to stop attending mass hadn't been easy. The first time, Doris got up on the Sunday morning, the first Sunday after telling Father Markham about Rainey, and she dressed in her usual church clothes. It was getting chilly, so she switched from a dress to nice slacks, but it was still warm enough for a long-sleeved button-down blouse instead of a sweater. Doris dressed, approved of herself in her mirror, a mirror Harvey made for her years before, and then she went downstairs for her Sunday breakfast. Pancakes with Tish and Rainey always came after church, and so she often treated herself before church with two doughnuts, bought especially for that purpose the day before. A strawberry and a maple. She liked to think of the maple as a warm-up, as a teasing invitation to what she would share later with Tish and Rainey.

But that morning, after eating her doughnuts, Doris walked to her car, stood there, and couldn't bring herself to climb inside. She pictured herself in church, in her usual spot in the second pew, on the aisle, but then it seemed like she just wasn't there anymore. She could see the spot in her mind, and it wasn't even empty. Someone else quickly filled in, and Doris' absence wasn't even noticed. Doris could hear the hymns, she could hum them, as she stood there by her car, but she could no longer see herself sitting, standing, kneeling, in rote in her spot in the church. She hit the button to relock her car and the car gave its usual honk, but to Doris, it sounded surprised. She felt surprised. But she returned to the house. She changed back into everyday clothes. When it was time for the pancakes, when Tish stood at the front screen door and peeked outside, waiting for Doris to pull into the driveway, Doris' car was still in the garage, and Doris herself was on the front porch, the paper spread open in her lap.

In the Sundays after, Doris slept a little later, had her doughnuts while reading the Sunday paper, then waited on the porch until Rainey and Tish were up to make the pancakes. Rainey never asked her why she wasn't going to church, and of course, Tish couldn't. But the maple kiss was still planted firmly on Doris' cheek.

Now, in the Garden of Prayer, Doris looked around, trying to find a spot to settle, to feel comfortable. She wasn't even sure why she came here on this day. It just seemed the place to go. Just as "Oh, thank God!" fell without thinking from her lips the day before.

"Come sit down, Doris."

She looked at the space on the bench next to the priest, then shook her head. She continued standing. Father Markham noticed her absence. She wondered if the priest, like her car, like Doris herself, was surprised.

As if he knew her thoughts, which Doris always suspected priests could do, he began to talk about exactly that. "You know, you've been to church every Sunday since I've been here. That's eight years already, Doris. Almost nine." Father Markham crossed his arms and leaned against the trellis. A vine flipped over his shoulder like an alien green braid. "When I give my sermon, there's this face missing. I always look to your face. If you're frowning, I know I'm not making much sense. But if your face is smooth, and you're looking at me and every now and then you nod, then I know I'm doing okay." He shrugged. "I haven't known if I'm doing okay, Doris."

"I'm sorry." Doris began to feel silly, standing there, and so she gave up and sat down next to him. It didn't seem appropriate, really, to sit next to a priest on a bench that wasn't a pew, in a place that wasn't inside a church, and particularly with the priest dressed in a t-shirt. But there was nowhere else to go. There was only this one bench. "Church just doesn't feel right."

"Is it because of your neighbor? Rainey?"

Doris nodded. It was because of Rainey. But Doris also knew that Rainey was only a part of it. Rainey was just the thing to make the teeny tiny prick in Doris' faith, scabbed over since Forrest's death, turn back into a chasm. Open into the chasm that had been running under her skin for fifty-three years. "Father Markham...it's just..." Doris stopped and took a breath. "I don't exactly know how to say this. Especially to a priest."

"Then forget I'm a priest. Just talk to me."

Doris glanced over at him, then down at his shirt. "That's kind of hard to forget."

Father Markham looked down too. Then he stood up, pulled his arms out of his sleeves, spun his shirt around, and tugged it back on. The plain back of the shirt, a solid blue, now transformed him into a man. Not a priest, with a white collar at his throat, or even white letters spelling out PTL anyway! on his chest. Doris was startled at the brief glance of hair on his belly. Somehow, priests weren't supposed to have hair on their bodies. They were supposed to be smooth.

She nearly laughed out loud. She had no idea where she ever came up with that thought. Father Markham was, after all, a man. Just as Jesus was a man.

And now, Father Markham sat back down. "Better?"

Doris smiled. She couldn't help it. "That is better. But…"

"But what?" He looked back down again. "These are jeans. Not black trousers. And you know what? I don't have a crucifix on me anywhere right now. I'm always afraid I'll drop it in the dirt. I don't even have a rosary in my pocket."

"No. It's just…it feels like your first name is Father."

"Actually, it's Bob."

"Bob."

He nodded.

Doris did too, then she crossed her legs. "Well, Bob," she said. And burst out laughing.

He did too, and they hooted together in the Garden of Prayer, leaning together like two old friends who'd known each other a very long time. Which they had. When they finally subsided to giggles and chuckles and then to deep breaths, both wiped their eyes. Bob took one of Doris' hands. "Okay then," he said. "Tell me."

Doris looked at their fingers, laced together, Bob's with a slice of dirt under each fingernail, her nails neatly trimmed and clean. "Is it…" she began. "Well. Is it okay to not like God sometimes?"

Doris had plenty of opportunities to be angry with God.

Bob sat for a second, then asked in a voice that blended in to the water bubbling from the fountain, "Have you stopped believing in Him?"

"No." The reply was automatic, as automatic as yesterday's "Oh, thank God," but Doris felt it. She felt the depth of that No reaching inside of her, a part of her skin, her heart, her soul. She wanted to know where God was that night. She wanted to know what kind of God would allow a monster to attack Rainey, to have Tish witness it and steal her voice, to let that monster leave a vestige of himself inside of Rainey, growing from her energy. She wanted to know what kind of God would let that happen again, three more times over.

And below that, under that new hurt, was the old hurt, the old wonder. She wanted to know what kind of God would take away a perfect baby boy after only five weeks and two days with his mother and father. And what kind of God would believe that baby was stained with original sin and leave him forever in a place called Limbo.

But she never questioned if God existed.

"That's good. That's a good thing." Bob let Doris' fingers go and he leaned back again. Doris did too and they faced each other. "You know, there's times I think that God doesn't always like us either. It's only fair then that we wouldn't like Him sometimes too, when He does things, or doesn't do things, that we just don't understand."

Doris tried to think of what to say next. The silence seemed to call for something. She wanted to put words to what she felt, to the anger, the disappointment, the confusion. But in the end, she just said, "It's hard. It's really, really hard."

As if he couldn't find the words either, Bob said, "And I wish I could give you an answer. Something that would make it all make sense. But I can't. All I can do is sit with you while you don't like God. Sit with you while you're angry. And understand why you feel that way."

"Rainey's pregnant." From the inside, from in Doris' thoughts, those words felt heavy. But outside, now that she'd spoken them, the words felt even heavier. They thudded to the ground like boulders. Doris knew if these words fell into the pond, the pond that soaked up people's prayers, the water would turn muddy and thick. "She doesn't know what to do. And I can't even begin to think of what to tell her."

Beside her, Bob shuddered. "It's the rapist's child?"

"Yes."

They sat like that for a while, and Doris felt like her confusion was reflected by his. She wished like he did that he could give her an answer, but in a way, she was glad he didn't. There was some comfort anyway in someone being just as confused as she was. Someone like Bob. Someone like Father Markham. Someone who was supposed to have all the answers. He was supposed to have the ear of God, wasn't he? And if he was confused, then maybe it was okay that she was too.

Though it sure didn't feel okay.

"Did you know that I had a son?" she asked.

Bob nodded. "I saw the headstone at your husband's funeral." He glanced away. "It was the first one I did, after I came here. It was how I met you."

"My son's name was Forrest. He was only five weeks old. He died before he was baptized. The priest back then said Forrest went to Limbo."

"Baby Limbo," Bob said. "There's been a lot of discussions on Baby Limbo. Most of the minds behind the Catholic church seem to think of it as a gentle place. Warm and loving. A nursery of sorts, I guess you could say, for souls that won't ever grow up."

"More warm and loving than Heaven?" Could any place be more warm and loving than Heaven was supposed to be?

Bob didn't say anything. Doris didn't really expect him to.

"You know, when someone dies," she said, "when Harvey died, there was some comfort in Heaven. In knowing that he went someplace and he's waiting for me. That when I die, I will walk down a path and everyone I know will be there, and Harvey will be there, and we'll be together again."

Bob nodded.

"But Forrest won't be there, will he. He'll always be by himself, in this Limbo. Without his mother. Without his father, even though his father is in Heaven right now. All because Forrest is a baby. All because of a sin he didn't even commit."

"I know that's difficult," Bob said. "But original sin needs to be purified out of the soul—"

And suddenly, he was Father Markham again.

Doris stood up. "Do you know how unfair that is, Father Markham? To take a little baby away, to put him in a place where no one, not even God, goes? Where he will never ever again be with his parents, and they won't be with him, even when they die? What kind of sense does that make?"

Father Markham leaned forward, held out his hands, imploring her to sit back down. "It's like I said, Doris. Things don't always make sense, and that's the hardest of times."

"But it's cruel, Father Markham. It's inhumane. It's vicious. It's mean." Doris found herself crying and she impatiently slapped away her tears. "How can I like a God who does something like that to children?" She looked at his blank shirt, pictured the letters that now sprawled across Father Markham's back. "How can I praise a God that brutalized Rainey? That tore Tish's tongue out of her mouth?" She pointed at the blank of his shirt. "How can I praise him anyway?"

Father Markham tried to take her hand again, but Doris pulled away and stepped backwards. "The rapist did that to Rainey, Doris, not God. Not God."

"But He didn't stop it." Doris started to walk away, but then some of the flowers in the Garden of Prayer held her still. Marigolds and begonias, pansies and geraniums, all splattered in colors that suddenly seemed obscene. Doris dropped her purse, stepped over the brick border, and stomped on the flowers. She heard Father Markham cry out, but she stomped anyway, pulverizing the blooms, mashing the colors, into a mess against the rich brown of the dirt. Perfumes released and mixed in the air and even the smell was violent. Father Markham took her arm, pulled her back, but Doris flung herself away.

"I am so angry at God!" she shouted. "I am so angry! And there's no one to yell at! How do you yell at God? How do you yell at someone you can't even see?" She grabbed her purse. "I will not praise the Lord for this, Father Markham. This is not praiseworthy. God should be ashamed. It seems to me He should be ashamed for a lot of things."

Doris spun and ran around the side of the church. Clattering down the thirty-three steps, she was amazed when she reached the bottom and hadn't fallen. When she hadn't been struck down for her own blasphemy. "Oh, thank God," she murmured, then realized what she said and she sobbed and leaned against her car.

After a while, she became aware of someone rubbing her back. Straightening, she found Father Markham there. She was startled to find that his face too was streaked with tears.

"I don't understand it either, Doris," he said. "I don't. I wish I did. But if you need to talk, I'm here. If you need to yell, I'm here. You can yell at me."

Doris swallowed. "I don't think…I don't think I'm going to be able to come to church for a while, Father Markham."

He nodded, then opened her door for her. After she sat down, after she buckled herself in, he shut the door and leaned in the window. "Then don't come to church, Doris," he said. "It's okay. But come talk to me. Or call me and I will come talk to you."

Doris felt a rush of gratitude. She wondered if she should thank God for this man. But instead, she whispered, "Thank you, Bob." As she drove away, she saw him in her sideview mirror. He turned and started up the thirty-three steps, moving slowly, his hands resting on his knees as if urging them to carry him upwards. On his back, in bright white letters, blazed, "PTL anyway!"

Praise The Lord Anyway.

"No," Doris said. And like before, just like when she was asked if she stopped believing in God, Doris felt that No deep within her soul, just as deeply as she felt that earlier one. Of course she still believed. There was no question about it. But right now, right here, Doris would not praise the Lord anyway. She just couldn't.

Doris felt bruised by the time she got home, and just as quickly as she thought that, she pushed it away. Watered it down. She was not bruised. Rainey was. Doris' bruises, if she was going to allow herself to think of it that way, were old. Fifty-three years old. If there was purple, and if there was blue and green and fading yellow, it was hidden and had been hidden for years. Rainey's were faded, just barely beneath her surface. And Tish's silence was a trumpet call.

And that baby? Did the baby have bruises? Doris wondered for a moment if a violent conception could hurt.

Was the child a bruise? Did it stain Rainey's insides with the color of blood and anger? Red?

Doris wanted to shove it all aside. She needed, she knew, a quiet night. With Rainey home, taking time off of work, Doris didn't need to pick Tish up from school or care for her right after. There was time for a quick sit-down with a cup of coffee and a leftover breakfast muffin, freshened with butter in the microwave, and there was time to give way to the blank stares for a bit. Doris did so, and when she heard the screen door on Rainey's side snap, signaling the arrival of Tish among today's stuffed animals, Doris came to with a start and with cold coffee and an uneaten snack.

Abandoning it, Doris went out and sat on the porch steps and sang nonsense songs to Tish while she danced. For the longest time, Tish crouched by the purple cow, her face pressed to its ear. Doris wondered if she was whispering. And then Tish came and sat on Doris' lap, curling into her body, her warmth weaving itself through Doris' blouse onto her skin. Doris hummed, and when she felt the reverberation on her chest, she knew that Tish was humming along, but so quietly that she couldn't be heard. Tish's hands were resting on Doris' arm and Doris noticed that both thumbs were dirty, but smooth and softly pink. No wrinkles. Tish's thumb hadn't been sucked since the day the rapist was caught.

In the days and nights since the rape, Doris tried to feel, in her rocking and humming, that she was offering comfort to Tish. But that evening, it felt like she was the one needing comfort, and she was siphoning it from Tish's warm body. The reverberation of Tish's silent voice, the softness of her hair under Doris' chin, the grit of playground dirt and smooth skin against her arm all brought about a sense of peace. Doris closed her eyes and sank into it.

When she opened her eyes, it was growing dark. It was getting later into fall and the nights were coming faster and seemed to be staying longer. Tish sat up, looked at Doris and smiled. Her eyebrows perked into an upside-down V.

"I'm okay," Doris said, answering the unspoken question, and hugged her. "Are you okay?"

Tish nodded, then stood up. As if on cue, Rainey appeared in her doorway. "Hey, Doris," she said. Then to Tish, "Time for supper, sweetie. Go wash up." Tish kissed Doris' nose, then ran into the house. "Would you like to join us, Doris? I made more than enough. Just ham steak and buttered corn."

"Oh, no thanks, Rainey." Doris got to her feet. "I think I'll just have some more of that vegetable soup. I seem to have made enough for an army." They'd shared the soup at lunchtime in Doris' kitchen. Rainey, Doris was pleased to see, even took seconds. She made a note to herself to put some of the leftovers in a container, bring it over to Rainey, and to Tish, so they could have some whenever they wanted.

"You should freeze some. It was really good. It would be great to heat some up in the middle of March, when it will be so cold outside."

The cold. Doris already felt the chill. March didn't seem so far away.

They stood next to each other on the porch, and for a moment, Rainey laid her head on Doris' shoulder. "Did you see that Tish still isn't sucking her thumb?"

Doris nodded. "She was humming with me, just a moment ago. Not so you could hear it. But I felt it. Her voice is there, Rainey. I think she just needs to find it again."

They said goodnight and went into their homes and Doris moved comfortably around her house. She ate her soup, filled it with the oyster crackers that Tish loved so much. It was warm and it was delicious, but right before she ate, when she folded her hands to offer a prayer to God, she stopped. Carefully, she moved her fingers apart, felt the mix of cool and warm air in the kitchen, then prayered her hands around her bowl of soup instead. Quietly, she thanked herself. She'd been the one to make the soup. She was the one to serve it, and now, to sit here on her own to eat it. But as she ate, and as she savored, she felt the missing words. The absence of her dinner prayer was a hole in the soup-laden air. It was as empty as the three other chairs tucked around her table.

One chair used to be Harvey's. One, she always planned for Forrest, for him as a young boy, then a young man. By now, he would have brought along a wife and grandchildren. By now, Doris might have even been a great-grandmother. But Forrest never sat at her table. He was never old enough to sit.

She glanced over at the window, where the bassinet used to be. Where she placed Forrest every morning while she made breakfast for herself and her husband. She remembered Forrest's sounds, his smell, the way his arms waved as he looked up at the sunlight playing on the ceiling and surrounding walls. Those five weeks and two days were the happiest of her life, she thought. She'd felt infused with warmth. The baby was warm against her body, tucked to her breast, and Harvey was warm with his kisses. She'd never felt such a sense of satisfaction before. Or since.

Taking care of Tish and Rainey was close. But Forrest and Harvey were hers.

Tish sat at her table now, and Rainey too. But Doris was alone on this night, the night she needed quiet. The chairs were emptier than ever. And for the first time in most of her long life, Doris' hands were not folded.

Doris filled the dishwasher and then she sat in her recliner and watched her shows. She laughed quietly, and even cried when it was appropriate. At nine o'clock, she made herself some tea and mixed it with a bit of brandy, to aid her sleep, and she ate a piece of her own homemade coffeecake.

The whole while, while she ate and laughed, drank and cried, her mind moved around, drifted upstairs, and eventually rested on her bedside table. On her Bible.

Doris got ready for bed, then pulled back her covers. She still slept on the left hand side, even though the right had been empty for eight years. She still fluffed his pillow. Harvey's things were boxed up and sent to Goodwill long ago, but the pillow remained. And so did his side, as if it still held the indentation of his sleep-warmed, and love-warmed, body.

Doris sat on the edge of her bed and rested her Bible on her lap. She touched the worn cover, moved her fingers over the nicks and grooves in the soft leather. Traced the golden swirl of the H in holy, the B in Bible, and looked at the faded illustration in the corner, of Mary holding Baby Jesus. Mary, holding a baby who lived for thirty-three years. She must have sat by his side as he slept, first in the manger, then in whatever was used as a cradle and crib back then. Mary heard her son breathe.

If Jesus had died of SIDS, would he have gone to Limbo? Or would God have been gentler with His own son? He was born of a woman, and he wasn't baptized until he was thirty years old by John the Baptist, so Jesus was stained as a baby with original sin too.

Doris shook her head. She didn't open the book at random, but instead, turned very deliberately to 2 Thessalonians 3:14—15. She read the words she knew would be there, silently at first. But then she read them aloud.

"And if any man obey not our word by this epistle, note that man, and have no company with him, that he may be ashamed. Yet count him not as an enemy, but admonish him as a brother."

She thought of her crazy dance in the flowers of the Garden of Prayer that afternoon. Her anger at God. For a moment, she was ashamed too. Not for her anger, but for taking it out on the flowers. She wasn't mad at the flowers.

Doris had many opportunities to be angry at God.

Carefully, she stroked the satin ribbon in place, then closed the book. "God," she said quietly. "You are not my enemy. But I am admonishing You." She remembered her words earlier that afternoon, words that she cried out to Father Markham in a torrent that felt truthful and right. *I will not praise the Lord for this, Father Markham. This is not praiseworthy. God should be ashamed. It seems to me He should be ashamed for a lot of things.* So many things. Forrest. Rainey. Tish. The little nameless one whose life floated in a whole new type of Limbo. And when Doris let herself think about it, when she dropped her guard and her Bible and her church for just a moment, it seemed a Limbo where that new baby should stay. "You made a mistake," she said now. "You should be ashamed." Tucking the Bible under her arm, Doris began to move through her house, down the hallway, then down the stairs. "I'm putting you in Limbo for a while, God." She thought of how Father Markham referred to Forrest's resting place as Baby Limbo. "I'm putting you in God Limbo. Because I'm not going to talk to You for a while. I'm not going to praise You. I'm not going to go to church and sing Your name."

God Limbo. Where in a house would such a Limbo be? What kind of Limbo was fit for God? Doris moved through her kitchen, opened the drawer beneath her stove which held her pots and pans, placed the Bible in a frypan. But it was a frypan she used, and so God would be released too quickly. Going into the living room, Doris hesitated by Harvey's chair, his sidetable, and she thought about putting the Bible there. She hadn't looked in the sidetable for a long time.

Opening the drawer, she found an ashtray, a long-ago leftover from when Harvey used to smoke. She could never get him to give up the ashtray, even when the cravings were gone, when the temptation was gone, and there'd been no cigarettes for years. He said he wanted it around, just in case. Just in case what? she asked. In case they ever find a way to make smoking be as good for you as it tastes and feels, he said. And so the ashtray went into the sidetable. On the last day in the hospital, even as Harvey slid away, his hand still rose every now and then, his fingers poised around an invisible cigarette, and he brought it to his pursed lips.

Doris hoped that in Heaven, Harvey could smoke again, and that it would bring him only glory.

Also in the sidetable was an unfinished crossword puzzle. Doris put it in there when she came home from the hospital that last night, before Harvey died, before she received the phone call in the morning. She was trying to convince herself that it wasn't the last time he'd be taken to the hospital, that he would come home and finish his puzzle. He always finished his puzzle, and in red ink too. The red felt-tip pen was in the drawer as well. So was a TV Guide from eight years ago, and next to that, a deck of cards that he would flourish suddenly in the middle of an evening, asking her if she wanted to play Rummy. She always said yes, he always won. It was a signal of sorts between them…what he won was her, up in bed that night. She always smiled when she lost.

Doris closed the drawer. This wasn't the place for Limbo.

She thought about the garage for a while and she even stood in it, leaving her house, stepping down the driveway, letting herself in through the side door, even though it was dark and the neighborhood was quiet and she had no business being in her garage that late. It was remote and cold, a place she didn't go to very much, except for getting in and out of her car. But then she thought of what Father Markham said about Limbo. *Most of the minds behind the Catholic church seem to think of it as a gentle place. Warm and loving. A nursery of sorts, I guess you could say, for souls that won't ever grow up.* At least God provided a warm place for the babies. It wouldn't be fair then to leave Him in the cold.

And then she realized the perfect spot. Going back upstairs, she went down the hall and into the room that used to be Forrest's nursery.

It wasn't a nursery anymore, of course. Harvey had taken the crib down, though he'd waited for a year after Forrest's passing, until it became apparent that there weren't going to be any more children. When the crib disappeared, on a Sunday morning while Doris was at church, she followed his cue and she made the room into a sort of study, with a desk and a reading chair and bookshelves. Sometimes she found Harvey up there in the middle of the day, usually on weekends before his retirement, but on any day once work was left behind for good. He sat in the chair and he usually held a book on his lap. But Doris knew he didn't go in there to read. Neither did she, when she slipped in there sometimes in the middle of the night.

It was Forrest's room. It would always be Forrest's room, no matter what the furniture implied.

Tucked inside the closet was the baby dresser. She'd bought it at Goodwill; even back then, she had a nose for a bargain. It was white, with one wide drawer running the length of the dresser, then four smaller drawers beneath, down the left side. Next to the drawers was a tiny door, and inside, a tiny closet, with a little pole for hanging baby clothes. The door held a picture of a smiling bunny, flecked like a pastel rainbow, in honor of the rabbit that died for the confirmation of Doris' pregnancy. Inside the closet were Forrest's clothes that he never had a chance to wear. She'd put the larger size clothes in there, to keep them safe until he grew. He never did; the clothes were there still.

The drawers were filled with his sleepers and the sheets and blankets for the crib. Doris opened the top drawer, the big drawer, and touched the quilt there. It was made by Doris' mother, for her grandson, and it was blue and yellow striped.

Doris could never give any of this up. When Harvey died, she was able to pack his things, except for his pillow, and send them off to charity. But these things, the baby things, were always right here, in this closet, in the room of what used to be a nursery. It was only a real nursery for five weeks and two days. Now, it was a secret. A disguised nursery, with a closet full of things for a beloved baby boy.

The crib used to be just under the window. The windows were high in here, in this old house, and the headboard fit just underneath. When she was pregnant, Doris pictured her baby lying in there in the spring and summer, the window open, a breeze breathing the sheer white curtains that hung like mist. Her son's hair would move as well, flickering in the sunlight. During her pregnancy, Doris yearned to watch her baby sleep. And after his death, she yearned even more.

The chair of the study was under the window now. The sunlight used to fall across Harvey's hair, his curls shimmering in the breeze. Doris imagined that Forrest would have curls, just like that.

She turned back to the closet, to the open top drawer and the homemade quilt. Folding it back, Doris slid the Bible inside, then covered it gently up. She closed the drawer, and then the big closet door, and stepped back.

In the dark, the words appeared to her mind, unbidden. Ecclesiastes 7:9.

Be not hasty in thy spirit to be angry: for anger resteth in the bosom of fools.

"I haven't been hasty," Doris answered. "It's taken me all of these years to do this. And if I'm a fool, well, then I guess I'm a fool. I'm admonishing you, God. You should be ashamed."

Around her, the silence felt complete. Doris didn't feel judgment in it. God was floating in Limbo with one of His mistakes. He was tucked in Forrest's things. And it felt to her like God was accepting of His punishment. Doris was grateful for that, even as she felt sad for the newest thing missing in her life.

Doris stopped by the bookshelves on her way out. She ran her fingers over all the titles she put there, found at Goodwill, rummage sales, the yearly used book sale at the library. Beautiful books, many of them leatherbound, many of them, she was told, classics. Dickens and Melville, Shakespeare and Yeats, Austen and all the Brontes. She thought about choosing a book and taking it to bed with her. Closing her eyes without reading first seemed impossible.

Yet so was eating dinner without a prayer. So was starting the day and ending the night without a random page from the Bible. So was admonishing God. She glanced at the closet.

Doris had many opportunities to be angry with God.

Returning to her bedroom, Doris forced herself to do the impossible. She closed her eyes. She slept.

CHAPTER TWELVE

Tish

Mama said the bad guy is gone. He's in a cage. He can't hurt us anymore. I'm glad.

Doris said Mama had to go look at a bunch of men, to find the bad guy. She called it a lineup. We line up at school. Sometimes I get to be the line leader and then all the other kids have to follow me.

Doris said there were ten bad guys. And Mama found him. He's in a cage.

In school, we count to ten. One, two, three, four, five, six, seven, eight, nine, ten. Now number ten is gone. One, two, three, four, five, six, seven, eight, nine. Nine left. Nine bad guys. Ten minus one equals nine, Mrs. Whitstone says. Mrs. Whitstone says that's math.

I don't suck my thumb anymore. I'm glad; it tasted yukky. Kinda like soap.

Maybe, if I make a sound, Mama will come get me this time. Maybe, if I make a sound, someone will come get her.

Maybe.

Maybe if I make a teeny tiny sound. Maybe I only had to be quiet for number ten.

But there were ten bad guys, Doris said. Nine left. That's math.

CHAPTER THIRTEEN

Rainey

Weeks 6 & 7: The embryo is about 1/8 inch long, about the size of a blueberry. The lenses in the eyes appear and inner ears start to develop. The digestive system becomes more refined, with the appearance of the stomach and intestines. The neural tube, connecting the brain and the spinal cord, closes. The lungs, the liver, the pancreas, the kidneys and the thyroid make their initial appearances. On the embryo's body, there are four buds, two to a side, and these will become arms and legs. The hands and feet are shaped like paddles, but there are indentations which will separate and become fingers and toes. The lower jaw and vocal cords begin to form, along with the opening of what will be the mouth. There is the start of the tongue. The brain is growing at the rate of 100 new cells a minute.

Within the embryo's heart, a dividing wall grows, preparing for the four chambers. On the 26th day after fertilization, one of these chambers begins to beat, but the heart is not yet functional.

Lying in bed, Rainey stared at the ceiling. The moon spilled in; the blinds were wide open. In the room two doors down, Tish slept, her teddy bear crushed to her cheek, her thumb still smooth and unsucked on the pillow beside her. Rainey thought that this fearless sleep was a sure sign that some stress was lifted. Rainey willed sleep to come for herself as well. There was no need anymore to lie awake at night and listen for every sound. Tires rolling to a stop.

A step, a scrape on the pavement, the stealthy turn of a doorknob. A creak on the stairs.

There was no longer need. He was caught now, wasn't he. Her rapist. She identified him and he would be put away for a long time. Forever? Rainey didn't know. How long was a rapist usually kept incarcerated? Incarcerated. What a harsh word. Like lacerated.

With a start, Rainey realized she wanted him lacerated. Strung up. She wanted him dead. But at least, he'd be incarcerated for a long time.

Wouldn't he? There were three other women besides her. And who knew how many before.

Rainey threw aside her blankets and headed down the hall. She stopped for a moment at Tish's door, listened to the steady breathing, and then padded down the stairs. Her laptop was on the little desk in the kitchen, where Rainey paid bills and sent emails and played on the Internet. Tonight, she kept the lights off as she booted up the computer. Its glow in the dark kitchen felt companionable. She put it on mute as well, wanting to hold the dark and quiet around her like the blankets she just tossed aside.

A quick trip to Google and a question typed in: "How long of a prison term will a rapist get?" And then she began to read. As she did, the dark around her changed its texture. No longer a blanket. But an anvil, heavy, square on her chest and squeezing the air from her lungs.

Rainey found a study released just a couple of months before, in July of 2006, by the U.S. Department of Justice. It showed that from 1990 to 2002, rapists received an average sentence of 120 months. The actual time served was an average of 5.4 years.

The Rape, Abuse and Incest National Network claimed that out of every one-hundred rapes, only forty-six were reported to the police.

Of that forty-six, only twelve would lead to an arrest.

Of that twelve, only nine would be prosecuted.

Of that nine, only five would lead to a felony conviction.

And from there, only three rapists would spend even a single day in prison.

Three. A single day.

Rainey sat back in the dark, now returned to dangerous. She reminded herself of Robert and Sarah, how they stayed by her side during the line-up, how they seemed so strong in their intent to catch this rapist, to make sure he stayed locked up. Her rapist had four women who came forward. Maybe that would mean he'd be one of the rapists who would at least get a sentence? Of at least 120 months? Ten years. And maybe he'd stay locked up more than five years. Even with good behavior.

Good behavior?

Only forty-six out of every one-hundred women reported their rapes. Which meant that Rainey and the three other women were a part of that, separate from the fifty-four who never said a word.

Why were the others silent?

Rainey left the lit screen and carefully, she moved around the duplex, checking the locks. The back door. The front. The windows. She went upstairs, looked in on Tish again, and then returned to the computer.

Rainey reported the rape. But she'd been found by a police officer. She wondered for a moment, if the rape happened that same night, the same way, but Tish wasn't there, if Rainey stumbled out from the bushes and had not found her daughter, held her, tried to warm her, would Rainey have sought out help? Or would she have run the rest of the way home, her breath tight and wheezing, looking over her shoulder, looking in front of her, looking side to side, run in the door, lock it, run up the stairs, and stay under the shower for as long as it stayed hot? And then stay under for even longer?

She thought of her body's climax, of the way her rapist forced her into a convulsing hated awful orgasm.

Would she have reported it?

No.

If she'd been by herself, if there'd been no child to protect, Rainey likely would never have stayed long enough to be found by the police. She never would have called the police, even after reaching home. She would have been too ashamed.

In the light of the computer, Rainey shuddered. If Tish hadn't been there, Rainey's rapist would have been one of the fifty-four who went on leading their lives as normal. Even though the women they raped never had a normal life again.

It was good, wasn't it, that Rainey reported it?

On this night, and for who knew how long, her rapist wasn't out there anymore. He was behind bars. And just like him, everything in the house, the doors, the windows, were locked up tight. Rainey wasn't in a dark park. Her child was asleep, tucked to the chin in a pink blanket. Her teddy bear at her side, all of her fingers firmly curled on her pillow. And Rainey was alone, and she should be able to go back to bed. She should be able to sleep now.

But she couldn't. Because her rapist, and how long he would stay in prison, kept her sitting by her computer. But that wasn't the only thing.

When her rapist walked away, when Rainey found Tish, when the policeman came, and hours later, when Rainey finally arrived back home, the rape didn't stop. The aftermath was still going on. Still growing.

From her pregnancy with Tish, Rainey remembered. All of the descriptions. And she remembered one in particular, because the number was just so fantastic. At about this time, an embryo's brain was growing at the rate of one-hundred new cells a minute.

Rainey sighed, a soft and moist sound slipping into the kitchen. She pictured her breath there, for just a moment, a white circle of mist. Then she put both hands on the keyboard again. She returned to Google.

Was this her fault? Did the orgasm create the pregnancy? If she'd just taken the rape, been the steak she felt herself to be, if her body hadn't suddenly arced in a pleasure she didn't want, would this conception have taken place?

She typed the question in. Can an orgasm make conception easier?

There were about 1,440,000 results. Rainey stared. All she wanted was a simple yes or no. This was 1,439,999 too many answers.

Rainey combed and she read. Some sites said yes, that the contractions from a woman's orgasm helped pull the sperm more quickly and deeply into the woman's body. Others said no, and compared ratios of how many women didn't experience orgasm during intercourse with how many got pregnant anyway. One site simply said, "Don't be silly."

Don't be silly.

There was an abundance of answers that led to no answer at all. Overwhelmed, over-tired, Rainey slammed the lid of her laptop down. Then she staggered up the stairs and got back into bed.

Her head spun on the pillow. Forty-six out of one-hundred rapes reported. Only three rapists in prison. 120 months, released in five years. Good behavior. Yes. No. Don't be silly. Despite being crowded with numbers, with facts that could be facts, but might not be, Rainey never felt so alone.

But she wasn't alone in the bed, was she. Her rapist was alone in his prison cell. But Rainey, in her room, in her house, anywhere she went right now, wasn't alone at all.

She'd tried everything to be the only person in her skin again. One afternoon, while Tish was still in school, Rainey drove to a remote spot outside of town where railroad tracks criss-crossed the country road. Repeatedly, Rainey drove over the tracks, urging her car to go faster and faster. Over the tracks, then a Y turn, over the tracks, then a Y turn. Twenty-five miles an hour, thirty-five, fifty. The last time, she hit the tracks at eighty-five miles an hour and the car soared as her seatbelt snatched her body in mid-flight, cutting deeply into her belly and chest. The car skidded to the side of the road, and Rainey sat there, her heart galloping, her hands fluttering on the wheel, waiting to feel what she hoped would be a welcome gush of fluid. But nothing happened. Rainey took a deep breath, reasoned that it could take a while, and then drove to pick up Tish at school. After settling Tish in front of the television with her snack, Rainey ran to the bathroom. But her panties remained unstained, that afternoon and that night and the days following; no sudden blood of miscarriage.

And every time Rainey went into the bathroom, whether to take a shower or use the toilet or to simply run a comb through her hair, she squatted on the floor and pushed as if she were giving birth. Even as she did, she held on to the sink for balance. To keep herself from falling.

It seemed there was always something there to rescue her. Or to rescue the fetus. The seatbelt. The sink. Things that Rainey really did herself. She clicked the seatbelt across her body, she grasped the sink's edge.

But still. Even as she grabbed at a multitude of last seconds, she worked at finding a way. Another way. Any way.

One-hundred new brain cells a minute. Time was passing.

As her mind slowed, Rainey focused again on the fetus. She wished it would just go. This fetus, this baby, this mass of cells, whatever it was. Go in a natural way. She pictured it packing up, grabbing some nutrients from her internal sea, putting them into the tiniest of leather suitcases, and moving down the passageway, through the doors that curved and tucked between her legs, and out on a warm, worn red carpet of blood. Rainey found herself wanting to assign the fetus a gender, so she could see who it was she was banishing. What it was. The face that she pictured, looking over its shoulder as it walked away on unsteady legs, the face that was at once angry, yet gray with loss, was male.

So was that what she carried? A tiny boy? Is that who was inside her, distilling life from her blood? Rainey thought about what Doris said, about evil begetting evil. It was dark inside of Rainey, she was sure of that. But did this child make it darker? Not by its skin, but by who it was? By its bloodlines, its pedigree, by a genetic path laid down by his father?

An animal. A beast. Locked in a cage, on the other side of town.

Was this baby a beast too?

Sitting up, Rainey looked across the room to the mirror on top of her dresser. Touching her hands together, thumb to thumb, forefinger to forefinger, she placed a circle over her abdomen in the exact spot where she was sure the fetus hid. There was always a stitch there now, as if it was digging in with its new fingers and toes, and Rainey felt the burrowing in the deepest of her tissues.

She remembered Tish as a baby, pink and moist and warm. She tried to put Tish's luminescence onto the child hovering in her mind, in her body, yet it remained as dark as that September sky on a Wisconsin night in the middle of a park where Rainey wasn't supposed to be. Where she took herself and her daughter, knowingly breaking the rules, the well-posted law, and where she now wished fervently she'd never been.

Rainey had to make up her mind, and she had to make it up soon. She knew that. The weeks were going by. Soon, it would be illegal for her to do anything and she would have to go along with what her body started, encouraged by the attack of an animal. Once she reached a certain week, she would have to go with the flow inside of her like the flow of the river that she sat by on that night where this all began.

Sliding back down in her bed, shifting in a search for comfort, Rainey tried to force herself into sleep. But the silence unnerved her and opened her thoughts to all sorts of paths that she hadn't intended thinking about when this night started. The nights were the worst since the rape. During the day, now that she was home, Rainey adopted Doris' schedule, becoming her shadow on her own side of the duplex. On days that Doris cleaned the kitchen, Rainey cleaned hers. When Doris dusted and vacuumed, Rainey's side roared with a vacuum as well. Following Doris' lead, Rainey kept herself busy, and her mind kept focused on whatever was the next chore, the next step. But at night…

At night, Rainey's mind became a centipede, all one-hundred legs stretching and reaching for different footholds. She moved from one fear to the next, from one secret to the next, often without a breath in between. Rainey kept opening her eyes to stare at her open doorway, which she didn't see so much as she stepped through to the next line of thought. Of memory, of recrimination, of fear for the future, and of thinking just how damn tired she was.

That open bedroom door led just about everywhere.

When she was little, her mother and father argued about her bedroom door. Her father said it should be closed, her mother said open. Her father argued over fire safety and privacy and how Rainey would actually be more protected because they would hear if her door opened in the middle of the night and she either crept out or someone snuck in. And her mother argued that when you were little and scared, sometimes an open door was like the open arms of a mother's hug. An open door let in the glow from the nightlight in the bathroom. It showed the path that led straight to her parents' room, if she needed them. And it let her tears be heard more quickly, instead of waiting for them to be soaked up by the door, washed out on the carpet, and then down the hall.

In the end, Rainey's door stayed half-open, a compromise, until she was old enough to decide to shut the door herself.

She did start shutting the door, when she was fifteen. When it became important to shut her parents out so she could dream of that boy in her life, of Jeff, of what he did to her, what she did to him. When it was important, for that awful couple weeks, for the aftermath then of her secret abortion, to shut out her mother, shut her away from the sudden rush of blood that overflowed Rainey's sanitary pad. The blood she blamed on a heavy, heavy period. And when that stopped and time slipped by, Rainey's door had to stay closed to hide the other boys, the new boys, that captured her heart and released it, captured it and released it. It became important to open an unheard window at two in the morning and slip outside for the warmth of lips and arms and pressed bodies. Or to let that warmth in, to her own bed, while her parents slept on down the hall. Their door half-open, a compromise, and Rainey's closed. Closed hard, a lock pushed in and twisted into place. Her father never had to worry about a creaking door. It never creaked. Only the window whispered with secrets.

Slut.

Rainey stared at her open door now. Down the hall, Tish's door was open too. A nightlight glowed in the bathroom between them. The path was clear.

Before her parents' sudden visit, Rainey talked with them on Easter, several months before, in spring. Before that, her mother's birthday. Before that, Christmas. Holidays meant a phone call, with Rainey doing all the calling, except for her own birthday. She and her mother always talked about Rainey's job, about Tish, about Tish growing impossibly fast. The conversations then were polite. Her father never came to the phone, but Rainey always told her mother to say hello, and she always heard a grunt in the background. Tish enjoyed talking with her grandmother, calling this woman Grandma, whom she'd never met, who was only a voice on the phone and an image in storybooks, a voice that caroled, "How are you?" and "Oh, you're such a big girl!" without ever laying eyes on Tish. At least, until she stopped for those few moments on her way out the door that sudden night a short time ago. Following that lit-up path. Rainey's mother saw Tish then, silvered by the moonlight, sweet in her sleep. Rainey's father, other than photographs, had never seen his granddaughter. He'd never spoken to her. Grandpa was a name Tish only saw on birthday and holiday cards. Signed by Rainey's mother.

Rainey left home over five years ago now. She'd never been back. Until the rape, her parents had never been here. Home. The word played with pictures of warm meals and quilts, laughter around a table, a swingset in the backyard. To think of her parents' house, where Rainey grew up, as home now was such an impossible thought. How could she ever find any comfort there? Home was here now, on her side of this duplex, and with Doris on the other.

And now, sometimes, her mother's voice on the phone. A secret cell phone.

In that moment, Rainey smiled.

Her relationship with her parents hadn't always been bad. Not really. Her mother supplied the usual band-aids, hot chocolate, crown-shaped bottles of perfume with names like Little Princess and Twinkle Time. Her father didn't do much, but every spring, on a certain day when a certain wind blew, he put down his newspaper and took Rainey to the toy store. He let her pick out whatever kite she wanted, and then he built it for her while she knelt by his side, in their garage. Across the street in the vacant lot, he launched it into the air for her and then handed her the spool of string. For an afternoon every spring, he stood there, his hands on her shoulders, and she flew the kite, a diamond with a rainbow on it, or a white bear, or a dolphin, and they watched it dip and twirl. Then he helped her reel it in and they hung the kite with the others in the garage. The next day, that certain wind would be gone and her father would be back behind his newspaper.

In Rainey's garage now, on her side of the duplex, there was a wall of kites too. But Rainey and Tish flew them on more days than just a certain one in spring. They flew them whenever the wind felt right and the urge came upon them, standing amid the leaves of fall or in a snowbank in winter or in the green grass in spring and summer. Rainey stood behind her daughter on those days, her hands braced on Tish's shoulders, and Rainey ached for her father. For who her father should have been. Even though he really wasn't bad. Not really. Not at all. Most people would say he was fine.

Even with the sneaking out, even with the hidden abortion, Rainey always loved her parents. But night-swimming changed everything. Her father, usually a quiet man, spoke loudly and forcefully, knocked-up, he said, slut, he said, and her mother cried and looked away, and they both seemed to think that the Rainey they knew was gone forever. And then she was.

But still, her mother supplied band-aids. She might not have come in person, but boxes showed up at Rainey's door, boxes filled with practical things, once she and Tish were living in Doris' duplex. Tins of formula and jars of baby food. Baby ibuprofen and an ear thermometer. Books on how to raise a child. Even alone.

Rainey wondered if her father ever knew about these care packages. Or if they were all a part of the blue tent Rainey and her mother put together on secret days. Rainey thought she might ask her mother about this during their next conversation. On a secret cell phone.

But now Rainey was hurt with a new and deeper hurt than she'd ever experienced and she didn't think there was a band-aid nearly big enough. She thought of her mother creeping into her room that night a few weeks before. Talking about how mothers make mistakes. All mothers.

Even Rainey? Even this kind of mistake? This was more than a mistake.

And what kind of a girl goes walking through a park late at night, Rainey, huh? What kind of girl?

Okay, what is this? Some kind of joke?

Who do you think you are?

Slut.

It wasn't a mistake. It was what she was.

Rainey glanced at her clock. There was no time zone difference between Waukesha and St. Louis, and so it was three-thirty in the morning there too. Rainey thought about calling, punching in the secret cell phone number, about hearing her mother's startled whisper, asking her if she was okay, asking her what was wrong. And at three-thirty in the morning, Rainey knew her only response would be to cry and cry and cry.

That, she could do alone. She had to. She wouldn't call her mother, not even secretly, not at three-thirty in the morning.

She wouldn't go knock on Doris' door.

She wouldn't even go stand again in her daughter's doorway, count the breaths, watch the pink blanket rise and fall.

Except for her secret, Rainey was alone. It was what she deserved. *Slut.*

But the next morning, Rainey's mother called her. Rainey was back from taking Tish to school, and she was moving around the duplex, busying herself with normal things, trying to take her mind off the fact that she had an appointment in a few hours with her doctor. And then her cell phone rang. Checking the screen before answering, she saw it was her mother. On the secret phone.

"Hi, Mom," she said.

"Good morning, Rainey." Her mother's voice was soft, but not a whisper, so Rainey knew her father mustn't be close by. "I was just thinking about you, so I thought I'd call. How are you?"

"I'm okay. I have to go see the doctor in a little while." Rainey pulled out a chair, sat at her table. From next door, she could hear the distant sound of a television and a closer sound of running water, and she knew that Doris was at work, cleaning the kitchen.

She and her mother sat in silence. Rainey could hear her mother breathing and it seemed to her the breaths were sharp and quick. Scared, like a rabbit. She wondered where her mother was, if she was standing where she could see out the window, if her father was gone and her mother was watching for the first sign of his return so she could hit the goodbye button. She wondered if her mother regretted the secret phone. If she wished she'd kept her face turned away.

"Mom? Can I ask you something?"

"Sure." There was the sound of pouring now and Rainey knew her mother was by the kitchen window, the coffee maker on the counter, just off to the right. Her father was definitely out then, doing some errand or another.

"Why are you doing this? Calling me. Getting a special phone. You've been…" Rainey stopped, choked up for a second. "Well, you've been gone for years."

A gasp. Then, "I know. And I'm sorry. I never wanted it to be like that. But your father…well, your father was so angry. And it felt like I was stuck in the middle and I needed to take sides. I didn't want to, it didn't feel right, but, well, I live with your father, Rainey."

Rainey nodded. She thought of herself that night she left home for good, slipping out of the house, getting in her car, driving to a spot on a map she'd only chosen on whimsy. The drop of a finger. "But I was pregnant, Mom. And alone. You know? There were so many times—" So many times she could have used her mother. Needed her mother. She had so many questions during her pregnancy. Was this normal, was that? What did labor feel like, would she be able to get through it? She took childbirth classes by herself, sitting in a room surrounded with couples, with men who coached their wives or their partners, counting their breaths for them, rubbing their backs and their stomachs, nodding seriously as they learned about "transition" and how the woman would likely become aggressive and irrational.

Rainey wondered who she would yell at, who she would blame at that point. Who would hold her hand, who would rub her back?

"I needed you, Mom," she said.

"I know." Her mother's voice broke and Rainey heard a clatter. The coffee mug must have been set down in a hurry. "I know. It was hard for me too."

Rainey always heard the expression, "My jaw dropped," but she never really felt it until then. Her jaw did drop, her eyes did widen. It was hard for her mother? The one who chose to look away? The one who sat on the couch in their comfortable living room and listened to her husband tell her only daughter that she was a slut. That she should never look to him for support or help with the baby that would be his grandchild. His granddaughter. Her mother sat on the couch and didn't say a word and looked away. She didn't look down, her chin remained level, but she looked to the side of the room that was empty, not filled with an angry father and a bewildered and scared daughter. Scared.

It was Rainey who left. Who went through her first full-term pregnancy alone, learning as much as she could from books at the library, articles on the internet. She haunted online chatrooms filled with pregnant moms, learning from them, listening to them, making some connections, but those connections were so far away, just names in a chatroom, no one she could really count on. The morning sickness, the backaches, the swelling of her feet and ankles. She asked Dr. Johansen at every visit if this was normal, if that was fine, and every month, she was reassured. But once back alone in her apartment, she asked the questions all over again.

The fear. The flat-out fear that she didn't know what she was doing, she didn't know what to do, what was right, what was wrong, and she had no one to tell her.

And it was hard for her mother?

Rainey thought again of that day in the supermarket, Tish a constantly wailing baby, in her cart, the world closing in and nothing to do but lean over her own child and wail too. Rainey remembered feeling like she couldn't move, she couldn't breathe, and the brightly colored aisles around her just showed how much she didn't know. And then Doris was there.

Doris was there still.

"Mom," Rainey said, and she spoke through the memory of her mother coming up the stairs that night, sneaking over after her husband was asleep. She spoke through the voice on the phone who hummed her to sleep, but did so quietly, so as to not alert the man in the next room. She spoke through now, her mother in an empty kitchen, one eye undoubtedly looking out the window, watching for that certain car. One ear too. Leaving just one ear for Rainey. "Mom, I don't think I can do this. You know? I feel like…like I'm your dirty little secret from Dad. But I'm not. I'm your daughter."

And Rainey hung up the phone.

In the silence of her kitchen, there was only the sound of the refrigerator running and the television from next door. Rainey pushed away from the table, went out her front door and in through Doris'.

Doris was scrubbing her counters. The television in the living room was on, loud, so that she could hear it. She looked up as Rainey came in. "Hey, hon," she said.

Rainey smiled. "I'm okay, don't stop. I just needed a little company before I go to my doctor's appointment. You do what you're doing, I'll help myself to a cup of coffee and a muffin, and I'll listen to your story with you."

Which is exactly what she did. Sitting at the table, she drank her coffee and munched on a blueberry muffin, listening with Doris to the dramatic storyline of the soap opera. Doris finished her counters, wiped down her appliances, scoured her sink. And every time she passed by the table, she touched Rainey, patting her back, stroking her hair, once stopping altogether to lean over her, wrap her arms around her shoulders, and hug.

Just the way Rainey did things around Tish. That touch, that glance, that hug.

Like a mother. Without Doris sharing a word, Rainey felt soothed.

When she lowered her head onto the table, when she closed her eyes, she felt her entire body relax. Doris would make sure she woke up in time for her doctor's appointment. Here, under Doris' watchful eye, Rainey could sleep.

All the way to the doctor's office, Rainey tried to tell herself that this was just a normal appointment, a check-up, not a visit to her OB/GYN to check on the rape. The product of the rape. This pregnancy.

In the waiting room, Rainey glanced around at all the women in various stages of gestation. Some barely showed at all, little tiny pouches under their shirts, but others straddled their legs out to accommodate the mound that threatened to take over their entire bodies. Rainey remembered being surprised at the sheer size of pregnancy, the weight of it, as she grew close to Tish's due date. She'd thought a pregnancy would only affect her middle, swelling her out like a beach ball during inflation, growing a little larger, and then a little larger, and then popping its plug and deflating. But pregnancy overtook Rainey as it overtook all women. Her hips spread, her legs widened their stance, her entire body became focused on growing and producing. Swollen ankles, swollen fingers, swollen face… Rainey remembered wanting to snatch a needle from a nearby bootie-knitting woman and puncture her own stretched-taut skin, letting everything out that had taken up residence, everything that wasn't Rainey herself.

Across the room now, there was another knitting woman and Rainey thought about snatching the needle again. She'd heard that knitting needles were used in at-home abortions, botched attempts that left women forever unable to reproduce, and even dead. Right then, as she sat there, that didn't seem so bad. This baby, skewered, gone. Herself no longer able to reproduce. But dead?

No, not dead. There was Tish, after all.

Rainey knew that since the rape, she'd wished herself dead a million times. Silently, secretly. And she also knew that a million times, Tish kept her alive. And would keep her alive.

Sitting in that chair, Rainey also wondered for the millionth time if she'd just made her decision. If she could consider a knitting-needle abortion, if she could consider rocketing herself over railroad tracks or forcing this fetus out by sheer will onto her bathroom floor, then why not abortion? Why not just take care of it and get it over with?

Rainey didn't know for sure. But there was just something so damning about making that appointment. About setting aside a time to keep this fetus from life, to drag this fetus to death, to bring the child out of her body before the child was even a child. If she could just get the miscarriage started somehow, it wouldn't seem quite so ugly. So forced. It would almost seem as if the fetus chose it.

But Rainey knew it was her responsibility to choose. She thought again about how she always snapped her seatbelt or grabbed the sink. She thought of how her hand seemed to automatically find its way to her abdomen.

"Rainey?" the nurse called, and Rainey got to her feet. All the faces in the room lifted and she knew that many wondered how far along she was. There was no bubble under her shirt yet. And maybe there wouldn't ever be. Maybe the bubble would burst, all on its own or by the force of Rainey's own decision.

In the examining room, the nurse did the usual things. Checked Rainey's blood pressure—a little up. Heart rate—a tad racy. Temperature—a little high, but pregnant women ran lowgrade fevers, their bodies transformed into living breathing furnaces, throughout the entire nine months. Nothing to be concerned about. She told Rainey that she could remain dressed, that Dr. Johansen would be just a few minutes.

Rainey waited, seated on the edge of the table. She swung her legs, her sneakers making soft popping and pinging sounds against the metal. Beneath her, paper crinkled. Posters were everywhere on these walls, posters of smiling babies, drooling babies, sleeping babies. They all looked so innocent. There was a pregnancy progression poster too, and Rainey slid off the table to look at it.

She was now at the end of the seventh week, starting the eighth. Rainey stared at the blob that was an eight-week old fetus. It didn't even look human, with its enlarged head and curly body. It looked, in a way, like a shrimp. There were four little buds sticking out of its trunk that Rainey knew would develop into arms and legs, fingers and toes. There was an eye of sorts. And in a small, shaded area, a heart. The baby had a heart.

Rainey felt dizzy and began to sway. She was staggering back toward the examination table when Dr. Johansen came into the room and caught her. "Rainey!" she said. "You okay? What's the matter?"

Rainey lay back on the table and the room spun. "It has a heart," she said. "It has a heart. I looked at the poster."

Dr. Johansen stroked her arm. "It's okay, Rainey, it's okay," she said, and she repeated it over and over again. "Yes, it likely does have a heart by now. But not a heart like you and I have, not yet. If the heart has started beating, it's only beating in one chamber. Not enough to support life. You still can decide whatever you want. It's not too late. You still can have an abortion. You can adopt it out. You can keep it. It's still up to you. That hasn't changed yet."

Yet. Not until twelve weeks. When one of those choices was taken away.

Rainey closed her eyes and she saw the bumper stickers. *Abortion stops a beating heart.* Maybe it wasn't beating yet. Or maybe, like its father, this baby didn't have a heart. Or maybe their hearts beat in the most violent of rhythms, together, in sync, with the intent and solid will to kill. To control. To dominate.

Dr. Johansen had Rainey take deep breaths. She stood by Rainey's side, coaching her, stroking her arm, until Rainey said the room stopped spinning. Then, when Dr. Johansen pulled up Rainey's shirt and undid her jeans to check on the pregnancy, Rainey put an arm over her eyes. She didn't want to watch Dr. Johansen mold her stomach, pulling the skin taut, exposing what was happening even before it could really be seen.

"Everything seems normal, hon," Dr. Johansen said. "How have you been feeling?"

"I still get sick pretty much every day."

"And this dizziness?"

"This was the first time."

Dr. Johansen walked across the room and Rainey took her arm away to see what she was doing. She picked up a bottle of gel and the Doppler stethoscope. Rainey quickly hunched her knees up.

Hearing the baby's heartbeat, if the heartbeat was already there. Putting that stethoscope on her belly could bring that heartbeat right into this room. Rainey remembered the wildly whooshing sound of her amniotic fluid, the stampede of Tish's heartbeat. She remembered how, the first time she heard it, Tish suddenly became real. A person. A baby. There was a baby wrapped all around that beating heart.

Rainey thought of the face she pictured the night before, looking over his shoulder as he walked out of her body, bearing a tiny suitcase. The fetus was real to her. She knew that. But she just couldn't stand to hear the heartbeat right now. It wouldn't be met with the same joy as when she first heard Tish, first heard the very real evidence that someone was tucked inside of her.

"Please," Rainy said. "Please, do you think we can skip that? Or can you use a regular stethoscope? I...I don't want to hear it if it's there."

Dr. Johansen hesitated, then put the Doppler back down. "Rainey, you have to make a decision soon, okay? You have until twelve weeks, but if you decide on an abortion, it really should be taken care of by then too. All right?"

Rainey nodded, her head ripping the paper.

Dr. Johansen helped her to a sit. "Rainey, have you gone to see anybody yet? To talk to about this, about the whole thing? Not just the pregnancy, but the rape itself."

Rainey heard the woman from the Rape Crisis Center again. *Okay, what is this? Some kind of joke?* "No. I've tried, but...no."

Dr. Johansen sat on her stool, scooted herself over to a counter and used a prescription pad to write. "I want you to call this woman. She's a friend of mine, and she's a therapist, specializing in sexual abuse. Rape isn't sexual abuse by its definition, but...well, it is, isn't it. Maybe not by black and white definition, but it certainly is in its physical action. In what it does to the woman. What it's done, what he's done to you. I want you to call her. Do you have a cell?"

Rainey nodded.

"Then call her now, while I'm here with you. I want to hear you do it, see you, and make sure you make an appointment." Dr. Johansen gave her the number, then sat and placed both her hands on Rainey's knees. "It's important, Rainey. It's important you get some help."

"But…" I did this to myself, Rainey wanted to say. I did this to us. I can't tell anyone. I can't tell anyone what a slut I am, what my body did. I can't. "But they caught the guy," she finally said. "I don't need to be scared anymore." She thought of her still sleepless night, her short nap on Doris' kitchen table that morning.

Dr. Johansen shook her head. "That doesn't matter. Well, it does, but that doesn't change what happened to you. Rainey, call her. I'm not leaving until you do. And there's a whole room full of women out there, waiting for me." She smiled.

Rainey looked at the name. Linda Henning. She was at the Women's Center, located right in downtown Waukesha. She knew just where it was, and she wondered if the familiarity would make this any easier. She dialed the number and got a receptionist. "Hi," Rainey said. "My name is Rainey Milbright, and my doctor, Dr. Johansen, thinks I should come see Linda. Can I have an appointment please?" Dr. Johansen kept her hands on Rainey's knees during the whole time Rainey fielded questions. Insurance information. How soon she wanted an appointment. Address, phone number, financial situation. Rainey recited it all and then set an appointment for the next week. The end of the eighth week, heading toward the ninth.

When she said the date out loud, confirming it, Dr. Johansen quickly and easily plucked the phone away and held it to her own ear. "This is Dr. Johansen," she said. "I'd really like Rainey to come in sooner than next week. It's very important, we're in crisis mode here." She listened, then said, "Day after tomorrow? Ten o'clock?" Rainey sighed and nodded. "Fine, thank you. She'll be there then." She flipped the phone closed and handed it back to Rainey. "Okay," she said. "You did it. That's huge, Rainey. You've got to start taking care of yourself. This is something that's going to require some healing, okay? Some recovery. Just like an illness."

Rainey thought of how slowly her body moved, how she ached, how fear seemed to jump on her at the oddest times. All the tears. The word illness seemed appropriate; it was like she was sick.

"I want you to come back in for a blood pressure check in two weeks, okay? And hopefully by then, you'll have a decision. You'll be just at ten weeks, Rainey. We only have twelve."

"Okay." Two weeks. Fourteen days. Rainey tried to calculate the hours, but couldn't.

"Now, there's just one more thing you have to know." Dr. Johansen looked serious and Rainey sat back. "While you were in here, we had some protesters show up."

"Protesters?" Rainey frowned, tried to wrap her head around the word.

Dr. Johansen sighed. "Remember how I told you that sometimes, we get anti-abortion protesters here? For some reason, they chose today. We never know why, there doesn't seem to be any rhyme or reason. Just suddenly, there they are. And right on their heels, the pro-choicers are here too. They're out front, on either side of our walkway, yelling at each other. We've called and canceled all of our appointments for the rest of the day, but we have to take care of those of you who are already here. Where did you park?"

Rainey's hand automatically went for her jeans pocket and her car keys. "In the lot across the street."

Dr. Johansen held out her hand and helped Rainey slide off the table. "We'll have you leave by the alley door. The last we looked, no one ventured back there yet. We'll check again before we send you out. From the door, turn right, walk down the alley, and you'll come out on another street. Cross it, then turn right again, come to the street that runs in front of our building, cross that, then walk slowly to the parking lot. It will look like you're coming from another direction, not from the clinic. They shouldn't even notice you. We'll be sending others in different directions, so there won't be a bunch of you all at once. It will look casual."

Rainey suddenly felt like she was part of a reconnaissance mission or an underground railroad. She had to escape undetected. "Okay, I'll try. But what if they do see me?"

Dr. Johansen sighed and shrugged. "Then you'd likely end up in a shouting match. Everyone yelling around you. You don't look pregnant, Rainey, so if they start up, just tell them you were here for your annual exam. They'll go back to shouting at each other."

Rainey watched her leave, then she put on her shoes, checked her jeans, adjusted her shirt. When she opened the door, the nurse was waiting for her. She smiled and wrapped her arm through Rainey's elbow. "Ready? It'll be okay, don't worry."

They walked together down the hall, toward the waiting room. Rainey could see into it, and she saw that the women still there had all moved away from the front windows. They stood by the receptionist desk and Rainey could see over their heads to the outside. She saw waving signs and posters. There were muffled shouts.

She wondered about the soon-to-be mothers she saw earlier in the waiting room. The ones about to burst. Did they know they were in a clinic where abortions were performed? Were they horrified? Was anyone there that day to have an abortion? Did they change their minds?

The nurse and Rainey turned left, and at the end of another long hallway, there was a steel brown door. The nurse pulled Rainey to a stop, and then she moved ahead and slowly poked her head outside. She seemed to look all ways. "It's clear, Rainey. Call us when you get home and set up your next appointment, okay? The receptionist is watching out the front windows. If she sees anyone disturbing you, she'll send someone to help."

Rainey nodded and scurried out. She could hear the shouts flying over the clinic's rooftop. The alley was deserted and Rainey did exactly as she was told, as if she was following a treasure map. When she crossed the street in front of the clinic, she began to stroll toward her car, as if she only just happened to be there. Nobody paid a bit of attention to her as she unlocked her door, slid inside, and locked up again.

Before starting the engine, she studied the protesters. Men and women lined both sides of the sidewalk. The posters on the right showed photographs of what the pro-lifers claimed were aborted fetuses. Rainey knew, from poring over books and websites while she was pregnant with Tish, and from the poster she just examined in Dr. Johansen's office, that what was inside her didn't look anything like what was depicted out here. There weren't arms and legs yet, just buds. There were no fingers and toes, not even hands and feet. There wasn't a face, there wasn't a neck to swivel, there wasn't a little round tummy.

But there was a beating heart. Or at least, a heart beating in one chamber.

Not enough to support life, Dr. Johansen said.

For all the photos, there wasn't a single one of a woman. And while there were bruises, they all belonged to the aborted fetus. There weren't any photos of the discolored skin of the woman who carried it.

On the pro-choice side, there weren't photos at all, but there were a lot of words. Rainey searched through them, and while she agreed with most of what they had to say, she noticed they were all about the woman. About all women. But there wasn't really anything there about the embryo. The fetus.

The baby.

Not a single word.

But Rainey knew there was a beating heart. A heart that started with just one living chamber, but if left alone, it would grow to thunder with all four.

She knew this for sure. Even without hearing it. She heard it with Tish. And she knew, if she'd allowed Dr. Johansen to lower the Doppler stethoscope onto her skin, she might have heard it with this one too.

Through her skin that was still faintly colored in sickly yellow. With traces of purple.

Rainey knew there were deeper bruises too. And she knew there was so much more to all of this than a newly beating heart. There was her own heart. There was Tish's.

Quickly, Rainey started the car and pulled out of the parking lot, away from the clinic and its rows of shouters and photos and words. None of which told the whole story. The real story.

Two weeks until the ten-week point. Then two more to twelve weeks. It seemed impossibly fast. And it also seemed like forever. Rainey wondered how many hours, how many seconds, how many heartbeats there were until then.

At three that morning, Rainey climbed out of bed and padded down the hall to Tish's room. Even though fall was now well underway, with its chilly nights, Tish still insisted on wearing her favorite summer nightgown to bed. A pink babydoll, covered with white sheep, and on the back, a black one that had a maniacal grin. One of Doris' Goodwill treasures. Tish's covers were completely kicked off, her nightgown, short to begin with, was yanked above her waist, and her bare bottom shone pink in the moonlight. When Rainey was potty-training Tish, the little girl insisted on sleeping without undies, claiming that if she didn't feel diapers, she wouldn't go to the bathroom in her bed. It made wonderful sense and Rainey bought into the theory and ever since then, Tish had dry nights. Rainey wondered how long it would be until Tish would abandon her nightgowns too, sleeping nude instead. Rainey was fifteen when she closed her door and shucked her nightclothes. She started wearing them again at twenty, when Tish was born. A few nights of feeding a hungry baby, only to end up with spit-up smearing her cleavage and rolling down into her crotch, convinced Rainey of the grown-up practicality of pajamas.

Now, though, she tugged Tish's nightshirt down, covered her with her sheet and blanket, made sure Teddy was close by, then returned to her room. Turning on the overhead, she stood in front of her full-length mirror, and stripped. Cover one, she thought. Expose the other.

Rainey couldn't decide if there was any sign of the pregnancy yet or not. She thought her tummy might be just the least bit pouchy. She'd read that subsequent pregnancies tended to show sooner than the first. She didn't show with Tish until the beginning of her fifth month.

Have it. Not have it. Have it. Give it up. Have it. Not have it. Have it. Give it up. Tish's rhyme: Eenie, meenie, miney, moe.

Rainey didn't look obviously pregnant. Yet she knew there was something there. And it was his. Her rapist's. She thought again of his picture on the table at the police station. His voice in her ear, then in that room, and the way it immediately threw her back to the night by the river. As if that sound would be with her forever.

"C'mon, baby. Sweet Jesus, girl, you know you want it."

And she thought of that website, the one with all the numbers, and the odds that her rapist would end up in prison for more than a little while. The small odds. And the multitude of websites that said that her body might or might not be an accessory to the crime. That while her rapist was definitely a criminal, she might be a criminal too.

Her breasts ached. The tiniest twinge of nausea rolled through her stomach. The pregnancy might not show yet, but the rape was there. Causing changes. Disturbances. Rainey felt the stitch in that certain spot on her abdomen. The digging in of little fingers. But then she thought of the poster she saw just that morning. The four little buds…no fingers yet, no toes. But there was digging going on anyway.

Turning off the light, she climbed back into bed, ignoring the nightshirt that waited for her under her pillow. While she kept Tish covered up, she kept her own covers down, exposing her skin to the air and the silvered darkness. The moon slid in, lighting her bed like a white-sanded island in the night ocean. And Rainey decided she had to know. She had to. She had to find her body's betrayal.

Closing her eyes, she pictured that night again. Only this time, Tish wasn't there. Rainey dressed herself as she remembered, the flirty skirt, the white blouse unbuttoned enough to show the lacy cami. She walked through the dark park, the river dancing on her left. There was the faint sound of crickets and a few night birds. The moon glowed on the water and she thought of night-swimming, of the night Tish was conceived.

Letting her hand drift down, Rainey flutter-touched her breasts, flattened her fingers over her stomach, then nestled just her fingertips into her pubic hair. Keeping her eyes closed, she pictured that night further.

He stepped out from the bushes and she saw him. Without Tish there, her first inclination was to run. He was frightening, the way he loomed, his size and shadow growing impossibly large, almost blotting out the moon. But when she turned, he grabbed her arm, thrust her through the bushes, pushed her to her knees.

She pictured it all. Every movement. She pictured it and poised her fingers at the edge of her sex and she saw it all again. She was amazed at how clear and focused the night appeared behind her eyelids. She saw it all in black and white, drenched in the moon and the darkness. And she felt every blow again, felt herself slip her mouth over him, taste him, roll onto her hands and knees, open her legs to him. In her bedroom now, her hand waited, fingers pointed, splayed, ready to pounce on any pleasure that presented itself, that suffused her with heat and need.

But there wasn't any. There was no pleasure at all. Behind Rainey's eyes, an impossible pressure built and in her chest as well. One by one, Rainey's fingers curled into themselves, balled, made a fist that rolled up and sat hard on her stomach. Her knuckles bearing in. Just at that one particular spot. Just beneath it.

When her rapist left, when he stepped out of the bushes and walked out of her mind, Rainey curled her entire body into a tight fist. And she cried. A deep cry, that left her racked and she felt waves of pain going through her body as the memory left its mark again. All of its marks, inside and out. She cried until she retched. And then she felt a hand on her shoulder.

Whipping her body straight, Rainey rolled over and found Tish, her eyes wide, her mouth round. "Oh, baby," Rainey said. "It's okay, Mama's okay."

Tish stepped backwards, her eyes zooming around the room, taking in the window, the open blinds, the moon, and then raking down Rainey's entire body. All elbows, she flung her own little lamb nightgown over her head and crawled into bed with her mother. Startled, Rainey cradled her, her arms tight around Tish's shoulders, cocooning her, and Tish's legs came up and wrapped around Rainey's waist. Skin to skin, they plastered together, and Rainey held her tight and didn't let go until Tish's arms and legs fell loose. Rainey settled her on a pillow, then pulled the covers up over them both.

Watching the shadows play over her daughter's face, Rainey wondered why her body didn't react at the memory. Why it did react that night. If she did want it, did want to be raped and manhandled, subconsciously or consciously, wouldn't the memory flare that desire in her?

And yet her body did respond, didn't it. The pressure in her eyes and her chest, her entire body contorting, her hand a fist over that one spot, every part of her curling over the core of her pain.

All those nights before the rape, nights when Rainey pleasured herself in the moonlight, she'd never fantasized about rape. Never fantasized about being under any man's total and violent control. She imagined soft touches, a warm, wet and knowledgeable mouth, deep and steady strokes while her body pressed against the man in her mind, and they kissed and kissed and kissed.

Now, her body went cold and rigid with the memory of that night. Even with the fantasy, the recreation of that night. Of being hurt, crushed, handled like meat. She remembered thinking of herself as a steak. A T-bone.

So why did it happen then? Because she remembered her body's sin, knew the response that made her mind and skin recoil in shame. She knew it. She didn't imagine that moment, she wouldn't know how to. She remembered the awful crash through her body, the way she willed the orgasm not to happen, but it did anyway. It overtook her. She could almost handle the rape, she thought, almost heal from it, maybe even deal with the pregnancy, if only the orgasm hadn't occurred.

Okay, what is this? Some kind of joke?
Just who do you think you are?
Slut.

Rainey reached under her pillow and drew out her nightshirt. She looked on the floor, where Tish had thrown hers, in that sudden and surprising and odd show of solidarity. Rainey wanted to put on her nightshirt, and then carefully ease Tish into hers, she wanted to provide one more layer of safety, of protection, between their skin and the world. But she didn't want to wake her little girl up.

On the bedside table, Rainey's cell phone buzzed. She checked the screen and saw it was her mother. Who else would it be at this hour? On a secret and hidden cell phone. Her mother, sneaking around the house, finding a dark corner, a place where she could covertly call her daughter, while her husband slept heavy in another room.

As if calling her daughter was a sin in itself. Something that had to be hidden from the world. Just as Rainey wanted, right there, to hide herself and Tish from the world.

How different was it, really? How different was it to have a mother who felt she had to hide her phone calls to her daughter, than it was to have a father who wouldn't talk at all?

Mothers shouldn't be ashamed to talk to their daughters. They shouldn't have to hold their daughters like a secret.

Eventually, the phone stopped buzzing. Rainey folded both of the nightshirts and left them on her dresser. Then she climbed back into bed, pulling the covers up, and reached beneath to hold Tish's hand. Tish's fingers wrapped automatically around her own, as they had since Tish was a baby, since that first moment when a blood-covered Tish landed firmly on Rainey's chest, squalling even then. Trying to talk, to make a noise. Tish was born verbose. Now, she breathed in sharply, then exhaled, letting out a hum as soft and sweet as a new bird's pinfeather. Rainey listened, drew it in to herself, then continued to hold Tish's hand as she slid into sleep too. Into a safe darkness, no water, no moon.

Her other hand draped over her abdomen.

Rainey went in to the school at lunch time. Tish's teacher called and asked for a meeting, to update Rainey on Tish's progress. The guidance counselor would be there, the speech therapist, and probably the principal too. Rainey hated these meetings, suddenly common in her life. While their purpose was reassurance, to let Rainey know that Tish was getting better, it felt instead as if the meetings only pointed out how much Tish regressed in such a short time. These meetings used to be unheard of, unnecessary.

Rainey heard voices as she approached the all-purpose room and she was relieved to hear their light tone and the quiet laughs. The first meeting she came to was like standing at the foot of a deathbed. Everyone was somber and no one seemed to be able to look directly at her. Between the end of that meeting and the beginning of the next, Mrs. Whitstone and the staff seemed to realize that Rainey only wanted to talk about her daughter, not about her own ordeal and her own recovery, and so the mood lightened.

Mrs. Whitstone looked up first when Rainey walked in. "Hello, Rainey!" she said. Crisis put them all on a first-name basis, though Rainey still had trouble calling Mrs. Whitstone Lynn. She was a teacher, after all. "I just saw Tish on the playground. She was with her group of friends and they were trying to jump rope. It looked like she was laughing, but I was too far away to hear if she made any sound."

The guidance counselor leaned forward. "Tish's friends have just been admirable through all of this, haven't they? They don't pull on Tish at all, they don't insist that she speak. She's found a comfort zone with them. I was talking with one of the little girls the other day, she pulled me aside in the hallway and she told me that Tish shrieked, just once, during a game of tag."

Rainey remembered when she used to cringe whenever Tish and her friends shrieked. That high-pitched shrill siren just made her spine vibrate and her teeth clench. Now, it was the sign of good and positive progress. Rainey wished so much that they were discussing how Tish was overcoming her difficulty with math, or that the letters of the alphabet that once appeared backwards on Tish's paper were now forwards. Being excited over a shriek…it was like Tish was barely able to function, like she was retarded. Rainey forced tears back down. "What did she do after she shrieked? Did her friend say?"

The counselor nodded. "The usual. Smacked her hand over her mouth and looked around like she expected a monster to come crawling out of the woodwork."

Or the bushes, Rainey thought. She thought of the night before, when Tish found her crying. The little girl's eyes snapped around the room like she was trying to trap an animal, or escape from one.

But the animal was in a cage. At least for now, and right at this moment, in this room, Rainey didn't want to think about how long he might be there. But how to convince Tish of that? How to convince herself?

"I should tell you," she said to the group, "the rapist was caught. He raped three other women after —" Rainey choked at identifying herself. Even though it was obvious. She skipped over the word "me." "They caught him and I identified him, and he's in jail, waiting for trial."

For a moment, no one spoke. They all looked blank, like they were wondering why Rainey was telling them this.

Rainey sighed. "I told Tish. I told her the bad man was caught. I'm hoping it will bring her voice back."

The faces brightened. As a group, they all exclaimed and offered their hope as well.

Then the speech therapist took her turn. "I really think she's doing better, Rainey. Her therapist seems to be doing wonders. Tish is beginning to hum more and more again, it's so good to hear her little voice when she's thinking. A few times, she started to say something to me, then stopped, but she almost did. She's on the verge. I was thinking about teaching her sign language, but I changed my mind. I think if we just keep going this way, maybe even finding ways of slipping in a little frustration for her, she'll talk again. Especially now that she knows the bad man isn't out there anymore."

"Frustration?" Rainey hated the thought of that. After what Tish had been through, she wanted it to all be easy for her daughter. "What do you mean?"

"Well, things like offering her two choices of something, but doing it verbally instead of physically so she can't point. Like at lunch, the monitor could say, 'Chocolate or white milk, Tish?' but not hold up the cartons, so Tish would have to find a way to say it." Rainey's face must have shown her discomfort because the speech therapist quickly added, "Oh, I don't mean a lot of frustration, just a few things here and there."

"What does her therapist say, Rainey?" Mrs. Whitstone asked.

Rainey looked at the table. These meetings always made it so clear to her how surreal this all was. Her four-year old had a therapist. There was an entire team of teachers and specialty staff discussing every sound Tish made, or didn't make. Suddenly, her little girl was a special case, a head case, a behavior issue, all those awful terms that Rainey always heard describing other people's children. Tish was never like this before; Rainey knew that this was not Tish at all. Her daughter spoke; she sang and she danced and she even talked in her sleep. Silence just wasn't a part of who she was, until now.

All because of Rainey herself. Tish's mother. Tish was barraged with all this, changed like this, because of what Rainey did. Because Rainey was in just too much of a hurry to wait for a bus.

And despite what the teachers said and what Nanci said, with her upbeat reports after every session with Tish, despite the rapist being behind bars, despite a sudden shriek while playing tag or a sighed tender note in Tish's sleep, Rainey knew this could be a forever thing. She might not ever get back that chatterbox Tish.

Mrs. Whitstone touched her hand, then rested her fingers on Rainey's arm. "Are you okay, Rainey?" she asked.

Rainey appreciated the gesture, the warmth of her skin, and she nodded. "Nanci says she's doing pretty well, though Tish isn't talking there yet either. Nanci feels that the first thing to do is try to figure out exactly what Tish saw, so we can help her to deal with it." The rape, Rainey thought. My four-year old saw a rape. "She thinks that the primary reason for Tish's silence is trauma, but also that she simply doesn't have the words to say what she experienced, because at her age, she doesn't know what it was. Only that it was…horrible.

But Nanci said that Tish has gravitated toward playing with dolls. And she's…well, she's showing some violence. Nanci thinks that this probably means that Tish saw most of it. The…attack. "

The room chilled. Rainey wondered what they pictured. If they all brought their own individual definitions to rape, of what it meant, what it would feel like, what they would do. Rainey was sure that they couldn't even begin to imagine what really happened. It was hard enough to think of the brutality of rape. Hard enough to think of a four-year old observing it. And harder still to think of a resulting pregnancy, which nobody but a handful of people knew about at this point. Hard, horrifying, but still conceivable. Possible. But orgasm?

Okay, what is this? Some kind of joke?

Slut.

Mrs. Whitstone squeezed her arm. "Well, I think she's really making good progress. We've got the whole school year to work through this and I'm hoping by the time she's ready to transition to 5-K, to kindergarten, this will all be a bad memory. I agree with the idea of frustrating her a little bit. Not too much, but enough to maybe make her start speaking by accident. And then more accidents and more accidents. And then she'll be back to being a constant chatterbox and we'll all be wishing she'd be quiet again!"

Mrs. Whitstone and the staff murmured laughter. Rainey, who couldn't imagine ever wanting her child to be so silent again, went still. She so needed to hear her daughter's voice spilling out in waves, spouting words and sentences and paragraphs and endless recitations of her day. Nonsense rhymes and sing-songs that made Tish giggle in mid-word and even shriek. That awful, wonderful spine-shattering shriek. Whispered goodnights. Boisterous good mornings.

When the laughter stopped, the meeting seemed to be over. Rainey ducked quickly out. The voices she left behind remained light and friendly.

Rainey walked by the playground on her way to her car. Stopping under the shade of a tree, she looked for a flash of pink and soon found it, with a group of towheaded little girls, all squirming and wiggling around a jump rope. They had it flattened on the ground and together, holding hands, they jumped left to right over it. In the middle was Tish, both her hands held tightly by friends, and her brown corkscrews bounced over her shoulders. Her head swiveled as she glanced from friend to friend and she just looked so happy. Anybody looking at her would think she was beautiful and very, very normal, just another four-year old little girl figuring out the rhythms and intricacies of jumping rope. Not a little girl who witnessed something she shouldn't even know about for years and years yet. A little girl who didn't even know about the possibilities of sex or the gentle side of it. She only saw the violence. And she saw it happening to her mother.

Nanci said that Tish had no words to describe what she saw. No words at all, and why should she? Rainey didn't know how to give these words to her. How do you explain a rape to a four-year old? How do you make it understandable when you can't understand it yourself? Rainey didn't even know yet how to explain sex to Tish, the birds and the bees, the way Tish came to be born. But she hadn't worried about it; it wasn't time yet, for years, maybe. But now, Tish had to know more. She had to know beyond courtship, conception, childbirth. And Rainey couldn't even use the typical definition of rape. It wouldn't work to say to Tish, "It's a crime of violence, not sex." Rainey never had a clue what that was supposed to mean. How did making it violent somehow make it different? How did that clear it of sex? Rainey knew full well that she experienced true and utter violence that night. But she also knew that the brandished weapon, the club, the gun, was sex.

Rainey looked at her daughter on the school's playground and relished her happiness. That sight, of Tish smiling and jumping and holding hands with her girlfriends, made Rainey feel better than anything the teacher and the speech therapist and the counselor said. And Nanci too. There wasn't any sign of violence in her daughter right then. No trauma, no fear. Just a gloriously beautiful and happy little girl.

Rainey slipped away for home before Tish could see her. After dropping off her purse, she walked over to Doris' side of the duplex, in search of a cup of coffee and company, something Doris always had plenty of. Rainey didn't even knock. The day was warm and the screen door stood open. Rainey knew that Doris likely heard her car pull up and she was probably already preparing the coffee.

Doris turned from the sink with a carafe full of water as Rainey came in. "Hey, hon. How're you? Coffee will be ready in a minute."

"Thanks, Doris." Rainey sank into the chair and watched as Doris poured the water into the coffee maker, then switched it on, the red light glowing cheerily into the fall afternoon. Fall was always Rainey's favorite season. It was so much more than the cooler temperatures and the landscape swiped with deep oranges and reds and yellows. It was a time to sit on the front porch, cupping her hands around a mug of coffee, or even hot chocolate laced with marshmallows, and she could wear her favorite sweater and watch the brilliant sunsets blend in with the landscape until the sky and the ground seemed all of a piece. Rainey always felt all of a piece in the fall. Peaceful. Held together. Ready to curl up in her chair with Tish, wrapping an afghan knitted by Doris around the both of them, and read book after book after book.

Why did the rape have to occur in fall? Why did this season have to become a time of violence and anger and fear? But then again, all of the seasons were threatened now. Rainey wasn't sure if she'd ever feel all of a piece again. Not sealed in winter's white and ice or spring's verdancy. She wasn't sure she would even feel safe and mellow in the surprise heat of a Wisconsin summer.

"So how did the meeting go?" Doris sat down as the coffee pot began its familiar groan and grind. She placed a plate of oatmeal raisin cookies between them. Rainey knew that they were baked just for this moment, for when Rainey came home from yet another meeting about her daughter, another reminder of all that changed, another reminder that right now, the world seemed to be only about loss and recovery and fear and healing, and how difficult this all could be. And about decisions as well. Difficult decisions.

More than difficult. Unthinkable. Decisions that no one should ever have to make. Just as no four-year old girl should know what Tish knew, Rainey felt that no woman her age should ever have to look in a mirror or look down into herself and make a decision like this.

No woman at all. Of any age.

"It was pretty typical," Rainey said, thinking again how the word typical meant something it never used to be. Rainey picked up a cookie and broke it in half, sending a sprinkle of crumbs to the table. "The teachers want to add a little frustration to Tish's day, things like offering her choices where she can't point, and make her come up with a way to talk. Force her, I guess. Make silence not an option anymore."

Doris nodded slowly as she lifted a cookie for herself. "You know, that makes sense, I think. Offer her the chance to have what she wants, but only if she talks. I can do some of that here."

Rainey felt her mouth turn down. "I guess, but not too much, Doris. I don't want her to be unhappy."

"Oh, of course not." Doris got up and poured their coffee. "But…you know, if Tish becomes happy this way, with getting what she wants even when she doesn't speak, then she might not ever speak again. A little unhappiness might not be a bad thing, in the long run."

A little unhappiness. Rainey wished for a little unhappiness. A little would feel so much better than this impossible load of concrete permanently settled on her shoulders. She warmed her hands around the mug.

Doris sat down again and leaned forward. "Oh, I know, Rainey, I do. She's already had to face so much. But I just can't imagine never hearing that voice again."

"Neither can I."

They sat quietly together. It was one of Rainey's favorite things about Doris. She didn't need noise, she didn't need chatter. She seemed to realize that sometimes the presence of another body was all that was necessary to take away the chill of loneliness. They remained quiet until Rainey finished two mugs of coffee and polished off six cookies. Then she leaned back in her chair, lacing her hands together over her full tummy.

Doris glanced at Rainey's entwined fingers. "So are you any closer to a decision, hon?"

Rainey shrugged. "Some days, I think so. Other days, not so much. And sometimes it can change minute by minute." She glanced at the clock, as if it was ticking off weeks instead of hours. The women in Rainey's office discussed babies over their lunches, when to have them, how long to wait. How often had Rainey heard these women click their tongues against their teeth in imitation of running clocks, biological clocks stealing away their fertile years? But the clock that ticked for Rainey now, clicked constantly in her mind and just below the surface of her skin, felt more like a time bomb. "I know I've got to decide soon. Dr. Johansen wants to recheck my blood pressure in a couple weeks, and she says I have to tell her then."

"Two weeks. That's all right, there's still time. You need to be sure. You need to be so sure, Rainey." Reaching over, Doris patted Rainey's hands, then let her own hands rest, just for a moment, on top of Rainey's, on top of her tummy. On top of what lay below. Their eyes met and Rainey looked deep, wanting to find an answer. But all she saw was herself, reflected in the blue of Doris' gaze. Only herself.

Doris squeezed, then collected their cups and plates.

Rainey pushed together a pile of crumbs, then swept them into her open palm. She walked them over to the trash can and tossed them in, brushing her hands off. Standing there for just a moment, looking at the closed trash can lid, she felt her shoulders roll forward, her head lower, her knees weaken. Just for a moment. Just as quickly, she caught a movement from Doris out of the corner of her eye, arms swinging out, and immediately, Rainey turned into Doris and allowed the older woman to hug her for what seemed like an impossibly long period of time. But a necessary one. There was strength there, and a comfort that Rainey wished would continue to flow over her, even after she stepped away. "Well," she said, looking again at the clock. "I should probably get ready to go pick Tish up from school."

"Would you like me to do it? You could go lay down for a bit. You haven't been sleeping, have you?"

Rainey thought of the nights spent in front of her mirror or lying in bed, staring at the ceiling. She thought of the wash of the moon. She shook her head.

Doris pushed her toward the front door. "You go back home. Curl up on the couch, tuck yourself up with the afghan. I'll get Tish and she and I will have some ice cream and a run to Goodwill. When we get back, you'll be ready for her."

It was as if exhaustion was just waiting for permission to appear. It landslided over Rainey, making her skin feel heavy, pulled toward the ground. "I'll take you up on that," she said, then squeezed Doris' hand. "Thank you. You're wonderful."

"And so are you."

Wonderful. The weight of that word's falseness only added to the exhaustion. By the time Rainey got to the couch, her eyes were already closed. There wasn't even time to pull the afghan from the back of the couch before she was asleep.

CHAPTER FOURTEEN

Doris

Doris was standing at the edge of the playground when the schoolbell rang and children charged through the doors. Tish flew out, then stopped and looked around, her glance going right over Doris. Doris knew Tish was looking for her mother. Every morning before Tish left for school, every morning since Rainey took time off from work, Doris and Rainey drilled her on who would be picking her up that day. As Tish scanned the crowd again, her mouth opened and elongated in a silent scream. Quickly, Doris stepped forward. "Tish! Tish! I'm right here!"

Tish saw her and ran, not stopping until she plowed into Doris' body. The impact nearly knocked Doris over, and then her body vibrated with the shudders of Tish's sudden tears.

"It's okay. Your mama's taking a nap, so I came to get you instead. I thought you might want some ice cream. And then maybe a trip to the Goodwill."

The child's grip loosened and she wiped her face on Doris' shirt. Looking up, she nodded. But her eyebrows remained upraised and she tugged on Doris' sleeve.

"Your mama's fine. She's not sick or anything, just tired. I told her to take a break and that I would pick you up. Besides, can you keep a secret?" She leaned down after Tish's nod and she whispered into the little girl's ear. "I just wanted you for myself. I just wanted to have some fun with you."

Tish smiled and the last remnant of terror fell away from her face. She skipped alongside Doris as they went to the car.

"Did you have a good day?"

Tish nodded.

"What did you do?"

There was no answer. Doris remembered when a question like that would catapult a twenty-minute long nonstop sentence of everything that happened, from pushes and shoves to bathroom breaks to gross accidents in the lunch room. Now, Tish just moved alongside her, her light feet telling Doris that the day was just fine, full of fun things. In the last few weeks, Doris had to become an expert in body language. Rainey mentioned this too, and sometimes, in the evenings, she and Doris compared notes, trying to figure out if they were reading Tish correctly. Rainey especially worried that she would miss something important; Doris secretly held the hope that something important would happen, and Tish's need and frustration would fling her voice from its hiding spot. Or its prison. Doris felt that Tish's tongue had been taken hostage. The rapist held her tongue. Maybe now that he was in prison too, he would give it back. No, not give it back; it wasn't his to give. Tish would snatch it back.

Even though it was closer to the school, Doris navigated away from the custard stand where Rainey and Tish went the night of the rape. Doris couldn't imagine ever going there again. Instead, she drove them to another favorite place, an ice cream shop right in downtown Waukesha. The place had the feel of the sweet shops Doris remembered from her own childhood, complete with chairs with heart-shaped backs and shiny white metal tables. In warmer weather, like today, Doris and Tish ate their ice cream on the scrolled bench just outside, so they could watch the cars and the people go by.

As they pushed open the glass double doors, Doris thought about what the teachers said about adding just a bit of frustration to Tish's day. Doris and Tish walked to the big freezer and Tish pressed her face against the cold glass. Doris knew that Tish would look at all of the flavors and then would inevitably choose her favorite, blue moon. To Doris, blue moon ice cream tasted like toothpaste, but to Tish, it was the greatest delicacy in the world. Waiting until Tish made her tour of the entire freezer, Doris grasped her shoulders and turned her away. "So what flavor would you like, Tish?"

Tish began to twist, to point toward the glass, but Doris held her firmly. "What flavor would you like? Tell me."

Tish struggled more, digging her feet into the linoleum, contorting her body under Doris' hands. Doris bore down harder, planting Tish in her spot. "No, Tish, stop it. Don't look at the ice cream. Just look at me and tell me. What flavor ice cream do you want? You do want ice cream, right? All you have to do is tell me."

And just like that, Tish sagged. Doris suddenly found her hands empty as Tish drooped to the floor, crawled behind Doris, and then ran out of the door. She didn't head for the street, Doris was relieved to see, but sat down on the scrolled bench.

Sighing, Doris went up to the counter where the clerk looked justifiably puzzled. She ordered a double scoop of the blue moon for Tish and a double scoop of the mocha chip for herself. She asked for both of them to be put into a dish, with whipped cream on top, and a cherry complete with a stem just for Tish. Smiling apologetically at the clerk, Doris left a good-sized tip in the Styrofoam cup, and went outside. Tish was still there, her elbows resting on her knees, swinging her legs as she studied the sidewalk. Doris sat next to her and handed her the ice cream. Tish held it, but didn't make a move toward the spoon.

"Go ahead and eat, hon," Doris said. "I'm sorry. It's just that I want so much to hear you talk again. I don't understand why you won't. I know you can do it. I've heard you talk for years. It makes me so sad not to be able to talk to you anymore."

Tish heaved a sigh so deep, it made the day seem darker. Then she slowly opened her knees and loosened her fingers and the bowl of ice cream fell to the sidewalk. Amazingly, it landed right side up, which Tish mustn't have planned, because she frowned and started to reach for it with her pointed foot.

"Oh, stop it." Doris leaned down and picked up the bowl. "Eat your ice cream and quit being silly. You know you want it. We're going to have a good time together, and that's that. We just have to figure out all new ways, I guess."

Doris saw from the way that Tish held her ice cream that she considered letting it fall again. But when she glanced up, Doris smiled at her, a smile filled with melting mocha chip ice cream, and Tish barked a laugh. Slapping a hand over her mouth, she looked quickly around, then back down at her dish. Within seconds, she was eating blue ice cream and bouncing on the seat next to Doris, as if nothing had happened.

Doris wished Tish could be that way about all of it. Just talk again, go back to bouncing her days away, as if nothing had happened. She wished Rainey could do that too.

But Doris knew everything had changed. There was no going back. And things might change still more, depending on Rainey's decision.

At Goodwill, Tish was still small enough to want to ride in the cart. She pointed at things and smiled, even opening her mouth in a laugh. Doris thought about how Goodwill trips used to be filled with Tish's chattering commentary on every person and every item, syncopated with, "Can I have that?" and "Please, please, please?" and accompanied by Doris' own, "Uh-huh, uh-huh, uh-huh." Now, there was a flurry of fingers and swinging legs, quick movement instead of noise, and Doris' vocal response felt lonely. Tish pointed to a Barbie doll, an odd thing all in purple, purple skin and purple hair and purple eyes, and dressed in netting, and when Doris handed it to her, Tish settled in to play. There was the smallest of hums then, quiet and easily rolled over by the cart wheels, but Doris heard it and relaxed. Remembering Tish's hand slapped over her mouth in front of the ice cream store, Doris decided not to comment on the hum. Instead, she just listened.

Tish was in there somewhere. Somewhere in the middle of all that silence. But oh, so quiet. Or maybe, with the hum and the laugh, maybe she was closer to the surface than before.

Walking through the aisles, Doris found some nice sweaters for Tish to wear in the coming winter, and a neat suede backpack purse for Rainey. There were even some new coasters for herself, ceramic, with pictures of coffee cups and wine glasses on them. Doris nestled them carefully into the sweaters so they wouldn't break as Doris and Tish completed their circuit of the store.

By the stuffed animal bin, Tish set aside her purple doll and looked expectantly at Doris. Doris rolled up her sleeves and dug in. Typical animals were tossed aside…teddy bears with one eye, kittens and puppies, ragdolls and cartoon characters. Doris saw several Winnie the Poohs and Eeyores and she carefully excavated these into deeper ground; Tish had an affinity for the Pooh characters and her room was well overstocked. From a corner of the bin, Doris suddenly unearthed a bright yellow tentacle, and she dug further. It grew longer and longer and added more arms and suddenly, Doris held the round body of a tie-dyed splashy orange and yellow octopus. She held it up for Tish to see and Tish beamed, holding out her arms. It filled her entire lap, the eight legs rolling over the cart edges to the floor. It was huge, almost life-size, but the sunshine colors gave it the feel of hilarity. It was as if a sunset bled onto the octopus, giving it a forever complexion of orange and yellow and red, and even a few snippets of white and blue. The front yard was about to take on a seascape feel. A seascape at sunset.

As Doris pushed the cart toward the check-out, Tish squeezed the octopus and rocked back and forth. People who saw her smiled and Doris smiled too. It was so easy to make Tish happy; all it took was a sunset octopus and a purple Barbie. If only these things would make her talk. If only happiness would make her talk. Why wasn't happiness making Tish crow with unabashed delight?

They checked out and walked to the car together, Tish clutching the purple doll in one hand and dragging the octopus with the other. Doris offered to carry it, to keep its legs clean, but Tish refused. In the car, buckled into her booster seat, she pointed at the opposite seatbelt until Doris buckled in the octopus too. Tish held one of its tentacles all the way home and Doris thought she might have heard a brief murmur of conversation, of comfort offered to the octopus that it was going to a safe place. Much safer than buried in a bin at the Goodwill.

When they arrived at home, Tish shot right to the front yard. Doris put away her new coasters first, feeling a sense of satisfaction as she threw away the old ones. Then she carried the sweaters and the purse out to the porch, intending to bring them over to Rainey, but Rainey was already there, seated on a step, watching Tish dance around the yard, the octopus' legs tangled with her own.

Doris sat down next to Rainey and placed the gifts on her lap. They examined the sweaters together and exclaimed over the bright colors, the cleverness of the little cat decorating one, the sweetness of a rainbow ending in a heart on the other. Rainey liked the purse too, and when she explored the pockets, she found a folded dollar bill, an added bonus. Then they watched Tish play. Doris told her about the ice cream disaster. Rainey hugged a sweater.

"That's what I was afraid of," Rainey said. "That frustrating her in this way would just make her sad, or angry, rather than encouraging her to talk. Doris, I don't think I can do that to her." Rainey hugged the sweater again. "I've already done too much," she whispered.

Doris wasn't sure if she was meant to hear, and she wondered what Rainey meant by that, but decided not to question her. Tish was too close. Maybe, she thought, I'll ask her later tonight. Instead of coffee, I'll bring hot chocolate.

Then Tish came up to them and held the octopus out to Doris. Doris lifted it onto her lap and Tish settled down on the step, tucking herself between the two women. "You want your poem?" Doris said.

Tish nodded.

And Doris thought. She had a poem already, that wasn't what she thought about. Instead, she remembered how it felt, putting her arms on Tish's shoulders, holding her in place, trying to get her to choose with her voice. She thought of Rainey's last words, about how she didn't want to make Tish more sad or more angry. Frustrate her, the teachers said. But what if the frustration was really small? Only a word? A tiny sound?

"Tish, honey, will you do something for me? Will you do it just for me?" Doris waited until Tish looked up, and then she decided to dive a little deeper. "Will you do it for me because I bought you the pretty sweaters, the purple doll, this octopus? Will you do it for me because you love me and you want to thank me?"

A question mark curled in the wrinkle between Tish's eyes as she frowned. But then she nodded. Rainey looked puzzled too.

"When I tell you this poem, I want you to let me know if you liked it. And I don't want you to smile or nod or shake your head. I want you to say yes or no. With your voice." Yes or no. Such small words. Much smaller than saying, "I want blue moon, please."

Rainey gasped and Tish slapped her hand over her mouth, her eyes instantly filling with tears.

Doris felt her own self tremble and she wondered if she should have waited, just a day or two, to put space between this request and the blue moon ice cream. "Just yes or no, Tish," Doris pleaded. "Just one little word. I won't ask you to say anything else. And you can whisper it. Just for me. Because you love me, right? Don't you love me?"

Tish nodded, but her hand remained clamped over her mouth.

"You can hold Mama's hand, and when you say yes or no, Mama and I will lean in very, very close, and so will the octopus, so we can hear, okay? It doesn't have to be loud at all. Just a whisper, really, really fast."

It seemed to take forever, long enough for Doris to look at Rainey, for Rainey to let a few tears spill over and roll in slow motion down her cheeks, and for the both of them to look again at Tish. Tish looked at the octopus. She looked at the sweaters and at the purple doll, now splayed out on the bottom step. And then she looked at Doris.

Her eyes were wide and full. Doris could clearly see the whites going all the way around Tish's dark brown irises. And that brown was rich with fear. Thick with it. Doris never saw such fear. She almost backed out, said it was okay, Tish didn't have to do this, but then Tish lowered her hand and she nodded.

Doris let out her breath as Rainey sucked air in. Tish scooted closer to her mother and grabbed her hand. "Okay," Doris said. "An octopus poem then." She stood up and faced them. She knew an octopus poem, thank goodness. She used to recite it when she babysat toddlers during church services. Holding the sunset octopus' head, she began to recite in a loud and clear voice.

> *I'm wrestling with an octopus*
> *and faring less than well,*
> *one peek at my predicament*
> *should be enough to tell.*
> *It held me in a hammerlock,*
> *then swept me off my feet,*
> *I'm getting the impression*
> *that I simply can't compete.*
> *I'd hoped that I could hold my own,*
> *but after just a while,*
> *I ascertained I couldn't match*
> *an octopus's style.*
> *It flipped me by a shoulder,*
> *and it latched onto a hip,*
> *essentially that octopus*
> *has got me in its grip.*
> *I tried assorted armlocks,*
> *but invariably missed,*
> *and now I'm in a headlock,*
> *and it's clinging to my wrist.*
> *It's wound around my ankles,*
> *and it's wrapped around my chest—*
> *when grappling with an octopus,*
> *I come out second best.*

As she recited, Doris moved the octopus limbs from place to place, around her wrist and ankle, her waist and her neck, until it appeared she really was grappling with the thing. As the poem went on, she saw the worry drop from Tish's face, replaced by a look of delight, just short of outright laughter. When Doris was done, she set the octopus on the step in front of Tish, and she and Rainey leaned in, so close that each one touched their noses to Tish's cheeks, their faces bookending hers. Doris could still smell the blue moon ice cream, wiped hastily from Tish's face with dry napkins, and there was still a touch of blue in the corner of Tish's mouth, which now fell from delighted to downturned. "Okay," Doris whispered. "Now, Tish. Did you like the poem?"

Tish squeezed her eyes tightly closed. She clutched her mother's hand and Rainey's fingertips began to turn white. Doris pushed in even closer, her nose denting Tish's dimple. But then, Tish threw her head back. Releasing her mother and flinging her hands to the sky, she bellowed, "Yes!" And then she slapped both hands back over her mouth and looked fearfully around, and Doris was struck by how much more intense this fear was, even more than the large brown eyes just a moment before. This fear was stark. It was white. It made Doris' own blood turn into icicles and the thought of a child ever having to feel that much fear made Doris want to just snatch that shouted yes back and stuff it down Tish's throat. So what if she never spoke again? Just let her feel safe. Without even thinking about it, Doris began to pray. Please, Lord, just let her be safe.

Tish continued to look around, and then Doris and Rainey did too. Nothing happened. Tish began to shake.

Doris took a deep breath. "See?" she said. "Everything is fine." She hoped she was telling the truth.

Tish rolled into her mother's arms, and Rainey scooped her into her lap. They both began to shiver. Doris picked up the octopus and wrapped it around them both. She wrapped herself around them too.

Doris thought again about wanting Tish to just pretend that nothing happened. That nothing changed. Maybe now, if the child's voice was there to punctuate their lives again, this could happen. Normal could happen. Maybe someday, Tish would stand by Doris' front door and wave as Rainey ran out for work in the morning. And Doris would take Tish to school and she would trot off without a backward glance. And after school, oh, maybe someday after school, Doris would say in exasperation, "Tish, hush just a minute! I can't hear myself think!"

Maybe. Exasperation would feel so good.

But when they went in for the evening, when they went in to their kitchens to make their separate dinners, when Doris hugged Tish and told her she loved her and to have a good night, Tish only nodded and offered her cheek for a kiss. Her wave over Rainey's shoulder was as silent as ever. And Rainey, Doris noticed, carried Tish high. Well away from where a new change, the possibility of change, hid tight within Rainey's womb.

Doris also noticed the exhaustion in Rainey's eyes as she turned to say goodnight. Any benefit of the afternoon nap seemed to be gone. Doris decided to stay on her own side of the duplex that night. Rainey needed time with her silent daughter, time to remember and relish that one shouted "Yes!", and time to just sleep.

Doris felt the need for sleep herself. For just closing her eyes and shutting everything away. As if nothing had happened at all.

The house was quiet as Doris prepared for bed that night. There were no sounds from Rainey's place; she must have already gone to bed. Usually there was the drumbeat of the shower or the low hum of the television in Rainey's bedroom as she watched a late-night talk show. But tonight, nothing. Doris hoped Rainey slept.

As she turned out her bathroom light and padded across the hallway to her bedroom, Doris' eye was caught by the upright mirror Harvey made for her while she was pregnant with Forrest. He carved out the frame in a beautiful oak, adding some filigree at the corners that made it clear that this was a feminine mirror, a woman's mirror. It stood on its own and easily rocked at an angle on its base so Doris could focus her gaze wherever she wanted. When she was pregnant, she wanted her gaze everywhere, she wanted to keep track of every change that Forrest's presence forged in her body. As the months passed, she stood naked before the mirror at least twice a day, before getting dressed in the morning and after undressing at night, and she looked and looked. There was the graceful swirl of purple veins in her legs as her blood capacity increased to accommodate not just her body, but her child's as well. Her ankles and feet became swollen, appearing almost cartoonish right before his birth. Her breasts grew dense and veins sketched a path there too, slim and curvy, spidering out from the darkening areolas and her thickening nipples which stiffened erect and stayed that way.

And there was the rounding, the wonderful rounding of her belly. At first, she could cup the pregnancy in one hand, but by the end, she braced it from the bottom, her fingers splayed, as if she were hefting a basket filled with fresh apples. She felt like a fresh apple, running with juice, ripeness nearly splitting her skin.

Standing in front of the mirror now, she wondered if Rainey did this when she was pregnant with Tish. If she did it now. Were there any changes yet, beyond the leftover yellows where bruises announced the brutal conception? Did Rainey see anything of this child's presence at all?

Was this a child? Could a child be created from such violence?

Pulling her nightgown off, Doris looked at herself in the mirror and tried to remember how it felt to be pregnant. How it felt to be ravenously hungry one minute, and horribly sick the next. How it felt to have breasts so tender, just the air on her bare skin hurt, so that even simple nudity didn't ease the shock and pain. She tried to remember the deepening in her abdomen, the feeling that she was hollowing into a great cave, a cave that hid and protected a special and new life in the privacy of her body, until the child had to come forth, until there was no more room for growth and so the child had to reach out. Burst out. Into the light, as the Bible said.

It was in that light, the light of an early morning streaming through a window, that Forrest died. Or at least, that he was found dead. Doris supposed it was possible he died in the milky path of the moon.

Doris remembered that morning. She remembered more than that; she remembered all of it. Every moment of her time with Forrest. The pregnancy and his entire life, the whole five weeks and two days, were locked into her body like a photo album.

Looking in the mirror now, Doris couldn't help but notice the definite erosion of old age. Her entire body had taken on a downward focus. She was moving toward the earth. For burial? Would her body be recycled in the loam of a grave while her spirit soared to Heaven? Or was all of her, her body, her mind, her soul, all of it fodder for future generations?

Doris liked to think that if she gathered her hair together on top of her head and gave a great yank, her body would pull back up like a marionette at the end of a string. She liked to think that, but she knew her body was on a path that couldn't be detoured. Soon enough, she would lie again next to Harvey, in the space for their little family in the cemetery. Well, not completely next to him. Forrest would be tucked between them. And her soul? Her soul would join Harvey's in Heaven.

Heaven, Hell, and Limbo. If Forrest was in Limbo, if he wasn't able to be there with Harvey, waiting for her at the end of that great tunnel of light, Doris wondered if she could stop at the gates to Heaven and ask to be transferred instead. To the floating place that was Limbo, filled with babies stained with original sin. Doris thought of the stain as a giant bruise, a deep purple, streaked with a muddy green and yellow, spread like paste over the babies' faces, running in a stream down their chests and tummies and legs. The pinkness of baby skin, her baby's skin, obliterated with colors not meant for children, not pastel, not soft, not pink and blue. Doris imagined holding all of these babies, filling a vat with clouds of soapsuds and warm water, scrubbing them free of their stain, and offering them up to the Lord. And then she and Forrest would cross over into Harvey's embrace.

God would listen, wouldn't He? How could anyone turn away from a million or more clean-faced babies, scented gently with powder and bubbles?

Doris had plenty of opportunities to be angry with God. Maybe a million or more. All accumulated since that morning, in the sunlight, that she looked on her baby's face and only saw stillness. Stillness and white.

Maybe Forrest did die in the moonshine.

After dressing again, Doris pulled back her covers and climbed into bed. She reached for the leatherbound book on her table, but held it unopened in her lap. The night after she sent God to Limbo, the night after she forced herself to sleep without the lullaby of reading a Bible verse, she returned to Forrest's nursery and chose a different book at random, just as she chose Bible verses at random. The book she chose to fill her table and her need to read before bedtime was *Wuthering Heights*. While the trials of Heathcliff and Cathy completely caught her attention, Doris still missed the Bible. She still missed the surprise of answers appearing from out of nowhere, to questions she didn't even know she had.

Yet God always ignored her biggest questions.

Why did Forrest die?

Why couldn't he at least wait for her in Heaven?

Doris wondered what she would do if she had to choose. If she died and ascended and at the pearly gates, she saw Harvey, waiting for her with a deck of cards and a smile. And then, on the other side of a gap in the sky, there would be the doorway to Limbo, she pictured it mahogany and arched and impossibly tall, and baby Forrest would be there, lying on his back on a silvery cloud and waving his hands at her.

Where would she go? Where would she go if there was no bridge? If even after washing the babies, holding them toward God in a pink and perfumed bundle, He turned His back. What if God decreed that she could only be one place or the other?

Doris imagined setting one foot in Heaven and the other in Limbo. With one hand, she would clasp the tiny fingers of her son, and her breasts would ache to nourish him. And with the other hand, she would find herself gripped up to the wrist by her husband, his skin rough and strong, tugging her toward a hug, the fullness of his body. She would straddle the universe forever, she thought, her legs wide over the breach, to touch the both of them, even if it prevented her from embracing either.

Doris didn't read about Heathcliff and Cathy that night. She didn't think there were any answers in those pages, answers to questions she knew she had, questions that haunted her every day, every week, every passing year. Instead, Doris returned the book to the table and simply turned out the light. She chose to close her eyes without filling them with words first. Just as she hoped for Rainey, she now hoped for sleep for herself.

As she waited for rest to come, she saw again the muddy bruises on the Limbo babies. On her own baby. And she realized with a start that those bruises were the same colors as all the marks that scattered over Rainey. The same discolor. And Rainey's skin would soon stretch over another child, a child who must surely be bruised too.

Two bruised babies. Both bruised by the fault of another. Her son, bruised by original sin, died without having that discoloration washed away with holy water. And now this new baby. Created by a rapist, a conception that was the very embodiment of a bruise. Was one bruise worse than the other? How could a child, created by a rapist, conceived in violence and hate and brutality, be allowed to breathe and play and grow, when her own child's breath stuttered and fell away?

Her love for Forrest, Harvey's love for Forrest, should have wiped away any bruising caused by the eating of a forbidden apple centuries ago. Their love was as clear and pure and reverent as any holy water the old priest could have sprinkled on Forrest's forehead and chest. How was any of this fair? God was supposed to be fair and loving.

Doris had many, many opportunities to be angry with God. Millions of them.

****

The next day, Doris decided to take a quick look through the resale shop, the Tres Chic Used Boutique. She didn't like the shop as much as the Goodwill as things were higher priced. But the store was pristine-clean and neatly organized and most of the items were just one breath away from being brand new. Besides, Doris was feeling antsy that morning; she couldn't concentrate. She didn't want to go to the church again, to see Father Markham. Bob. She didn't want to be a bother. But she needed to get out.

As she sorted through the children's clothing, Doris found herself drifting closer and closer to the baby section. She tried to tell herself she wasn't, there was no need to look at baby things, but finally, she gave up on her own denial. She just stood in the aisle and looked, maintaining a distance so she didn't actually touch. To touch would make it real, would mean she was window-shopping for a possible baby. There were a few nice cribs and some changing tables. A beautiful cradle hugged one corner. It looked homemade, with a little star and moon cut out of its side. Doris didn't know if Rainey had a cradle or a bassinet. She didn't have much, that was for sure, when she moved into Doris' duplex. There was a crib for Tish, purchased at a rummage sale, and Doris remembered worrying over the space between the slats. Were they too wide for the tiny baby? Rainey also had a few sleepers and a car seat, and that was about it. If she chose to have this baby, she would need more things. Better things, this time around.

As if better things could make the situation easier.

And if the baby was a boy, Rainey would need so much more.

Doris looked at the cradle again and imagined a little boy lying within it. She made his face sweet, his lips puckered in sleep, black hair tight in sweat curls around his head. A tiny fist pressed against his cheek.

Tiny fist. Doris shuddered. She just couldn't help it. She tried to imagine herself cuddling this baby, singing to him, holding him by the armpits as he struggled to stand on her lap, his knees alternately elastic and stiff. If Rainey had the baby, she would ask Doris to provide daycare, just as she had with Tish. And of course Doris would. Yet when Doris looked at this imaginary child, bouncing on her lap, all she saw was a bruise. A bruise different from the Limbo babies of the night before, when she compared this new child with Forrest. This baby was all bruise, head to toe, with no pink of innocence shining through. In her mind, when the child stiffened and cried, his mouth became a gaping black hole, without even the relief of baby pearl teeth or pinkish-red tongue. The Limbo babies wept. This baby screamed.

What would Rainey see? What did Rainey see as she automatically pressed her hand against her abdomen? Did she feel a separate heart inside?

Was there a heart? How did it beat? Did the baby's heart echo the rhythm of his father?

What if that heart had no right to be beating to begin with? What if that heart was beating a drum solo of violence, of an anger bred in so deeply, born from a conception of rape, of saying no, of screaming it, and then of being brutalized, that there was just no way this child could ever be peaceful?

What if this child was like his father? How could Rainey possibly look on this child's face and not see that father? Not relive that night?

Doris tossed the clothes she'd selected for Tish onto a nearby shelf and fled from the store. Quickly, she drove to the church.

Father Markham wasn't in the prayer garden and Doris didn't see him inside the church either. His office was in a quiet corner downstairs, near the community room and reception hall, but his chair was empty. The coffee cup on his desk still steamed, so Doris knew he must be close by. She looked down the pair of hallways leading to the Sunday school classrooms, but the lights were off and everything was still. Doris chose an aisle and walked slowly down it, listening outside of each room's doorway, wondering if the priest was hidden inside.

In the room just before the exit sign, she heard a low drone. Looking through the tall and skinny window above the doorknob, Doris saw Father Markham move from one side of a square table to the other. She heard the muted hum of his voice and his hands rambled, from tapping his chin to waving, but Doris couldn't see anyone else with him. Cautiously, she opened the door.

It creaked and he looked up. "Oh, Doris! You startled me! Were you looking for me?"

Doris nodded and looked around the room. They were alone. On the table was a checkers board and the pieces were already in play. "What are you doing?"

Father Markham blushed and quickly grabbed a game box from the shelf beside the table. He swept the checkers into it. "I really like a good game of checkers, and sometimes, if I can't find someone to play with, well, I just play myself. I overheated my coffee in the microwave, so I thought I'd catch a quick game while it cooled." He smiled. "A coffee break without coffee, I guess. I'll drink it when I get back to work."

"And you talk? To yourself?"

"Well, sure." Father Markham closed the lid on the box and carefully stacked it with the other games. "You have to try to psych out your opponent, you know."

"But your opponent is—"

"So what can I do for you today?" Father Markham slipped his arm through Doris' and escorted her from the room. "Let's go get comfortable."

They walked down the hallway toward the church. Doris didn't say anything, just let him lead, and eventually, they stepped out into the Garden of Prayer. Father Markham seated her on the bench, and then he excused himself for a moment, going to fetch his coffee and bring Doris one too.

Doris stared at the little fountain. Around it, there were the remains of the plants she stamped on. The blooms were gone, but the stems and leaves, while bedraggled, looked like they would live. Doris regretted hurting the plants now. They hadn't done anything to her. And the little place didn't look quite as pretty without the color and puzzle of blossoms. She resolved to stop at a greenhouse and get some nice fall plants to replace what she trampled on. Zinnias, maybe. Asters.

When Father Markham came back, he handed her a ceramic mug. "I didn't heat yours nearly as long as I did mine. I made mine boil," he said. "It's a new microwave. I hope it's hot enough."

It was. Doris wrapped her hands around it and set it on one thigh, sending a circle of warmth through her. "It's fine."

"So tell me. What's happening with your neighbor?" Father Markham shook his head. "I think of her often. God, what an awful situation."

Doris was startled, hearing him use God's name in such a way. He clearly wasn't calling on his Maker, but making an exclamation. She didn't know priests were allowed to do that. "Nothing has really changed," she said. "She hasn't made any decisions yet, but she has to soon. Tish, her little girl, still isn't talking." Doris corrected herself. "Well, she said one word. I got her to yell one word. But now she's quiet again."

"Decisions," Father Markham said. "You mean whether to keep the child or adopt it out?"

Doris sighed. She turned toward the priest and looked him full in the face. "You know that's not it, Bob. There is another choice. She has to choose whether or not to abort this...fetus." The word felt strange on her tongue; it was a word she never used. Yet somehow, applying the word baby to the child she imagined before, the child who stiffened on her lap and shrieked, didn't seem right. The child that Rainey surely didn't choose to have placed inside of herself. Maybe that was the difference between a baby and a fetus. Doris herself was only able to use the word baby until now. But now...it was different.

Like an echo of her thoughts, Father Markham said, "Baby. Baby, Doris."

Doris decided not to argue the point. It wasn't what she wanted to talk about anyway. She suddenly knew what that was, the unfairness washed over her like a spring rainstorm. But Father Markham wasn't ready to be derailed yet.

"She's considering abortion then," he said.

"Well, of course she is. She was raped, Bob. She was brutalized."

And Bob, the good Father Markham, a priest, a Christian man, flinched. Just as Doris knew he would. Just as she knew anyone would, even if they tried to cover it. And Doris knew they would continue to do so, if the child was born and lived his life in Waukesha. It wouldn't take long for everyone to know that this child was conceived on the bank of the Fox River, to a mother who didn't ask for it and to a father who demanded her submission. Forced it. And who now sat in a jail cell.

"Does she talk to you?" Father Markham asked. "Have you counseled her against abortion?"

Doris shook her head. "That's not what I want to talk about. I need to ask you something. And I want you to answer absolutely honestly, not necessarily from the Bible or from your education, but from you, okay? From your gut."

Bob sat back. "Would you like me to remove my collar?" His fingers played with it, the white glowing at the base of his throat like a dog's identification tag. "I can, if you'd like me to not be a priest right now. Just like the other day. Whatever you need."

Doris considered it, then said, "No. It's fine. You're a priest, and I want you to answer as you." She waited until he appeared settled. He scrooched a bit on the bench, then rested both of his hands on his knees and looked at her expectantly. "What I need to know is… well. What I need to know about is fairness. About God's fairness. Why would it be fair that this…fetus be allowed to live when my baby, my Forrest, didn't?" She stopped and took a breath, thought deeper. "Why is it fair that my Forrest is sent to Limbo, never ever to see me again, never to get to Heaven, while this fetus could live out its life and experience everything, and I mean everything, that Forrest didn't? Why is it fair for Forrest to die when he was conceived in love, when he was wanted, and then for this one, this new one, to live when it was conceived in the worst possible way, in hate, in fear, in violence, and it's not wanted at all?" Doris turned away, looked at the fountain, read the inscription: *Peace be to all who enter here.* She wanted peace. She wanted promise. She wanted to know that she would have Forrest back again, someday. She shook her head. "I guess I'm not even really thinking about why is it fair. It's unfair. It's as unfair as it can be. I guess I'm wondering why, if it's so grossly unfair, would God even think of allowing for it to happen?"

She turned back and found Bob with his eyes closed. He rocked gently back and forth. His face was quiet…he wasn't frowning or smiling or anything. She waited and wondered if he listened at all. Or if he was still stuck at the harshness of the word fetus. If he closed his eyes to it.

Then he stopped rocking and looked at her. "Gut level?"

She nodded.

"I don't know."

Doris startled, grasped the bench.

He sighed, leaned forward, let his hands dangle between his knees. Doris knew that look. Her husband did that a lot, when he was trying to explain something and wasn't quite sure how. "You know how I could answer, Doris. It's like the first time we talked about this. I could give the mysterious ways speech. But really." He shook his head. "I don't know. I don't understand it. I wish I did. Your little baby shouldn't have died. He should be safe in the arms of his mother, on this earth and in Heaven. Rainey shouldn't have been raped. Her little girl shouldn't have seen it. And never, ever should a pregnancy have occurred. A baby, conception, isn't supposed to be about force and violence and, well, everything evil. Yet there it all is." He cupped his chin in his hands and looked at her. "Forrest is dead. He wasn't baptized before he died, and so he's in Limbo. Rainey was raped, her daughter was there, and now there's this baby. And I…I just can't explain it. I really wish I could. I would love to make you feel better."

Doris felt tears swim to her eyes. She'd wanted honesty, she asked for it. She expected Bob to respond with his great belief in God, his faith, and even his knowledge, all three working toward proving that this was the right thing, that this was what was supposed to happen, that something good would come out of all of it. Everything happens for a reason. God's will be done.

Doris realized she wanted to hear those arguments and stomp on them. Just like she'd stomped on the flowers. That was one way to be angry, to work that anger out and set it loose in the world. But all Bob said was he didn't know. Neither did she. How could she fight against that? She went limp and cried.

Bob held her and for a while, they rocked together, the sound of the fountain and Doris' tears blending together. Eventually, Doris sat back up. "You know, through all of this, I just feel like the most selfish creature on earth," she said.

Bob offered a handkerchief. "Selfish? Why?"

"Because." She mopped her face. "This has all happened to Rainey, and to Tish. And I feel so awful for them and I'm trying so hard to help. But the whole time, the whole time, this thought just keeps running like a banner through my mind. Like one of those electronic banners, you know? Like the ones in stores with all the bright colors?"

"The streaming signs," Bob said and Doris nodded. "Well, what thought is it, Doris? What does the banner say?"

Doris shuddered. "I just want my baby back. That's all I've ever wanted, ever since the morning I found him."

"Oh, Doris. Oh, Doris, I'm so sorry." He held her again as a fresh bout of tears was released, tears held for years in the corners of her heart, as clear and pain-filled as the day Forrest died so many years ago.

"You know...he'd be fifty-three now. Older than Rainey. Old enough to be her father. But I can't think of him that way at all. He's just a baby, lying on his tummy in his crib. He's wearing a baby blue sleeper. It has a little bunny on the right side of his chest, a little brown bunny. And...I just want to pick up from where we left off. I want to sing to him and feed him and bring him down to the kitchen while I make breakfast for his father."

Bob released her, but held her hand. "I wish I had answers. God, Doris, I really wish I did, but I just don't. This is absolutely the hardest part of my job. I feel like I'm supposed to know these things. I feel like I'm supposed to know the answers." He dropped her hand and then scrubbed his own face, tried to wash away something that just wasn't there. "How do I give a reason for a baby that died? How do I explain a woman getting raped in the dark, or her pregnancy, or her daughter watching the whole thing? I just can't. And I so wish I could." He looked at his feet. "The only thing I can do is pray on it. And I will. Maybe God will tell me something that you and I don't know."

Doris looked at him. "You talk to God?"

Bob smiled. "All the time."

"And He talks to you?'

Bob held still for a moment, then he nodded.

Doris stood up and returned the handkerchief. She looked for her purse, then remembered that in her hurry to get to Father

Markham, she'd left it in her car. She hoped it was still there. Then she looked back at the priest. "What does God sound like?"

Bob stood up and shoved his hands in his pockets. He tilted his head, as if he was listening to God right then, right that moment, with Doris beside him. "Not like you'd expect," he said. "It's the softest voice I've ever heard. I'd miss it completely if I wasn't listening really, really hard."

Doris blinked. She wondered how hard she'd been listening. It seemed to her like she was always straining to hear. But then, anger made your blood pound in your ears, didn't it? And too, could she believe a man who talked to himself, who bullied himself and made fun of himself, while he played checkers with himself? If he played with a fake opponent while he was at the checkerboard, how was she to know if he talked with a fake God?

Father Markham seemed smaller now, standing there with his hands in his pockets and his *I don't know*. Impulsively, she stepped forward and hugged him. His embrace was warm and strong. "Thank you," she said.

He shrugged. "I wish I could do more."

"I know. That's why I'm thanking you, but also for being honest. Go back to your checkers game. I hope you win." Doris listened to his laugh and then she walked slowly out of the church, the day and the last few weeks dragging on her body. She thought of her advice to Rainey the day before; take a nap. It sounded like a good idea, even though the only time Doris took naps was when she was sick. And maybe she was sick right now, a little bit. But first, she wanted to make one more stop. She needed to see Forrest. And she needed to see Harvey.

Doris knelt at the graves, plucking away the old flowers, settling in the new ones. She never knew what kind of flowers to get for Forrest…he didn't live long enough to even know what a flower was. Doris sat back and considered. During the baby's five weeks and two days, he was cranky in the late afternoon, and she learned to put him up on her shoulder and stroll through the house, bouncing him gently, bringing up bubbles. She pointed out things to him, saying what they were. Chair. Couch. Mirror. Light. Cup. Forrest liked the mirror and the lights best. Sometimes, if she was tired, Doris would lay a blanket on the kitchen table, put him on his back upon it, and then swing the simple chandelier that hung from the ceiling. Forrest was entranced by the spinning lights and, since he was too little to roll, Doris felt free to step a few feet away from him, heat up a cup of coffee, settle down at his feet and drink it, accompanied by some store-bought cookies. There was no time to bake in those five weeks. And two days.

She tried to remember if she took Forrest to the window, if she pointed out the flowers to him. But she just couldn't bring to mind a picture of herself, looking outside, her baby's fat cheek pressed firmly to hers, both of them rapt at the light and the color. Those five weeks and two days seemed telescoped into the walls and halls of the house. And into the photo album she held within her body.

But it was different with Harvey. She knew his favorite flower. Doris tucked a bouquet of black-eyed susans into the plastic holder by his headstone. He'd always loved this flower, always stopped to buy it for her on his way home from work on Fridays. He never stopped to ask her what her favorite flowers were, which were daffodils. He just exuberantly shared his own. Every now and then, Doris bought herself some daffodils, usually from the grocery store, and put them on the kitchen table or at the window over the sink. But on Fridays, she welcomed the black-eyed susans and she loved her husband.

So she brought Forrest black-eyed susans too. And daffodils, when they were in season. She had them tucked round with baby's breath.

Putting a hand to Harvey's large stone and Forrest's small one, Doris lifted herself up. Standing with one foot on each grave, she folded her dirty hands and looked down at her boys. "Harvey," she said, "if Forrest is there, I hope you're taking care of him. If you grow up in Heaven, after you die as a baby, he'd be a man now, and would provide you with some nice company. But if he's still a baby, remember that he used to like being held upright on your

shoulder, rather than cradled at your waist. And if he's not there…
well, if he's not there, I hope you're figuring out who you can talk
to, to change things." Harvey was always one for fixing. Whenever
there was an issue with a mistake on a bill or with a contractor, Doris
always stood back and let Harvey do the arguing. His no-nonsense
attitude usually worked.

But with God? Could you use a no-nonsense attitude with God?
Didn't God himself express that kind of attitude?

Doris decided if anyone could, it would be Harvey. He had a
charmer's way about him. But then she saw that posture again, the
one that Father Markham used just a bit ago, the one she remembered
Harvey using, while they tried to explain something they had no
words for. Leaning forward, elbows on knees, hands dangling useless
between their legs. Would Harvey be sitting like that, next to God?

She wondered if God ever sat like that.

She shook her head.

Doris stood and looked at Forrest's headstone, his name carved
in graceful curlicue near dead center, an angel above to his left and an
angel below to his right. Harvey was afraid the curlicue was too girly,
but Doris convinced him that it showed that someone special rested
here. Someone loved. Someone who was only a baby.

Shifting her gaze skyward, Doris wondered about Heaven,
about where it was and what it was like. The sky certainly seemed big
enough to house such a place, though Doris always pictured the sky
as the underside of the great marble floor of Heaven, blue and creamy
and exposed toward the earth. Most of the time, the sky seemed
like a friendly and peaceful place. There were ripples, of course, the
gray slate of winter, the shattered black of a thunderstorm. But peace
always returned in the blues and whites of sunny days, the oranges
and reds of sunrise and sunset.

Could she, Doris wondered, wish Forrest through that blue and
white marble floor to Heaven? Could she hope him there? Could she
pray him there?

If so, then Doris knew he must already be in Heaven. Already
with Harvey. And Doris couldn't imagine the other mothers of little

Limbo babies not hoping and wishing and praying for the same thing. In which case, Limbo was empty.

Doris just wished she knew for sure.

"All children," that old priest said, *"are born with the stain of original sin. Baptism purifies. Without baptism, the baby stays stained in sin and won't be allowed into Heaven."*

"I don't know," Father Markham said.

Neither did Doris. Once more, she straightened the flowers, making sure they were cheery against the solid gray of the stones. Then she patted both, kissing her fingers each time, and headed for home, maybe for a nap. Well, probably not. But at least a cup of coffee and a sweet and a break at the kitchen table. And maybe some company from next door.

CHAPTER FIFTEEN

Tish

It felt good to yell. Like a bubble. But then I was scared.

What if the bad guy got out of his cage? The hamster got out of his cage at school once. We couldn't find him *forever*. It was like *days*. And then we found him when he bit Amber on the toe. She took off her shoe to scratch her foot and when she put it down, he was there and he bit her, right through her sock. So he got out.

What if the bad man comes back? What about the other nine? The teacher said the hamster was our responsibility. Like the rhinoceros in Doris' poem. The one that rhinocerusted. The bad man is my responsibility.

Best to be quiet. Doris said that. Used to be all the time. Best to be quiet, shhhhh.

But it felt so good to yell. And nothing happened, really.

Not yet.

But it's been like *forever*. It's been *days*.

CHAPTER SIXTEEN

Rainey

Weeks 8 and 9: The embryo is the size of a kidney bean and is growing about a millimeter every day. It is in constant motion, waving the newly webbed fingers and toes that are growing longer. The embryo is developing lips, a nose, and eyelids. Ossification, or the hardening of the bones, begins and the elbows, wrists and other bones and joints form. Skin is paper-thin and see-through. The intestines are growing longer and run out of room in the abdomen, so they protrude for now into the umbilical cord. The gonads are changing into either testicles or ovaries, but externally, the gender is still impossible to determine. In the brain, nerve cells branch out and connect, forming primitive neural pathways.

The aortic and pulmonary valves are clearly present in the heart, which now has four fully functioning chambers. It gallops at about 150 beats a minute, twice the rate of an adult heart.

Rainey sat on a hard plastic chair in the hallway of The Women's Center, waiting amidst the bustle of ringing phones and voices and women and children running by. Her therapist, she was told, was just beyond the closed door to her left and would be with her in a minute. Rainey knew this place from the outside, but inside, it was all unfamiliar, all strange, and so different from Nanci's child-friendly office where she took Tish. There, the colors were rainbowy, bright, safe and happy. Here, the colors were muted. They were earth tones, browns and soft greens and a barely-there adobe red. Rainey wondered if the colors were designed to relax, if she was supposed to look at them and take a deep breath and curve herself gently into the plastic contours of the chair. She didn't. She felt hidden, like she was being hidden away from the bright sunshine, the same sunshine Nanci was trying to lead Tish to. Rainey was surrounded by camouflage. There was a fountain burbling away in the corner, water spilling out of a stone nude woman's hands, over her body and into a pond at her feet, and it made Rainey feel like she had to go to the bathroom. She already went twice; once before she sat in the chair, and once five minutes later, after listening to the fountain. She didn't want to leave again, she might miss her name being called. So she tried to let the muteness work on her. Make her relaxed instead of wanting to pee. Wanting to stay hidden.

The door opened and a blonde woman looked around the corner. She smiled at Rainey and held out her hand. "Rainey Milbright?" she said.

Rainey nodded and stood up, accepting the woman's hand. She never knew how firmly to shake; she didn't want to come across as weak, but she didn't want to be seen as aggressive either. "Linda?" she said, though it was obvious.

"Yes, I'm Linda Henning. Thanks for coming. Come on in."

Thanks for coming? As if Rainey was invited. She caught back a snort and followed Linda into the small office. She settled onto a couch. The colors were different here; not childlike, not earthy, but vibrant. Paintings of women were scattered over the walls, some dancing wild tribal dances, others looking pensively at the sky or at their own feet. The paintings were surreal and gentle and Rainey decided that she liked them. She shifted her gaze to Linda, who sat in the chair across from her.

"Well, let's get the necessary stuff over with," Linda said, and together, they ran down a clipboard filled with pages of questions. Rainey breathed a little easier when she was told that her status as single mother and her low-tier job allowed her to see Linda at no charge. Rainey was already struggling with the bills from the emergency room visit and with paying for Tish's therapist, so this was no small relief. When Rainey was asked the reason for her visit, she said simply, "Rape," and Linda's hand didn't hesitate when she wrote it down. Rainey appreciated that. Linda took Rainey's signature, added her own, then set the clipboard aside. "Okay then," she said. "Let's talk, and you only need to tell me what you're comfortable with. When was the rape?"

"Eight weeks ago."

Linda's eyebrows went up. "You're counting the weeks?"

Rainey nodded. She decided it was best to just come right out with it. This was what Dr. Johansen sent her here for. She was running out of time. Linda didn't flinch at the word rape. So it didn't make any sense to keep anything else from her. "I'm pregnant. By the rapist. And I have to decide what to do by week twelve. Dr. Johansen would really prefer that I know what I'm doing by week ten, so we can have a plan in place."

They sat in silence for a moment, but Linda's gaze didn't shift. She didn't look away or glance down at Rainey's belly. Rainey was the first to look away. "Can you tell me about the rape?" Linda asked.

Rainey nodded and started in. To her relief and surprise, she found she could recount the facts now without breaking down, without her voice even shaking. Instead, her words were quick and flat. A memorized recitation that she wanted to forget. But she couldn't look directly at Linda as she talked. If she did, she knew the tears would come back from their not-so-far-away spot behind her words, and she didn't want them to. Not today. Not ever. She wanted the tears to be placed firmly away so that she could feel some sense of stepping aside, just like she did that night, when she stepped out of her body to sit next to the river. Rainey felt it was time to step aside again; she didn't know that she'd ever be able to make a decision if she didn't. She had to stop crying first. So instead, Rainey looked down at her own hands, folded in her lap, and said everything she needed to say.

She hesitated for just a moment when she came to the part where she reached orgasm, but then she just said it out loud and plowed on. From what she could tell, there was no reaction from Linda. No gasp, no jump, no jerk.

So maybe there truly wasn't a reason to hide. Maybe she really could say it all.

When the story was finished, Linda leaned forward. Rainey leaned back. "Your daughter was there?" Linda asked.

Rainey nodded.

"And how old is she?"

"Four." Rainey felt the crack before she heard it in her own voice. "Shit." Like a leak in a dam, tears trickled down her cheeks and washed her voice away. Rainey couldn't even speak to apologize for swearing.

Linda took her hands. Rainey was against the back of the couch, there was no place she could go, so she just let her fingers fall limp. "Oh, Rainey," Linda said, and there was such sadness in her voice. "Oh, Rainey, I am so, so sorry."

And so the tears. Rainey gave way and hated herself for doing so. Rocking sideways like a pendulum, Rainey cried and cried, and Linda, holding onto her hands, became an anchor, her pivot point. Linda didn't let go until Rainey was done, subsiding into soft hiccups, and her face was a mess. Then Linda retrieved a box of tissues and deposited them in Rainey's lap. "You have a lot to deal with," Linda said quietly.

Rainey understood now the muteness of the outside walls. Hard to be bright when things talked about here were so harsh. Yet she appreciated the vividness and relief of Linda's dancing ladies. They felt like Rainey's desire to step away.

Linda waited to continue until after Rainey was done wiping her nose and eyes. "My biggest concern is that I help you to heal from this. What happened to you was horrible, Rainey. Horrible. And it will take some time to recover. You have to give yourself that time, and I know that's hard, especially since you're trying to help your daughter recover too."

Rainey nodded. Her voice was still gone. She wondered if this was how Tish felt, if Tish's voice was washed away too, not in tears, but in fear.

"Your daughter is in therapy, right?"

Rainey nodded again and felt like an idiot. She tried to clear her nose and her throat. The noise was terrible. "Yes," she squawked.

Linda sat back. "Okay, that's good, that takes some of the pressure off of you. And initially here, while I want to focus on your recovery, I think we temporarily have to work on helping you to make a decision. That's got to be weighing heavily on you. Once that decision is made, then we can move forward."

Which was exactly what Rainey wanted. Stepping away. Moving forward. "Okay." Rainey closed her eyes for a minute, took a breath, tried to settle more comfortably into the couch.

"What do you see as your choices?"

Rainey clicked them off instantly. "Abortion. Have the baby and keep it. Have it and give it up for adoption."

Linda nodded. "That's good. That's clear thinking. Did you list them in any particular order? I mean, do you lean more toward one than the others?"

Rainey smiled. "Yes. And then five minutes goes by and I lean the other way."

Linda laughed. "I'm glad you can still smile, Rainey. That's a big, big thing. Well, let's talk about the choices. I want to make sure you know all the facts about each. Have you ever had an abortion before?"

Rainey looked away. "In high school."

Linda's voice didn't shift and again, Rainey appreciated that. "Things haven't changed that much since then, so you know what you'll experience if you choose that. Was that conception different than this one?"

Rainey knew she was being asked if she was raped before. And she wasn't. It was worlds apart. "Oh, yes. I was with my first boyfriend. I loved him. But he didn't think we were ready to have a baby." She took another tissue, wiped her cheeks for what she hoped was the final time. "Now, I know he was right. I was only fifteen. But then... well, I guess you could say I was in love with the idea. Two young people and a baby, struggling together to make a wonderful family. So that abortion was hard. It wasn't just the end of that baby, but the end of that relationship too. He broke up with me right before he drove me home from the clinic."

Linda rolled her eyes. "Nice. What an idiot," she said, which made Rainey laugh outright. "So yes, the emotions are totally different this time. But the procedure will be the same, you'll know what to expect there. So what about the second option, have the baby and keep it?"

"I've thought about it." Rainey untied her fingers and ran her palms over her jeans. "I love having Tish. But this is so different. I'm afraid I'd look at this baby and always see that night. And…I hate to even think about it, but there's money. I'm all by myself, and having two children, well, one alone is expensive. And …I worry about what this baby will look like."

"Look like?"

"What if he looks like his father? What if…" Rainey stopped.

"What if he acts like his father?"

Rainey agreed. "The rapist…well, it wasn't just the rape. It was the meanness. He didn't just do the job and run, you know? I really got hurt." The bruises were a physical memory and Rainey's body was suddenly wracked with pain. She tried to hug herself, calm her skin back down into its returned healthy color. "And there's having to explain it to Tish too. Why the baby looks different, if it looks different. The rapist was black, so the baby could look very different than me and Tish. And having to explain to her who the baby's father is. Tish hasn't even asked about her own father yet, but it's bound to come up. And she was there. She saw the man. She's terrified, even though he's locked away now. Imagine having a brother or sister whose father is the man who you saw rape your mother." The tears threatened again and Rainey shook her head impatiently. "For that matter, imagine telling that baby."

"Again, good thoughts. You're thinking really clearly, Rainey."

That was a relief to hear. Rainey wondered sometimes if she was thinking straight at all.

"Okay. The third option. Having the baby and giving it up for adoption."

"I've thought about that too. My main problem with that is again having to explain it to Tish, having to explain what is happening to Mama's body, without giving away that there's a baby inside, and then suddenly my body will change again. She's a smart girl, she's not going to accept simple answers. She's seen her friends get baby brothers and sisters, and she's seen their mothers pregnant. She doesn't know the facts of life, but I think she could easily make this connection, apply it to what is happening to me. And I worry about my job, about what they'll think." Rainy shook her head. "I got just huge with Tish. I can't imagine being able to hide this pregnancy. If I let it continue."

They sat quietly for a moment, while Rainey let her thoughts roll over and over. "And I guess there's another thing too, though it feels so selfish to me."

Linda smiled. "At this point, let's not think about selfish. What's the other thing?"

Stepping aside. Stepping away. "I just want things to go back to normal. I want Tish to talk, I want to feel better, I want things to be like they were. How can they ever be normal if I go through this? If I have the baby and keep it, nothing will ever be the same again. And if I have the baby and adopt it out, it's another seven months before I can go back to normal, and in that seven months, everything changes. My body changes. Every day, there would be a reminder. I just want…I just want normal." Tears threatened again, and Rainey fought them, taking deep breaths and squeezing her hands into fists. Linda seemed aware and she waited.

Finally, Linda said, "This isn't an easy decision. Not by a longshot."

Rainey shook her head. "Not at all. I wish it was. The first two times I was pregnant, it wasn't this hard. In high school, my boyfriend made the decision." She sighed. "And the second time, I made up my mind right away. I mean, right away. Even before I told her father, I knew what I was going to do. Even though it meant giving up college. But I didn't want—" Rainey choked suddenly.

Linda leaned forward. "Didn't want what, Rainey?"

Rainey forced her voice through. "I didn't want to do that to another baby. I didn't really know what I was doing the first time, in high school. I mean, I did, but somehow, it wasn't real. It was just love, being in love, being with him. Nothing was supposed to go wrong. In college, though, when I got pregnant with Tish, I felt really responsible. I knew what I was doing, and I knew what could happen, and I ignored it anyway, in the heat of the moment. It didn't seem fair to make the baby leave, just because of my own mistake, my own thoughtlessness. So I had Tish." Rainey smiled. "I don't regret it. She's amazing."

"But this time…" Linda let her voice trail.

"I don't know. I mean, it's really different this time."

"It is really different. It couldn't be more different." Linda's firmness made Rainey sit up straighter. "You're not responsible for this pregnancy. It was done to you. This conception was inflicted on you."

Inflicted. What a word. Like a punishment. But Rainey remained quiet. She felt the truth pounding at her. It pounded from the inside out, from between her legs, as if the baby was smacking a gavel against a courtroom desk. Rainey knew the truth. The baby, if it was cognizant, knew the truth too. Rainey wasn't completely innocent, after all.

Sweet Jesus, girl, you know you want it.

"Rainey?"

"I feel responsible." She whispered it, hoped that Linda would just accept it, would remember what Rainey described in her story of the rape. The secret Rainey exposed quickly, but into the room aloud, surrounded by many, many words, hidden like the camouflage of the walls.

"Why? You didn't ask to be raped."

Tears again. Always tears.

"Rainey? You didn't ask for it."

"But I—" It was there, ready to say again, but maybe Linda didn't hear it the first time. Maybe that was why there was no flinch, no immediate sending her out the door.

Okay, what is this? Some kind of joke?

Rainey shook her head. "I can't say," she said, her voice clogged. "I can't say, not now."

"Okay." Linda took her hands again. "Deep breath, all right? Deep breath and relax. We don't have to talk about that right now."

Rainey breathed and chased the subject away. She hid it behind her, between her back and the couch. She really didn't want Linda to see it. She liked Linda. She suddenly didn't feel so isolated. She wasn't alone, she knew that. Her doctor knew about the rape, so did her parents, and Doris, and even Tish. But when it came to the orgasm, there was only Rainey. And the voice from the Rape Crisis Center that shamed her into hanging up the phone. She didn't want that to happen with Linda. Rainey needed help, and she knew it.

Linda sat back. "Well, you seem to have a pretty good grasp of the situation. But I want to tell you a few things, make sure you do know about them. It may help you to make your decision. You already know about abortion, so I don't have to tell you too much there. I know your doctor, and Dr. Johansen would help you with that, you wouldn't have to worry about finding someone new, and you truly wouldn't have to worry about her judging you. But you do need to know that if you decide to have this child, even if you decide to adopt it out, Wisconsin law requires that the child's father know about it."

Rainey jolted back on the couch. It banged against the wall.

"You said that the rapist was caught, right? The police have identified him?"

"I identified him," Rainey whispered. "And I think the other women did too. I haven't heard otherwise."

Linda leaned forward again. "That's a good thing, Rainey, really. I'm so glad he's locked up. And he's waiting for trial?"

Rainey started to sweat. She felt it puddling on her throat as she nodded.

"Do the police know that you're pregnant?"

"I told them. At the line-up." Rainey immediately began wondering if she'd done the right thing, if she should have kept her mouth shut, not allowing the pregnancy into the room with her and Officer Stanton. Robert.

Linda sighed. "Well, that means it's on the crime report now, in the case file. When it comes to prosecution, the prosecuting attorney will want to use the pregnancy, if you keep it, as a way to ask for stronger punishment. Even if the lawyer doesn't disclose it, by the time the case comes to court, you will likely be showing, and as a single woman, it won't take too much to put two and two together. The rapist could figure it out, his family, if they're there, could figure it out, and ask for a DNA test. Plus, if you have the baby and keep it, you'll receive child support when the rapist gets out of prison."

Rainey found herself wanting to lift up her hands, push the air in between her and Linda away, force the information back into Linda's mouth and brain and keep it out of her own. It was too much to take in, too much to think about. But Linda kept talking.

"So if you decide to adopt the child out, the father would have to agree to give up his parental rights. Usually, that's not a problem. Most rapists aren't any too thrilled to become parents. But there have been cases where the father has used the mother's desire for adoption as leverage to not be incarcerated. In one case that I know of, a father bargained his giving up parental rights with his victim agreeing to drop all charges against him."

Rainey gasped. "Did she agree?"

Linda nodded. "She did. She was too far into her pregnancy to have an abortion. She waited too long, and her rapist wasn't caught until she was well into her second trimester. She didn't feel like she had a choice; she didn't want to keep the child. So yes, she dropped the charges, he gave up his parental rights and walked free, and she gave the baby up for adoption."

The rapist walked free. And who knew how many other women were hurt? For a second, Rainey wondered if her rapist was the same man. He seemed experienced, and he'd raped others. She shuddered.

Linda settled back in her chair again. "Now if you have the child and keep it, Wisconsin law will see to it that the father pays child support, as I said. Hopefully, he will be convicted and imprisoned soon, but once he's served his time, he would need to find a way to provide you with financial support, just as I'm sure you receive for Tish."

Rainey nodded again, moving her head as little as possible. She was afraid if she moved too much, she would shatter. Her rapist would have to know? She didn't want his support; she didn't care about the money. Why would he have to know? Why did he have any rights at all?

Linda continued and Rainey felt like one thing after another was being heaped on her shoulders. "As the father, he would be able to go after visitation rights, and it is possible he would get them. Even if he doesn't, his family, his parents, his siblings, could also go after visitation, and it's conceivable that would be awarded too. If you choose to adopt the child out, he has to know. He wouldn't be able to keep the child himself while he's in jail, but his family could come forward and claim the child, and a court could conceivably give the child to them."

"But—" Rainey struggled through the shatter and tried to find the words. There were only the most obvious ones, and she finally got them out. "But he's a rapist! He didn't rape just me. There were others! Three other women!"

Linda nodded. "I know. And I know it seems unfair. I think it's unfair. But there are probably fathers and grandmothers and grandfathers and aunts and uncles and cousins who would argue with you and with me that it's unfair that they not have the chance to keep their blood kin. There might even be half-brothers and half-sisters."

Rainey couldn't say anything else. She let her hands flutter uselessly above her lap and then fall. She hadn't thought about this baby being related to anyone but herself and her rapist, and she couldn't even begin to think of the rapist in terms of being a father. But he did have family out there. Somewhere. Bloodlines. Family that raised a rapist.

But family. He had a mother. She would be the baby's grandmother. Rainey suddenly pictured Doris.

Linda sighed and reached for her appointment book. "I know it's a lot to think about. But I want you to be able to make an educated decision. And I'm here with you, Rainey, I'll listen to you as you talk about it, figure it out, and whatever you decide, I'll support you in it. Do you have others that will stand by you?"

Stuttering, trying to get her words to bring herself back into this room, back into a place where all these thoughts weren't swirling around her like a flock of dark crows, Rainey told Linda about Doris. She decided to leave out her parents. For now.

"Okay, that's good. Let's make another appointment. If it's all right with you, I'd like to meet with you twice a week until you make your decision and either carry it out, in the case of abortion, or sit back with it, if you let the pregnancy grow. I really want to help, Rainey."

Despite everything running through Rainey's head right now, those words sounded so good. Rainey tried to focus on them as she stood up. When Linda threw out some dates, Rainey agreed and set another appointment for that week, and eight more for the following four weeks. At the end of those, the 12th week would be over and something would be done. Something. Or something wouldn't be done, but either way, a decision would be made. Rainey didn't know what it would be, but she suddenly felt like she had a road map with a definite destination at the end, a big red X. She accepted the card Linda gave her and shoved it into her jeans pocket. When Linda opened the office door, Rainey immediately heard the fountain and her bladder echoed it. This physical need brought Rainey back to herself and she stopped in the doorway. "Linda," she said. "Linda, I have to ask you something."

"Sure." Linda waited, her hand on the doorknob. She kept her eyes on Rainey's face.

Rainey tried to force the words out. I climaxed during the rape, she wanted to say. Doesn't that mean I asked for it? Did my body help to make this baby? Doesn't that make me responsible for it? Are you sure that I didn't know what I was doing that night?

And what kind of a girl goes walking through a park late at night, Rainey, huh? What kind of girl? Maybe the same kind of girl who gets herself knocked up swimming naked with a bunch of boys at college?

Slut.

Rainey leaned against the wall. "I guess I can't."

Linda touched her elbow. "Okay. But it seems pretty important. Give yourself until our next appointment in two days, and then you will be able to ask me. You will. We'll sit and we'll work it out, word by word. Okay? It'll be all right. I promise."

Rainey wanted so much to believe her.

The evening was cool and sharp-aired and even after Tish went to bed, the sky was still streaked with the remaining reds and purples of sunset. Rainey didn't know if it was the autumn leaf colors in the sky or the promise of cool air against her skin that beckoned, but she found herself drawn back outside. She nearly sat on the front step, her usual perch, but instead, she chose the chaise lounge. Something about having her feet up and her head cushioned as the night air blanketed her seemed exactly right, seemed exactly what she needed to temper the events of the day and the thoughts in her head. From this seat, she could see out past the overhang of the porch and she waited to discover the stars beginning their scatter in the sky.

The television was on next door and then Rainey heard it fall silent and so she expected Doris when she came out of her side of the duplex. There was a gap of about ten minutes, and the tray loaded with a teapot, two cups, and a plate of sliced poundcake didn't surprise Rainey either. But it suffused her with a warm wash of contentment and comfort.

"Hi, Rainey," Doris said. She pulled over a chair from her side of the porch and set the tray down on the wicker table between them. She prepared their cups and soon the night was filtered with the aromas of lemon and sugar and the particular organic and woodsy scent of tea.

Rainey scooted up a bit and accepted her mug and a huge hunk of the poundcake, iced with a layer of butter. It was still warm from the oven and the butter quickly oozed golden. "This is wonderful, Doris, thank you." Rainey inhaled the steam and the quiet and she relished this moment of peace with Doris. Tish was upstairs, sleeping, a time when she was supposed to be silent, when it was normal to be silent, when her silence didn't feel like another open wound still needing to heal from the rape. Right now, on the porch and under these new stars, Tish's wild yell from the other day felt hopeful, the silence following it less foreboding. Doris gifted Rainey with company and heat and sweetness and, for the moment, Rainey felt her body melt like the butter into relaxation.

Doris' chair rocked and it sent a creak out into the night, a slow rhythm which matched Rainey's mood. But then Doris had to speak, even if it was quietly. "How did it go at the Women's Center today? Did the therapist help?"

Rainey sighed and set aside her cup. "Hard to say. It was only the first visit and she said I'll need a lot of time to recover." Rainey felt silly, saying that out loud. The rape was an event, an awful event, but it was over and done with, it had a beginning and an end and it was over. Suggesting that she needed to heal made Rainey feel as if she were still covered with cuts and bruises. As if she was ill. And she wasn't.

Though she knew she was. The wounds and sickness were just hidden under skin that looked clear, but held every second of that memory. That night. Deep inside.

"She did tell me some things I didn't know." Rainey told her about the issues she'd have to face if she chose to have the baby, even if she decided to give it up. The father's rights. The grandparents' rights.

Doris stopped rocking. "You're kidding."

Rainey smiled at the echo of her own reaction. "That's pretty much what I said. I guess there's a lot of support for father's rights. Extended family's rights too."

"Well, yeah, father's rights, I can see that," Doris said. "But this man, if you can call him a man, this man is a—"

"Rapist," Rainey finished.

"Actually," Doris said softly, "I was going to say monster." She resumed rocking.

Monster. Rainey thought of her rapist's size, the growl in his voice, the pressure of his hands holding her down, the impressive weight of his body on hers. She'd been thinking of him as an animal. A wolf. She looked around the yard; it was stark and empty at night, after Doris brought in all the stuffed creatures. Toys meant to bring the animal kingdom to children, share the softness of their fur, the warmth of their skin. All of Doris' animals were huggable.

Maybe monster was a better word.

"I agree with you," Rainey said. "But I guess even monsters have mothers. And fathers. All sorts of family. And they would be related to this…" Rainey didn't know what word to use. Baby? Child? Was it? And even if it was, what did that mean? She left the word blank. "They might want it, even if I don't."

Doris' rocking became faster. "It's not right," she said. "That just feels wrong. They have no right to this child after raising that… that…"

"Monster."

Doris nodded. "What are you going to do, hon?" she asked. Again. How many times had she asked that question already? How many times had Rainey?

Doris' voice was soft, but Rainey could hear the tension in it. The decision weighed heavily on everyone. Doris. Dr. Johansen. Tish, who didn't even know there was a decision to be made. Nanci, and maybe even Linda. And Rainey herself, of course. It did more than weigh on her. The decision threatened to drag her under. "I still don't know. I just keep looking at Tish, you know? I could have said no to her too." Rainey never told Doris about her first boyfriend, the first pregnancy in high school. Doris didn't know that Rainey already said no once.

"This fetus isn't Tish, Rainey."

Rainey startled at Doris' choice of word. She'd never heard Doris use it before. "I know. But still. When I found out I was pregnant with Tish, it didn't seem fair to get rid of her. Her conception was my own mistake. It wasn't fair to punish her for what I did." The night was growing darker and the chill began to seep under Rainey's clothes. The cold felt damp and she shivered. "And now…well, I don't even like referring to Tish's pregnancy as my mistake. Tish isn't a mistake. God, just look at her." Rainey motioned to the yard, as if it was lit up with daytime and dotted with crazy-colored wild beasts and one corkscrewed bouncing nymph. That little girl. Rainey couldn't even begin to think of life without her.

Doris got up and went inside. When she returned, she brought out two afghans. One, she tucked around Rainey, making sure she was covered from her feet to her chest, leaving her hands free. The other, she draped around her own shoulders like a shawl. "You're right, Tish wasn't a mistake. But this pregnancy…this wasn't a mistake either. In a whole different sort of way. You were responsible for Tish's pregnancy. This one, you're not. You didn't do this, Rainey. You didn't ask for this."

And there it was again. Everyone kept insisting this wasn't Rainey's fault, but only three people knew the details. Only three, since this afternoon. Linda, who didn't react, and maybe hadn't heard at all. The woman on the telephone at the Rape Crisis Center. And Rainey herself.

Just who do you think you are?

Well, four. The rapist knew too, didn't he.

See, baby, you want it. Oh, yeah, baby, that's a good girl.

Rainey felt the tears start again, effortlessly pushing their way up through her eyes. There wasn't even a sound with the tears now. They worked their way through her body like an escalator, rolling up and over, only to reappear again.

"You didn't do this, Rainey," Doris repeated.

In two days, Rainey was supposed to tell Linda, again, that she'd achieved orgasm during a rape. If Linda would answer her, if Linda didn't throw Rainey out in disgust, Rainey was going to find out once and for all if her own body's reaction somehow eased the sperms' journey, if she'd somehow impregnated herself, if her guilt impregnated her. If she'd wanted the rape, asked for it. Google couldn't answer her. But maybe Linda could.

Slut.

Two days until Linda.

But Doris was here now. And Rainey knew Doris and Doris knew her. Doris loved her. She loved Tish. She was as close to a mother as Rainey had since leaving home five years earlier. Rainey hadn't spoken to her own mother since Rainey said she felt like her mother's dirty little secret and hung up on her. There was only silence.

Rainey was a dirty little secret. Not just her mother's. But her rapist's too. And her very own.

"Doris," Rainey said and choked. She cleared her throat and tried again. "Doris, I think I did do it. It's my fault."

Doris stopped rocking. She leaned forward and grabbed one of Rainey's hands. "What are you talking about, hon? You were raped, Rainey, you didn't do this!" She squeezed Rainey's fingers. "You're not thinking straight. Did that therapist say something to you?"

Rainey shook her head. "No, I've felt like this for a long time. See, Doris…well, that night. That night. He did…" Blackness threatened to close in around Rainey and she felt like she was gasping for air. She felt like she was going under, the water of the river closing over her head. Her words were the river, or the lake, and this time, night-swimming was dangerous. "He did a lot of things to me. He forced me…and he hurt me." Rainey could hear the current roaring in her ears. This night was dark, just like that night. Tonight started out so nice, just like that night, and now it turned bad. She couldn't stop talking now, her words were jerking out like a rapids and getting ready to fly over the falls, and Doris had Rainey's fingers in a death grip. "I dressed like, you know. The short skirt. The cami, the lace. And then when he was doing stuff to me, when he was doing the last thing to me, I…he touched me. He touched me in this certain way and I…came."

"You came where?" Doris rocked backwards and nearly pulled Rainey from the chaise.

"I came, Doris! I climaxed! I reached orgasm!" Rainey's voice went up with each word and she wrenched her hand from Doris'.

"You—"

Covering her eyes, Rainey swayed back and forth, again like a pendulum, her shirt rubbing against the back of the chaise. But this time, her hands weren't held by an anchor. There wasn't a pivot point, but she waited for one. She waited for what seemed like forever.

But there was only a soft sound. A click.

When Rainey uncovered her eyes, she was alone. The teapot was still on the table beside her, the cups empty, a slice of lemon at the bottom of each. There were still two slices of poundcake left. The butter melted into a dark yellow, darker than the sunshine of the pound cake itself, and it wasn't even a puddle anymore, but a stain. Rainey waited, but Doris didn't come back out. There were no more afghans. There was no more tea. Her lights were still on, but the house was silent.

At this moment, on this porch, with her daughter sleeping upstairs and her friend disappeared, this new silence felt heavier than Tish's.

Rainey ate another piece of poundcake. Doris never let her eat one of her treats alone. But when she was finished, when she was licking her fingers, there was still one piece left for Doris. Huddled in the afghan, Rainey sat and looked at the sky. She was alone, but not alone at all. She was surrounded by voices.

And what kind of a girl goes walking through a park late at night, Rainey, huh? What kind of girl? Maybe the same kind of girl who gets herself knocked up swimming naked with a bunch of boys at college?

Okay, what is this? Some kind of joke?

Slut.

Oh, yeah, baby, that's a good girl.

Just who do you think you are?

Eventually, Rainey stood up and folded the afghan, leaving it neatly centered on the chaise. She straightened the plates and cups and utensils on the tea tray, leaving the final piece of poundcake, just for Doris. And then she went into her side of the duplex. In the darkness of her living room, she sat on the couch and kept watch, peeking between the curtains and the window.

Ten minutes later, Doris came out and gathered all of her things. She still wore the afghan draped over her shoulders and the way she clutched it at her throat, the way she moved so slowly, she suddenly looked like an old woman. She was an old woman, Rainey realized. When Doris went inside, the last square of light on the porch went out. Because of the overhang, not even the stars could be seen. The night was only split by the lights in the houses across the street and the occasional headlights of a passing car. Those lights only ran alongside the yard; the porch remained in darkness.

One by one, all of the houses went dark too. There didn't seem to be any sound, no more passing cars, no barking dogs. Rainey just sat and looked out at all the emptiness. It didn't come anywhere close to the emptiness inside of her. An emptiness that was created by an intruder, and now was inhabited by an intruder.

Like father, like son. A monster?

Okay, what is this? Some kind of joke?

Rainey shuddered.

The next day, Rainey felt like she was walking behind Doris' shadow. She heard Doris moving around her side of the duplex, she saw her setting out the stuffed animals, then taking them in. Doris played with Tish after school, just like always, just like nothing happened, and sent her in at supper time. She stood on the porch and waved at Tish through the screen door and then went into her own place. After Tish went to bed, Rainey sat on the porch and hoped so hard, she wondered if she was actually praying, which she thought Doris would like, but the television in Doris' living room remained on until the square of light on the porch floor flickered and disappeared. .

Doris was there. But she wasn't there for Rainey.

Rainey felt a whole new ravine of grief open up inside of her.

When Rainey went inside, she kept the lights off, the television off, and just slouched in the dark, her feet up on her coffee table. Out of her peripheral vision, she could see her front door, and she waited for the knob to turn, the door to swing open, and for Doris to walk in, delivering late night tea and a sweet and a simple reason for taking so long. As it stayed still and empty, Rainey began to think about what it would be like to see someone else on the other side of that unlocked door. Unlocked because she was so hoping, praying that Doris would come, and she wanted to make Doris' way as easy as possible.

But what if her rapist was there. On the other side of the unlocked door.

Rainey's hands went immediately to her abdomen, cupping it. She had two weeks left to decide. Well, four, really, four weeks until she hit the 12-week Neverland. The Never-Go-Back Land. But two until Dr. Johansen wanted her to make up her mind.

Rainey imagined what it would be like to hold an infant, a toddler, a four-year old, carry him to the door, open it, and then hand him over to his father. Hand their child over to him. Theirs. Because this child was theirs, hers and her rapist's. They were the parents. Daddy was a rapist. Mama was a victim. The conception a fiery stream of black and blue. And red.

Rainey tried to picture that face in the photograph, those arms that treated her so brutally, reaching out. And she tried to picture herself letting go of that child, letting him be taken away, even if it was only for a visitation. She imagined what Tish's face would look like, seeing that man there, recognizing him as the man who hurt her mother that night by the river. The man that took Tish's voice away. If Tish's voice came back, would it disappear again, if that man was ever on the other side of the door?

The door in Rainey's mind shut so hard, she felt the impact.

So maybe he wouldn't get any sort of visitation. Maybe there would be a smart judge who would have some common sense and know better than to do that. But then, what about the rapist's parents? His brothers and sisters? They could come forward, demand grandparents' rights, extended family rights. And then Rainey would have to open her door and turn the child over to them, as they promised hard, as they promised earnestly, not to let the child have any contact with their son, their brother.

Rainey would never believe them. She knew that.

She let her hands drop to her sides. So adoption, maybe. But then the rapist would have to know and he'd have to give up his parental rights. Would he?

Rainey thought of his voice, his hands, the way he manipulated her, controlled her. This baby connected her to him, and right at the moment, the baby felt like a collar around her neck and the rapist held the leash. He would yank on the leash and bring her right back to him. To his side? Under him? To her knees.

The baby was a connection to him. He was their child. And as long as this baby was in the picture, the rapist would be a part of her life. A part of Tish's life. For that matter, a part of the baby's life. The baby would always have a father who was a rapist. A mother who was a victim. And a half-sister who might never talk again.

Rainey wanted to bury herself under the afghan, head to toe, and not look out at the world, but she also wanted to pace. To walk this situation away. She grabbed the afghan, wrapped it around her like a shawl, like Doris did the night before, and she paced the dark living room. She knew it well, knew just how far away to walk from the coffee table so that it wouldn't bark her shins. Knew where to step aside from the basket that held Tish's toys.

I don't know what to do, she thought. And "I don't know what to do!" she said out loud.

Having this baby meant giving herself over, giving Tish over, even giving the baby over, to life with a monster. But not having this baby meant no life for the baby at all.

Rainey stopped dead center in the room and looked at the curtained window. The curtains were closed for the night, but Rainey knew what she would see out there. Her porch. The yard, silver under the moon and bereft of its animals. Next door, Doris' television went silent.

Moving to the door, Rainey stood in front of it, the dark sealing around her like a cape. She kept one hand on her abdomen and she imagined the baby weight in her arms, a soft cheek against her neck, a diaper bag hanging from her other shoulder. She opened the door and pictured his face there, on the other side of the screen. That face. The one she didn't see clearly, but that haunted her every night for weeks now. What would he say? What would she say?

"Hi, how've you been?"

"Good, good. You?"

"Oh, fine. He's had a bit of a cold, so I put some infant Tylenol in his bag, and some decongestant too. And a bulb. You have to suction out his nose from time to time. He can't blow it yet."

Laughter.

And Rainey handed the bag over first, waited until he slung it over his shoulder, and then she held out the baby. As her rapist took him, she felt those hands gliding over her own. Her rapist's hands.

And Rainey was immediately immersed in cold.

That would never happen. That would never ever happen. If she opened the door, he'd push her down. He'd push the both of them down, and Tish would be there, and it would happen all over again. All over, in her home. While a baby screamed and Tish looked on silently.

Rainey gasped, turned away from the door, intending to fly upstairs to her room, but instead, she slid down to the floor. Her back braced, she drew her knees to her chest, wrapped her arms around as much of herself as she could, and she held on. There was no one else to hold on to her right now, and so she held on to herself, and felt completely inadequate.

But then, she just wasn't holding on to herself, was she? Her legs and arms protected her middle. And what was inside.

"I don't know what to do," she whispered to the darkness. "I just don't know what to do."

Except cry. And that wasn't getting her anywhere. Tears didn't bring answers and decisions. But Rainey was overcome.

When she was able, when her legs grew cramped and her tears stopped, she locked the door and walked up the stairs to her bedroom. She thought she heard the echo of Doris' footsteps on the other side of the wall. She wondered if Doris heard her crying, heard her slide down the door, heard her repeated lament of "I don't know." Doris' footsteps were slow and Rainey listened and climbed in unison with her and felt a small comfort from their matched steps. From walking with her friend's shadow. She whispered goodnight to Doris at the top of the stairs, then checked on Tish before getting herself ready for bed.

The next morning, Rainey sat again in the Women's Center hallway on a brown plastic chair and she shivered until Linda came out and waved her into her office. Rainey sat stiff and straight on the furthest corner of the couch as Linda sat down. She scooted her chair closer so that her knees touched Rainey's. She held Rainey's hands with a touch that was cool, but in a comforting way. "Okay," she said. "Let's get right to this. I can see you're under stress and I want to relieve it, so let's not wait. Tell me what you wanted to say. Ask me."

Rainey took a deep breath. She closed her eyes. Which was a mistake. With that night so profoundly in her thoughts and her question so close to asking, the darkness swooped in from her mind and from that night and the park and the river and then it was all there again.

The shadow stepping out from the bushes and her whispered warning to Tish. And then the weight of him, the rock beneath her, the knife shiny in the air, reflecting the stars and the moon, and the sounds, his grunts, her own caught breath, her cry, his slice.

"Rainey!" Linda gripped tighter, shook Rainey's hands. "Where are you? Talk to me!"

Rainey leaned back, but Linda held on, pulled her arms like yanking a drowning body to safety. "He was on me!" Rainey cried. "He said suck! I did! I thought he would go away! Then he threw me on the rock and when I cried, he slid the knife in me, there was a knife in me! Inside me! He cut me, he hurt me and then he was on me!" Rainey was gasping, trying hard to pull in air, the weight so full on her again, pressing on her back, the darkness all around. Where was Tish?

"Rainey, open your eyes, look at me, focus on me!"

But Rainey's eyes wouldn't open. She searched everywhere in the darkness for Tish, listened for a sound, then heard a small rustle, a whimper. Was that Tish? Was she there then? "He took so long to finish, why didn't he finish? Oh, the rock, the rock hurt so much, there was grass in my face, I couldn't breathe!" She sucked in again. "He was in me and his hand…his hand!"

Linda pulled harder. "His hands? What about his hands?"

"He reached around! His thumb…" And Rainey remembered the rush, remembered the heat, remembered her own throb in the palm of her rapist's hand as he slammed against her, his satisfaction dripping from her and from his guttural sigh. And was there another rustle? Was there another sound? Was that Tish, parting the bushes? Did Tish see her just then, did she see her mother's face suffused in fear and in the physical bliss of orgasm? Did Tish see?

Rainey fell forward and Linda caught her. She wrapped her arms around Rainey and rocked as Rainey sobbed and retched, her body caught in the dry heaves. Linda rocked and rocked and Rainey kept her eyes closed until the darkness fell away and became the pink and red of her own closed eyelids. She shuddered and sat back.

Linda stayed leaning forward, her knees touching Rainey's, her hands resting there too. "You told me the other day that you reached orgasm during the rape. Did you think I wasn't listening?"

Okay, what is this? Some kind of joke?

Rainey nodded. "You heard?"

"Of course I heard. I heard everything you said. Tell me what you're thinking."

Linda's hands were firm on her knees, but Rainey pictured Doris' retreating back. "Did that help the pregnancy happen? And did I... did I want it? The rape? I came, I must have gotten something out of it—"

"Stop it," Linda said, the words sharp, cutting off Rainey's voice. "Don't say anything else like that. Don't say it to yourself. Don't think it. Rainey, he manipulated you into orgasm. His thumb. He knew just where to go, didn't he? Your body didn't have any choice."

"But it was a rape, Linda!"

Linda nodded vigorously. "Of course it was! But think about it. What was his thumb doing?"

Rainey twisted her head away. She didn't want to picture it again, but Linda pressed. Rainey followed Linda's words, she followed her voice and closed her eyes again and trailed after the memory to the spot right outside the bushes. She tried to remain an outsider, placed herself like Tish, looking in. Just like she herself was, when she stepped away from her body and sat by the river. Just like then, she saw the rapist slamming into her, violently, hard, and the pain immediately reverberated through her hips and lower spine. But then there was his hand. Rainey ducked and looked under, looked between her own legs, where his hand was buried. And there was his thumb. Moving slow. Moving soft. An even and careful rhythm. No pain. In the middle of all that violence, one spot of pleasure. A deep spot. Caressed by a thumb that knew exactly what it was doing.

Rainey recoiled. Her legs slammed together, her kneecaps cracking loudly.

Linda sat back. "He manipulated you, Rainey. And it's really, really common. It happens in a lot of rapes. Your mind disassociated and your body took over."

Rainey shook her head, trying to understand Linda's words as the last bits of memory slid like gray from her eyes. "I'm sorry?"

"Disassociated. Your mind removed you mentally from the event. And your body responded. It took over. Your body gave you back something, to relieve all the pain."

Rainey thought of the odd sensation of her elbows and knees coming unhinged like an eggshell and how she crawled away to the edge of the river, leaving her body behind. How she looked over her shoulder at herself, saw her own face pulled back in a death mask, and how the moon rippled on the water. And then the shock of being sucked back into her own body, the awful sensuality she didn't want to feel peeling her away from peace and from safety.

Linda leaned forward again. "Listen. There have actually been lots of studies on this. You know the hormones released during sex? During intense pleasure? Do you know when else those exact same hormones are released? Those exact hormones, Rainey."

Rainey shook her head.

"During intense pain and fear. That's when. The body responds in the same way. Your body was just being a body. You can see it as your own body was trying to rescue you, remove you from a physical and emotional pain so intense, it first released you, allowed you to crawl away, and when that failed, it gave you one shot of pleasure to try to cushion you from what was happening. That's all, Rainey. That's all it was. Anesthetic."

For a moment, Rainey stopped breathing.

"Rainey." Linda rubbed Rainey's arms. "Your body did absolutely nothing to cause this. Okay? Not the rape, not the pregnancy. Your body is not to blame. You are not to blame." Linda rubbed harder. "Take a deep breath. It's okay. Breathe."

Rainey did and Linda breathed with her. Slowly, Rainey's shoulders eased, her neck loosened. She was surprised there weren't more tears.

"Rainey, are you aware that hundreds, maybe thousands, of rapes go unreported every year?"

Forty-six, Rainey thought. Out of every one-hundred rapes, only forty-six get reported. Rainey nodded. "Sure. I remember learning that in college, in a women's studies class. And I looked it up the other day." She ducked her head. "I was trying to figure out how long my rapist could stay in prison."

"Not nearly long enough."

The profound venom in Linda's voice made Rainey look back up.

"Do you know why the rapes go unreported?" Linda took her hands again and squeezed, reminding Rainey of Doris' grip on her fingers two nights before. Before Doris knew the truth. Before she went inside and closed the door. "Because the victims reach orgasm during the rape. And they feel ashamed and guilty and like they somehow asked for it." Linda released her. "You didn't ask for it, Rainey. You didn't want it. And your reaching orgasm has nothing to do with the pregnancy. It just happened. It's a byproduct, a remainder. You were raped. And you didn't want it."

While Linda kept talking, Rainey listened. She heard the sincerity in Linda's voice, she heard the knowledge and the experience. She saw the compassion on Linda's face and her absolute belief in what she said. And while Linda talked, Rainey felt the truth roll over her like a river in the afternoon of a summer day. Warm and slow and rich and clear. The same river that rolled by her that night.

For a moment, Rainey let her hands clasp her stomach. But then her fingers slipped apart and up, and she criss-crossed her arms over her chest and grasped her own shoulders in a hug. Her elbows, akimbo, her hands, gripping, left her stomach exposed and unsupported.

Tightly, Rainey hugged only herself.

CHAPTER SEVENTEEN

Doris

Doris glanced at the clock. Tish's school would be out in forty-five minutes and Rainey still wasn't home. Doris didn't know if Rainey planned to pick Tish up or not. She knew Rainey had the appointment with that therapist and she assumed that's where Rainey was going when she drove out an hour and a half ago. But what about Tish?

Normally, Doris would know. Normally, there was a schedule; Rainey was at work and Doris was in charge of Tish. And in this surreal new normal, this post-rape normal, Rainey was home, on leave from work, and there were decisions every night as to who would bring Tish to school, who would pick her up, and then check-in points during the day where Rainey came over for coffee or Doris brought tea over there, and the previous night's decision was checked and rechecked and confirmed.

But there was no plan for these last couple days, and Doris knew whose fault it was. She hadn't made any move to talk to Rainey since Rainey told her the secret. Told her the truth about the rape. Because Doris just couldn't. She couldn't even look at Rainey without hearing those words again. Those impossible words.

I came. I climaxed. I reached orgasm.

During a rape? How was that even possible? Rainey described horrible brutality from that night, her words a battering ram all of their own as she told Doris what happened. But if Rainey reached orgasm, was it still a rape then? Doris remembered picking Rainey and Tish up at the hospital. She remembered the bruises, the cuts, the wild, almost animal look on Rainey's face. Doris remembered thinking that Rainey was destroyed. She was just destroyed.

But how could there be destruction with pleasure? How could Rainey have felt what she did and come home looking like that? Like death. Rainey looked like she wanted to die. So how could she...?

Doris moved to the window in her living room and looked out. A car went by, but it wasn't Rainey's. She went onto the porch and sat down on the top step. Where she and Rainey usually sat together, watching Tish dash in and out of the animals.

It had been eight years since Harvey died, but Doris still remembered relations with her husband. Of course she did. Forty-six years of relations, until Harvey died, and while their flexibility changed, while the duration changed, the frequency, all those things changed, but the climate never did. The warmth and the sincerity of their intimacy. The nights started quietly, then their breaths grew deeper, their hands touched here and there, and the covers had to be thrown back to make room for their passion. Doris remembered the simple rhythm of it, and the complete contact of skin to skin afterwards. The soft kisses, the murmurs, the limbs tumbled together and left to recover, to revel, rejoice. There was desire; the intimacy was something that Doris wanted, it was something she and Harvey shared, and their bodies joined in.

But rape. How could desire be a part of rape? How could pleasure be a part of it?

Another car went by and Doris craned her neck. No Rainey. She figured if Rainey wasn't there in a half-hour, she'd go after Tish herself. If Rainey was waiting in the school yard, Doris would just slip away.

Rainey said he did horrible things to her. He forced her. He hurt her.

But then how could she...?

Harvey never hurt Doris. He never forced her, not even on those nights when she didn't rise to meet him, when she whispered no and spoke of early mornings, late nights, a body worn with fatigue. He just held her then, spooned her to sleep, and the press of their skin was enough.

Doris thought about what Rainey said she wore that night. She remembered the skirt, it was new, and Doris thought it was cute with the little pleated flounce going around the bottom. And Rainey did let her cami show, but it wasn't that deep cut. Rainey dressed a little provocatively sometimes, but she was young, they all dressed that way, and Rainey never pushed it too far. Doris dressed provocatively herself, when she was young. Rainey was so pretty. There was nothing wrong with looking pretty.

Those bruises. The way Rainey held herself afterwards, like every inch of her, inside and out, hurt.

But then how…?

Doris sighed, rested her chin in her hands, and looked out at her animal kingdom. It all just didn't make sense. But then, neither did a neon green ape sitting in the middle of a front yard in Waukesha, Wisconsin.

Neither did a baby who stopped breathing, just like that, in the middle of the night, five weeks and three days after he was born.

Neither did not letting a baby into Heaven.

So many things didn't make sense. But there they were.

Rainey's car showed up with fifteen minutes to spare, parked in the driveway instead of the garage because, Doris guessed, she'd be heading right back out to get Tish. Doris started to get up, to go into the house, but then she lowered herself back onto the step and waited. She heard Rainey come up on her side of the duplex, hesitate, then walk over. She sat down next to Doris, but left a gap between them. They looked out at the animals.

"I was afraid you wouldn't be home in time to get Tish," Doris finally said.

"I didn't know if you would be available to get her, so I hurried," Rainey said.

Doris wondered if she should offer coffee. There wasn't really time before Rainey had to leave again. "How did it go?" she asked.

Rainey shrugged. She gripped the edge of the step. Doris thought about the night, just a few nights before, when Rainey came out and rested her head on Doris' shoulder. As natural and easy as it could be, between them. Now there was this gap, like a canyon, and Rainey's words were quiet and cautious. "I told Linda what I told you. About the rape. About reaching...well, you know. And you know what she said?"

Doris shook her head.

"She said it was common. She said it happens in a lot of rapes. The woman does this thing, called disassociation, where her mind kind of leaves the scene. And her body takes over. The body tries to get rid of the pain, to bury it. Like a painkiller, like an aspirin. Anesthetic. And then things just happen." Rainey let go of the step, folded her hands in her lap. "It just happens. It wasn't my fault, Doris. He manipulated me. Linda said that. And I...well, I just have to believe her. She knows what she's talking about. She's seen lots of women like me."

Rainey continued to talk, her voice flat, full of facts, and so full too of exhaustion that she had to stop, gather her lungs, and force the words out again. Doris thought about that night. She thought about what it must have been like, to walk through a dark park with your child, to sing and laugh with her, to play games of pretend. And then to see that man step onto the path. That monster. The rapist. When Doris thought of Harvey, when she dreamed of him, as she dreamed of him still, eight years after his death, it was always with a gentle sinking, a slipping into warmth, like a hot tub at night when the dark hangs close outside. But that night, with Rainey, that was a different kind of dark. Doris thought of fists. She thought of knives. She thought of curse words and heavy bodies and the thought, just the thought, that a little girl could have been on the other side of the bushes.

What mind wouldn't want to step away from that? And bodies... well, bodies without minds were just bodies, weren't they?

Rainey got up and started to walk toward her door. Doris wasn't quite sure when she stopped talking. "I'll go get Tish," Rainey said.

Her voice was low, and Doris detected a new kind of sad in it. Rainey's voice had been so sad lately, in so many ways. But this was a new way. This was because of Doris. This was because of loss.

"Rainey." Doris didn't move. She patted the step next to her and waited until Rainey sat back down. "I don't understand it all. I don't. But I don't think I need to. I saw you that night. I saw how hurt you were. And I just…I know you. I know you, Rainey. And I'm so sorry. I'm just so sorry."

The gap between them closed, seamed together in a mixture of arms and welcome pressure. They rocked and Doris wasn't quite clear who was comforting who, but it felt good. The tears that fell were silent and warm. Doris shifted into the rhythm that they both knew so well, that they both used on Tish, that Doris used on Forrest, and now they used on each other.

Rainey pulled away first and looked at her watch. "I'm going to be late," she said. When she got to her feet, she held out her hand. "Come with me. It'll be a treat for Tish to be picked up by the both of us."

As Doris followed Rainey to her car, she thought about all there was that she just didn't understand. But sometimes things just were the way they were. She thought about how good it felt to be talking to Rainey again, to be near her, to sway with her, to share her daughter with her. Doris wouldn't feel all of that if Rainey wasn't a good person. She wouldn't feel that at all.

So some things would have to just be left not understood. Some things you just had to accept on faith. She looked over at Rainey as they drove down the street, and out of habit or providence, Doris couldn't say, but a Bible verse ran across her mind. Hebrews 10:39.

But we do not belong to those who shrink back and are destroyed, but to those who have faith and are saved.

Doris wasn't shrinking back. And Rainey wasn't destroyed.

Thank God, Doris thought automatically, and then she shook her head.

Rainey looked tired, her hair was unkempt, just pulled back into a scraggly ponytail, and her eyes were streaked with pink. But there was a smile flitting around her mouth as she drove toward her little girl. Her hands were steady on the wheel. And Doris knew that when Tish saw her mother, she would spin into a run and her face would break open with glee and a love so absolute, it would show on every inch of her body. It would show on the way she launched herself at Rainey, in the way she literally left the ground for her hug, wrapping her arms and legs around Rainey's thin and still-healing body. There would be a special smile and a hug for Doris too, but the joy, the joy was purely for her mother. For Rainey.

A good person. A good woman. Some things you just had to accept on faith. And then you were saved.

The next morning, Doris was just getting ready to start a fresh pot of coffee and set out some blueberry muffins in case Rainey showed up, when the phone shrilled and Doris startled. She wondered why the rings of a phone could never sound merry.

It was Father Markham. "Good morning, Doris," he said. "I hope I didn't wake you."

She looked incredulously at the kitchen clock. "At ten?" she said. "Not hardly. You called just in time for my mid-morning break. I'd offer you some coffee, but that's hard to pour over the phone."

Father Markham laughed. "And I'd take you up on it, if I was there."

Doris glanced at the pot, filled with water, just waiting to be poured into the machine. "Well, why don't you?"

"Why don't I what?"

"Come over. You're only a few minutes away." Looking around, Doris tried to figure out if her kitchen was clean enough for a priest. She shrugged. "There's fresh warm blueberry muffins…"

"Oh, well, then I'll be right there. Give me the address."

After hanging up the phone, Doris quickly took the garbage out to the can in the garage, then washed off the table even though it was already clean, and switched the placemats to ones with an autumn theme. She was just arranging the platter of muffins and the sugar bowl and creamer pitcher on the table when Rainey walked in the door.

"You're amazing," Rainey said. "You always know when I'm coming." She pulled out her usual chair and sat down.

Doris thought about correcting her, but then changed her mind. "Coffee will be ready in a minute," she said. "Oh, and someone else will be here too."

Rainey straightened. "Who's that?"

"Father Markham, the priest at my church. I just got off the phone with him." Doris stopped in the middle of placing the butter dish, with a new stick of butter, on the table just so. "Come to think of it, I don't know why he called me. He just called, and before I knew it, I was inviting him over." Doris frowned. "You know, I don't think a priest has ever called me before. At least, not out of the blue."

Rainey started to stand up. "Maybe I should go. Maybe he has something he wants to talk to you about. He's probably not expecting me to be here."

"Oh, no, sit. I doubt as it's anything important." If Father Markham was coming over to talk about Rainey, he surely wouldn't do so in front of her. Doris decided to mention Rainey's name right away, as soon as Father Markham came in, as soon as they were all in the room together, so he would know who Rainey was. She wondered what his reaction would be. She knew he could control his words, but she wondered if he'd be able to control his face.

Father Markham was true to his word and he rang the bell just minutes later. Doris let him in and there were a few moments of bustle in the kitchen as introductions were made and seats were taken and coffee was poured and prepared. At Rainey's name, Father Markham glanced quickly at Doris and then his eyes swept over Rainey's face. Rainey didn't seem to notice. Doris wondered if the priest's eyes would have dropped to Rainey's tummy as well, if it wasn't safely tucked under the table.

Doris waited until the muffins were passed around, sliced and buttered. "So, Bob," she said, "I'm afraid I cut you off on the phone. You never told me why you were calling."

"Oh, I just heard something that I knew you'd be interested in." He set down his muffin. "It's about Limbo."

"Limbo?" Rainey's muffin was thick with butter; Doris noticed that since the pregnancy was confirmed, Rainey ran toward butter the way ants swarm to sweets. "What's Limbo?"

Quickly, Doris explained. As she talked, she listened to and thought about her words. And suddenly, she thought, I sound quite ridiculous. She stopped in mid-sentence and Bob picked up easily, apparently not noticing that Doris was frozen around her own explanation.

Rainey frowned. "Dead babies don't go to Heaven?" She turned to Doris. "Well, of course they do, if there is one. Why wouldn't God let a baby into Heaven?"

Bob tried again to explain about original sin and stained babies, but while his mouth moved, his voice began to twist and blend. These were just sounds, sounds that didn't seem to have a beginning or an end or a plan or a meaning. The confused expression on Rainey's face didn't go away. She looked at Doris and shook her head.

"So anyway," Bob said. "I was on the phone this morning, talking to the Archbishop, and he said he'd heard that Pope Benedict is going to eliminate Limbo."

"Eliminate it?" It was Doris' turn to frown. "Can he do that? How do you eliminate it?"

"I guess—" Bob chose another muffin, sliced it in half, spread it with butter, "—if the pope says it's so, then Limbo would cease to exist. Would never have existed, actually. He's questioning the whole concept."

"But...wait..." Doris grabbed onto the side of the table. The room suddenly threatened to sway. "He's questioning the existence of Limbo? How can he do that? Shouldn't he know? Doesn't it say so in the Bible?" Her old priest seemed so certain. *All children are born with the stain of original sin. Baptism purifies. Without baptism, the baby stays stained in sin and won't be allowed into Heaven.*

Though there was Bob. Bob said himself that he didn't know. That he didn't understand.

Now, he looked at her, his muffin raised halfway to his mouth. Doris noticed that he wasn't wearing his collar. He looked like any man, just sitting there. A man with a nice red polo shirt and blue jeans. Doris didn't know that priests could wear red. "Well, no," he said. "You know that, Doris. You've read the Bible. All it says is that anyone who doesn't accept Jesus as their savior, anyone who doesn't confess their sins to God and repent, will not be allowed into Heaven. Babies who die shortly after birth don't have time to repent from their sins—"

"They don't have time to sin either." Rainey sat back now, her face aghast, her muffin returned to its plate, her coffee only half-finished.

"Well, no, but everyone is born with the stain of original sin…"

While Bob droned on again, Doris ransacked her brain. She shuffled through an impossible number of Bible verses, passages she read every day for so many years, and no matter where she looked, no matter what quote she heard in her head, the word Limbo was not there. How could she have not noticed that? Horrified, she threw herself back into the conversation, interrupting Bob in mid-sentence. "So what does that mean? That Limbo will be eliminated?"

He turned away from Rainey and leaned toward Doris, offering his hand across the table. She took it; his skin was warm and she could feel the calluses from gardening on the pads of his palm. "It means," he said, "that your baby is in Heaven, Doris."

"Baby?" Rainey, who just started to lift her coffee cup, set it down. "What baby?"

Rainey didn't know; Doris never chose to tell her. When Tish was so tiny, a screaming, kicking little spark of life, and then later, when she filled both sides of the duplex, filled the yard with liveliness and energy and light, it didn't seem right to bring up an empty crib, a silent grave. It would be like the sudden shade thrown by a cloud covering the sun. There was just no need. "My husband and I had a baby, Rainey. A long time ago. Fifty-three years. His name was Forrest." Doris blinked rapidly, trying to push tears aside. She wasn't sure what they were for yet and she didn't want to cry them until she knew. "He died when he was five weeks old. They said it was crib death." At Rainey's blank look, Doris added, "It's called SIDS now.

Sudden Infant Death Syndrome." Rainey's face cleared; of course she'd heard of this. "Back then, it was known as crib death." She hated those words. Pairing what should be a baby's safe place with death. She turned back to Bob. "He's in Heaven?"

"Yes. With Harvey."

Doris pictured gates opening and babies, like a river, a racing upward current to Heaven. Forrest would be in the lead, his arms flailing, and Harvey would be ready to catch him, to scoop him out of the river like a fish in a net. "And Pope Benedict sent him there?"

"No, Doris." Bob squeezed her fingers. "You're not understanding. The pope isn't saying that Limbo should be opened. He's saying it never existed."

"But then who put Forrest into Heaven?" Doris struggled through her tears which now rolled down her cheeks like the river of babies. She only felt confusion, not joy. Not yet. Not joy that her baby was in Heaven where he belonged. How could he be there when he hadn't been there five minutes ago? How could he have been there this whole time when yesterday, he was in Limbo? When just a few days ago, Bob said he didn't understand Limbo, but that's where Forrest was; when fifty-three years ago, the priest said Forrest was stained? How could Forrest suddenly be unstained? What happened to original sin?

Bob used both hands now, clasping Doris' in his, and she felt his skin growing warmer even as hers fell cold. "God did. God did, Doris. Forrest has been there all along. There is no Limbo. There never was."

And Doris felt her tears turn red. She felt the tide turn, no longer a river, but a rapids, churning down her face, soaking her shirt. For fifty-three years, she thought Forrest was in Limbo, floating just beneath Heaven's great floor, surrounded by other babies like him. Babies that cried constantly for their parents, for comfort, for a God to reach out and sweep them up and deliver them into the arms of love and caring and devotion. For fifty-three years, she wondered how God could turn His back on such cries, how God couldn't look past a simple stain, placed on the babies' skin long before they were born.

And now this. Father Markham saying there was no Limbo, even after another priest, an old and learned priest, told her there was. Suddenly, there was the pope, Pope Benedict XVI, deciding, out of the blue, it seemed, that there'd never been a Limbo all along.

So who decided there was one? Did a pope decide? Who created a Limbo for babies in the first place? Who locked the babies behind the gates of prison?

Not God.

God didn't bolt the gates of Limbo. It was the Catholic Church. Her church. The church she went to every week. Every week of her life, all the way back to when she was a tiny baby herself, carried in the arms of her mother, bounced on her father's knee in the wooden pews, soothed to sleep by the sound of a sermon. The church where she married God, where she became His little bride, where she accepted Jesus onto her tongue and into her body for the first time, where she accepted Jesus into her body every Sunday for decades. The church where she volunteered her time and her skills, cleaning, baking, organizing fundraisers and coffee groups and newcomer welcomes. The church she believed in.

God never held the key to Limbo. And He'd been trying to tell her all along.

Father Markham offered a handkerchief, Rainey murmured words of comfort, but Doris shoved her chair back. "I have to go," she said. Father Markham started to say something, but Doris cut him off. "Rainey," she said, "I have to go now. I'll be back later. Would you please show Father Markham out and lock the door for me if you go anywhere?" Without looking back, without putting a comb through her hair or refreshing her lipstick, or turning off her coffee pot, or even clearing her table, Doris grabbed her purse and her keys and she left.

The drive to the cemetery was swift. Doris stumbled up the hill, blinded by tears that were no longer red, but filled with the blue of remorse and the clarity of joy. When she got to the two stones that she knew so well, she lowered herself to her knees and wrapped her arms around Forrest's little headstone, and she cried. Forrest's name, his birth and death dates, and the faces of two angels pressed against her body as she slid into the familiar sway of comfort, but the one she was comforting was herself. Because Forrest was in Heaven. He was in Heaven! He was with Harvey and with God and she would see him again. She would see him and hold him and rock him through all eternity. It would be as it should be. Her family was waiting.

Eventually, the tears slowed and then stopped and Doris dropped to a sit in the grass. Her breath caught and she steadied herself by holding onto Harvey's stone too. Turning, she rested her back against him, as she used to do when he was alive and they went on picnics when they were courting. She imagined she felt his arms go around her waist, nestle under her breasts, his fingers reaching up for sneaky little strokes that no one else could see, but she could feel, and she heard the secret deepness of his chuckle in her ear. She stretched her legs out, then curved one arm protectively around Forrest. Around his stone.

Forrest wasn't there. He was in Heaven. And Harvey's arms curved around him even now.

When Doris closed her eyes and breathed deep, she heard the words. There were no words of Limbo in the Bible, but in the book of Luke, Chapter 8, Verse 48, there were words that suddenly came unbidden. Without even opening the Bible, without even holding it in her hands, the words were there. Just as the words were there when she was in the car with Rainey, heading to school to get Tish, and Doris accepted that some things, you just have to take in faith. She accepted Rainey's goodness in faith, she accepted that Tish would talk again in faith. And now, she accepted herself in faith. She saw these words, heard them, and felt them reverberate through to her soul, streaming through her body in the great riverway of her veins. Quietly, she said them aloud, brought them into the air, and made them real.

"And he said to her, Daughter, be of good comfort: thy faith hath made thee whole; go in peace."

Doris waited a while, waited until her breath came easy and the need to get back to business returned to her bones. Carefully, she got up and brushed off her slacks. She brushed off the headstones too, then gave them each a pat. "I'll see you Sunday," she said, the rightness of that day and this destination suddenly settling onto her shoulders. She nodded toward the sky. "I'll see You then too."

As she picked her way back down the hill to her car, Doris checked off the next steps in her day. First, she would call Father Markham and thank him for telling her his news. And then she would tell him to not expect her in church anymore. Ever. She would spend Sundays with Harvey and with Forrest and with the One who watched over them for her. And then she would retrieve her Bible from Forrest's dresser drawer.

The Catholic Church stuck Forrest in Limbo. Doris stuck God in the drawer, in a Limbo of her own making.

It was time to destroy Limbo, for Forrest and for God.

It wasn't until that night that Doris finally found herself in the nursery, opening the closet door, the dresser drawer, and digging beneath the baby quilt for the Bible. When she'd returned home, Father Markham was still there, waiting for her. He stood in front of the green ape, studying it. He turned when she stepped onto her porch.

"Hi, Doris," he said. "I just wanted to make sure you were okay. I'm sorry if I upset you…I thought the news about Limbo would make you happy."

She shook her head. "It does make me happy, Bob. I just don't understand why I had to feel like this for fifty-three years, why anyone had to feel like this. But I'm fine now." It was harder to tell him to his face that she was leaving the church than it would have been over the phone. But she did it. "I just can't support a church that would create such a place," she said. "Who would make their members suffer so."

"I'm sorry," he said again.

She shrugged. "It's not your fault. You didn't invent Limbo. You didn't tell me and thousands of other mothers that their babies were going to float forever in a non-Heaven, non-Hell." She patted his shoulder. "At least you had the wherewithal to tell me that you didn't understand Limbo either, that you didn't know why it was there, why babies wouldn't be allowed into Heaven. That's something."

He smiled, shuffled his feet. "Well, I guess by saying I'm sorry, I'm apologizing for that. Apologizing for the church. My church. I don't know that they'd back me on it, but I need to say it anyway. I'm sorry for the church's part in adding to your sorrow at the loss of your child. And I hope…well, I hope you'll find your way back. Things are changing. I hate to see you lose your church."

Doris thought of the graveyard, the two stones, the peace she felt when she leaned on Harvey, the bright blue Heaven-floor of the sky. "I don't think I've lost my church at all," she said. "I think I've found it."

Father Markham hesitated, then embraced her. She hugged him back and realized as she did so that he was about the age Forrest would be, if Forrest had thrived and grown and lived. "You find your way back here too," she said, "whenever you need a blueberry muffin. Just because I'm not going to your house anymore doesn't mean you can't come to mine." She watched as he left, going down her driveway into the cute bright red VW Beetle parked at her curb. He waved at her as he pulled a U-turn and headed down the street.

Doris didn't know that priests could wear red, or drive cute red cars. She always pictured priests in something staid and classic, like a black Cadillac.

But then, she didn't know until now that priests could be friends too.

She'd only been in the house a few minutes when Rainey was back, and there was a long series of questions and answers and tears and explanations. And of course, after all the questions were answered, after all the tears were dried, it was time for Tish to come home, and then nothing could be done until playtime was over, suppertime was over, and Doris heard the house so connected to hers quiet down and settle in for the night.

Doris closed up her house, darkening the first floor, before she went upstairs to bring God out of Limbo. She lit her bedside

table lamp and unmade her bed. She moved Wuthering Heights to
Harvey's table and changed into her nightgown. Then she went into
Forrest's nursery.

Turning on the light, she was flooded with the softly blue walls,
the white wainscoting. When it came time to paint the nursery, once
her pregnancy was so far along, she kept expecting her skin to burst,
she'd insisted on the blue, even though Harvey cautioned to use
green or yellow for whoever the baby might be. But Doris knew it
was a boy. She knew it was Forrest. After he was born and when she
held him for the first time, her body curved around him in instant
recognition. He was who he was all along and he was as familiar to
her as her own skin. He was her own skin.

A year after Forrest's death, when the room was converted into
the study, Doris insisted that the color had to stay. And the dresser,
with its sleepers and overalls and sheets and blankets, had to be
tucked away in the closet. The scent of her baby, the softness of his
skin, the feel of his cheek tucked into her neck, were all gone. But
not all of him could go. Doris needed some of Forrest to stay. She
needed his presence to comfort him, and to comfort herself, as he
hung in a Neverland between Heaven and Earth.

A Neverland she knew now that was as fictitious as Peter Pan's.

She crossed over to the closet and opened it. The top dresser
drawer slid silently open, and carefully, Doris reached into the folds
of the baby quilt and pulled out her Bible. Its worn leather fit easily
into Doris' hands and when she clasped it, when she brought it
to her body and cradled it against her chest, she ached again with
recognition and familiarity. The word of God was there and God was
there too. Like Forrest, He was who He was all along, and He too
was as familiar as her own skin. Her own heartbeat.

Before closing the drawer, Doris picked up the quilt and held it
to her nose. There was no scent of Forrest there, only age. Fifty-three
years of being tucked away, unused, in a drawer. Doris stroked the
quilt, returned it, and then one by one, opened the other drawers
and looked at and touched their contents. Sheets brittle and stiff
with age, covered with fuzzy animals and pastel stripes. One-piece

sleepers, most blue, some yellow and green, most never worn, but also old now, neatly folded and tucked away for a baby that left her womb and then her home and never came back.

Forrest was in Heaven now. He was safe. She could let him go.

Closing all the drawers firmly, Doris then shut the closet door. In the morning, she decided, she would box everything up and drive it to Goodwill. She would donate the dresser too, but she'd have to find someone to help her carry it down the stairs. Rainey couldn't, not now. Not in her condition.

Doris wondered at her own protection of this fetus. It felt odd to protect something that Doris found horrible to think of. Something that might even be going away. But Doris knew she wouldn't let Rainey lift anything heavy, particularly down the steps.

She considered, for a second, offering the dresser to Rainey, in case she did keep the fetus. But then she shook her head. It was time for the dresser to go.

Turning off the light in the study, she and the Bible returned to her bedroom. Doris settled into bed, folded the covers around her, then rested the Bible on her lap. Clasping it with both hands, she closed her eyes and prayed for the first time since God's banishment. She asked for forgiveness. She asked for answers. And she asked for God to return to His place in her life. Then she opened the book.

> *"Ye shall not respect persons in judgment; but ye shall hear the small as well as the great; ye shall not be afraid of the face of man; for the judgment is God's: and the cause that is too hard for you, bring it unto me, and I will hear it."*

The familiar settled around her and Doris knew without looking that she was in the book of Deuteronomy. Folding in the satin bookmark, Doris closed the Bible, then brought it to her lips. I'm sorry, she thought, and then "I'm sorry," she said aloud. "I should have known better. I should never have doubted. You take care of the great and the small, and Forrest is safe in Your hands." She thought again of that morning, fifty-three years ago, of finding the baby still and quiet, peaceful in what she thought was sleep. "I don't understand why You took him. I guess I won't ever understand that. But I do know that he is in Your care. It's enough to know that he is in Heaven." *The cause that is too hard for you, bring it unto me, and I will hear it.* "Thank you."

Doris put the Bible where it belonged next to her bed, where it would greet her in the morning. She would take it downstairs to the breakfast table, and she would read it again as she had for innumerable mornings. She would start her day with a random message from her God and she would answer Him with a prayer of thanksgiving.

Doris turned out her light. As she rolled over and then into sleep, one more Bible verse floated into her memory. Behind closed eyes, she reached out, grasped the verse, and held it in the palm of her hand.

Everyone born of God overcomes the world. This is the victory that has overcome the world, even our faith.

1 John 5:4.

Doris overcame the Catholic Church. Her faith was no longer based on words that were chanted every week, or on rules, demands and ideologies thought up by men. Catholic men. Men who thought it made perfect sense for the most innocent in this world to be barred from their place in Heaven.

Doris' faith was in God. And in herself.

She slept.

CHAPTER EIGHTEEN

Tish

I whisper at night and I hear myself. I pull the covers over my head and I curl up tight and I whisper. I say hello and my name and I say all the things I wanted to say during the day, but I couldn't. I tell Emma that she needs to take turns with the puzzle. I tell Mrs. Whitstone that eleven comes after ten, and twelve comes after that. I tell Mama that I want two hot dogs, not just one, and then I'm not hungry anymore. I say all these things and they feel so good and I hear my voice and I remember.

"Tishy, Tishy, Chatterbox," Doris used to say. "Why do you talk so much?"

Because it feels good.

When I take the blanket off my head, I hear a sound. I know what it is. "Don't cry, Mama," I whisper. Every night, she cries. All the time now. I want her to stop.

I walk to her room and she is sitting on her bed. She is rocking and crying. I go to her and I touch her knees and she looks at me, but she keeps on crying. It's like she can't stop. I want her to stop. I hug her, but she keeps on crying. So I say it. "Don't cry, Mama."

It feels good.

She stops rocking. "What, Tish?" she says.

"Don't cry, Mama," I say, a little louder.

And she stops. Her tears pop and go away, like bubbles when you blow them. "Tish," she says. "I will stop crying if you keep talking. If you keep talking and talking and talking."

It feels good. "Okay, Mama," I say.

And then she laughs.

No more tears. No more tears ever. I laugh too. Loud.

It feels so good!

CHAPTER NINETEEN

Rainey

Week 10: The embryo transitions into a fetus. It is the size of a prune, about 1 ¼ inches long. Vital organs, including the kidneys, intestines, brain, and liver, are in place. The stomach produces digestive juices and the kidneys produce urine. The liver is now making red blood cells as the yolk sac disappears. All four limbs can bend. The hands are flexed at the wrist and meet over the heart, and the feet may be long enough to meet in front of the body. The fetus can kick. The outline of the spine is clearly visible through still translucent skin, and nerves begin to stretch out from the spinal cord. The forehead, bulging over the developing brain, sits very high on the fetus' head. The basic divisions of the brain are now present. The fetus can swallow fluid. The webbing has disappeared from the fingers and toes and tiny nails are forming. Hair begins to grow. Inside the mouth, buds of baby teeth appear under the gums. The inner workings of the ears are complete. The fetus can hear.

The fetus now resembles a baby. The word "fetus" comes from the Latin fētus, which means offspring, or bringing forth or hatching of young.

Rainey quietly padded past Tish's bedroom. She moved just as carefully down the stairs, making sure to avoid the fourth and the seventh steps, which had a tendency to squeak. Since her promise to Tish that she wouldn't cry if Tish kept talking, Rainey's nighttime forays into grief were more difficult. At times, Rainey felt like she was just going to dissolve right in front of Tish, into a torrent of unshed tears. In the past week, Tish's voice returned to normal and it was like she'd never gone through a period of long silence. She chattered about her day, her thoughts, her playtimes, her dreams. Rainey listened to it all, every vowel, every syllable, every silvered shriek of laughter. But if Rainey made the mistake of sighing deeply or letting even the corners of her mouth turn down just a bit, Tish froze and stared. Rainey felt as if her face was developing the rubber dexterity of a clown; she sprang quickly back into a contented smile or wide-eyed grin. It didn't matter if it was fake. The contortions were worth it since Tish was talking.

Rainey made her way through the dark to the laundry room at the back of the house. There was a window there and she'd set up a stool a week earlier, so she could come downstairs at night and look outside and if she had to cry, she would be out of Tish's earshot. Even so, she'd learned to cry quietly; no deep breaths or gasps, no sobs or stutters, not even a moan. Just tears washing from her eyes down her face into the safety of a clutched tissue. Rainey didn't even want to risk the soft plop of a tear against her robe. She gladly traded Tish's silence for her own, even if the darkness inside of her just kept growing deeper without release.

Tomorrow was the ten-week appointment. Tomorrow, Rainey would tell Dr. Johansen her decision. And Rainey knew what it was.

Settling herself on the stool, Rainey looked outside. There was a definite chill that evening and Doris predicted snow by the end of the week. Thanksgiving was a week away and snow at Thanksgiving in Wisconsin wasn't all that unusual. Still, last week had given way to Indian summer and Rainey hoped the warm weather would last. Even though she knew it wouldn't. Tonight, she could see her breath.

Carefully, she wrapped her arms around her middle.

The moon was in and out, draped with the clouds, and Rainey saw infrequent glimpses of stars. The backyard was mounded with leaves, raked earlier by Doris and Tish, though Tish did more jumping than raking. At one point, Rainey went outside and when she asked Doris where Tish was, she shrugged. Confused, Rainey turned and Tish burst out of a leaf pile, leaves scattered through her corkscrew curls, held there like autumn barrettes, and she yelled, "Surprise, Mama!" Rainey was surprised and she kissed Tish's bright red and cold cheeks. She reminded herself that it was time to buy a new set of mittens and stocking cap and scarf. In pink, of course.

Looking out at the yard, Rainey tried to imagine what it would be like to have two little children playing there. Well, Tish wouldn't feel so little anymore, if there was a new baby. One big child and one little child crawling through the leaves, earning Doris' good-natured scolding as yet another mound had to be re-raked. But Rainey just couldn't see it. There was Tish. There was only Tish.

Rainey closed her eyes and pictured Tish as a little baby. At first, she only saw the pink and white mottled infant that seemed to be all open mouth and squeezed-shut eyes. The mewling was constant. Rainey remembered the exhaustion and the frustration of not knowing if she was doing anything right and not having anyone to ask. Did she feed Tish too much or too little? Was she dressed too warmly? Not warmly enough? Should she sleep on her back or her side or her tummy, and should there be music playing? Was it wrong to try to soothe her daughter with the Winnie-the-Pooh waterglobe music box Rainey splurged on at the hospital gift shop when there was no one else to bring gifts for the baby?

Throughout Tish's pregnancy, Rainey only called home once, and then she got the answering machine. She left a message that day, giving her new address, and saying she could still be reached by cell if necessary. She said she was all right. Shortly after that message, her cell phone stopped working. When she stopped at the phone company's booth in the mall, she was told her service had been disconnected. Up until then, her father paid Rainey's cell phone bill. On that day, she stared at her phone in disbelief, and didn't breathe fully again until she signed herself up for the most basic plan offered and her phone sprang back to life. Under Rainey's own power. The phone company even let her keep her old number, given to her by her father, but now supported fully by Rainey alone.

Rainey didn't call home again until well after Tish's birth. She figured her parents could count as well as anyone, and they knew when the nine months were up. But there'd been nothing. She only called after she settled into Doris' duplex. She had a new job, a permanent address and her own child. Rainey wanted her parents to know she was making it, she was doing fine. She wanted them to know she had help. It was only after that conversation that the practical packages started showing up from her mother.

Now, Rainey thought about calling her mother, using the secret phone. At this time of night, Doris was asleep and even though she told Rainey that she could call at any time, Rainey didn't want to wake her. Doris was dealing with this situation side by side with Rainey during all of her waking hours. Rainey wanted to give her the gift of sleep.

But that memory of having all those questions during her pregnancy and during Tish's first three months and no one to ask them to drew up alongside the present and parked itself next to this night. Rainey wanted to talk to someone.

Her cell phone was right there with her, resting on the windowsill. So quietly, even though Rainey told her mother she didn't want to be her dirty little secret anymore, Rainey picked up the phone and called her mother's secret number.

And then she listened as a recorded voice told her that number was no longer in service.

Just like her own number, so many years ago. But this one, her mother's secret number, Rainey just didn't have the power to restore.

She set her phone back down on the sill. Apparently, her mother was gone again. Like her memory sidling alongside the present, her mother was alongside her father. And both of them had their backs turned. Rainey wasn't even a dirty little secret anymore. She wasn't anything at all.

At least, to them. Rainey shook her head. She knew she was something to the little girl upstairs, and to Doris next door. She'd been nothing to her parents before, and she survived it. She would again. She knew she had help. Just like then. And Doris, she knew, would never turn her back. Never.

Rainey folded her hands on the windowsill and rested her forehead against them.

Back then, Doris showed her how to be a mother. She showed her what a wonderful thing motherhood was. As Tish grew, she pointed that out to Rainey as well, constantly comparing who Tish used to be with the marvel that she was now. All in all, it was an amazing thing to be a mother.

But not to this one.

There was only one way to step away from all this, Rainey decided. One way to step away from the memory of the horrible night and the aftershocks of such pain and fear and worry. Step away from the weeks of silence from a little girl who should be chattering nonstop and singing at the top of her lungs. The only way to step away from all this was to step backwards into what was normal. Which was what Rainey had been trying to do all along. Tish singing and talking and dancing. Doris setting out her stuffed animals in the morning and bustling around Rainey and Tish with coffee and sweets and homemade soups. And Rainey going off to work in the morning and coming back at night. Just the three of them.

Not a fourth.

Not a fourth created in such a nightmare way. A fourth conceived in violence and perversion and hatred.

When this was over, it would remove the last scrap of reminder of that night. Rainey could pretend it never happened as she needed to, and deal with it when she could, as she could. Around her, there would only be her life, the way it had been, the way it needed to be again.

Even though she knew that deep inside of her, for a few weeks now, there was a second heart beating. She knew it, even if she'd never heard it. But she also knew that if she allowed that heart to beat apart from her, her heart would never beat the same way again. Neither would Tish's. They would live with the shadow of fear, the shadow of a reminder. Even if that heart was beating in someone else's home, in someone else's arms, the shadow would still be there. The memory of the pregnancy, the memory of the birth. The memory of the conception. It wouldn't go away.

And possibly, the rapist might not allow for that to even happen, if that heart was allowed to continue to beat, whether inside or outside of Rainey's body. The rapist had the right to keep that from happening. His right, his choice, mattered more than hers, in this world. Even though he was a rapist. Even though he was in jail. Even though he took what wasn't his to take, and he left behind what shouldn't be his to have.

Rainey just couldn't do it.

She wanted to howl. She wanted to lift her face and howl to the moon as it peeked out between the clouds. She wanted to throw the darkness inside of her to the darkness outside, blot out the moon, blot out the stars, and drown herself when there was no more light.

Instead, the tears followed their usual tracks down her face. Rainey waited until they slowed, then stopped. Then she walked back upstairs, avoiding the seventh and the fourth steps, and paused outside of Tish's room. Tish slept, her teddy under her cheek, and Rainey returned the blankets to her daughter's chin. Then firmly cloaked in her own silence, Rainey returned to her bedroom.

She would howl, she knew it. At the appointment tomorrow, and at the appointment that had to be made. When Tish was away at school. When Rainey could safely hear her own voice without losing the sound of her daughter's.

The next day, Rainey prepared herself to announce her decision to Dr. Johansen. She practiced the word. Abortion. She said it silently to herself as she got Tish ready for school, as she drove her there, kissed her goodbye, watched her run inside. She said it out loud as she drove to her appointment. "I've decided on abortion," she said in her car. She kept her hands firmly on the wheel, refusing to touch any part of herself, refusing to acknowledge the pressure where her abdomen pressed against her jeans. She said the words to the air. But she didn't tell Doris. This way, it could all be set. The appointment, the date, the time, all of it. Underway. So not even Doris' expression could stop it. Though Rainey could no longer predict what Doris' expression would be.

When Rainey was finally at the clinic, finally seated on the examination table, and she said the words out into the air and to Dr. Johansen, Rainey wasn't prepared for Dr. Johansen's response. Not at all.

"Okay," she said. "We can set that appointment up right away, anytime within the next two weeks. Or if you would prefer, if you're ready, we can do it today. I have the time."

Rainey sat stunned on the examining table. "You mean now?"

Dr. Johansen nodded. "I deliberately left my schedule clear. I knew that this was a difficult decision for you, and if you had your mind set, I wanted to be able to offer you this option. We could relieve some of your stress by just getting it over with. You wouldn't have to wait and worry and second-guess your decision. It would just be taken care of."

Taken care of. That brought forth images of warm blankets and hot soup, good long hugs and kisses goodnight. It would be wonderful to be taken care of. And it would be wonderful to not have to think about this anymore. To have it over and done and be able to step back into her life. Which was exactly what Rainey said she wanted to do. And it was the way it should be. Just Rainey and Tish, and Doris too. And Tish talking. No more pregnancy. No more bruises, inside or out.

Rainey took a deep breath. "Okay," she said. "I think that's a good idea."

Dr. Johansen stood up. "Do you have anyone here that can drive you home?"

"No...I wasn't expecting this."

"Is there anyone we can call? I'm sure you remember that you'll be groggy afterwards. You could come back for your car tomorrow... it'll be fine here."

Rainey did remember. She remembered the fog that descended in the doctor's examining room when she was only in high school, the fog that started at her head, then gradually caped itself over her body as the procedure went on and on, it seemed like for hours. She remembered leaning on Jeff as they walked out of the building, leaning on him to the car, and then his telling her, through the gray, that they wouldn't be seeing each other anymore. The dark came then. Now, there was no one else but Doris. And Doris would know as soon as she received the call to come pick up Rainey. The next time Rainey saw Doris, Doris would know Rainey's decision and it would already be carried out. Rainey would lean on her, walking beside her out of the office, and Doris would help her into her car. And then home.

Would it stay home? Or would the dark come? What would Doris do? Would she brandish her Bible, quote from her memory that seemed to go on and on forever? Or would she just let it go, carry on the tradition of silence that started with Tish, and now transferred to Rainey? Would they just not talk about it at all?

Rainey shook her head. Even through her fear, which she realized was irrational, she knew Doris would never turn her back. Not ever. To Doris, Rainey was too important. She, like Dr. Johansen, would take care.

Rainey gave Dr. Johansen Doris' phone number.

"The nurse will be in in a few minutes to get you prepped." Dr. Johansen put her hand on Rainey's shoulder. "Rainey…I'm behind you on this, okay? I would have been behind you, no matter what." She nodded toward the counter, where a white plastic bottle stood. "I had pregnancy vitamins all set for you, if you were going to keep the baby or give it up for adoption. There's a pamphlet there too, for support groups on single parenthood, although I know you already know about that." She squeezed. "Really. Whatever you decided, I was behind you, and I was ready either way. Your decision, whatever it was going to be, was the right decision. This whole situation has just been horrible."

And now the last bit of horror would be scraped from Rainey's body, leaving her clean and empty and back to herself again. Just herself. Her connection to her rapist would be severed. There would be nothing shared between them anymore.

While the nurse bustled around, helping Rainey change into a hospital gown, settling her back on the table with her legs up in stirrups, starting the IV, Rainey didn't howl like she thought she would. She trembled. She kept her hands away from her midsection. The tears flowed without restraint in their usual river, soaking the gown and the paper beneath her. She thought about afterwards, about walking outside, her body only her body again, feeling the air and the sun and heading toward home. Yet even as she pictured herself doing this, something didn't feel right. It didn't feel finished. It felt like she was doing the right thing, but she wasn't done yet. She had to do something. Just like she had to buy that Winnie The Pooh waterglobe for Tish in the hospital, at a time when there was no one else to do anything for the new baby.

Something for the fetus. Something for the baby. She had to do something.

Taken care of.

When Dr. Johansen came back in, Rainey raised herself on her elbows. The IV was taking effect and she swayed a bit, causing the nurse to come to her side, place a steadying hand on her shoulder. "Dr. Johansen, I have to ask you something. And it's going to sound sort of weird."

Dr. Johansen turned on the spotlight, settling it between Rainey's legs. Warmth tumbled down her thighs, but it made her tremble more. The nurse covered Rainey with a warm blanket and Rainey remembered the warm blankets from the hospital's ER on the night this all began, Tish curled asleep in the chair, the kindness of the doctor and the nurse, the watchfulness of the police officers. "Go ahead and ask me, Rainey," Dr. Johansen said. "I don't care if it's weird. With all you've been through, you deserve a little weirdness. You've been amazing through this."

Rainey allowed herself a small smile. She tasted her own tears and realized she was still crying. Crying had become such an everyday routine for her, she didn't even notice it anymore. Except when she was around Tish, and then Rainey became a weeping watchdog, sniffing out any sign of possible tears. Rainey squeezed her eyes shut, forced the tears to stop. She didn't want to have a life where crying was as routine as brushing her teeth. "Would it be possible for me to have the...well, the remains? Of the fetus?"

Dr. Johansen sat quickly down. The silver stool squeaked and rolled backwards.

"See…I think maybe I want to bury it. Take care of it that way."

"Rainey…" Dr. Johansen looked at her nurse, now frozen by Rainey's side, and then back at Rainey. "Oh my god, Rainey. I've never been asked this before. I mean, we usually take care of the disposal ourselves—"

Rainey winced. "Please. I don't want it disposed of. I want to bury it. I want to put it to rest. I think…I really think this will help. Please."

Dr. Johansen hesitated, then nodded. "Okay." She sent the nurse out to find a container. "You'll have to do it fast though, Rainey. It won't…well, it won't keep."

Rainey lay back. She closed her eyes and for a moment, she allowed her hands to rest on her stomach, cup her abdomen. Then she folded her fingers together, brought them up to her chest, just under her chin, and she waited. The IV dripped slowly into her vein and she let herself spin under.

When Rainey walked out, supported by the nurse, she heard the whoosh as a chair was vacated and she knew Doris was flying to her feet. Rainey didn't look at Doris, but when Doris' arm wrapped around Rainey's waist, she sighed and thought again about being taken care of. She also thought about the fog, about Jeff saying goodbye, and she struggled to clear her thoughts so she'd be ready for whatever Doris did, whatever she said. Rainey clutched a paper bag with both fists, and inside was a small, almost weight-free container.

"Doris—" Rainey said as soon as they stepped outside.

"It's okay," Doris said. "I know. And…it's okay."

Rainey dared a quick glimpse. Doris' face was firm and quiet. She caught Rainey's glance and she smiled. "Really," she said. "It's okay. I understand. I mean…" Doris helped Rainey down the steps. "I just don't see how you could have done anything different. It… well, it just makes good sense. Sad sense…but good."

Rainey felt flooded with relief. Her knees went weak and she felt Doris' grip tighten around her waist. Rainey wanted to close her eyes, they kept drooping, and when Doris finally lowered her into the car, Rainey immediately put her head against the back of the seat. The world spun for a moment, then settled back down.

Doris buckled her in. Taken care of. But when Doris reached for the bag in Rainey's lap, she resisted. "I'll hang on to this," she said. "I have to."

There was the thump of the car door, then the other door opened and Rainey heard Doris slide in behind the wheel. "What is it? In the bag," Doris asked. "Do you have meds to take? Or is it bandages? Pads?"

Rainey shook her head and it felt like the car wobbled. "It's... well, it's the fetus, Doris. The baby. I asked if I could bury it." When Doris didn't respond, Rainey opened one eye. Doris sat straight behind the wheel, her hands clutched at ten and two. But the car wasn't moving. It wasn't even running yet. "Doris. I just wanted to bury it. It seemed right." The weight of explaining pressed down on Rainey and her eye drooped again. "The doctor said it has to be fast."

"Okay." The engine started. "Let's go."

When the car lurched forward, Rainey grabbed the bag and it crinkled. She looked at it. It was a small bag, one that you would find at a grocery store or a liquor store. Even a lunch could be packed in it. "Doris, do you think I should get a box? I mean...I can't bury it in this, can I?"

Doris glanced over. "You said it has to be fast though, Rainey. I don't think you're up to shopping."

"Well, no, but—" The bag was ugly. It was generic. And the container inside...Rainey couldn't even bring herself to look. "Could you buy me one? I could stay in the car."

Doris remained quiet and the car's motion quickly lulled Rainey to sleep. When she opened her eyes, it felt like hours later, but Doris was just pulling into a parking space at the mall. She shut the car off and turned to look at Rainey. "You'll be okay out here?"

Rainey nodded. "Sure. I'll just sleep."

"And...you trust me with this?"

Rainey forced her eyes open. She was amazed to find Doris in tears. Like a domino reaction, Rainey began to cry too. "Of course I trust you. Just make it something simple. But beautiful. You know?"

Doris nodded. "I know." She got out of the car.

Rainey settled back to sleep when her door popped open. Gently, Doris reclined the seat. Then she found a blanket in the trunk and covered Rainey. Rainey felt her body relaxing and, under the blanket, she even let go of the paper bag. They were both safe, under the covers. Rainey heard the car door close and lock and then she returned hard into sleep.

CHAPTER TWENTY

Doris

Stunned, Doris walked into the mall. The bright lights and canned music made her wince and stagger. She felt like she was blindness in motion, hands out and grasping, not knowing at all what she was looking for.

Yet she knew exactly what it was. She knew. Something small. Something delicate and lovely. Something to bury a baby in. Only this time, a baby that never breathed. A baby that never stopped breathing. A baby that was never a baby at all.

As she moved down the mall's court, she fell into step with the scattered and infrequent weekday shoppers. Their stride was casual and so she slowed herself down, tucked her hands in her pockets, and began looking in the windows. She told herself this was just a morning of shopping, that's all it was. Dresses and blouses. Shoes. Gray and black business suits, punctuated in between by bright sweaters meant to keep the winter blues at bay. Rock posters and CDs. No boxes, no jars, no vases with lids. Doris thought of the little bag on Rainey's lap, tucked under the blanket, and she held her hands out, trying to approximate its size. It wasn't big. It couldn't be big. Dizziness swept over her like a sudden undertow and Doris sidestepped into an alcove and leaned against the cool and smooth concrete wall.

She remembered the quiet of the funeral home, fifty-three years ago. Harvey's voice was gruff as he explained their loss of a five-week old baby. Their son. The funeral director's vowels became sonorous and molasses as he melted in heatwaves outside of her tears. There weren't many coffins to choose from. White, white and more white. Some carved, some planed so smooth, they looked like a brand new stick of butter. In the end, Harvey chose and she just nodded. An impossibly small white coffin, no bigger than the bassinet tucked under the window in their kitchen. A Roman cross was carved above where Forrest's heart would be. Inside, the purest of baby blue silk lined the sides and the underside of the lid, and there was a matching little pillow and a quilted blanket.

Harvey made the decision, not Doris. And now Doris had to make the decision for Rainey. For a never-born baby. A baby that couldn't be born, and shouldn't have been conceived in the first place.

A fetus, Doris corrected herself. A fetus. Unloved. Unwanted. A reminder of a night so violent, so dark, that no amount of sun on an infant face would ever make it right. A bruise, not a baby at all.

Doris took some deep breaths, then forced herself away from the wall and down the aisle. She reminded herself that Rainey was in the car, sleeping, probably bleeding, and she needed to get home to rest. To finally heal. To draw her body back around herself like an old and comfortable dress that fit just right, even if it was no longer in style.

But no matter where Doris looked, there just didn't seem to be anything that would fill this purpose. More clothes, more shoes. Athletic equipment. Doris paused and considered outside of a store filled with things to commemorate events. She thought about a small box, engraved in filigree, rich crushed red velvet inside. But what would she have engraved? She glanced through the gifts, pens, pocket watches, music boxes, silver cups and banks, and she thought about a few. But they all seemed too bright. She didn't want anything that would reflect or sparkle or glow.

Coming to the end of the mall and working her way back down the other side, Doris started to pay attention to the kiosks in the center. Lots of jewelry. Cell phone services. But a few other things too. Artwork, paintings and sculptures and photographs. Near the middle, Doris found a kiosk whose shelves were scattered with wooden knick-knacks and wall-hangings decorated with Norwegian rosemaling. The light colors and graceful swirls attracted her and she wandered by two times, going slow so she could study the items without being conspicuous. Each time, a flash of blue caught her eye, and so she moved closer.

There was a small rectangular box. Its lid was domed like a treasure chest and hinged and on the top and around the sides, blue swirled like ocean waves. No, not an ocean...it was too gentle, too quiet. A lake. Maybe even a river. The blue was tempered with streaks of white and here and there, a surprise of yellow. It stood on four squat little legs. Doris opened the lid and looked inside. Baby blue crushed velvet.

This baby, this fetus, was conceived next to water. By a river.

"Can I help you?" asked the bored-looking woman at the cash register, situated on the short end of the kiosk. She set down her paperback.

Doris held up the box. "I'd like this, please."

The woman wrapped it in bubble wrap, then tucked it into a brown sack with rope handles. Doris blinked at the price, but then shrugged it away. Ignoring the rope handles, Doris held the bag in front of her with both hands and carried it like an offering to the mall entrance.

The old priest had asked Harvey and Doris if they wanted pallbearers at their son's funeral. Doris remembered nearly laughing... pallbearers for a coffin so small, one person could carry it! Then she looked up, the first time in days she looked beyond her entwined fingers clenched in her lap. "Can Harvey and I do it?" she asked. "Can we carry him to the altar? And carry him to the grave?"

Harvey didn't flinch, but the priest looked away and shook his head. He said it wouldn't be appropriate. In the end, Harvey and Doris sat in the front pew of the church while Forrest was rolled in on a little cart, his coffin already closed. Doris thought about the wheels of the cart, how they rolled like the stroller she'd never had a

chance to use. Later, Forrest was rolled back down the aisle and out
of the church into a waiting hearse and his parents rode behind him
in a limousine, escorting him to his resting place. Doris watched as
two men from the funeral home, dressed in gray suits and baby blue
ties, lifted the coffin from hearse and carefully lowered it into the
grave. She wondered for a wild moment if Forrest was really in there.
But she knew he was. She'd seen him. Before walking into the church
for the funeral, the priest invited them to that final private moment
with Forrest. She and Harvey held hands and stood by the casket,
their free hands perched on the edge. Forrest's skin was so white
against the baby blue pillow. Doris blessed him with the hidden holy
water and then she tucked the quilted blanket under his chin, and
it was Harvey that closed the lid. He cried then, and for the first
time since the morning when Forrest stopped breathing, Harvey
leaned on Doris, his weight nearly toppling her, and he cried on
her shoulder as she'd cried for days against his chest. Doris held him
then, she dropped the holy water and wrapped Harvey in her grief
as he wrapped her in his, and she rocked him and didn't step away
until the priest came in and told them it was time. Time for what,
she'd wondered. Time to feed the baby? To put him down for his
nap, to give him a bath, to wrap him in a fresh diaper, a clean sleeper?
It would never be time for anything again. She'd thought Forrest
floated in nothingness, in a place that wasn't Heaven and wasn't Hell.

Doris knew now that for years, she and Harvey floated there too,
and then she was there by herself. Uselessly. Needlessly. They lived
in a world that was neither Heaven nor Hell when both places were
there all along, and Forrest waited for them both.

She walked to the car, the little blue rosemaled box held before
her. She slipped into her seat, closed the door, and turned to the
sleeping Rainey. Carefully, Doris removed the box, taking it out of
the bag, stripping it of the bubble wrap, which she quickly tossed
into the back seat. Tish would want to play with it later, stomping
on it to get the most pops at one time, finishing it by holding the
individual bubbles between her thumb and forefinger and squeezing.
Then Doris patted Rainey on the shoulder.

Rainey's eyes split open and for a moment, she stared blankly at Doris. Doris watched as memory slid in, bringing the fresh shine of tears and a wince of pain, and Rainey struggled to sit up. Doris reached behind her and tugged on the latch, returning the seat to an upright position.

"Did you get it?" Rainey's voice was sticky with sleep and drugs and sadness. Doris held out the box.

Rainey took it, ran her fingers over the top and the sides. She lifted the lid, closed it, lifted it again, and stroked the soft blue velvet. Then she tucked it under the blanket. Doris heard the crinkle of the bag as the box settled into Rainey's lap. "It's perfect," Rainey said. "It's just perfect. Thank you."

Doris nodded, then started the car. "Where should we go?"

Rainey stared straight ahead. "Oh. I hadn't thought. I guess…I guess I can't bury this in the back yard, can I." She brought her hands out from beneath the blanket and rested them, folded, protective, on her lap. "I don't know. The river?"

Where the rape occurred. But that was what caused all of this. Rainey's pain, Tish's silence, and in the end, this little one's death. It wasn't Rainey at all. And the fetus needed release too, from his bleak beginning and sudden and fitting end.

Doris buckled her seatbelt. "I know where," she said. "It'll be all right. He'll be in good company. And he'll be shown the gateway to Heaven." As they drove away from the mall, Doris patted Rainey's hand, then curved her own fingers over Rainey's clenched knuckles.

CHAPTER TWENTY-ONE
Tish

At recess, I scream. I scream and I holler and I yell. When a ball hits me on the head, I cry, and when the boy says he's sorry, I say okay. I call my friends' names and we try to jump rope. We trip whenever the rope goes over our heads, so we just lay the rope down and jump back and forth over it. I laugh and sing as loud as I can!

Mother, Mother, I am ill
Call for the doctor over the hill.
In comes the doctor,
In comes the nurse,
In comes the lady with the alligator purse.
Measles, says the doctor.
Mumps, says the nurse.
Nothing, says the lady with the alligator purse.
Out goes the doctor,
Out goes the nurse,
Out goes the lady with the alligator purse.

When we go inside, I ask Mrs. Whitstone what an alligator purse is. She says it's a purse made from alligator skin and my friends and

I go, "Ewww!" I think Mrs. Whitstone is making it up. I decide to ask Doris for a stuffed alligator for the yard. And I will ask Mama if that's what an alligator purse is. I will ask her loud and clear. And she will tell me the truth.

CHAPTER TWENTY-TWO

Rainey

Abortion: Word Origin & History
The word abortion first appeared during the 1540s.
It came from the Latin word abortus which means
miscarriage. Originally, abortion was used for both
deliberate and unintended miscarriages. In the 19th
century, there was an attempt to distinguish miscarriage,
abortion, and premature labor. Miscarriage occurred
within six weeks of conception, abortion between six
weeks and six months, and premature labor after six
months, but before the due date. Abortion eventually
came to be used primarily for intentional miscarriages.
The word foeticide appears in 1844 as a medical term
for deliberate premature expulsion of the fetus. The word
abortionist is first recorded in 1872.

On January 22, 1973, Roe vs. Wade was passed in the
Supreme Court, deeming abortion a fundamental right
for women in the United States.

Rainey wasn't startled when Doris pulled into the cemetery, though she did wonder what they were going to do. Drive to a remote corner and dig a hole there? Borrow someone else's stone? Maybe find a lone tree on a hill to be the marker?

She didn't know why she needed to bury this pregnancy away. This fetus. She knew she made the right decision. The deep ache in her body, the way the muscles in her back were giving away one by one, told her that. Yet this need for burial was right too. The pregnancy could not be allowed to continue, but Rainey had to acknowledge that for a short time, this little being had a heartbeat separate from hers and it echoed off the walls of an interior darkness that Rainey could only imagine, but knew intimately. That heart was stopped now, and it was all over. That night was all over, the rape was all over. There was nothing left to do but pick up from where she left off. And heal. She made a mental note to call Linda right after a nap, to let her know that not only was her decision made, but everything was already carried out. Finished. Beginning to middle to end, done.

Taken care of.

Doris pulled over along the side of the little gravel road that ran throughout the cemetery. Rainey waited for her to come around to her side of the car and she welcomed and accepted Doris' arm, her body to lean against for support and strength. Rainey carried the bag and Doris carried the box and together, they trudged up the hill.

Rainey could feel that the pad between her legs was soaked through. But it was okay. The blood seemed appropriate somehow, like that dark night was flowing out of her body, flowing away, leaving her, only her, behind, fresh and clean.

Doris stopped by two headstones and Rainey read the names. Harvey. Forrest. She clutched Doris' arm.

Doris lowered herself to the ground and eased Rainey with her. "This is where my husband and baby are buried," she said. "And over here, next to Forrest, that's where I'll be. There's no stone yet, but it's already set up, chosen and the engraving picked out, even the script. I could have had it put in place when Harvey's stone got here, just left my final date blank, but the idea of visiting and seeing my own stone each time…well, it just sort of bothered me." Doris patted Rainey's shoulder. "Are you doing okay?"

Rainey nodded and felt the thickness between her legs. "You think that it's all right to bury this here?" She touched the bag.

Doris shrugged. "This bit of land is mine, isn't it? And there's a baby here already. It's a restful place. And this little one—" Doris touched the bag—"needs the rest. Until it's his real time to come."

Rainey noticed Doris' use of "his," and she pictured again that baby boy face as he looked at her from over his shoulder, right before he walked out on the red carpet from her body, carrying his small leather suitcase.

He. A boy. Rainey didn't know. But she did.

From her jacket pocket, Doris produced a hand trowel, the kind used to plant seeds in a garden.

"Where'd you get that?" Rainey asked.

"I always keep it in my trunk, so I can put some plants in here if I want to." Doris looked quickly around, then began to dig. "If anyone shows up, we're planting some late fall flowers."

Rainey nodded and kept watch. She held the bag with both hands and she glanced from time to time at the box Doris picked out. It was beautiful and reminded Rainey of the waves of the lake at college, where she and Tish's father went night-swimming. She looked back at the paper bag and thought of this conception's dark night and the river and she shuddered. It seemed right to bury this fetus in the gentle blue swirls of a lake.

Doris finished with the little hole and then she set aside the trowel and took up the box. Placing it next to the new and tiny grave, she opened the lid and looked at Rainey.

Rainey held the flap of paper that locked the fetus inside. She had no idea what kind of container Dr. Johansen chose and she had no idea what she would see when she opened the bag. She carefully peeled the paper back and reached in, shutting her eyes.

She felt hard plastic. Pulling it out, she opened her eyes and looked at it, a plastic food storage box, sealed with a lid. The sides were frosted and she couldn't see inside.

A wave of grief hit her then and she held the container to her chest. The howl that she hid in the laundry room, the howl she thought she would release at the doctor's when she said the word, abortion, seared out now, starting at the pit of her stomach and moving up her throat. Her head drew back of its own accord and it felt like all the pain she'd felt in the last ten weeks, all of the pain and the terror and the depth of it all that had no name, surged from her in a voice so raw, it burned her throat. Her eyes clenched shut and squeezed out hard, hard tears that fell trackless to the ground and left her breathless and arid.

When the sound stopped, when her neck released itself and she gasped and fell forward, her elbows unlocked too and the container bounced to the ground. Doris grabbed it, then grabbed Rainey too and she held them both. Together, simultaneously, Rainey and Doris began to sway, and Rainey felt soothed and protected and alive.

With Doris' arms still around her, Rainey took the container and lowered it gently into the rosemaled box. It fit, its edges not quite touching the velvet walls. Then Rainey closed the lid and set the box into the small hole.

Doris released Rainey and began to carefully return the dirt. Rainey lowered herself from her knees into a sitting position and she leaned against Harvey's headstone. Doris had carefully peeled away the top layer of grass and when she rolled it back into place, smoothed it over, the hole completely disappeared.

And the fetus with it.

The late autumn sun shone on the headstone and Rainey felt the warmth radiate through her jacket onto her skin. She soaked it in as she watched Doris fold her hands, lower her head, and pray. Rainey closed her eyes too, but Heavenward words didn't come. Instead, she felt her body reach for sleep, for a place where it could find its own peace, where Rainey could find peace, where she could smile again, laugh with her daughter, sit on the front porch with Doris and watch Tish bounce and sing through the jungle of stuffed animals, through the rest of the fall, the winter, the spring and the summer.

Doris got slowly to her feet, then helped Rainey to hers. They walked down the hill, Rainey carrying the empty paper bag and leaning into the older woman. Rainey dozed during the car ride home, then walked with half-shut eyes up to her bedroom with Doris' hand at her elbow. She allowed Doris to move her like an adult-sized doll, lifting her arms to undress her, then fold her into her flannel nightshirt, bending her onto the toilet, changing her soaked-through pad, then replacing it with a new one inserted into fresh and clean panties.

Rainey climbed into bed, felt the blanket tucked securely around her shoulders and under her chin, then felt the warm pressure of

Doris' lips against her forehead. *Taken care of.* The door clicked softly as Doris left the room.

Huddling down, Rainey let sleep overtake her like a fever. She felt her body slide into a waiting rhythm, deep and slow, waiting for the bleeding to stop, waiting for the healing to complete, waiting for her life to notch itself back to normal.

Two weeks later, on what would have been the twelfth week of the pregnancy, the week when Rainey would no longer have had a choice, her mother called. It was early evening, and Rainey was in Tish's room, unmaking her bed and setting out her clothes for the next day, while Tish sang at full volume in the tub. The last time Rainey heard this song, Doris was singing it, and there was no joining voice from the little girl. Now, Tish delighted in singing, "Rubber ducky, you're the one!" over and over, changing the tempo, changing the octave, but singing with a joy accompanied by splashes of water. When her phone rang, Rainey checked the caller ID, then checked it again. It wasn't from the cell phone, the one with the now out of service number. It was from her parents' landline.

"Hi," her mother said after Rainey's quiet greeting. "It's both me and Dad. We wanted to see how things were going."

"Things are fine," Rainey said. She wasn't sure how to answer. Her mother knew some things that her father did not.

"Rainey," her mother said. "he knows. I told him. And we're here. We wanted to know what you decided to do."

Rainey hesitated, then said, "Dad?"

She heard his throat clear. "I'm here, Rainey," he said. His voice was flat.

From the bathroom, Tish's voice rose even higher.

"Is that Tish?" her mother asked. "She's talking?"

Rainey laughed. "That's her, all right. She's...back to normal. We both are."

Her parents were silent. Rainey wondered if they were listening to Tish sing, or if they were trying to figure out her meaning.

"So then you came to a decision?" Her mother's voice was soft, just above a whisper. "What was it, Rainey? What are you going to do?"

Rainey took a deep breath. She placed Teddy on Tish's pillow and then she stood straight. "It's already done. I had an abortion two weeks ago."

There was a click. Rainey clutched the phone tighter and braced herself for dead air. But there was only one click, and the air, while quiet, wasn't dead. She could hear her mother breathing. "Mom?" Rainey said.

"I'm here, sweetheart," her mother said. "He's gone, but…I'm here. Okay? At any time. At this number." Her voice broke. "At this number."

"Oh, Mom." Rainey sat down on Tish's bed. Through her own broken voice, she told her mother all about it. When she hung up the phone so she could get Tish out of the bathtub, she knew her mother would call again. And Rainey knew she would call home too. After a while. It would take a bit. But as long as her mother called, Rainey would answer.

Healing just worked that way. It always took time.

EPILOGUE

Rainey

One year after the rape, Rainey Milbright walked quietly and alone through the dark park. She wore black jeans and sneakers and a heavy sweatshirt, the hood drawn over her head. She still remembered that night so well, even though she wished she didn't, and she set out at the same time she and Tish set out the year before, talking of jungles and deserts and camels and elephants. Rainey tried to guide her feet into last year's rhythm so that she would arrive at that spot as exactly close to one year later as possible.

Rainey was breaking the rules again. But her pace was filled with purpose.

Tish was at home, with Doris, getting ready for bed. Once Tish regained her voice, she never spoke of that night, and Rainey saw no reason to bring it back into her memory on this awful first anniversary. Instead, Tish spoke of a 5-year old's world, filled with the excitement and mystery of addition and subtraction, learning to tie letters into words, learning to tie shoelaces into bunny-ear bows.

But Rainey felt she had to acknowledge this night, and when she asked Doris if she would bathe Tish and settle her into clean pajamas and then into bed, Doris agreed. Doris remembered what night this was; Rainey knew that without asking.

When the curve in the path loomed ahead, when Rainey saw the familiar bushes, she hesitated and tried to push down the wave of nausea that rolled through her. She stopped right beside the spot and her memory and the present blurred together and joined. There was no whine of a bicycle tire, no clink of a chain. There was also no heavy breathing, no hard voice, no bitten-off and crude commands. Rainey stood for a moment, tried to move on, but then plunged through the bushes to the small clearing she still saw at times in nightmares.

On the other side, next to the river, there was the rock. Rainey circled it, reached out and touched it, drawing her hand back at first as if she was burned, and then, finally, she sat on it. She drew her knees up, nestled her chin and looked out at the river.

The moon was headlight-white and its glow scored the river in dozens of struck-match flickers. Rainey listened to the burble. The river was gentle tonight and its song was a hum. A lullaby.

This night was beautiful.

It was dark, like last year, and quiet, but the heaviness was lifted and sifted away through fall-crisp air. Rainey tightened her hood, pulled her cuffs over her hands. The grass was full and silver-green, there was no sign of any flattening, any tearing, any struggle. Even the rock, when Rainey looked down at it, gave off the tiniest of sparkles.

There was nothing left of that night a year ago, nothing left of the weighty dark, the fear, the rage. The only thing left of that night was Rainey. And a little girl who, a short distance away, was likely singing a Winnie the Pooh song through her toothbrush and toothpaste and laughing as white and minty foam circled her mouth and dripped down her chin. Beside her, Doris would be laughing too, even as she admonished Tish to behave herself.

Rainey sat there on that rock, alone. She let the cool grace her face, listened to the river croon.

Soon, she stood up and pulled her sweatshirt over her head. She removed her shoes and socks and stepped out of her jeans. At the edge of the river, she stood cleanly naked, not a bruise or a slice on her body, and then she waded in.

The river was already preparing for its transition to winter ice and Rainey gasped at first, but then allowed the current to embrace her up to her neck, zinging every inch of her skin alert and alive. The water didn't get much deeper and she paddled out to the middle. Turning to float on her back, she slowly waved her hands in figure eights to anchor her position as the water lapped past her. She looked up at the moon and then at its blanket floating over her. She was draped in moonglow.

She thought of fresh spring nights spent playing in a lake, swimming over and around her lover's body, flirting through touch and tongue and the softest laughter, the gentleness and innocence of that mating. The glow of her own youth. Then she thought of that night a year ago, the violence, when Tish could have been killed. When Rainey could have died. When in the most shame-filled of moments, she wanted to.

And now she floated here in the path of the moon, in the lazy flow of the river, alone, but not alone. She could hear Doris' goodnight to Tish, Tish's sleepy answer, and Rainey knew when she walked in later, Doris would be waiting for her, sitting on the couch, a leatherbound book open in her lap, fresh coffee and warm mint brownies in the kitchen. Tish, upstairs, would be asleep, but her lips would pucker anyway when Rainey kissed her cheek. They were all here, they were all okay, they were all alive.

On the other side of town, there was the cemetery, which Doris visited every Sunday and Rainey, never at all. But Doris told her, quietly and in passing, of the flowers that she brought to the graves. The circus yellow of daffodils. The sunny gold of black-eyed susans. And from time to time, the barely-there white of baby's breath.

In the river, Rainey tingled with moonshine.

When a mourning dove called from a tree on the opposite bank, Rainey rolled over and swam back to the rock. She wrung out her hair and dressed swiftly, not giving herself time to shiver. She tugged the hood over her head, then moved quickly down the Riverwalk.

Not the way she came. She kept moving forward. As she intended that night one year ago, she walked the rest of the way through the dark park. Following the moon's path, she celebrated this awful one year anniversary, celebrated that she was there to see it.

And then she left it behind.

THE END